The Losses

The Losses

A Novel

Cully Perlman

New York, New York

Published by MidTown Publishing Inc.
1001 Avenue of Americas
12th Floor
New York, NY 10018

Library of Congress Control Number: 2016914536

ISBN 978-1-62677-014-0 (print book)
ISBN 978-1-62677-015-7 (eBook)

Praise for *The Losses*

"I've just read Cully Perlman's hefty, ambitious, and radiant debut novel, *The Losses,* and I was flat knocked out. This is much more than a promising first novel by an inordinately gifted writer; it is a dazzling literary achievement. Perlman is an enchanter, casting his spell with lyrical prose, evocative details, and spellbinding characters. He explores familial chaos, reckless behavior, and tragic love with poise, savvy, and tenderness. What talent, what nerve, what a wondrous and spellbinding novel."

—**John Dufresne,** *I Don't Like Where This Is Going*

"Rich in character and plot, *The Losses* is a hard-boiled literary romp sure to send you scurrying for anything that Cully Perlman writes next."

—**Jeff Parker,** *Where Bears Roam The Streets, Ovenman,* and *The Taste of Penny*

"Cully Perlman's debut novel, *The Losses*, examines the ways that intricate fissures can erode relationships. The more we learn about the characters, the tauter the truth is stretched. Before all hope is snapped Perlman stitches the sorrows back together with nimble fingers and a surgeon's care. He makes the binding stronger. The culminating result is an unforgettable portrait of a complex family. With *The Losses* we gain an elastic new voice which will surely help us weave through these strange new days."

—**Jason Ockert,** *Wasp Box* and *Neighbors of Nothing*

"Cully Perlman's *The Losses* is the rare kind of novel by a young American writer that will continue to work on you long after you've turned the last of its pages. It will likely leave you breathless. Raw in its sheer narrative power, it packs an uncommonly potent psychological punch, unfolding with the quiet inevitability of a Greek tragedy burnished by the slow glow of Cormac McCarthyesque embers."

—**Mikhail Iossel,** *Every Hunter Wants to Know: A Leningrad Life*

Dedication

For my mother, Zoraida Rivera-Sehnert,
who's always been (and still is) my lighthouse

The most beautiful people I've known are those who have known trials, have known struggles, have known loss, and have found their way out of the depths.

–Elisabeth Kübler-Ross

Acknowledgements

To my wife, Susan, and daughters Meena and Nylah. My stepfather, Trent. The members of John Dufresne's Taos Master Class, including friends Teddy Jones, Hector Duarte, Peter Stravlo, Laura Runyan, Lydia Webster, Sharon Oard Warner, Eva Lipton and the Taos (now Santa Fe) Writer's Workshop. Dan Cox and Ryan McConkey. Rob Walker. Kevin Griffith. Arlo Grady. My father, Lenny, and stepmother, Doris. Sisters Rose and Elizabeth, my brothers Davin and Brett, and Michael Zealy, publisher of MidTown Publishing, a true professional. And of course my friend, professor, mentor, and one of the best writers and teachers of writing out there, John Dufresne. It's been a long road and I hope there's an even longer one ahead.

The Losses

Harv and Julianne

On the morning he was to tell Julianne that he was a liar and a cheat, Harvey Lipscomb walked down the hill into town and had breakfast with Roscoe Vance, who by last count had more divorces than Elizabeth Taylor. Roscoe was on his second cup of coffee, stirring three sugars round and round with his spoon, watching Lucille Meunier's bottom as she pushed a broom under a booth. Harvey thought he looked like he was considering adding Lucille to his future ex-wives club. And he didn't doubt it could happen. In Helen, three of Roscoe's wives lived as amicably as anyone could, nodding to each other, holding doors on occasion when by chance they'd happened to be leaving the Edelweiss Inn or the Southern Comfort Quilts shop (two of his wives were knitters) at the same time. When Harvey walked in and sat opposite Roscoe, a few of the men and all of the women turned their eyes, but no one said a word. Harvey and Roscoe's breakfasts raised eyebrows early on, but now, a year in, everyone just turned by habit when they heard the bell over the door, when they saw who walked in, then turned right back around.

Roscoe pushed the sugar over to Harvey's side of the table, said, "You grow your balls yet, or you expecting to up and croak and get out of it that way?"

"Your vocabulary is always delightful," Harvey said. "It's like dining with Flaubert."

"Flo who?"

"No one." Harvey smiled at Lucille. Lucille brought him his cup of coffee and half a bagel.

"Yeah yeah," Roscoe said, eyeing Lucille as she said morning to Harvey, kept her rear out of Roscoe's reach to avoid his accidentally bumping into her. When Lucille disappeared to the back, Roscoe said, "You ain't the saint of candyland yourself, sweetheart."

Harvey sipped from his coffee mug. He spread a pat of butter on his bagel. "So, Mr. Vance," he said, "shall we begin lesson number three in breaking hearts?"

"We shall," Roscoe said. "Giddy up."

It was like that with Roscoe. Crass as could be, but a good old boy. Predictably, Roscoe had plenty of the same experiences as Harvey in certain departments, namely the wrong ones. They talked about wives and lady friends, all of Roscoe's in town, all of Harvey's spread all over. And sure, they were different, the two of them. Roscoe all his life fixing things, first as a handyman, then home builder, motorcycle mechanic, auto mechanic, and finally back to handyman once he retired. Roscoe had grease on his hands all his life. And Harvey, all his life except one summer a hundred years ago as a camp counselor, working in academia, writing papers, speaking, teaching. Riding the clean-hand gravy train, Roscoe called it. But the two of them, they shared that thing, that love of women, that got them into trouble. The thirst that you just couldn't quench. So different they were, yet oh so very much the same.

But as happened—and had been happening for a while now—every morning after their weekly breakfasts, Harvey wandered off, lost his train of thought, even as Roscoe led the way. He forgot what he'd said the week before, and then when Roscoe reminded him, Harvey just agreed, pretended that everything Roscoe said—about the families, about what Harvey's families knew of him—that it was all true, even when he wasn't sure himself. Bits and pieces, sure. He could remember that. The names of his boys, where he met this wife, where he serenaded that lover. But it was like reading a novel, like watching a television show. Things changed each week. Plots morphed, scenes blended. The weeks, they just went on and on. Life was, and then it could be and had been, and it is, all at once.

This morning, on this particular day, like and unlike so many other mornings, he has woken, flat on this bed—his bed and Julianne's—as he has so many times before. It is his fifth year in the cabin, his fifth December in Helen, his fifth, he is sure, of many other things, but it is also his tenth wedding anniversary to Julianne Lipscomb *formerly* Beasley *née* Talmadge. And he knows this day, like the rest, is possibly the end of everything they've built together as man and wife.

He knows, as he always knows, and as he repeats to himself sometimes, that he is an esteemed professor of gender, of sexuality, that he teaches one *online* class a year for Ypsilanti (no more flying to Michigan) and not once a semester in overcrowded classrooms, as he has for many years. He has published numerous books and dozens of articles, too many to recall by memory, but alas, no bestsellers. Above everything he is sure, or believes wholeheartedly, that his children despise him for who he is, but mostly, who he is not. He knows they believe he is a fake, a charlatan, an imposter, an abandoning hooligan and play-actor posing as a compassionate liberal of the genus Academicus. But somehow the pain they can cause him has dulled. And he is afraid of this; this, after so many years of not caring. It is this that he thinks about more every day. It is this that drives the neurosis.

The morning goes on, tic toc. After he shaves, if he is alone, if he's feeling *off*, he may look in the mirror as he's taken to doing, stare at his aged face, and say, "Professor Lipscomb, I presume," and walk away. And Professor Lipscomb may, later that evening, share his pickled baby shrimp, perhaps the pork rillete, with his wife of ten years, Jules the beautiful, the sun warming his neck and shoulders through a window, her in the shade in a buttoned sweater, sunlight resting atop a single, ivory-colored hand. And they will sit there, the two of them, listening to the clang of fork tines and soup spoons, their early bird specials consumed, until slowly (and as they had planned it) the sun falls behind the restaurant's placard out on the lawn: *Nacoochee Grill,* Live Fire Grill, sinks below the level mound of cedar chips along the ground, and another day has passed.

When she, his second wife, brings him coffee in his mug, his *"What would Gilligan do?"* mug, she hands it to him carefully, knowing he will not look away from the cardinal sitting on the barbecue. He has watched it now for an eternity, its crimson form and twiggy legs majestic and strapping, its beak dipping and pulling from a pool of water trapped in the folds of fabric where the grill cover bunches and then stops, like a gypsy's skirts, at the ankle. The mug is a shared secret, or perhaps not a secret but a joke of sorts, because it is not Gilligan on the island but Gilligan as in Carol Gilligan, whom he wrote a paper with when they'd been at Harvard—her on her way out to Cambridge, him to a small community college in upstate New York for a stint before Ypsilanti eons ago. It had been his best collaboration, his ideal academic coupling, really. Though they—he and Julianne, not he and Carol Gilligan—could, they never tell about the mug. It's *their* secret. Unspoken, the Gilligan mug means Harvey has a sense of humor, albeit a quirky one. A humor that lives in his world, in their cosmos. Because while the joke is arguably humorous, it is certainly not a joke that is funny *ha ha*. But it is, and not unnoticeably so, something Harvey holds on to, clutches with desperation, and thus something that touches Julianne when she spies him holding. Not simply the humor, per se, but the modest ambition that's part of it, that has splintered, that has withered, that has been compromised by neglect or, more abstractly, destroyed by a lack of serendipity along the way. The *ganas*, he calls it, which is what, he has divulged to her, they had called it in Spain. The particular yearning, which he had for so many years, and that has now faded. It was a yearning that rumbled his stomach and stole his breath. It was a fire that burned, but now seems to have found its grave. And he remembers, *Yes*, what a time that was, my little stint in Andalusia, in Granada, Madrid. To go back and relive the good times, perhaps this time without regret, because there were so many. When he picks up the glass of water, the ice cool on his lips as he takes a sip, feeling lonely though he is not alone, he thinks, *Why* have I not been invited this year to the Universidad? Has someone in Madrid forgotten? Have they cancelled the conference? Has my invitation been lost? What fool has forgotten? But he knows that maybe it is he that cannot remember, and not everyone else. Knows that maybe, the way things are, everyone knows, precisely, incontrovertibly, what he, the great Harvey Lipscomb, really is.

Julianne, herself, dreamed of children home for the holidays, in particular Christmas and New Year's, and for the past few years her dreams came true. After the girls' father, Joseph "Jo" Beasley, a.k.a. "Measly Beasley," disappeared (in spirit, perhaps, and not necessarily in body), left kids in diapers and a wife lost in debt, she locked the door and listed her grievances while the girls—and only briefly—wallowed in their filth.

Grievance 1: Joe's mother, the repugnant cunt Mrs. Beasley, blocking any contact whatsoever, over the financial obligations, of course, of her good-for-nothing. She isn't fooling anyone, thank you very much.
Grievance 2: Herself. How in God's name, dummy, did you let him talk you into bed but not forced the issue of bettering yourself when you could have, before he'd started with the whiskey, before he'd blown his loot?
And **Grievance 3:** written a few months later, perhaps not a grievance but an observation: Women don't just need men. Men need women too.

Soon after she'd written Grievance 3, Julianne picked herself up, got educated, and the rest, as they say, is history. Rachel rebelled, and Sammy rebelled, and Lettie, well, she did her rebelling in her own ways, Julianne supposed. Maybe didn't get in trouble with school, maybe didn't get caught necking with boys behind the gym or at parties, smoking doobies, but there were other types of trouble. Other types of shortfalls and missteps that maybe didn't get you just then but came around later, when certain things others experienced early paved the way for a smoother ride later on. But they grew up well, the three of them, Lettie and Rachel excelling in school, Sammy little Miss Entrepreneur for a time.

She sat down with her mug too, next to Harvey, who leaned over, sweet hubby Harv, brushed his lips against her cheek. He peeped the contents of her mug (she did not have a special mug), said, "It must be Tuesday," and she said, Yes, it was. But it could have been Thursday as well, and if he was having a day, he might have said, "Thursday." But he had not.

"Kids coming soon, huh?"

"Yes," she said.

"Good," he said. "We'll have a full house."

"We will," she said. She said, "Are you ready for a full house?"

A touch of something. Concern, perhaps. "Why wouldn't I be?" he said.

"I mean, with your work and all," she fibbed.

He said, "Almost done. It's going out Thursday, end of day."

"The gender-class-race one?"

"The feminism and marriage one."

Julianne nodded. "Oh," she said. "I like that paper." Which was not completely true.

Harvey said, "So who all is coming again?"

"My daughters," she said. "Samantha, Rachel, Lettie. Their husbands, Clifford and James. Michael. And of course Lettie's son, Aaron. And little Hadley, Rachel's daughter."

Harvey thought for a moment, took a sip of his coffee. He said, "I thought James and Rachel were having problems."

"Sam and Cliff are."

"Mmm," he said. He looked to say something else, but nothing came.

He finished his coffee, left his mug teeter-tottering on the arm of his chair. He said, "I think I'll take a walk," and she said, "Have fun, Love." She watched his sweet face perk up like it did when he was thinking, when he was wondering if there was anything she wanted to remind him, because so often now that was something she did, and which he did not necessarily object to. She gave him her smile, which made him smile too. She said, "Shall I fix you a snack?"

"I'll take an apple. Maybe one of them granola bars with the cranberries or some of them fruit paper things."

"Coming right up," she said, and she watched Harvey go into their bedroom to change.

Sometimes the days and weeks flew by, and other times it was like he watched everything in slow motion, every little thing, like the God he knew didn't exist was telling him, *Look, Harvey,* pay attention, keep your eyes open, because it's all going to go away soon enough, and there's not a darn thing you can do about it (the God that did not exist for him did not cuss). And so he looked. He looked closely at everything now, like he was studying all the details, wondering how everything was made, how the nuts and bolts and wheels all worked together, allowed everything to move, to be set in motion. He saw the shades of color that maybe he had never noticed before, the scarlet and lime green and even the browns of the leaves, which could blend together like a million grains of sand, pellucid against the sky. And it was okay; people did not pay him any mind. Because maybe he blended in as well. He was a *Professor,* and it was his job to study, to prod, to poke, to analyze. He was an expert in his field. Did not the word itself, did not "Professor," mean to be, or *profess* to be, an expert in an art, in a science? Did not his very actions follow exactly what he, by definition, was? In his opinion, they did, and always had.

It's all related, he justified. And once even out loud to Julianne, whom he caught staring at him one evening, seemingly from another planet.

"What's related?" she'd said.

And he had said, "Everything is related," and she could not argue with that.

But Harvey was no nincompoop. He was not good at pretending something like this didn't exist. He knew this ship of fools—this emptying vessel that was Harvey Lipscomb—was manned by someone, or had once been manned by someone. Someone who got that ship of fools away from shore and sailing away after the crazies had boarded. So now maybe Powell's sent him books *about* him and *for* him alongside books by Jane Pilcher and Judith Butler, Michel Foucault and Oyeronke Oyewumi. Now maybe he turned inward, read up on how to deal with the inevitable, which funny enough was not death but losing the person you were, which maybe was worse than death. There were so many unresolved issues to consider, how could one keep track?

Julianne tucked a bottle of water into his cargo pants' pocket, put sun block under his eyes, pinched it all over his nose.

The clouds would come out later, but right now the sky was bright blue and the sun would sear his skin like bologna, even with his cap. Harvey said he would be an hour tops.

"I'll have lunch ready when you get back," she said. "Liverwurst okay?"

"Perfect," he said. "I don't make it back in an hour, please don't call the Mounties." He smiled.

"I promise," she said. The real Harvey talking. The Harvey she fell in love with talking. She said, "Can I sell your books?" and he said, "Just the ones I've written," blew her a kiss, and walked out the door.

They ate lunch between ten-thirty and eleven these days, earlier than most, but considering they were up at the crack of dawn they did not find the habit peculiar. She spread the liverwurst over the slices of bread, sliced some pickles. The phone rang and she stopped what she was doing, sat at the kitchen table, twirling the phone cord. Her attorney again, but nothing crazy, nothing that wasn't part of doing business. She just didn't like the term: *Mail Fraud*, because that wasn't what it was. Was your electric bill mail fraud? Was your gas bill? Your mortgage? No, it was not. She remembers when she had first hired him, Dustin of *Dustin Kitchens, Attorneys-at-Law*. She'd said, Look, Mr. Dustin, I am fully aware of what my products are and what they are not. They are healthcare and cosmetic products, not necessities. But it's right there, in plain English on the website thingy. You are *signing up* for quarterly orders, and you *are* being charged for refills. Period. I don't hide any of it. And Mr. Dustin had smiled and said, Of course, Mrs. Lipscomb, and they'd shaken on it, and she officially had representation. He had cashed the check later that afternoon.

She was never going to get rich on her sales, but the site more than paid for itself. Two kids from town sent out the hair gels and the nail products and the henna powder straight from their homes, where they'd agreed she would deliver them once a month. All they had to do was stick her labels on, print out customer addresses, drop everything off at the post office once a week. The easiest two hundred a month the kids could ever expect to make. And she did not have to worry about bills, not with what was coming in and what Harvey had stashed away and still made on his books. Mail fraud was a bit over the top.

Mr. Dustin said, I'll need a bit more to keep going, and she said, *But of course, Mr. Dustin*, and said she'd be down later to give him his check, which she was already signing, payable to *Dustin Kitchens*, wondering if indeed a Mr. *Kitchens* truly walked this earth. Just leave it in my mailbox or over with Myrtle at United Community, he'd said. Going fishing, Mrs. Lipscomb. Oh, she said, thinking, well, that must be nice, mustn't it? Fishing in the middle of the day.

As soon as she'd hung up, the phone rang again, this time Sammy. She could hear exhaustion in Sammy's voice, not exasperation or surrender or anything else she heard recently, just exhaustion. Exhaustion from working multiple jobs; exhaustion from the roller coaster of her and Cliff. Exhaustion from some new diet she was on, not enough carbs, too much meat, eating things that bloated her like a Thanksgiving Day parade balloon. Julianne said, "And how is my number one, today?"

"Tired," she said.

"Still coming up on Friday?"

"Trying. Maybe Saturday. Still figuring it out."

"Cliff still coming?"

"Yep."

"Still trying to talk him out of it?"

"Yep."

"Well, you just take some deep breaths and don't stress too much about it. You can kick back up here. Get you right in the Jacuzzi under the jets."

Sammy was quiet for a second, like she was moving something or rearranging something. She dropped the phone, said, "Mom, I gotta call you back," and Julianne said, "I'll be here," and hung up.

It was like that recently. Talking in codes, Julianne assuming scenarios, Sammy with one-word affirmations and negations. Quick two-minute calls, quick hang-ups, because she had to discipline their ornery dog, which was half beagle, half devil, or maybe because she was already late for work. All her daughters did it, though. Really it was just to speak to her. Called when they just wanted to hear her voice, know she was there, when they wanted a shoulder to lean on, an understanding ear to just listen, and not try to fix. They did it for the same reasons: a fight with the hubby (we had a "disagreement" is what Lettie and Rachel called what they had with theirs), a question about a recipe. But they also had their own reasons. Recently, Sammy's questions were about leaving, and Rachel's were about fulfillment. Lettie's, bless her soul, were about sex, which Julianne was glad, though she could never have dreamed about talking of such things with her own mother. But Lettie had always been her little bitty Chicky, her reticent child and peek-a-boo-kid. Lettie was the baby, and she played the role well. Lettie was the introspective one. Her reader and little artiste, writing away in her little notebooks as if she were George Eliot or Virginia Woolf.

When Harvey strolled in, Julianne looked up at the clock. She said, "Sixty minutes flat," and Harvey winked at her and tapped his watch. "I set the timer," he said. "Raced back when I fell behind some." He bent down, brushed the side of his ankle, rubbed his shin. "Nearly beefed it around a corner though."

Julianne said, "*Slow down*, Indiana." She put the sandwiches onto two paper plates, put napkins under them where the pickle juice bled through. She said, "One of these days you're going to break your neck and someone's going to come up and run you over by accident."

Harvey took a bite of his sandwich, guzzled some water. Julianne said, "Help me make the beds after lunch?" and Harvey nodded. Julianne wanted to mention Mr. Dustin's call, but kept it to herself. No need to get Harvey all riled up at what a shyster the man was, even *if* he kept the hounds at bay. Harvey did not think lawyers should have ponytails, in Helen or anywhere else for that matter. She wanted to mention Mr. Dustin's going fishing, it sounded like such a pleasant thing to do, even if it was the middle of the day. And a workday, which as a client seemed irresponsible. But maybe Harvey could go fishing too, get out of the house. Get some more of that beautiful mountain air in his lungs. Drive out a ways, catch whatever was up there flipping around in the Hooch, throw it on the grill for supper like they did years back when they'd first bought the cabin and were newlyweds. But that did not happen. And somewhere inside she had already prepared for it not to happen. Not that it bothered her, because it didn't. Just that she noticed it, which she did more and more. Harvey wound down and she slowed up, and he changed out of his outside clothes into his inside clothes. They made the beds and swept the deck and took their little catnaps, and soon they were sitting on the front porch eating caramel covered popcorn and drinking sweet tea until it got dark without them realizing it, and it was time for bed all over again.

It was comfortable, if it was nothing else. That's what she liked. That's what made her life good. Not just that, of course, but because good was not bad. That was also good. Being able to just be, to walk barefoot over the smooth hardwood, stare out at nothing in particular for as long or as little as she wanted. To be able to release focus and relax and know that everything would still be just as you left it, unmoved, solidly in place where it had always been, planted firmly into the ground. To know that the leaves would fall but that others would still be clinging to the branches outside of their window, waiting for her (and only her) to watch them loosen up and fall, flutter to the ground, feed the earth. Or so she liked to think, anyway. What did that hurt?

Friday morning they wake early and begin going through the checklists Julianne has written up so they don't forget any of the details. Julianne has written "Harvey's To Do's" on one sheet, "Julianne's To Do's" on another, and she has set them side by side on the kitchen counter with half pencils that have made their way from one of the local gas station lottery counters. It has begun drizzling outside, rain mixed with bits of hail. As they wet mop the floors, the rain is their music, and when it stops, Harvey does his *60 Minutes tick tick tick tick tick* to keep it going.

As he completes each task, Harvey crosses them off the list one by one, a clean pencil line through the middles of the words, cutting them in half. It is not a race, but he does notice that his tasks are being crossed off at a much faster rate than

Julianne's, which is perhaps not normal but definitely not unheard of. When he finishes dusting over the fireplace and resupplying the bathrooms with rolls of TP from the garage, he moves to the last task on Julianne's list, starts working on that, scratching each task off her list and then initializing them with smiley faces. Julianne does not correct Harvey, does not say, "Harv, dear, you've missed a spot here the size of Guatemala," does not point out that no, he did not, in fact, already fold the linens that he did not remember to pull from the laundry (though yes, he probably heard the timer buzz). There is no point to it, unless the point is to make him feel bad. So she runs through his list again, later, when Harvey is in his study, reading his books a third time, writing articles that, somehow (and to Julianne's surprise), still find homes. He goes days like this, as half a Harvey, misplacing, forgetting, and when people come around, withdrawing. But then, other times, he's the old Harvey, the whole Harvey, and everything is as good as it always was. She knows these weeks, the half-Harvey days, are the beginning, and she is glad it's a slow process, which allows her to get used to it, to acclimate. Last year, all was well, and the kids were in and out. This year, what, a month? They'll know; and it won't take long. But she won't say it. Won't admit it before they have a chance to pick up on it themselves. Not because she wants to fool them, because that would be distasteful. But rather to see how noticeable it all really is to those who do not live it every day. To those whose problems and issues are not hers, not every day, not in the here, not in the now. Those whose worlds are not overshadowed by the whirlwind that is Harvey Lipscomb.

For a time, she thought, maybe it is brilliance that afflicts him. Maybe Harvey is like Einstein. She has read or maybe she'd seen it on PBS that Albert Einstein often walked right past his house without realizing it. This was how deep in thought the man could be, and how could you blame him, solving the problems he solved? So much so that they'd had to put an "X" on his front door to remind him where he lived or he'd just keep walking. Probably drove his wife batty. And sometimes, Harvey was like that. He could go on trips to Ypsilanti and to conferences in

Madrid and Barcelona and be lost for days. No call, no e-mail, nothing. Just silence, as if he'd walked off into another universe where they didn't have phones, where time stood still. She thought maybe the change of scenery exacerbated his condition, this condition, which seems to have come on full throttle all of a sudden, or at least what seems all of a sudden, because it has probably been there for some time, now that she is capable of admitting it. Now that she knows what's what.

When the lists are crossed off and then crossed off a second time, Harvey puts his arm around Julianne and says, "You ready?" and she says, "Yep. Round one, here we go."

And Harvey says, "You want to pull a couple bottles of red?"

And Julianne, unbelieving that she herself could forget to remember, throws her hands over her head and exclaims, "The wine!" Which, of course, tickles Harvey so.

He watches Julianne rush off to put her jeans and socks on. He says, "We, toots, are a twosome destined for disaster."

Julianne grabs the first notepad she can find, scribbles her hasty yet expressive *Be-right-back*, signs it with a happy face like Harvey's. She tells Harvey to tape the note to the door while she ties her boots. She says, "Stick it on there good. It's windy and wet." Harvey says he will. He says, "We'll probably be back before they get here anyway, but we can just leave the door open."

Julianne says, "All my girls have keys," and Harvey says, "Oh, right," remembering when they had mailed the keys to New York and Florida and someplace else, folding them in newspaper and then tucking them into multiple sheets of scratch paper from the printer. It's like a clandestine communiqué, Harvey had said, pointing out the mumbo jumbo typing all over the sheets, where Julianne had tested out the new ink cartridge. Not "asdf ;lkj," as he would have thought, but "10001 1001 101," which he found curious.

When they pull back up to the guard gate, tired from shopping, Jim tells Harvey and Julianne they have guests waiting for them at the cabin. They had not expected to be gone so long, over two hours, but they had not expected to have driven to

Cleveland to go to the Walmart and the Piggly Wiggly out there, because Betty's was out of peach syrup and Harvey had said they couldn't come all the way out to Georgia and not have peach syrup on their pecan pancakes. And then they had bought nearly all of the Cabernets and one Riesling from the young woman at the Bavarian Bottle Shop, Petra or whatever her name was, who wouldn't shut up about the new Riesling until they'd agreed to buy a bottle. *So pushy*, Julianne had said, as they drove out the parking lot and through their little Freistaat Bayern.

When they pulled in they saw the giant of a truck hogging the driveway, a sliver of moon at its back, reflected off the windshield and half-acre hood. Harvey pulled in behind it, pulled the emergency brake, and Julianne hustled off inside with an armful of grocery bags and one of the bottles of red, hollering hellos to everyone. Julianne's daughter came out, threw an arm around Harvey, and then James, her husband, came out and helped him unload, and soon they were in the house putting all the groceries away.

Harvey, to cozy everyone up, lit a fire, put the stereo on, searched for Christmas albums to listen to. Later, when Julianne's granddaughter, who, it was true, was also his granddaughter, had gone to sleep, Harvey told James about all of the work they had done over the past year on the house, upgrading this, re-caulking that. When he stumbled, Julianne helped him along, reminding him about the subfloor they'd put in the guest bathroom, the new vanity in the master, what a disaster it had been, maneuvering the hulking cabinet around that corner and all. "Nearly lost some digits," Julianne said. And Harvey concurred.

In bed later that evening, Harvey not snoring but not *not* snoring, Julianne thought, No, they had not noticed. Or they were good at not showing that they had noticed. Maybe they had been so tired they hadn't been able to notice. Or maybe, which was very possible, they had simply not wanted to bring it up. And if that were the case, then it was pity they felt, and no, she could not be pitied. But Rachel would not do that. Rachel would not pity them. Not even if James steered her that way would she pity them. Rachel did not pity; Rachel stood up. Rachel helped. Rachel drove straight through, pulled everyone along with her, kicking and screaming. Rachel always said, Hey, make lemonade. That was her Rachel. That was her number two daughter. Soon Julianne fell asleep to the music of Harvey's low breathing.

Everyone fell in like they always fell in. They did things as a family, at certain times of the day, but for the most part they left Harvey alone, let him hide in his room, in the garage, the study. James had his *Crackberry,* and Harvey had his computer and his word processor, and more often than not James had wires hanging from his ears as he paced through the rooms, returning calls, joining meetings and then muting his little microphone, stepping outside where he worked his calves on the steps they'd stained a shade too light a few summers back. Harvey did not avoid anyone, did not shy away when asked to participate, but he changed few of his routines when they had guests. He woke early and went for walks in the morning, read the paper, had his coffee, did his writing, corresponded with students about the upcoming semester, what he expected from them, what they could expect from him. He made pecan pancakes with peach syrup and cinnamon butter (his specialty), and he helped Julianne cook when she needed his help (he acquired great little hors-d'oeuvre recipes from his trips to Spain [tapas he called them, which everyone always heard as *topless*]), especially when her fingers swelled up, when her migraines kicked in, and her only savior was a cool rag over her eyes and dead silence. He spent time with James and he spent time with Hadley, who loved Harvey like she seemed to love all old men who played dolls with her and who taught her cool new things. Hadley seemed to like Harvey the most, probably because he taught her how to pretend she was levitating when really she was only tiptoeing on one foot. That particular trick she still did, months and months after he'd taught her. An optical illusion, is what it is, Rachel heard Hadley confide to her friends on more than a number of occasions. "It means it fools your eyes." But mostly Hadley loved the stories he told her about the journeys of the chivalrous Don Quixote de la Mancha and his buddy, the fat Sancho Panza, galloping away on their silly but ultimately melancholy quests across the unforgiving landscapes of La Mancha.

In his books, Harvey felt important. In the forewords and on the back covers, where his fellow authors and academic colleagues praised his work, he felt as if he had indeed made his mark. He felt a measure of accomplishment, and he felt that, Yes, he had given something back when for many years, and perhaps ashamedly so, he had only taken. Taken childhoods (those of his son, his daughter), and stolen youth (that of his ex-wife's, he had to admit), and god knows who or what else, for surely he left victims in his wake. Not out of malice, but definitely, absolutely, out of selfishness. Yet what could you do? What were the rules? How could he suppress a talent, a gift, a *calling*, that had always wanted to emerge, even if the collateral damage was his own flesh, his own blood? How could he rationalize cutting off insights the world over should know, theories yearning to be shared in lectures, in text? Truths about something as important as gender, as universally essential and as necessary as sexuality? The answer was simple: he couldn't.

And yet, while he saw need in his books, in the physical nature of dirt, Harvey saw the world. In tilling the earth, Harvey felt *connected*. In planting seeds that grew, Harvey built life, and like the work in his field, this life was more than compulsion. Like everything he did, the seeds he planted kept his heart beating, kept his lungs breathing, kept his blood pumping. It kept him alive. The garden, unlike other things in his life, *had* to grow. The garden was the yang to his yin. Sure, it was a young garden, newly planted, still artificial. It had its difficulties. It was not the previous one he had cultivated over a decade, thriving fully, contributing on its own to its prosperity, because that one was gone. That was an Eden that no longer existed, at least not for him. Someone else tilled that earth. Someone else reaped the fruits it bore. But this garden, his and Julianne's, was a cosmos unto itself, an early utopia split between two beds, a fragment of the previous but good enough. Two planetary systems peeking at one another from across a universe of gravel, pitchers of water like travelers in space floating from one planetary system to the next, sprinkled gently to the earth like rain, moistening the skin like dew. *Working.*

Until a voice from the heavens, singing across the universe, rattles everything. "Heading in," the voice says. "Starting supper."

Plain. Simplicity itself. Julianne's voice aligning the planets again, and topsoil is topsoil, fieldstone is fieldstone, river rounds are river rounds. And the invaders, the nematodes he knows are there, hiding in his sandy soil, cloaked in their microscopic camouflage, are having their last supper. They are done, because he has rotated his okra, and he has rotated his tomatoes and, for the coup de grâce, has laid his chitin. With their demise comes life. All of these things, this miniature microcosm of wars and battles, make his garden grow. Wonderfully.

A truth without question: Harvey enjoys all of Julianne's children. He appreciates their husbands, the family men they are, though never would he want to be like them. Their careers are not careers, in his mind, not what he considers worthy ones, anyway. They are money machines, yes, but these careers leave empty lives, hollow souls. These careers do not construct, but shuffle. This goes here, that goes there, and the chime in the register dings and dings. And the house expands. And more and more and more.

They are sitting in the dining room now, he and James, Rachel's husband, the corporate man, the driver of the tank in his driveway. Today he will attempt to mingle, and tomorrow he will attempt to actually socialize, but Sunday, all hellos and small talk exhausted, Harvey will read the New York Times, and he will try (and fail) to sleep late, and he will sit in bed and jot down ideas for the future, as he always does. The work before the work begins.

"You guys should come up some time," James is saying now, not looking at him but at the little machine in his hand, the little computer he knows was invented by a college dropout, which seems unfair. "In the summer we can take the boat out, go sailing."

"That would be nice," Harvey says. "Appreciate it."

James works his thumbs over the little machine, tapping away on the tiny little buttons. He presses one of the larger keys, puts the machine down on the table. He looks up at Harvey, his eyes wide, a smile across his chiseled face. It is a kind look, Harvey thinks. It is probably the same look he shows clients. It is a look that makes you feel like there's only the two of you in the whole world. He says, "I mean it, Harv. Walk right from the backyard onto the boat. Head out for the day, come back in and barbecue. It's awesome."

"All for it," says Harvey. "I enjoy sailing."

James puts his hand on Harvey's elbow, squeezes, like Barry over at the car lot does whenever he and Julianne walk by on their way to the post office. Harvey does not look at the hand; it's just James being James, talking how he talks.

"Just got the new Hunter 50CC," he says. "Hull and rig is the same as the H-49. But the cockpit, it's elevated. More style. More function." He says, "You'd love the aft stateroom, Harv. Custom divan, cedar storage. *Un-f'in-real.*"

Harvey says, "Sounds like it." He buttons his lip, gives James the thumbs up. "I'll talk to Julianne this evening, see if I can't convince her to pop up there next summer."

But James is already back to his computer, typing away. He says, "What was that, Harv?" and Harvey says, "You want some sweet tea?" and when James says one sec, Harv, Harvey says, "I'll go get us some sweet tea," and goes wandering off into the kitchen.

Rachel says, "I apologize in advance for my husband," when Harvey walks in. She has been watching James and Harvey, whom she can see completely from her seat beside Hadley at the kitchen table. Hadley is taking rabbit nibbles from the corner of a Rice Krispies treat.

"No worries," Harvey says, using a term he knows he's picked up from his students. He pulls two glasses from the cabinet, grabs the pitcher of tea from the fridge. Pushes the soy milk to one side.

But Rachel says, "No, I know. But it can be annoying, that damn thing always pressed to his face. It's like where did that come from? All of a sudden everyone has this growth at the end of their arms."

Harvey says, "The duplicitous nature of technology," and walks off with the glasses of sweet tea. He drops one of the glasses off on the table in front of James, and James thanks him, and Harvey is off to another room, out of sight. Julianne looks at Rachel, says, "Apparently work calls," and sits down beside Hadley, who licks her fingers, says she would like another one, please, Nana.

Rachel digs in her travel bag, which is on the kitchen counter by one of the larger bowls Harvey has carved up in his little workshop. She pulls a big Ziploc of snacks out, hands a packaged Krispies treat to Hadley, tells her that's it, no more. Hadley smiles, and when she can't tear the plastic, Julianne tears it for her. Bon appétit, she says. Hadley says, I will *teet*.

Rachel says, "So what else is going on around here?" She means here, in the house, in their cabin. She means with them, with Julianne and Harvey. She means *their* lives.

Julianne says, "Well, you missed Oktoberfest, which was a few weeks back, and the Festival of Trees, but coming up I think we have some glass blowings the kids might like. And we have the lights downtown, of course."

Rachel remembers the lights from last year, how much the kids enjoyed walking around Helen. She says, "Hadley has been getting into *RE LIGI ON* at school." She spells the word out, one letter at a time, slowing down and speeding up, throwing off the normal pattern she would normally use around children, around Hadley. Hadley looks at her mother, gives her the, I'm *seven, Mom.* I'm not dumb, look. She says, "Helloooo, I'm right here. I know what you're talking about!" with as much exaggeration as she can, considering her mouth is full of toasted rice and marshmallow.

"Someone can spell," Julianne says.

"Apparently," says Rachel, pinching Hadley's side. "Now we just have to get her to read more than one book a year with her own two eyes and her own half a noggin!"

Hadley gets up, lets Julianne wash the sticky marshmallow off her fingers. She says, "Can I watch TV?" But before Rachel answers, Hadley says, "K. Thanks," and walks out of the room smiling, one hand up in the air waving bye, which is something she's learned from Bridgette, her babysitter. Rachel tells her just for a little bit.

Julianne starts a small saucepan full of milk, says, "I'm making everyone some hot milk and honey. Be a dear and get the Christmas cups from the other room." Julianne has always made hot milk, but more during the rough times, when tempers flared, when there was loss.

Rachel says, What room? And Julianne says, "The only other room with cups in it." Rachel heads to the dining room, spots the china cabinet she's looked at dozens of times and notices there's actually Christmas cups and cutlery and even Lladro Christmas-themed porcelain figurines sitting right there behind the glass. After she moves the Lladro snowman-with-girl from the center of a wooden tray, she grabs the tray, stacks it full of cups, and brings the tray to the kitchen. She says, "Lladros, right?" and Julianne says, "Yes. Harvey got me started on them a few years back. He sends for a piece every year on the day of our first date. Romantic boy, my Harvey." She does not tell Rachel that this year no Lladro has arrived. That this year there was no heavily-taped white box with *Correos* or *España* stamped over Juan Carlos' face.

When the milk begins to boil, Julianne turns the fire off, pulls the skin off the top with her fingertips. Rachel passes her an empty cup each time Julianne fills one, and soon they have a miniature assembly line of sorts going until they fill up the tray, hands touching hands touching hands. Julianne pours the last of the milk into the last mug, says *Perfect*, and Rachel heads off to play the kind and generous holiday assistant to Julianne's host. When she returns, there are two cups still on the tray, one for her, one for Julianne.

Julianne pulls the stools from under the kitchen bar. They sit down on opposite sides of the counter, sipping the milk, tasting the sweet honey on the tips of their tongues. Julianne says, "When you and your sisters turned one, I fed each of you a little bit of honey on my finger, for your birthdays. I wasn't able to buy you anything, not that any of you would have noticed anyway, but come your first birthdays, you each got fingertips of honey."

Rachel says, "You're not supposed to give that to babies. Gives them botulism." She is smirking, another one of those *Oh my God, how did I ever survive childhood?* smirks.

Julianne says, "You're here, aren't you?" She says, "I know that. I knew it then. But after twelve months, honey isn't going to kill you."

Rachel says, "Mom? Can I ask you an odd question?"

"Shoot," says Julianne.

"I mean, maybe it's not odd, but just odd for me." She says, "What do you think of me? Of my family?"

Random, Julianne thinks, but not completely so. Without hesitation, she says, "I think you're great, dear. I think they're great." And she means it. If they aren't, who is?

"But I mean, like what we've talked about on the phone. The eight hundred ways thing?"

She means the eight hundred paths any family can take, the end result, what's left after all of the pieces have been moved, at least up to a particular point in time. The mathematics and the statistics of it, of life. Person A marries person B; A plus B produces C; A plus B plus C move to a particular town on a particular island in a particular location into a particular environment, where they begin talking in a particular way, living a particular life. Leaving behind, of course, the seven hundred ninety-nine other possibilities that could have been their lives if they had decided it should be, if they had simply altered one input or another.

Julianne says, "You have good lives, dear. You are successful. You are the dream, whether you know it or not. You are privileged, and you are healthy. Never forget what you have." She puts her hands on her daughter's cheeks. "No one is ever completely happy," she says. "Not absolutely."

Rachel nods. "I know. I think the older I get, I start questioning is all. Not always. Just sometimes. I look at Had and I want her to have it all. Not everything, but *everything*."

Julianne says, "You're a mother. That's your job."

Rachel sips the last of her milk. She says, "Did you have these thoughts? Or were you too . . . *busy*?" It is not meant as a dig. Julianne knows her daughters well. Even when Rachel digs, her scoops are shallow.

Julianne says, "You mean because I had to work three jobs?" and laughs. "No. You were my babies. Still are. I have those thoughts now." She says, "You have to remember, when I was your age I had three teenage daughters. Three daughters who were very different from each other. *Very* different." She finishes her milk, hands the cup to Rachel, who puts the cups in the sink. She says, "Try *that* for a weekend. Try that *and* going on a date with someone you like without your daughters knowing. Talk about tough." Julianne is smiling now. She says, "Hmph," walks over to where Rachel is sitting.

Rachel says, "I shudder to think."

Julianne says, "You do what you have to do." She is hugging Rachel now, holding Rachel's head to her chest. "Remember that, dear. You have a good life. Enjoy it. That's all the advice in the world that matters."

As a family, Rachel and James and Hadley head to town and then on the road, to wander and sightsee as they always do when they're away. A month is a long time, and separation is good, even from those you've come to spend time with. Even from family. Or especially from family.

They drive and walk along the Smithgall Woods Conservation Area, along Otali Road and Tsalaki Trail, and even Boca Hills Road, which makes Hadley go into a sing-song, repeating *Mouth Hills Road* until she is simply humming one long hum that starts with M and ends with what sounds like "ode." For Harvey and Julianne, the quiet time is good. They spend the early morning hours after breakfast tending to the garden, where everything is ready to go but in an intermediary state of dormancy, awaiting the frosts to thaw and the heat to come. They sweep and mop and do what laundry there is, which is not much. They run the Jacuzzi and open the heating vents in all the rooms (which they keep closed when it's just them), Julianne supporting the ladder while Harvey points the grates just so, a little this way a little that way, maximizing and directing the dispersion of heat like traffic police.

By noon Harvey is sealing manila envelopes, putting too many stamps on submissions too important to send via e-mail. A day late, but not a dollar short. He will walk into town, pick up a paper, drop his manila envelope with Eugene at the post office, who calls him *Professor L.* Eugene who has, in fact, read numerous papers Harvey has written over the years, and even one of his books, God knows why. Eugene who reminds him that, in a way, he is one of Helen's minor celebrities, transplant or not. Eugene, whom he has seen, on more than one occasion, using his high school Spanish to read the Spanish correspondence he has written, carefully, with a dictionary, prior to slipping into España-bound envelopes.

"Article or chapter?" says Eugene, weighing Harvey's envelope.

"Article," replies Harvey, quietly, a little Salingeresque reticence in his tone.

"Good luck," says Eugene, waving at Harvey, who is walking out the door, having held it open for Mrs. Coggeshall, who Harvey knows, at one point in time, has also worked in academia.

Hand in hand they walk, he and Julianne, for she has decided a walk with Harvey will be good for her now, before daughter number two, Lettie, and her husband and not-so-little Aaron, their son, come rolling in later that afternoon, though she had planned on their being here earlier. After they arrive, she knows, there will be too much to do, too much minutiae to manage. Conductors cannot walk in on their symphonies. Ringmasters do not show up late to their circuses.

She is holding Harvey's hand, the old couple walking around town, Harvey's keys and wallet and cough drops and lip balm tucked sloppily away in his Buffalo pouch, which James teasingly calls a fanny pack. They are on their leisurely walk today, not their exercise walk, not their errand walk; there is nothing to buy, no ingredients to pick up, no prescriptions to refill. They go up and down the stairs, in and out of the shops, saying their hellos, promising their attendance at upcoming community events, the crab boil at the senior citizen center, the potlucks at people's homes around town and out in the hills, when a few of them get scrunched up into the Moss's brown van like they're schoolchildren, get nauseated zigzagging up to whoever's house so they can eat salty brisket and over-boiled potatoes.

They stop into Louise's little shop, tell her their kids are here, more on the way, Harvey admiring the amethyst pendants while Julianne and Louise stare at the ascending rows of Matryoshka dolls that look like rainbows crashed into armless women wearing babushkas. Harvey says, "It means *not intoxicated*," and looks back at Julianne, at Louise. "What does?" says Julianne, looking over her shoulder but still bent over the rainbows. "Amethyst," says Harvey, pointing at the purple crystals behind the glass. "It comes from the ancient Greek. 'A' is 'not,' and 'methustos' means 'intoxicated.' Not intoxicated. Not drunk."

"I didn't know that," says Louise, surprised. "Been here years and that's the first time I ever heard that."

"He's a wealth of knowledge, my Harvey," says Julianne. And Harvey, moving down the glass display, says, "You have half the gemstones on planet earth here, Louise."

Louise says, "And yet, no one's buying!"

He wants to say, "You can't charge an arm and a leg for pretty rocks," but says, "Tough times, I suppose," as if the words have ever really had much meaning either to her or anyone else with wares to vend. For a moment Julianne tenses, thinking, and horrified, that Harvey may bring up Louise's impending foreclosure.

Instead, his words only serve as signifiers of other things, other entities, other topics, which is all some days are meant for. Perhaps this is one of those days.

So Louise now confides in Julianne some of Helen's newer gossip, it's more scandalous tittle-tattle, which is Harvey's cue to make his sweet little exit, his *be right back*, and walk along the Chattahoochee, where he can kneel by the rocks, check for the familiarity of the wriggling bodies under the stones along the river. He has not fished in Georgia, but old habits rarely die. He allows himself to recall the summers he spent in Montana, fly fishing for trout, dissecting stoneflies and pale morning dun, and then tying his own flies. He remembers working at Many Glacier, the beauty of the landscape, the bear and gray wolf, the red fox and moose and goat. He remembers paddling out to the middle of the lake, on one side Many Glacier's giant cabin, a thousand times his and Jules' cabin, and on the other side a sheer wonderland of western larch and subalpine, snowy peaks slicing the blue sky like ice; a snaking trail hugging a smaller lake just beyond the brush.

"Sweetheart," she says. "It's time to go home." A voice calling from up the bank. "Lettie and Michael should be getting here soon, okay?"

Julianne, smiling, waving at him from beside a garbage can, where the little footpath stops, meets the slope down to the river. He waves at her, starts heading up. He kneels, picks up an oddly shaped twig the size of a chopstick, lets her pull him up the last little bit. He says, "We walking or they picking us up?"

"Who?" says Julianne.

"James and Rachel?"

"No," she says. "We're walking." And they head home, Harvey's shoes leaving dampened footprints along the sidewalk behind them, his socks wet at the shins, but his feet dry and warm, Julianne looking at him but saying nothing, wondering how, in all God's earth, can he be comfortable like that.

He knows that they were just there, walking around Helen, he and Julianne, but now he and James are walking into town again. Now the road is clear, the wind is cool, and it's like the fog that had been there before is simply passing through. James is Julianne's daughter's husband, *Rachel's* husband, which makes him his son-in-law, and this is a fact that he knows without pretending. James is a money man, a big wig, carries burdens much unlike any he has ever known. The places he wants to go, they have corner offices, and they have concrete titles, titles like you have in Washington, salaries that are negotiable and probably obscene. James is discussing vacation homes, but that's not what he is talking about. Harvey knows this. He knew it back at the house. He has always found James a hint overly transparent.

James says, "It would be a pretty big move, Harv."

James is talking about becoming President of his company, and he is talking about becoming COO, Chief Operating Officer. Both big titles, Harvey knows. Both important. For James, who Harvey knows will never be an entrepreneur, who will never risk that much without a guarantee, CEO, Chief Executive Officer, is all that's left. That and the prestige of sitting on the boards of different companies later on, when perhaps, like him, he is too old to work at the rigorous pace he's become accustomed to.

"That's something," Harvey is saying. And it is. Because while maybe he would never go that route, others do, and goals and hard work are goals and hard work. Accomplishment is admirable in any occupation, regardless if earned through persistence or prowess.

James claps his hands for some reason, like he can't control his nerves, and Harvey's ears ring painfully. James is talking now about when he was younger, moving up through the company ranks, putting in the hours, sacrificing while his friends were out getting laid (excuse the language, Harv), and painting the town. But Harvey can't get the ringing out of his ears, like he's had a heart attack sometime in the past, and now, just as Buzz Callaghan's ears ring when someone claps, so does his ring. James does not notice anything, does not see Harvey squint his eyes and put one hand up to his ear. He does not see Harvey shake his head to one side, as if loosening trapped pool water. And he does not see Harvey hold his nose and blow, faintly, as you would on an airplane. Instead, James continues talking about himself, about who deserves what, about merit in this world and no free lunches. It is not until James completes his monologue and there is no response that he looks back, sees Harvey digging into his weathered fanny pack (which he loathes), and says, "Harvey? You okay?" and Harvey says, "I can't hear you. One second, David."

When Harvey is finished digging in his fanny pack, when the eye drops are in his eyes and he has wiped them dry, and when he has glossed his lips with his medicated Chapstick, he says, "Sorry, what was that? The wind picked up a little. I lost what you said."

There is a brief hesitation in James, which Harvey believes is thought, but James picks right up, says, "You okay? You looked a little something right there." Waiting. Expecting something. Expecting it from him.

"Oh sure. Sure," says Harvey, smiling, mimicking James, mimicking Barry the car guy, his hand on James' elbow. "My age you just have to keep yourself oiled and moving or all hell breaks loose." Harvey smacks James on the back, hard, like keep moving, buster, the storm is coming. There's nothing to see here, pal. *Nada*.

Maybe he has never paid much attention, but James has never heard Harvey cuss, much less use a word like "hell." He does not mention it to Harvey. He likes that Harvey is loosening up some, which is how he interprets Harvey's little blaspheme. And maybe Harvey's little error, his calling him by the wrong name, maybe he reminds Harvey of someone named David. Maybe the age *is* catching up.

James says, "You have to make any stops, Harv?" meaning to buy more ChapStick (which looks like it itself has been through hell). Meaning to wrangle anything old guys like him need wrangling. Aspirin, Neosporin. Antifungal cream.

"Not that I can think of," says Harvey, thinking, looking around, running his eyes along the rooms back at home, his and Julianne's bathroom, the garage, his study, imagining lists floating in the trees, pasted on the clapboard signs along Helen's fabricated Strasses. He says, "I'm sure something'll hit me along the way. You just do your thing. I'll be all right."

And it occurs to Harvey, though he makes sure not to assume anything, that maybe he has gone someplace, become something faster and sooner than even he was prepared for. Has morphed into something more rapidly than what he had been expecting. Than what he had been planning on. Maybe Julianne has already made her decisions, already laid out his future, Harvey Lipscomb walking Helen a has-been, a loony-tunes, or worse, a wandering, mindless, wispy-haired once-was, whom people look at, not with admiration but with sadness. But he is not sure. He is not certain. And so he tells himself to hold off, that James is not to blame, that if indeed that is the case, James is simply an accomplice, James is not someone he needs to confront. Not because he is afraid, not because he could not handle himself with James in the art of verbal sparring, but rather because, he knows, it is of no consequence. A discussion with James would matter little, have no bearing on his situation. In his story, James is a fly-by-night, a drive-through, a *good-seeing-you*. If Harvey Lipscomb has been sent out to pasture, pushed out into the fields to walk his days away, the trickery lay with Julianne. The blueprints have been drawn by her, and her alone. But even this he cannot be sure of.

James says, "Bla bla bla," and Harvey follows him into Henkenberns. The rubber on Harvey's boot gets stuck on the gray carpeting, and he bumps smack into James' back, nearly knocking himself and James into a rack of wooden candlesticks. James says, *Whoa*, and Harvey apologizes, chuckles his aw shucks chuckle. He says, "That would have been ugly," and lets James get a few steps on. James is checking out birdhouses and swans carved in glass, rubbing the smooth glossy surfaces of picture frames made of pewter, admiring the carved handles of letter openers. Harvey walks around a display of black chrome and teal and copper Eycatchers, which chime pleasantly in the little breeze he makes on passing them. He thinks, What is it they say about a butterfly's wings here is a hurricane there? James looks at his BlackBerry, puts it back into this pocket. He walks over to a display of salad bowls, wooden plates stained with swirls of milk chocolate and blonde horsehair.

"Lipscomb originals," says a voice, and James turns to see Harvey standing beside an older couple, probably Harvey's age, a year or two younger. The man, wearing jeans, a light blue tie-dye shirt, says, "That whole row is Harvey's."

"I didn't know you sold your stuff, Harv."

"I don't."

"He does," the man says, jutting his hand out. "I'm Ken. This is Prima."

James says hello. He is reading the little placard sitting behind Harvey's bowls and wooden spoons and salad tongs. He says, "Local artisan and renowned author, Harvey Lipscomb," and Harvey says, "Gobbledygook," and slaps at the air. "The Henkenberns make me out to be the Prince of Arabia."

"Harvey's bowls are our number one seller online," says Prima. "He's going to have to start pulling some of them bowls off the walls back home to keep up. You keep him turning," she tells James.

James says, "Harvey the artisan. Well well." And Harvey says, "I support local, but I'm no artisan. That's a skill I have yet to be worthy of."

Prima says, "Nonsense." Says, "I'll be right back. Got me a customer." She walks off behind a glass case, to the register, where a woman holding a kneeling porcelain fawn is opening her purse. Ken says, "And you are?" and Harvey says, "Oh, sorry," places his palm on Ken's chest. "Ken, James. James, Ken."

James says, "Nice to meet you, Ken."

"Which sweetheart are you married to?"

"Rachel," he says. "Daughter number two, as Mrs. Lipscomb puts it."

"Oh sure," says Ken. "I know'em all. Lettie the best, but we know Rachel and Samantha, isn't it? Numbers one and three. For a while there she was down here all the time, Lettie was."

Harvey looks at James. "Ken means when Aaron was a little tyke and Michael was traveling."

"Ah," says James. "Michael's little South America sabbatical." Besides it being listed on his resume, he and Michael have spoken of their time working abroad, the exotic places both of them have had the opportunity to pretend to be expats. It was good for Michael's career, and Lettie hadn't minded. She had stayed with Harvey and Julianne, being nature girl Lettie, writing in her notebooks at pull-offs on the tops of mountains, visiting places nearby like the Margaret Mitchell house in Atlanta and Flannery O'Connor's place outside of Milledgeville, Aaron staying behind with Julianne and Harvey for long stretches while Lettie lived her literary dreams.

James' BlackBerry buzzes. He excuses himself, tells Ken it was nice meeting him.

Harvey and Ken watch James walk outside. Harvey says, "How's business?" and Ken says, "Come on back," and the two men walk over to a small table in a back room littered with boxes and plastic bubble wrap, coffee mugs stained beige.

They had both nearly jumped out of their hides when the horn blared at them, but now they saw smiling faces behind the Suburban's windows, Lettie and Michael and Aaron whooping it up at their expense. Harvey said, "You trying to kill him or me?" as he stepped over to the passenger side window smiling his warm smile.

Aaron was laughing so hard he looked like he would piss himself. Harvey said, "Kid's going to laugh himself silly," and Lettie said, "How are you, Harvey!" and hugged him around his neck. Michael told them to hop in. Sandwiched between James and Harvey, Aaron was in heaven, being tickled by James, and Harvey, *Magic Man* Harvey, was teasing him, telling him he had a new trick for him that would top any of the many tricks he had taught him and his cousin Hadley the previous year. James was asking Michael how his tooth was, did he get everything straightened out. All good, Michael told James, changing the subject. "So what have you troublemakers been subjecting this pretty little town to?" James said, "Did you know Harvey here is a renowned artisan?" Harvey, shaking his head enough that James could see him in the rearview, said, "Ken and his big mouth."

When they got to the cabin everyone went inside, Aaron leading the way, yelling his little head off, announcing to the world that yes, he had indeed arrived. He and Hadley jumped around like greyhounds off to the races, hugging each other and then sprinting to their bedroom, working themselves up into a cyclone of frenzy and giggles, and then heading outside to torment whatever God's creatures crossed their mischievous trajectory. Harvey lingered a bit, picked up a paperweight, set it down, walked off, said he had some work to do. Julianne fell into motherhood all over again, loving every minute of at least two of her babies back home, letting themselves go, becoming children anew as they always did when she was around. Need was absolutely one of the things Julianne cherished.

Before long, Julianne and Lettie are sifting flower, mixing ingredients to bake their goodies when the doorbell rings, Jim delivering a cardboard box, the same cardboard box that arrives every year for Harvey. Inside, Julianne knows, is a bottle of Chardonnay that Harvey will drink, alone, over three days, December 16, 17, and 18, as he does every year, only this time perhaps with a little more ominous of a tinge to the timing, because, according to the papers, they were but days from the impending doom of this Y2K thing. He will pour one fourth of the bottle on the sixteenth, and one fourth on the seventeenth. But on the eighteenth, she knows, Harvey will force himself to finish the remaining two glasses, to finish half the bottle, and that he will drink himself a tad loopy to remain faithful to his little tradition. Why, however, is something he has yet to disclose. And why, Julianne does not ask. She believes everyone, no matter what, should have a little piece of something, whatever they like, whatever suits their fancy, whatever floats their boat, to themselves. She says, "Thank you, Jim." And Jim says sure thing. She says, "Jim, I know, I *know*, but the offer still stands," and Jim says, "Thanks, Mrs. Lipscomb. If I could, you know I would." Jim waves and heads back down the road to the guard gate, where she knows he will read old issues of *Reader's Digest* and do his crosswords, where he will fall asleep before dark and watch the *Late Late Show* on a small black and white television when everyone is sleeping soundly in their beds. But she hopes he does not spend Christmas alone. She hopes Jim does show up, dressed in his best, eats Christmas dinner with them, her family, because she could not allow a poor old man to spend Christmas all alone, no matter who he was or if his only boy and daughter-in-law were stationed in Germany or Japan or wherever.

When Julianne sticks the box on top of the fridge, standing on her step stool, Lettie says, "Harvey's mystery box?" and Julianne nods.

"Still no clue?"

"None. But I think it's kind of cute, don't you?"

Lettie says, "I don't know if cute is the right word." She wipes her nose with the back of her wrist, wiping away at a smudge of flour tickling her. "And you're never going to ask, huh?"

"Never ever," she says. "Harvey is a big boy. I'm sure there's depth there."

Rachel says, "Do you care if *I* ask?"

Julianne says, "Don't you dare." She folds her stepping stool, clicks the little metal clasp. Slips the stool between the fridge, the cabinet where she keeps her cookie sheets. She says, "Just because you're grown doesn't mean I can't put either of you over my knee."

Lettie says, "Have you seen Rachel's waistline? You may want to rethink that."

Rachel says, "I'll rethink you," and dips her finger in the sweet red filling in one of the bowls on the countertop.

Julianne pulls the bowl towards her, covers it with a tear of Saran Wrap. She says, "That's all you get," pushes the cherry jam to one corner. "Once Sammy gets here we'll have a bakefest and eat ourselves sick."

Lettie tells Rachel to help out, and Rachel says, Okay, pulls out a plastic container, a metal rack from one of the bottom cabinets. She says, "There you go," and takes off to the back deck. Lettie says, "You'd think she'd thrown a grenade."

Julianne says, "I think she and James got something cooking. Something about a rental property or something."

Lettie says, "Martha's Vineyard. For a week. On the water."

Julianne says, "Hmm. I thought they'd said the Cape. Maybe I misheard."

"Nope. Same place they rented last year."

"Hmm," says Julianne again. "I believe I'm losing my mind. I thought they said they were buying the place." Julianne, scraping a lemon for its zest.

"Buying? No, not unless you know something I don't."

And Julianne, familiar with the waters of deception, for whatever reason deception has presented itself just then: "Nope. My fault. I need to listen more carefully."

The tarts in the oven, her kitchen warm and sweet with baking sugar, Julianne joins Harvey and her grandchildren in the living room, pulls a blanket over her legs, tells Hadley to come sit by Grandma, warm her up some, which Hadley does. In the reflection of a framed photo of the Grand Canyon, the one in Yellowstone (not the one in Arizona), Julianne watches Michael peek into the kitchen, then walk out the front door to join James, whom she knows is yearning to be free. Free from the snail's pace of their cabin, and free to work his muscles, which are too big and whose veins are too prominent, at least in her opinion. She pulls Hadley in close, kisses her on the side of her head. And Hadley, wrapped in another world, pulls away, but not completely, which is a compromise to them both. This is evening one.

Harvey walks off in the morning, extra early, to be alone. He has worn a light windbreaker, his cargo pants. Underneath nothing but a white undershirt, which is normally enough. But the sun has not risen strong this morning as he had hoped, does not warm him as he had thought it would. He can feel a draft on his legs, which no longer fill these same cargo pants as they once had. He breaks a sweat within minutes, walking fast, moving his legs like pistons, keeping his arms by his side so as not to look like the crazies he sees every now and again, swinging their arms like Olympic speed walkers, strutting around in their women's shorts, making sure one foot is always on the ground, as if someone is watching, waiting to disqualify them from the Nationals of an everyday sport.

He walks up and he walks down. He waves to Mary in her booth, which is Jim's booth later in the day and late into the night. He nods when he passes other early morning strollers, waves hello to those whom he is more formally acquainted—Mrs. Kim, who works at the real estate company where he and Julianne first went looking for a home; Susan and Lizzy Birk, the cute fraternal sisters who work at the yarn place Jules sometimes pops into; Rose, whose last name escapes him, and who oversees operations for Caterpillar for the whole state of Georgia. And they all wave back, neighborly as always.

He wanders for a period of time that escapes him. For a time, in the shady places, maybe he's trembled some, but he's always had paper thin flesh, so what's new. It is not strange for him, floating, hovering, destination-less, and then, with an almost palpable mania, focusing like a homing pigeon headed home.

When he returns, Jules is all over him, yelling about catching cold, getting pneumonia, what's wrong with him? She tells him he has to take a shower, take some of the Vitamin C tablets she's always raving about. Maybe take that other stuff he hates taking, supposed to *prevent* a cold from coming on. She says, "Next time, wear your boots, *please*."

He looks down at his feet and he acknowledges, openly, that yes, she is right. He should not have gone out on his walk, in this weather, in boat shoes. Without socks. In shorts. Not a good idea in general, hiking around in boat shoes, much less at this time of year, in this type of weather. Surely, he will remember next time.

In the steam, he sits down, rubs his feet, which are sore. He shampoos his hair, soaps himself, rinses. He can see his ribs, his wrists, his legs, too thin, not enough meat on them. His belly goes in, not out. A product, he knows, of the walks, of his inability to sit still, which is a great habit, but only to a point. He tells himself he will have to eat more, or he will have to walk less. He remembers a quote: "*My Soul is dark with stormy riot, Directly traceable to diet.*" Samuel Hoffenstein. He will make a point to eat more. He will remind Jules to remind him. The little things, he knows, add up. The soles of my feet hurt, he thinks. And that big toe. What throbbing!

He eats with Jules' family and retires to his study, where he has been meaning to finish the last few chapters of a textbook someone has sent him to review. Competently written, sure. But lacking. Lacking. He pulls the little gold chain on his reading lamp, taps the light bulb, which flickers and then illumes his little space in bright white. He puts on his reading glasses and begins reading, remembering other books he has yet to read, that he has left unread throughout the house, like decaying fruit.

"I think she just needs to go back and get an education," Rachel is saying. "She's smart. Just needs to jump in. Get something for herself." She is talking about Sammy now, the three of them are, Rachel, Julianne and Lettie, sitting in Julianne's "office," which is a bedroom stuffed with Harvey's books and Julianne's skeins of yarn, boxes of picture albums and Hobby Land clearance items, various other past times and businesses she has picked up over the years and dropped soon after. Lettie holds a half-knit centerpiece of some sort to her chest, lays it back where she found it. Rachel says, "We offered to help her, pick up some tuition or books, but she said no. Said school wasn't her thing."

Lettie says, "Very generous," tucks a strand of black hair behind an ear. She says, "That offer hold for sister number three?"

"Sorry," she says. "Only for the needy and uneducated."

Julianne says, "Have some couth, Rachel."

"I didn't mean it like that," she says. "It's a joke, mother. A joke."

Lettie says, "Did it not cross your mind that maybe your offer was insulting?"

Rachel's eyes go up, down. "Not really, no," she says, shaking her head ever so faintly.

Lettie just keeps on, says, "Sammy is stubborn. But I think Cliff is a good guy. I think his problems aren't specifically his. I think his problems are their problems."

Julianne says, "They're both good." She looks over at Lettie, who is gently pulling a piece of loose yarn from another unfinished something-or-other. She says, "Everyone matures at their own pace. There is no manual for life, my dears. What one does at twenty, another does at forty."

Rachel says, "Always good in everyone, mother, huh?" She is being facetious.

Julianne says, "Youth is wasted on the young."

Rachel says, "Okay. Okay." Her attempt at changing subjects, however weakly. She says, "Let's clear some of this junk out of here, shall we?" She is looking at Lettie.

Julianne says, "This is not junk, thank you very much. If you want to help your mother organize her possessions, your mother would greatly appreciate that type of assistance."

Lettie says, "Okay. Let's help mother rearrange her junk," and laughs.

Julianne says, "Oh one day, my children, one day, I will be a very old woman. And one day, I will be sitting in one of your homes, quiet as a feather, rocking in my old lady rocking chair, minding my business. And you will—I'll bet you right now—you *will* have accumulated more than ever I had in my whole life. And I will not laugh. I won't. But I *will* sit there, and I *will* smile, and you'll ask me why I'm smiling. And I'll just say, Remember when . . . and you just remember today, sugar pie. You just remember today."

Rachel says, "Mom, please. You know that will never happen. I will *never* get as old as you."

And Julianne: "Laugh it up, dearie. Laugh it up."

"Girls," says Lettie. "Can't we all just get along?"

"My daughters will be the end of me," she says. "And don't think you're going to get off on that comment either, missy. Violence isn't funny, in jest *or* insinuation."

After the room was straightened, after the yarn was squished into two plastic bins and the homemade soaps were scattered to different bathroom drawers around the house, after Lettie and Rachel made Julianne promise to donate the dozens of *tchotchkes* she'd planned to sell on websites she never got around to building, they pulled out the flour and cocoa powder and red food coloring to make Sammy red velvet cake with cream cheese frosting, which was her favorite and had always been her favorite. Lettie asked Aaron and Hadley did they want to bake a cake for their aunt Sammy. They did.

Sammy has always been her number one, will always be her number one. Not because she loves numbers two or three any less, because she does not. But Sammy will always be number one because she, Julianne, can never shirk the blame—of learning by trial, of erring too much too often, of being perpetually too many steps behind. Sammy is her, and Sammy is her father, a product of the two, a victim of them no less. Yes, Julianne admits, Sammy came to them as a blessing—and No, her beautifully damaged daughter was not an accident. Yes, she was young, but no, she was not careless. Not intentionally. Not with malice. She did her best, and sometimes, by today's standards anyway, her best may not have made the grade. But back then? Back then, she was a good mother. Back then, no one could fault her for anything.

When Sammy arrives, Julianne literally stumbles to open the door. The red velvet cake they baked for Sammy is on the dining room table, guarded by a glass cake cover, and Julianne, checking one last time on it, catches her foot on dirty gardening clothing Harvey has left by the front door. For some reason someone has locked the door, God knows why, even though she knows it was probably Harvey who did that as well, on purpose or more likely by accident, his subconscious locking out whatever craziness he may have believed was after him. Julianne sees them both, Sammy and Cliff, standing in front of the glass window. They look like they're waiting in line at the DMV, Sammy's hair windblown, looking like a crow's nest, like she's had her head out the window all the way out from the airport. She opens the door and they're all smiles, but quiet, like they're happy to see her but someone's thrown a library around them.

Everyone says their hellos, gives their air kisses and hugs, Julianne watching Sammy, trying to read her, see if there's anything new going on beyond all the new always going on with her and Cliff. She thinks: Tsunami? Hurricane? Earthquake? But no. None of them. Maybe just a tornado rolling through town, headed on its way out.

Soon after their arrival, Michael and Cliff take off to drop Cliff's rental off over in Cleveland, which everyone knew Cliff would want to do. Julianne watches Michael's big black truck follow Cliff's little dinghy of a car out of the driveway, her biting her lip and grimacing as she watches Michael nearly run over Harvey's garden he's going so fast. When they're gone, she walks over to Sammy, puts her hand on her lower back, pinches her side like she used to do when she could get her hand around her daughter's like she was no bigger than a Raggedy Ann.

For a few days the kids go nuts, dirtying every single piece of clothing they've brought for them brown with the mud and clay all around them, but sleeping heavily nearly from dusk until dawn. Everyone settles into their routines, and even Harvey seems nonplussed with all of the upheaval and commotion. But one morning Julianne is awakened by something and when she leans over she knows it is the empty bed that has stirred her. She opens her eyes and listens for anything there is to hear. But all there is is silence, and maybe the slight creaking of wood here or there in the rafters. And so she rises and goes in search of her husband, who she knows is entering his own new sort of life, if that's what it is he is going through. Changing, she thinks. Becoming someone else without wanting to become someone else.

When she finds him, she finds him sitting outside in the cold, sipping tea, mesmerized by the stars. It is three in the morning, almost four, and everyone is asleep. He thinks he hears the sound of water, and maybe he does, but it's not from a river or a stream, because there are none close enough to hear, even now, when everything is sleeping. In his youth Harvey loved the stars, memorized the constellations like other kids memorized the statistics on baseball cards. When other kids were trading Ernie Banks and Sandy Koufax, Mickey Mantle and Ted Williams and Yogi Berra, Johnny Logan and Satchel Paige, he and his father were figuring out the ascensions and declinations of Hydrus and Triangulum, listing the abbreviations of Fornax as well as the genitive, which were *For* and *Fornacis*; reciting, from memory, the funny names of those wacky men who'd named them. Fornax, he recalls, was named by Abbé Nicolas Louis de Lacaille, and also named the *Chemical Furnace* in honor of someone whose head was severed from his body in the French Revolution. The silly facts you remembered decades later, tattooed in your memories like ink.

He did not hear the door creak open, and he did not hear Julianne's bare feet shuffle out onto the deck until she said, *Harv, dear. Everything all right?* Her voice a whisper.

She put the back of her hand on his neck, and now it was her warming him, when usually it was the other way around—him warming her, rubbing her chicken skin flesh, keeping her toes warm, defrosting the tip of her nose. "It's a bit cold," she said. "Let me get us a blanket."

"He killed himself," Harvey says. "I wanted to tell you. I want you to know that."

For a moment, Julianne is silent. "Who did?" she says. She takes a step back, closes the door behind her.

"David," he says. "My son."

She kneels, holds his hands to her face. She says, "Oh, sweetie. Your son is alive. His name isn't David. It's Harvey. Like yours. He lives in South Carolina. Harvey junior. You remember, don't you?"

Harvey says, "We had a son before him. Before Harvey."

Julianne says, "Oh," surprised that her hand has jumped to her mouth.

"I'm sorry I never told you. I should have told you. I'm sorry."

In the moment, she believes he should have as well. She knows well, however, that pain comes with no manual, that common sense has loose footing in death, no path on grieving. She says, "Tell me about him, dear. Will you? About David?" His name on her tongue is strange; how can her husband, this man she thought she knew so well, this man who is vanishing right before her eyes, whom she reminded daily to brush his teeth and to eat, because he could forget to eat, how could he have a son she has never known about? It makes no sense at four in the morning; it can't make sense in the middle of the day.

But she does not ask. Harvey is crying, the tears glistening on his cheeks in the silvery light of the stars, the white of the moon. They are quiet tears, running his face in silence. He does not wipe at them, but Julianne hurts for him, and she wipes away his tears with her palm. She says, "Oh, Harv." She has never, in all their years as a couple, seen Harvey cry.

"They blame me. His mother, his siblings. They don't say that, but they do. They always have."

"I'm sure that's not true, Harv." Julianne kisses Harvey on his cheek, hugs him close. Harvey's hands do not leave the armrests of his chair. She says, "Tell me about David, Harvey."

She thinks about all her family, inside, asleep in their beds. Dreaming, she hopes, about pleasant things.

"He took pills. His mother found him in his bathroom, slumped halfway in the tub. She could see him from outside, from the window. His feet." He puts a hand to his face. "I'm a bad person, Julianne. I'm abhorrent."

Julianne is sitting in his lap now, like a child would sit in her father's lap, listening to a fairytale that has suddenly become a horror story. It is her way of keeping him warm, because reckless as he has been with himself, he is bound to catch cold. But it also lets him be close to her without her seeming to try too much, which she knows he would not like just then.

He says, "She thought he was vomiting. She thought he was out drinking again and she went over to try to help him when he didn't answer the phone. She'd tried all morning." Harvey is quiet for a moment, adjusts his legs under her, holding on, balancing her, him. He says, "He was always troubled, David. Even when he was small we knew. You could just look at him—he was beautiful, that little kid, my boy, him and his big brown eyes, his fat legs. You could just see it. Something lingering there, staring at us. Waiting behind everything. It was like looking at black water in the middle of the day. You know you shouldn't be scared, that everything will be fine, that the sun—it's right there, everything's lit up, what can happen? But that black water. You just never knew what was in there down deep." Harvey shivers, but Julianne cannot tell if it is from the cold or something entirely different. He says, "He held on as long as he could. We all did. And then it just happened." Harvey shakes his head. "He was naked when she found him. Broke down the door and found her son naked in the bathtub."

Julianne imagines this naked boy she has never known, sees what Harvey's poor ex-wife has seen, what she has gone through, and everything she has ever thought—about Harvey, about her, about their children—is no longer the same, has been altered. She cannot think of Harvey's ex as irrational or unreasonable, and now everything Harvey has told her—about his ex, about his son, his daughter, all of it is now in question, as if the man she knows and loves, whose name she has taken, is perhaps not the man she thought he was. She says, "Is there anything else I should know?" regretting, the second she says it, that she has said anything at all. That perhaps, in a few words, she has dropped the anchor a bit deeper than she would have liked.

Harvey is silent, as if he could fill the sky with thunder, as if he could tear the earth from under the oceans. "No," he says. "That's it." He looks at her, his eyes shimmering in the cold winter air. He has the look of a child who has spoiled his dinner. He knows what she is thinking. He knows she is thinking, If he has kept David from me, what else is there he has kept, not told her about, in this drama that is Harvey's previous life. What machinations has he taken upon himself to build this new existence for himself, with her and her family, with those she loves more than anything in the world? He says, "I swear, Jules," and stares into the darkness, searching the blackness for whatever is there. And she thinks, What timing the man has. What timing indeed.

"The Chardonnay," he says, remembering now, not wanting to forget to tell her, because later, perhaps on its next arrival, she would ask. "I drink it because that's what David was fond of. Chardonnay." He is laughing now, shaking his head slowly. "My sweetheart was fond of Chardonnay and woodwork. Odd, don't you think, Jules? A young man liking Chardonnay?"

Julianne is smiling now too, because Harvey is coming back to her. It does not matter how he comes back now when he does because she knows to enjoy the good moments when they come. "It's not that strange, Harv. He was probably taking after you, don't you think?"

Harvey says, "I do it because of him. He showed me. He taught me. Like we were in class and he was the facilitator." He does not tell her that their last class, just weeks before David's mother found him in the tub, David had presented him with his own lathe, his own chisels, his own calipers, spear points, round points, roughers, gouges and parting tools, that all the bowls all over the house, all the ones being sold by the Henkenberns at their shop and online, that really they are just products of conversations he has with David that take place during lessons Harvey cannot bear to quit. That at the end of those conversations, when he is sitting there on his stool inhaling that wonderful smell of sawdust, missing that sweet voice of his boy's, the one that had deepened so but which he still heard high-pitched, unsure of itself, trying not to forget the long black locks of hair, the almost-muscled body in the rock-n-roll T-shirts, that he's always surprised to find this freshly finished bowl sitting on the table, smooth as silk, waiting on some purpose, yearning, he knows, to be stained beautifully. But he also does not tell her that sometimes, when he thinks these things, he also wonders if he is not mistaken, if the memories he has are not of David but of someone else.   Am I confusing something here, like I confuse everything these days? he asks himself. But no, it's in his heart, cemented there like everything is cemented within him, pulling tightly and hugging everything together, knowing that at any moment everything could all fall apart, just like that.

"Oh," she says. "Well."

Harvey says, "I'm sorry, Jules. It's my heartbreak. I just haven't been able to share it."

"You keep it," she says. "When you need to share it, I'll be here." She smiles. She says, "Why three days, dear? Why do you drink the wine over the three days?" She thinks, perhaps because he has three children. She thinks, three somethings that have meaning, this is why. But Harvey, laughing, says, "Because I hate Chardonnay, and it's all I can stomach."

Later that day, when the phone rings, Harvey is asleep and Julianne rises quickly to answer it. Julianne says, "And how is my little worker bee doing this morning?" She has seen on the caller ID that it is Millie Oliver, probably calling for more labels, another box of hair gel or cuticle cream. Millie says she is fine. She says, "I can't work for you anymore, Mrs. Lipscomb. I'm sorry."

"I see," says Julianne, employing that surprised older woman's inflection that works so well on the young in town. "May I ask why?"

There is hesitation, and then silence. Julianne says, "Dear?"

"I'm sorry," Millie says. "My mother will bring up your stuff later."

Julianne hangs the phone up, says, *hmm*. She thinks, I wonder what the poor girl has gotten herself into now. She thinks, surely it cannot have anything to do with the whole attorney thing.

Sammy says, "What's going on?"

"Nothing," Julianne tells her. "I think one of my helpers got herself into trouble."

"Who?"

"No one. Just a young girl I have helping me sometimes with my little business."

Sammy says, "And how is that going?"

Sammy, like Julianne, had been a serial entrepreneur her whole life, ever since she was a teenager. While Julianne dabbled in cosmetics and healthcare, Sammy was into visual art and crafts, driving from town to town along the east coast, selling glass block art and American folk art, drawings and paintings and framed prints at Arts & Crafts shows in places like Ft. Lauderdale, Florida, and Durham, North Carolina, Winchester, Virginia, and West Long Branch, New Jersey. For a number of years she packed her car with knickknacks and plastic bins full of her wares, Cliff as her companion and assistant when he wasn't employed. And for a while there it went well, though no, they never had ten dollars to spare after it was all said and done and they were back home again, one more adventure under their belts. Once her car died, that was it. She gave it up. When Julianne asked her if she didn't want to set up a website and sell her art online like she sold her cosmetics, Sammy had said no. Wasn't for her. It was like a light turning out for both of them—Sammy's desire to do her own thing, Julianne's to do hers with Sammy.

Julianne says, "I don't know. Maybe it's run its course." And in the back of her mind Julianne thought, well, yes. Maybe it has.

"Mmm," she says.

Soon after Julianne's call with Millie, Millie's mother, Pearl Blount, schoolteacher over at the White County Middle School, ex-wife of Rusty Oliver, welfare abuser and recluse up in his fancy new Bayview modular home (which Pearl called his BM with a view of jack shit much less a bay), drives up in their old beat-up station wagon with the wood paneling and the nine thousand stickers on the back claiming half the population of North America is on the White County Middle School Honor Roll. Pulls up slow but somehow still manages to slide haphazardly along the gravel, nearly right into James' rented tank, so close a call Julianne can see Pearl's eyes bug out nearly halfway out of their sockets, she's so scared. Not scared of hitting the car, she's sure, but scared of having to pay for any of the damage, thrifty lady she is. She looks behind Pearl's bouffant to see if Millie is with her but the car is empty, just Pearl and that monstrous hairdo from god knows when. She would have liked to have seen Millie, let her know it's okay, I understand. Not your fault or choice, sweetie. Water under the bridge. But not today. Maybe some other time.

"My ex-employee's mother," Julianne says to Sammy. "Come to rid her daughter of the devil's makeup."

Rachel says, "I have to ask her where she does her hair."

"Almost thinking maybe you should," says Julianne, but quickly adds, "but I don't need anything with her after whatever's coming."

Julianne and Sammy and Rachel, who has joined them at the window with a glass of pomegranate juice, watch Pearl and her helmet hair empty the back of the station wagon of what must be a dozen boxes of varying size. Some of the lids on the boxes are open and flapping around, and in the wind a handful of packing peanuts leap out, hit Pearl in the face. Some of the white peanuts cling to her hair. But Pearl is resolute. She keeps pulling the boxes out of the back of the wagon, stacking them up on the front porch. When she is done, she slams the back door of the wagon, walks up to the door, and rings the doorbell, one, two, three, and knocks twice.

Rachel says, "Nice display of something right there." She shakes her head, chuckles. "You know she knows we're watching, right?"

"It's her way," says Julianne. "Leave her be."

Julianne opens the door. Before she says a word, Pearl hands her a stack of invoices that Millie has yet to fulfill. Sammy and Rachel listen from the kitchen. Sammy wants to join Julianne for support, but Rachel holds onto her elbow.

"Check it and make sure everything's there," Pearl says, a tone of what sounds like arrogance or condescension meant to jab at Julianne somehow. But Pearl cannot hide being flustered, hard as she might wish. A thin sheer of sweat shimmers on her upper lip, the sides of her neck. Sammy and Rachel can see Pearl's mom jeans, her gray windbreaker in the crack of the door, ruffling like the feathers of some angry hen. Julianne stays quiet, reading through the invoices, looks down at the boxes. When she says Yep, all here, it's clear that she has not checked at all to make sure that everything is indeed all there. Good, Pearl says, in a way that is meant to scream no, everything is not all good.

"Pearl," Julianne says, her voice low, not quite submissive but not quite not. Sammy and Rachel struggle to hold their breaths, because Julianne is speaking so low that even the breeze makes it hard to hear.

"I have to admit, Pearl, this comes as a little surprise. Millie doing all right in school?"

"Nothing to do with school," Pearl snaps. "You *know*—," Pearl says, but she says it too loud, her voice raised like she's fixing for a confrontation, wanting whatever wrong to be righted right then and there, as if what is roiling Pearl goes back years and years, has finally spilled over. Julianne steps outside, pulls the door behind her, like come on, Pearl, not the time, nor the place. Sammy wants to walk right out there, tell the old hag to shut her mouth, who does she think she's talking to. But Rachel says, "Just listen, Sam. Don't make things worse." And so Rachel and Sammy tiptoe over to the door, just close enough so they can hear whatever it is Pearl wants everyone to hear.

"No," Julianne is saying. "Listen to yourself, Pearl. You know that can't be."

"Julianne, we're friends. We've been so for a long time. But she ain't lying. Trust me. You think I'd come up here with something like this? Just like that? Nothing behind it? Lord, Julianne."

"No," Julianne says. "I don't. But I'm sure things just got a little mixed up in the telling is all."

"Things got mixed up all right, Julianne. In that rattled head of his. That's what's mixed up."

"Watch your tongue, Pearl. He's still my Harvey."

"Still or not, Julianne. I can't have it. I just can't."

"Let me look into this, Pearl. Give me some time here. I'm not saying something did or did not happen. But what you're telling me, sweetheart, is crazy. Just let me sit down with him on it." Julianne says a few more things, but they can't hear it she's speaking so low. It continues for a few minutes. Hushed mumbling and head nods. And then things seem to ease up.

Pearl's voice is calmer, quieter, like the engine's run out of steam, and Sammy and Rachel already know the why, the how. Because their mother, because Julianne, is able to calm people who seem inconsolable, able to turn the flame down on boiling water with a look, some words. "Oh I don't know, Julianne. I don't know," Pearl is saying, almost apologetically. But in the silence now they know their mother, the matronly Julianne, whether Talmadge or Beasley or Lipscomb, whether now or last year or two decades ago, has draped her hands around Pearl's, has given Pearl that wide smile, no brilliant whites but undeniably an abundance of warmth, plenty of everything's-gonna-work-out-just-fine, and the hullabaloo she came up with falls back off the porch, breaks up into the dirt and bits of asphalt that have made their way from town in the treads of visiting tires. The pink flush in her cheeks has turned pale again.

"I'll call you, Pearl. Or I'll come down, whichever's best for you."

"Well," Pearl says. "I guess the either or. You do what you have to do."

"I'll come down then, Pearl. We can talk over one of Imogene's sweetbreads, dear. On me. One of them cappuccinos, too. I know you like them so."

And Pearl, never one to shun away free anything, matting down the sharpened quills she'd come up with but still keeping one or two out for posterity, says, "Well, I can meet you, but not later than Friday, Julianne. Not later than that. This is serious business, you know. *Serious* business."

"Of course, Pearl," Julianne says, walking Pearl to her car, kneeling at the window while Pearl starts up the station wagon once and then twice, when it stalls in a disharmony of thumps and knocks. And when Pearl rolls the window down and Julianne is talking but Sammy and Rachel can't hear a word, they know their mother has won Pearl back more than just a bit, if not completely. And so it is not surprising that when Julianne sticks one of the boxes back through the window, Pearl accepts. She even squeezes their mother's hand in goodbye, as if everything, no matter what it was, no matter how awful or bad it could be, could not be bad enough to not get over.

Julianne waves to Pearl as she backs up, wheels crunching over the gravel, rainwater skidding off the camouflage-green hood, down the wood-paneled doors, hightails it back down the hill into town careful, Julianne is sure, not to slip off the embankment as she descends their ritzy, gated drive. But afterwards, she doesn't walk back in. Sammy and Rachel watch their mother walk out into the garden, pluck a few Star-of-Bethlehem from a bunch Harvey had been meticulous in trimming just the day before. She holds the flowers to her nose as it begins to rain. They watch their mother close her eyes; they watch the rain loosen the bun she's tied in her hair earlier that morning; they watch the rain, like tears against her un-tanned skin, pick up speed just before the black, inevitable downpour comes Helen's way.

Though she knows her daughters are watching her just as they'd all watched Pearl put on her little show, has known it all the while, she does not care because they all three are but pieces of her, and how can you be shy in front of you yourself. She just wants to feel the rain right then, to let it cool her face, to let it freshen her up (or refresh?) because at least in the rain, in its cold pitter-pattering sweetness, there is familiarity, and she wants to drink some of it just then, even if only for a bit, to remind herself of the simple pleasures in life, those things that have always been free, that you can purchase when you're one or twenty or ninety. Even if she looks like a mad woman out there in the rain, soaked to the bone, dripping to the ground, it's okay. It's fine. It's the here and it's the now and no one or nothing can take that away from her no matter what.

"Nothing," Julianne says, to no one in particular. It is morning, and the occupants of the cabin are just now rousing from bed, crowding the bathrooms, starved for coffee. "Nothing," she says again, and neither Sammy nor Rachel nor Lettie, who is also curious to know what *nothing* is, presses for more. Because Julianne's nothing, it is clear, is not meant for their ears, even though their mother has said it aloud. She feeds them scrambled eggs and chocolate chip pancakes for the kids, rests a large pitcher of orange juice in the center of the table, next to the butter, the syrup. She washes the frying pan and dries it and puts it back in its place in the cabinet beside the oven. She wipes down the counter and wets a paper towel, starts wiping down the inside of the microwave, pulling crumbs from under the circular glass tray that swivels round and round when the microwave is cooking. She keeps busy feeding and cleaning and making sure everyone is okay, and Harvey, who's already eaten before the sun came up, is already hidden away in the garage, door closed, turning something from hunks of wood into something else, listening to NPR, not showing his face even after the kids are calling for him.

After breakfast is over, after she has done all of the dishes and put the syrup and the milk and the bottles of jam and ketchup and Tabasco away, wiped down the table and wiped it down again, she announces that she has to run a couple of errands and disappears alone, telling Lettie no, no, you stay here, honey, I just need to visit a few of my old fogies, dear. They don't like strangers. It scares them, new voices, new faces. Which they all know is a lie. Which Julianne knows they know is a lie.

And they watch her, Lettie and Rachel and Sammy and Michael and Cliff and James and Aaron and Hadley. Watch her go out walking down the hill in her sneakers and little getup, big-brimmed hat over her drooping face, dark grandma sunglasses with the side wings and shimmering black plastic. Jackie O 'a the hills. Mother Theresa of White County, heading down to help the less fortunate. The in-need. The retirement holdouts, and the white-haired rebels who would rather pass the first time around in their own homes alone than be jumpstarted back by white-slacked heathens making less than they should. Or so they've all agreed to pretend to believe that this is what she was doing, because why would Julianne lie?

When they—all of them—peek in on Harvey, he's sitting on a stool, listening to *The Diane Rehm Show*, bandaging up what looks like a cut on his thumb, winding green and yellow electrician's tape round and round. He does not hear them, not with the radio sitting on a stool a foot away, aluminum foil crumpled up like a broken arm, jutting out from the bent antenna. James shakes his head, leads Aaron and Hadley back to the living room, where they set up a few of the board games for game hopping, three full games in an hour if they can manage. Sammy and Rachel and Lettie follow right after, but Michael stays behind, staring at the back of Harvey's head, the sun-burned bald spot, the straggling white hairs along the sides of his wrinkled neck. Harvey picks up a whittling tool, sheds two short curls of wood, puts it back down. He grabs some wood glue, squeezes (or tries to squeeze) some of it into a wooden dowel hole, gives up after turning a light shade of red. Just as Michael is about to close the door, head back and join everyone else, Harvey turns around, stares at Michael for a second, blinks, and turns back around, which makes Michael think that yes, maybe Harvey looked at him, but no, he did not really see him. Like maybe his eyesight has gone, or maybe, somehow, he was looking somewhere else, seeing something different. Michael closes the door, slow so he doesn't make a peep, and joins everyone else by the fireplace.

When Julianne returns, half the day is gone, but no one says a word, because Julianne has returned red-eyed and soaked to the bone, strands of silver hair pasted to her cheeks, over her eyes. It had rained on and off, but Julianne could have been swimming fully-clothed in the Chattahoochee from the looks of her. Neither Aaron nor Hadley remind her that they were supposed to bake blondies with white chocolate chips, that they were going to watch *Twas the Night Before Christmas,* that they were going to do the karaoke machine James surprised them with from the trunk of the car after he'd said he was going out for vitamins but really drove back over to the Walmart in Cleveland. Even they sense something is wrong.

Michael tells them to go play in their room. Aaron grabs a deck of cards and Hadley grabs a Game Boy, and they head to the room without hesitation, Hadley brushing her head up against Julianne for her to get a quick squeeze in, let her know, in her child way, she cares. Sammy follows them with a red *Barrel of Monkeys* game, dropping some of the monkeys along the hallway. Instead of bending down, Sammy kicks the monkeys along the hardwood until each and every one reaches the room. Cliff comes out of his bedroom, walks over to Julianne, asks if she's okay?

"I'm fine," she says. "Just a little damp is all." Sammy comes back with a towel from the linen closet, hands it to

Julianne. Julianne wipes her face, drapes the towel over her head. Sammy and Cliff start pulling off her jacket, the hat that's plastered flat and dangling at her back, strangling her with its knotted cord, which makes Julianne cough just a little. Lettie collects Julianne's feet with her hands, starts unlacing one and then the other sneaker, throwing the clunky wet Reeboks into the foyer a few feet away. Lettie says, "Got yourself caught in a little storm, Ma."

"Looks so, huh?"

"Looks so." Cliff pulls Julianne up, one arm under both of hers, supporting her back like a big bear, leaving the others behind. He walks her over to her bedroom, leads her into the master bath, her saying let me go let me go the whole way, kidding, of course, but now smiling, now remembering the young man Cliff, the suitor, the one that used to sit with her outside on late afternoons, waiting on her hand and foot, trying to get in good with her back when he was courting Sammy. All *Yes ma'ams* and *How are yous.*

Cliff sits her down on the edge of the tub, tells her, Mom, turn the heat up, pour some of them purple salts in there. Take yourself a catnap. I'll go get you some floaties. Ha, she says. She nods. But he's right. A warm bath is what she needs. And while maybe all was not good when and since he and Sammy had come up, all's gotten much better. At least the tensions seem to have moved around some, shifted from someplace to someplace else. Settled, for the time being.

She finds herself looking at Cliff, more lines in his face, more leather, at how age has touched him as well, how he is still a man and a boy all at once. It occurs to her she's always had a place for him in her heart, damaged as he is. Not all bad, she thinks, this one.

She turns the hot water on, drops the stopper in the drain and almost falls in, Cliff grabbing her arm, holding her up. She hands him a box of Epsom salt, watches him pour the crystals in, swaying an arm from the front of the tub to the back, like he's some kind of professional Epsom salt pourer.

She says, "I do, Cliff. I do hope things work out for you two."

"I know you do," he says, walking over and grabbing a couple of gray towels sitting on the vanity. Steam rises from the tub, fogs the little stick-on mirror stuck to the wall between the shower and the tub. Cliff leans over, holds his wrist under the water, adjusts the hot, the cold. He says, "All I do is my best, Mom. It's all I can do."

"I know, Cliff. We all do."

"All I can do," he says again, pulling the shampoo and the soap and the back scrubber from the shower, as if he did not hear what she'd said, which maybe he hadn't.

He puts the half-empty plastic bottles next to the faucet, hands Julianne the back scrubber. "You want any wine or anything before you jump in?"

She considers everything there is to consider, having forgotten what it was like, taking a bath for pleasure, to relax. "Wine," she says. "My, if that doesn't sound good."

"White?" he says. He has a smile on his face.

"White," she says. "But not the Chardonnay, Cliff. Something else."

"Riesling?"

"Or Sémillon. I think there's a bottle in the fridge there somewhere. Check for me?"

"Okay," he says. "Back in a jiff."

Cliff closes the door, but why, she doesn't know, because she won't get undressed until after he comes back, until after he leaves again. Maybe he's trying to trap the steam, keep it all toasty for her. She lets her shoulders relax. She takes a breath, lets it out. She listens to the water run. She doesn't look over at the mirror, because she knows she won't like what she sees. She hopes it will fog up, but she knows it will take much too long, that the space in between is too large, that the fog will never reach her other self. The one sitting behind the shimmer of the mirror, behind the reflection, lost in the black backing. Waiting for her to turn her neck, look her eye to eye, see herself at just this moment in time, sitting there, looking back.

She looks down at her ankles instead, puffed up as they are, swollen and not particularly attractive. She analyzes the varicose veins, which look like fissures in marble, running in a hodgepodge of tributaries and dying thunderbolts, thinning out, sinking into deeper flesh. She turns and looks out the small window, through the sheer curtains that look out over the mini forest to the northwest of the cabin. She remembers that at one point in time they considered tearing out that window, installing either an arched one or, as Harvey had suggested, a large bay window, where they could sit together in the tub and stare out at the colors of fall, or at the night sky and all its constellations, hit the Jacuzzi bubbles and watch the trees shed their leaves. Harvey had even sanded down one side of the window frame to test different shades of white. But none of that will ever happen, she knows. Pipe dreams come in all sizes, in all shapes. And she had always thought the windows would strip away some of their privacy anyway. Some things could be good ideas, but maybe, too, they were ideas better left undone.

She can hear Cliff opening and closing the refrigerator doors, the suction of rubber jangling the other side of the wall, the salad dressing bottles on the refrigerator door clinking. Hears him speaking with Sammy (or is that Rachel or maybe Lettie?), asking, surely, about the Sémillon. She looks back out the window; it is growing darker, as if a curtain is being drawn, pulled down from the heavens with the rain, which is falling harder now, big drops crashing against the window, hurled by a southerly wind. Hears the rain gutters filling up, cold rainwater rushing each section. Down through leaf screens and elbows, hitting splash blocks in a loud, persistent rattling of aluminum, of plastic. Running down the side of the house, away, off into the dirt, darkening the pine cone that lay across the forest floor. She hears the thunder, but it is a long ways off, the low grumble of Harvey's stomach when he's forgotten a meal.

When they met, she and Harvey, she wasn't all that sure. He had his little quirks, his eccentricities. Could he be called odd? Sure. Different? Absolutely. But she never had any doubts about him. There was a difference between the two, between doubt, between surety. It was smart, knowing the difference. Because it let her be her. And let what needed to materialize materialize. She wasn't sure if it was love at first sight, but she didn't doubt she would come to love him. She wasn't sure he'd get along with her kids, but she didn't doubt any of them wouldn't try. That's what had made everything so easy for so long. It was the glue that was always there, even when you didn't know it was there. But Harvey took her and she took him, and that's all there was to it. She learned about him and he learned about her, and it worked. It just worked. Night and day compared to Jo. Night *and* day. Harvey didn't yell, didn't get all Tasmanian Devil at the slightest of things. Didn't drink, not really, not like Jo did, her ex, the kids' father, and he was just a kind-hearted, sweet, sweet man. Wasn't erratic like Jo, not in the ways Jo was, anyway. Not anything wild and unpredictable. Or hadn't been. Maybe still wasn't. But now, she didn't know. Now, with his little episodes. With this thing ravishing (was it ravishing?) him. Oh boy, she thought. Well.

There is a knock on the door, Cliff with the wine. "*Finally*," she says, exasperation in her voice, playing with Cliff, who is being extra kind. He hands her the glass, watches her take a sip, pucker up. *Tart*, she says. Cliff takes the glass back, rests it on the side of the tub by an unscented candle. He holds a lighter over the candle, flicks, and the candle flame glows bright against the tile. He takes a small bow, one hand behind his back. Thank you, Cliff, she says, standing up. Madam, he says. He walks out of the room, closes the door behind him. Holler if you need anything, he says. But she will not need anything, not with the wine, not with the heat, which is already loosening her neck, her arms. Letting her mind just stop thinking.

She pulls off her blouse, lets it drop to the floor. Not on the bathroom rug, where the soaked blouse will not leave a slippery surface, and not hung up on one of the three silvery hooks behind the door (which were already there when they bought the cabin, and that initially she'd wanted to replace with brushed nickel, which Harvey had actually fought her on), but right there on the tile, an aging person's hazard, perhaps, if she were to leave it there. She does the same with her slacks, her bra, letting them fall carelessly, sloppily, in little mounds before the tub. She steps into the tub, holding on to nothing, lets herself slide down, slowly, into the too-hot water, which she does not adjust. Cliff had adjusted the nozzles just so, but he did not know that, like everything around them, the nozzles have their own minds, their own personalities, that just because they were this hot now did not necessarily mean they would remain that hot for long. That they had their own prerogatives, if nozzles could have such things.

She slides even farther, taking the pain of the heat as it rises from her rump, along her sides, over her breasts—breasts, which she notices, are so very white, so very different, but thankfully there— *still there*—right below her chin. At her age, breasts can very easily be gone, lost forever. Can be taken away by doctors, nurses. She thinks about Jane Kelly, two first names but zero boobs; and Sandra Cortez, that beautiful woman (she'd die for her hair), walking around the Habersham Winery with just the one now, giving tours of the place, making a statement maybe, but what that statement is Julianne is not quite sure. I'm a survivor, look at me? One boob or two, it doesn't matter, I can still lead you to tipsy-ville? Julianne does not know. But she will not question her motives.

She thinks now of Harvey, and of what Pearl has told her, but no, she cannot believe that woman, not now not ever. No, she thinks, taking a long sip of the wine, holding the side of the glass up against one cheek, and then the other, closing her eyes to the world, or at least to this one little corner of it. Inhaling through her nose the wine sitting in her mouth, tasting the tannins—or maybe not, if that's not what you taste in white wine, in Sémillon. *Mistaken* is what Pearl is. That's what Millie is, too. Confused. Their brains are scrambled by the dumb that runs in their family, she mumbles, for her ears only. But then, and with something that feels like regret, she takes it back, brings her fingers to her mouth, and pulls the invisible words from her lips, tosses them out the window. She has never been one to blame.

She drinks the rest of the wine. She wants to yell for Cliff, but that would attract too much attention, and besides, she's already feeling light-headed from the one glass, and neither Cliff nor anyone else out there needs to see any of what's there in her bathroom, namely she in all her glory, soaking like a raisin inside while the world shrivels up outside, splashing around in its own problems.

It keeps raining—for hours it rains, and the sun, which had only peeked at them earlier in the day, never returns. In her robe, pinched tight all the way up to her neck, drops of water still dangling from her heavy lobes, she watches the rain fall under the porch lights, against the one light they installed up at the Smith's turnoff, where it would have been impossible to see the gravel road to their place otherwise, which for some reason now seems too perfect, too utterly wholesome, when before they could not hold a candle to her and Harv.

At night, Harvey falls asleep in his recliner, his legs splayed like broken chicken wings, and Julianne, preferring to sleep alone this evening, does not nudge him on his arm, does not say, Harv, honey, it's time for bed, c'mon you sack of potatoes, let's go. But instead lets him fend for himself, even if it makes her feel a little guilty. She could throw a blanket over him, or straighten his neck out some, because in that position, he's sure to wake up with a kink the size of a cheese ball. But she does nothing for him, big boy he is. Let him get himself up this time, she thinks. Just the once. And Julianne, tucking herself into bed, worrying only about herself for once, slept.

It was a few days later, by accident, that Rachel sees her mother standing in the corner of the laundry room. She could see it—the shiver in her shoulders, the pause. The hesitance in what she was doing, or what she was supposed to be doing. Rachel knew her mother had been crying. Perhaps she was still crying. She glanced quickly around her, making sure they were alone, said, "Mom?" And Julianne raised one finger, as if she were just trying to calculate a simple arithmetic problem, two plus three equals five, and said, "One sec, dear." But Rachel had already come through the door, already had an arm around her, tilting her head, questioning. Julianne regained her composure now, and she was laughing. Actually laughing. She said, "The game's up," and laughed even more now, a heartier laugh, and Rachel could not help but join her. She said, "What game?" and Julianne said, "The big one," and shook her head and sunk her eyes into the sweater she had been folding. She said, "He looked me dead in the eye, and I knew. I just knew. Who he was, who I was? All of it? Gone. And then he did it. I knew it was coming, and he didn't disappoint." Julianne peeked out the laundry room, closed the door. She said, "For a moment I knew what it was to be him, and

I'm glad it happened at the same exact moment." She said, "Harvey looked right at me, like this, like we're looking at each other right now, and said, 'I know we're married, but remind me again who we are?' And Rachel, dear? Oh Rachel. The funny thing is, I just couldn't say." And Julianne thought, Oh, and *Harvey*? Harvey dear? What have you done that cannot be undone to that poor little lost child, Millie? Did you know what you were doing? Or were you just being . . . you?

James and Rachel

The bags were packed—two suitcases, two carryon's, two laptop cases, one for Rachel's MacBook, one for James's PC. Pick up time for Hadley at Holy Angel's was between eleven and eleven-thirty (*Please be on time*), when Hadley would be at lunch and her removal from school would not be a distraction to the other children. Hadley was adamant about not wanting to go; all of the other kids at school, she said, and complained, and moaned, and grumbled, would be having fun doing all of the Christmas stuff—decorating classroom trees, having gift exchanges, acting in the school play. Hadley said she had waited all year for the play. She knew she was going to be chosen to be Mary this year. But Rachel told her she could be Mary and anyone else she wanted when they performed not just the one play, but as many as they wanted to perform at Grandma's in Georgia. Hadley had cried, but her tears, as they always were, were temporary. An hour of changed scenery and the play would be forgotten. Hadley would pick up on something else, stick with it, get lost in it like it was the only thing on earth. A plane with TVs tucked in the seats was as good as ten leading roles.

They were on the plane, first class as usual, James sitting in 2A, typing an e-mail, *Outlook* open to next month's calendar as he checked his availability. They tried but couldn't get seats together, even this early before the holiday rush. But they had plenty of miles to spare for Rachel and Hadley to not have to sit in coach. And besides, they were close, 3D and F, and the space provided James with the freedom to get some work in while he still could. Next to James was a young sales guy, a marketing manager or something, newer sports coat, clean shaven, a bit too much cheap cologne. Under the sports coat James could make the edge of an embroidered golf shirt, the logo of some technology company he had never heard of, a logo Rachel could have designed blindfolded if she were still pursuing the graphic designer business. But she wasn't doing that anymore. She had lost the desire, not to create the logos and designs but to seek out the business, put the little advertisements in the local paper, push-pinning her cards on top of all of the other cards on the board at Lessing's or over with the host staff at The Snapper Inn, who probably threw the cards away as soon as she was gone. When James had made that comment, calling it—what she'd taken classes for, taken seriously as a possible new life path (a little bit business, a little bit art)—*cute*, that was it. She was done. No more logos. No more nothing.

The sales guy had an IBM like him, the newer BlackBerry. James asked him if he liked it. The guy told him it was a big improvement, great features. The memory goes, though, and I'm history. Thanks for playing, know what I mean? Please uninstall. James thought, we lose our data, we're all history, pal. Every last one of us. The sales guy smiled, put his headphones on, and closed his eyes.

Every now and then, after they were airborne, Hadley stood up, and James could see her thin torso and her little wave and her little toothy smile. He would wave back until the flight attendant had Rachel sit Hadley back down, buckle back up. Once Hadley fell asleep, the earphones went in, the MP3 turned on, and both of them, James and Rachel, escaped into their own worlds, James to Hip Hop and Rap (which did not suit him completely), and Rachel to old Disco tracks, (which suited her absolutely). Twenty minutes from landing, Rachel stopped by, asked James if he'd given it any thought, adopting, if when they tried in the not-so-distant future, a biological baby wasn't in the cards. But there was turbulence, the plane jolting up, down, and the flight attendant asked her to please return to her seat.

When they landed everyone ducked into the bathroom, washed up, got ready for the two-hour drive. James stood in line for the SUV they rented for the month, all of their bags leaning against the car rental desk. Rachel and Hadley bought snacks for the road at Starbucks. They walked over to James, Hadley nibbling on a chocolate doughnut, Rachel balancing two Grande drips, a bag stuffed with a fruit and cheese plate, a cruller with powdered sugar sticking out of the bag, listing against the side of her nose. James took the bag from Rachel's teeth, said, "They didn't have the Suburban so we got a Tahoe."

Rachel wiped sugar off the tip of her nose. "I think we'll live," she said.

Hadley said she was tired, didn't want to walk anymore. James told her they were almost at the car. Hadley threw herself over one of the suitcases, said, *My. Legs. Hurt!* and James said, *Hadley.* But Hadley was plugging her ears with her fingers, pretending not to hear him. Rachel threw her laptop over her back, pushed James to the side. Go, she said. Get the bags. She swooped Hadley into one arm, steadied the coffees with the other hand, and walked off towards the exit. James followed behind, dragging the wobbly suitcases, apologizing whenever he thumped someone's heel.

Hadley fell asleep before they were out of the airport. Rachel opened her laptop, closed it. James said something unintelligible, and Rachel said, "I can't work with you driving anyway. Who'll steer?" James said, *Hardy har.* He pushed some buttons on the Garmin, waited for the route to show. Followed the signs out of the airport until the voice took over. Rachel watched him do that thing he did when he was anxious, rubbing his fingertips over his upper lip, his chin. She said, "Stop thinking about it. It'll come." James looked at her, back at the road. "You just think I would have heard something already, no?"

Rachel slipped her boots off, put her socked feet up on the dash. "The more you think about it, the more you're going to drive yourself and me crazy. Just relax. *Please.* We're on vacation." And they were.

But their vacations were defined differently. They had been on vacations before, or what they thought were going to be vacations. Because James turned everything fun into work, into business. He made everything he did about work. Wrote off anything and *everything* he could. Anytime he could get himself away because everyone else was away—during Christmas, Thanksgiving, spring break, Easter, they weren't really getting away. They were just pretending to get away. Sometimes Rachel thought it was a little too much, his ambition. But she wasn't complaining. Not with the lifestyle they lived. She relished that lifestyle. It was a lifestyle of privilege. A lifestyle *to die for.* A lifestyle, she admitted to herself and her inner circle, she could no longer live without, now that she was accustomed to such opulence, if that's what it was called. Sometimes, though she would not admit such a thing, it really could be too much, even for her.

For James, the anxiety seemed to drive him, to put fuel in his fire. The sense of urgency, the need to succeed—that was what made him who he was, who he had always been. For James, failure never had been an option. Not when he was Hadley's age playing stickball behind the ShopRite, aiming for the black cantaloupes in the shopping cart of the ShopRite logo because if you hit it, it was a guaranteed triple. How many hours had he sat there, alone, swinging away, improving? Nor was it an option when he played quarterback for the Redmen in high school, when his stomach churned and churned so much he'd vomited behind the bleachers before games—games, of course, where he'd led the Red and White to victory. Games, he remembers, when he'd imagined a father in the stands just like the other kids had fathers in the stands, cheering them on, rah-rahing, giving them 'atta boys and high-fives, their voices deep, commanding. A father maybe who worked with the local union or jumped on the LIRR at the crack of dawn, trudged to his big city job through sleet, through snow, in his suit and his tie, came back home in the evening to great big plates of veal and pasta, everyone sat around and listened as pops told everyone of this guy or that guy, what a schmo Carlisle was down in Sales, how much Abruzzo was pulling in a year, the schlep, and how you just had to *know* someone, that's it, know someone and you were good as gold. Zoom. Straight to the top.

But none of that, none of the woe is me nonsense, was ever going to stop him from making it, dad or no dad. Nope. Not a chance. While sure, he excelled at football and baseball and even basketball for a time, he still kept an eye on the smarter kids in school, the nerds if that's what they were. And then eventually, and not so secretly, he asked to join their study sessions, their social clubs. He asked because he saw where it could lead. He knew high school success did not real-life success make. He felt like it was the natural order of things, like transferring energy from where it was lacking to someplace where it would thrive. Instead of going out and getting hammered four or five nights a week, he held it to one or two, compartmentalized the time for play against the time for work, for study. If the two went head to head, it was the studying, the working, that won. Being Mr. Popular, who was going to question him? No one, that's who. Yet succeed as he did, the anxiety never went away, as he thought it might. It stayed there in his stomach, ebbing, flowing, emerging and rising to the back of his throat like fire, propelling him to strive and work until, as always, his efforts paid off. And they always paid off. *Always.*

It was this ambition, this full-throttle need-to-succeed rocket that scared her. It brought what they wanted when they wanted it, but it maybe was also James' hubris. Their hubris. Or almost had been. Because but for her, without her reaching out (and maybe with some desperation), James would have been gone long ago. Would have just walked out of her life like any of his other girlfriends, and there were plenty. And truth be told, all cards on the table, he'd almost ended it—this, everything they'd worked towards—over the phone, which she could not believe at the time. Which she could still not believe now. Moving, he'd said. She could hear it, whatever it was, in his voice. Moving where? she'd said. Look, he'd said. I don't think it's going to work out. But she never heard that. Or never let it sink in, because she'd already sunk in, in her mind, with him, and it wasn't anything that ended like that, with him saying goodbye over the phone and walking away. Not even remotely like that. She wouldn't let him just walk away. For a job, out of confusion on what to do (take the new job somewhere else or keep the steady [and slower] corporate climb going where he was), or any other reason. And eventually, when everything worked out, when it was all said and done, he thanked her. Actually said, "Thanks, babe, for not letting me ruin this." And she did. Said, You're welcome, knucklehead, and that was that. They stayed together and got married and here they were. She good for him, and he, in his ways, definitely good for her.

A woman's voice told him to merge onto I-85 North for thirteen point five miles. Then she said something about continuing on something, but James was listening to Rachel. She was saying he should be more patient, that good things come to those who something-or-other, which he assumed she said *wait*. He played bongos on the steering wheel, put his fingers in his ears like Hadley. Rachel said, *Moron*, pointed her fingers to her eyes, to the road ahead of them. She said, "Just drive, idiot. Try not to get us killed," and leaned back in her seat.

But she was thinking about it too. Wondering why they hadn't gotten the phone call yet, the e-mail buzzing on his BlackBerry. Congratulations, James, you're it! You're our new President and COO! Nothing. And what was it now, three days since he should have known? The board knew about his vacation plans. They'd known about it for months. And his buddy, his pal, Thorpe? He could at least have the courtesy to give a buzz, tell James they were still figuring out the compensation package, tweaking the bonus structure. But nothing. Just cold, icy silence. Torturous, nerve-wracking, ulcer-inducing silence. Like they didn't care that she, Rachel, ever bubbly wife-at-home-with-child, loving spouse—who always said, Sure, honey darling, abandon your family once more for three weeks for work every couple of weeks, no way is it a problem, no how is it an inconvenience—that she might have also been expecting to hear word? That maybe their decision had other consequences that might affect not only James but those he loved. What kind of wife expects to see her husband, the father of her child, more than three times a year? What do you think I am, needy? This is normal, people. These expectations are not excessive. They are normal, people. *Normal.* Look it up!

Because didn't they know how these things went? Didn't they know she had given up more than any of them? Given up her career, her independence, her *self*, really, if they got down to it. But no one checked grade point averages. No one wanted to know who had the better grades in school. Because if they did, they'd see that she, Rachel, outdone-by-no-one Rachel, had always scored higher than James. *Always.* He knew it and she knew it, but, truth be told, she just did not want it as much as he did. Not even close. Never had. And besides, once they'd gotten pregnant, it wasn't like he could go and take a year off for her. In that sense, it *all* made sense. When they'd put it all down on paper (not because they had to but more as a matter of ensuring they did their due diligence), all it did was make more sense. Ninety percent James goes the corporate route and ten Rachel does the stay-at-home thing versus, well, no other alternative, really. It was settled early on in their courtship. *Everything* they wanted lined up. They had run down their checklists (which they'd written up without hesitation, pulled out the Excel spreadsheet and laid everything out when others may have thought it a deal breaker from the start):

James	R&J	Rachel
	Exercise	
Career		Homemaker
Yard work		Baking (no cooking)
Weekly sports		Weekly girls night out
Boys travel	Travel together	Girls travel
	Homeownership	
	Family (*although not James', of course*)	
	Own private bank accounts, no questions asked (notice the bold)	

Maybe a little stereotypical, but it had always worked. Even the bank accounts. James had twenty percent taken from his check, direct deposit straight to Rachel's private account every two weeks. When he got paid she got paid, and there was never anything to talk about ever. And once, without her even knowing he'd done so, she found out he had set it up that if the deposit didn't go through for whatever reason the bank had to call her and explain why. Not him, even though all the money was coming from him, but her, because, as it said on the account, she was in charge. Marie-Ann Ciampi, their banker down at Chase, Coach Ciampi's wife, called to apologize for the mistake that had been made before Rachel even knew what had happened. Technical error, Marie-Ann told her. Rest assured, she'd said, we've put the money into the account even though it hasn't cleared. Sorry for any inconvenience. Rachel had said thank you, and hung up. And though the thought had crossed her mind to mention it to James, she never did. It was kind of him, sure, but that was the deal, and a deal was a deal. You work; I stay at home. We both get what we want. Period. Finito.

It was dark before they made it north of Atlanta. They were twenty minutes past Gainesville when Hadley woke up, said she had to go *Now*. James said they were almost there, but Hadley insisted. She said, *Now, Dada*, made an agonized face, put her knees together, holding the flood. James looked back at her, said he'd pull off at the next exit. They pulled into the parking lot; Rachel sprinted with Hadley into the *QT*. James went in, bought some Teriyaki Turkey Jerky, an onerous-looking energy drink in a tall black can. *Monster Energy*, it said. A green neon *"m"* like someone scratched it into the can. Rachel and Hadley came out of the bathroom. James asked them if they wanted anything. Rachel put her hands over Hadley's eyes, said, "No one here wants anything," and led Hadley past the chips and candy, past the rack of Georgia maps, out the glass door, Hadley protesting and then laughing and pretending to cry but jogging alongside her mother anyway until they were both laughing. *Daddy!* she yelled as the door swung slowly behind them. *Help me, Dada!*

And then they were lost. James had been ignoring the female voice, because he thought you just had to loop back the same way you came, turn left, jump back on the Interstate. Rachel told him he was going the wrong way. Hadley said, "We're lost?" And James said, "Shh, please, ladies," and kept driving. They were riding along the edge of what looked like a country road, and they could see the Interstate right there on their left, running north. James was leaning forward, hovering over the steering wheel, like that was going to help him see better. The female voice was telling them to make a U-turn, head back the other way. Rachel wished she just said, Hey, Dumbass, pull a Bitch already! But James kept driving, as if if he willed it hard enough, perhaps the earth would right its course.

The *QT* was out of sight now, and besides a sliver of moon and some foggy white from some outside lights in houses set way back from the road, it was dark. After a few minutes the Interstate disappeared, but James kept going. Rachel turned the interior light on, said, "You want a map, because clearly you're not paying attention to the Garmin." James said, "We're heading north. We're all right."

"Why did you get that thing if you're not going to listen to it?"

James said, "I got you, didn't I?" but quickly added, "I kid, babe, I kid," in his jokey voice. In the voice he used when he put his foot in his mouth. The one with the higher pitch. The one followed by the puppy-dog eyes, the hand on her cheek.

James leaned over again, panned the night sky. Rachel said, "Tell me you're not." James smiled that silly smile he always smiled when he was doing something that was probably going to annoy her or piss her off in some form or fashion. She knew he was doing his Boy Scout thing again, looking up at the stars, figuring out his coordinates based on the shiniest or the largest one or whatever, which she loathed. She thought it was the epitome of male idiocy, trying to wing something you didn't need to wing. Proving . . . what? That he could get lucky? That men had an acute sense of place? Irritating as it was, though, she had to admit, his stupid little trick had never failed them.

They veered a couple more times, past a couple more houses, James going fifty-eight in a forty-five. Sure enough they came up on 384. Within a few minutes they were back on 75. James had a smile on his face now, and Rachel said, "Don't even look at me." But she was smiling too, and James did a little dance on the dash with his index fingers, the *Charleston* maybe, put his hand back between the seats and Rachel said, "Don't encourage him, Had," but Hadley gave him five anyway.

She loved watching them, Hadley and James, how they got along, typical father/daughter stuff, hugs and kisses, lots of tickling. He doted on her and spoiled her and she loved him unconditionally, which was very different than how Measly Beasley had treated her and her sisters. James bought her whatever she wanted, and maybe she was spoiled. But so what? That's what childhood was for. Once you became an adult and had all the responsibilities, you lost that carefree joie de vivre. And Hadley, their little baby, deserved all the spoiling that came her way. All of it and then some because, well, you just never knew what could happen. And much could happen.

When the doctor told them that everything was not *completely* normal, James had almost died. He sunk down, deflated, shoulders crumpled, like he was ready to jump off the Verrazano if everything didn't turn out all right. Rachel assumed she looked the same. A one-in-fifteen hundred chance, their Hadley. That's what the doctor said. Just stood there, not smiling, not pretending to be devastated, definitely a little too clinical for their preference. Rattled off terms and concepts that changed their understanding of who they were, how the world worked. *Congenital heart defect.* Those the doctor's first words. No introduction, no lobbing of softballs. Just out and out says, *congenital heart defect.* That's what your daughter was born with. Like a thunderclap reverberating in the hospital room. All of the planning, all of the reading up on everything you needed to do before birth, not eating this, not drinking that, they'd never given a second's thought what could happen *after* Hadley was born. Never heard of Atrial Septal Defect until Hadley already had the damn thing. No one ever mentioned venous blood or interatrial communication, left-to-right shunts. No one said peep about any of the possibilities, so of course they were not prepared for dealing with any of it. It had been a foregone conclusion, their baby's—Hadley's—health. They had painted the room neutral colors, and they had baby-proofed not only her room but the entire house, putting up padded gates between the doors and blocking the stairs, installing outlet covers with cord shorteners, Mommy's Helper Toilet Seat Lid-Locks on all the toilets, and KidCo cabinet locks, so their little babe would not get into anything she wasn't supposed to get into. They were ready. But not for this. It was only yesterday they saw that little white peanut with the big head sitting against that black background, all the promise in the world wrapped up in maybe two inches of faceless, jiggling arms and legs.

After the doctor had left the room, after he had closed the door and it was just them and James sat down beside Rachel, he wiped not tears from his eyes but sweat, as if it were physically strenuous, receiving this news. As if he'd just been dealt a bad hand at Texas Hold'em and he was going to have to ride it out. He looked up at her and said, The best laid plans, huh? Not knowing how to respond, she simply nodded her head, and then lay it back down on the fluffy hospital pillow until she fell asleep and James had gone home. Alone, in the hospital room, she would not let her thoughts think of anything but her baby. Not the bad that was possible, not the lack of whatever it was James was capable of.

But then they had dealt with it. Agreed that nothing was going to get in the way of their baby growing up normal, being okay. Not this. Especially not this. And in time they conquered it, at least as far as they could tell. Or they prayed they had conquered it anyway, so that it went away. Disappeared. Out of sight, out of mind. Just dealt with it as you would anything else. Took care of business.

On the recommendation of specialists they'd gotten Hadley evaluated and treated, which meant surgery to correct her defect. Or *their* defect; neither of them liked to say it was hers. They couldn't blame their baby, which is what that was, saying it was Hadley's defect and not their defect. Putting it on her like that, when clearly it was borne of them.

According to the doctors, surgery was the right choice. Better sooner than later, they'd said. After twenty-five, the risks of complication, well, that's not what they wanted to be faced with. That's not the situation they wanted to create for their daughter. The doctors told them Hadley could expect to live a healthy, long life. As long as everyone else, really. But for a long time Rachel imagined all of the symptoms her baby could develop. Paradoxical emboli. Migraines. Decompression sickness like divers got. She could not help babying Hadley sometimes, and even James, who felt the same way for a while, was able to back off, let their baby live her life without constantly worrying she would implode. And that, Rachel knows, is when Hadley started loving James more than she loved her. When treating her like even a hard sneeze would shatter her into a million little pieces. Because *that* was not telling her she loved her but instead that she could break, that she was fragile, that she was destructible, and in some abstract, paranoid way, she, her mother, did not want that responsibility, even if she'd give her life for her. Even if all of it was untrue. Even if for years Hadley would not be able to put that into words and Rachel, too much love in her heart, would never admit it. How depressing it was. And she and James, both could imagine very early on how it would all work out. Rachel, in the end, would be the loser. And neither of them could ever stop that ball from rolling, no matter what. Not because they didn't want to, but because they couldn't.

Rachel used her key to open the front door. They said hello to the guard at the gate, who said, Oh sure, sure, I remember you. Go on up. He raised the wooden arm and waved them through. But James and Rachel were sure they'd never met this particular guard before. The guard's name was Jim, and Jim was probably upwards of seventy. Until they'd pulled up and actually honked, he hadn't opened the sliding glass door. Rachel had said, Just toot, because if you give him a full on beep we'll probably get convicted of scaring the poor guy to death. He had been watching television, or sleeping in front of it, they couldn't really tell. Hadley heard the word "death" and said, What? And James looked back at her. "Nothing, baby. Your mom just wants to kill grandpa." And Hadley said, What? again. "Nothing, baby," Rachel said. "Your daddy's a doodie."

There was a note Scotch-taped to the door. Her mother, Julianne, had written the note, which she could tell even before she'd stepped out of the car. Julianne had taken to fancy swirls and underlines, messing with different fonts. She told Rachel on the phone one day that calligraphic practice was "the art of giving form to signs in an expressive, harmonious and skillful manner," and Rachel had looked it up on Dictionary.com and sure enough, word for word. Rachel assumed it was something she'd learned in a new class at the university where Harvey taught (free classes for family members), perhaps something Harvey had taught her himself, one of the little quirky things he'd picked up somewhere over the years. Any cards or correspondence from Julianne over the past few months had these new ornate markings, the peculiar words, which Rachel found oddly appealing.

Home in a bit. Shopping.
Give Harvey a call if you guys need <u>anything</u>.
Mom & Harvey. ☺

James said, "That's gotta take some time to do."

Rachel said, "Don't start."

"We can outsource them to Hallmark. Great opportunities in Venezuela for greeting card makers, I hear."

Rachel said, "Just get the bags." She handed Hadley a small Ziploc bag from her suitcase, told her to brush her teeth, get ready for bed.

After they'd unpacked, after he'd scoped out the cabin and walked around the perimeter as if he were fortifying his castle, James set up his computer. He opened his files and set up a corner where he could work and stay connected and, Rachel thought, disengaged, but considerately so. Where he could jump in and out of work at will, slide his finger over the mouse pad whenever the screensaver came on, and he couldn't monitor his inbox. Once all of that was set up, James grabbed a glass of cold milk, scoured the cabinets until he found a box of double chocolate biscotti, and sat on the couch in front of the television.

They were watching the news when they heard Harvey and Julianne pull up in the driveway. James flipped the channel, found an old black and white cowboy movie. Rachel jumped up, went to meet them at the door. She turned the outside light on, which she'd forgotten to do after they'd stumbled around in the dark. She opened the door as Harvey and Julianne climbed up the two wooden steps, both of them lugging too many grocery bags.

Julianne said, "My sweeties are here," and dropped her bags at her feet, hugged Rachel to her, squeezed to where Rachel's chest felt like it would collapse. Harvey put two bags down on the porch. While Julianne strutted quickly inside with hers, he hugged Rachel, told her, Welcome, glad they made it. As he started to say, "Where's James?," James came walking out in flip flops, shorts, a T-shirt that was too small for him, made his chest stick out too far into their faces.

Rachel said, "Hope it's okay, but we took the same room we had last year." Harvey said, Of course. "Let's get these bags in before we freeze to death." While Julianne smothered Hadley with kisses in a back room, Rachel, James and Harvey unloaded too many bags with too many groceries and definitely too many bottles of wine for their needs.

In the kitchen, after Julianne tucked Hadley in for the night, after she'd turned the heat up and closed the front blinds and turned the stereo on and Merle Haggard was singing "If We Make It Through December," Julianne heated up Irish Coffees for everyone, and they sat around the kitchen table and talked. James kept reaching for his BlackBerry whenever it vibrated, and when Julianne noticed Rachel's eyes bopping over to James', she said, "You two are bugging out. What's up?"

Rachel was about to say, Well, we're waiting to see if James finally makes President, but James said, "Nothing, Jules. Just put in for a small house on the Cape. Waiting to hear back from the Realtor."

A lie, but Rachel went right along, because in a way it *was* true. Yes, they had put in for a house—but only to rent it for a week in August, not to buy it. It wasn't on the Cape; it was on Martha's Vineyard, but what did it matter which parts of a lie were more lie than others?

Julianne said, "Well well," and raised her coffee cup. She said, "Congrats," and Harvey raised his cup too. But neither James nor Rachel lifted theirs soon enough, and for a second there was an awkward pause, Julianne and Harvey with their mugs in the air, Rachel and James hesitating. But then they all had their mugs up, clinking merrily and sipping away at their steaming coffees, each of them wondering what that—what just happened—was.

After a sip, Rachel said, "I think we just don't want to jinx it, is all."

"It's a nice place," James added, now more humbly, erasing the Viagra e-mail he got to his Hotmail account, and not the *Yay! You're El Presidente!* e-mail to his work account. He said, "Anyway, you've done some redecorating since last year?"

Julianne let Harvey go into it with James about the dropped lighting and the new wainscoting, and how he'd wanted to finish up with some new glass backsplash tiles but they hadn't arrived yet, being special order and all, like they were asking for Eye of Newt or something.

In the morning the fog was so dense outside you could barely see in front of your face. Rachel had slept in the other room with Hadley, because Hadley had wanted to sleep in the bunk beds, which Rachel would not let her do alone. James got up early. Rachel knew he would get up early because he wasn't one to sleep when he was anxious, and like clockwork she woke too, for she had always been afflicted with the same ailment. She stared at the ceiling. She listened to him get dressed and ready for his morning run. She listened to his sneakers squeaking along the hardwood as he walked down the hallway.

The room was stuffy, radiator hot and too warm for the covers, and Rachel peeked down at the bottom bunk, careful not to move the bed too much. When she thought about it though, it would probably have taken a blow horn to actually wake Hadley, deep as she slept. Hadley had kicked the blankets off, pulled her shirt up, exposed her belly; her long hair was damp with sweat, little dark curls above her forehead, stuck to one cheek. One sock clung to the tips of her toes, the other lay scrunched like a tiny accordion on the floor. Hadley brushed the back of her hand against her face, turned on her side. She stuck her little behind half off the side of the bed, balancing, somehow, midair. Rachel heard the front door click, footsteps crunching over the gravel driveway. For some reason she looked up, feeling a draft, feeling something, and when she did, there was Harvey, or Harvey's eyes anyway, peeking in through the door, staring at her, at Hadley. "Morning," he mouthed to her. But she did not mouth anything back. He stood there for a few seconds, and eventually, after what seemed a bit too long, pushed the door closed. She heard Harvey walk into his room, heard the door click behind him, and soon it was quiet again. It occurred to her that he must have been there for a few minutes, staring at them, because when he walked away the floorboards creaked, and she had not heard them creak when he'd approached.

Sweet, peculiar Harv, she thought. Checking in on his guests, the old oddball.

When she woke up again, she could hear James, Harvey, and her mother cooking breakfast. She could smell the sweet musk of sausage and thick-cut bacon, the acrid perfume of coffee. The door was cracked, and when she looked back down all she saw were mussed sheets. She walked down the hallway wiping her eyes of sleep. Hadley was the first to see her. "Sleepyhead is awake!" screeched Hadley, and everyone turned to see Rachel standing in the doorway in her sweats, the same baby blue "*Word to your Mother*" sweatshirt Lettie had given her the previous Mother's Day. Julianne read her sweatshirt, said, *Oh boy*. James said, "The nuns at Holy Angel's *love* that sweater." Julianne shook her head. "I bet they do."

Julianne scrambled eggs in a Teflon pan. Harvey was cutting up some sort of sweet pastry loaf, sawing at the layers of yellow and white and red, laying the slices into a bread basket with a couple of paper towels as liner. Every so often he stopped, agitated something off his fingers, stared at the stainless backsplash. Harvey said, "Everything's in the same place, Rachel. May have to look in the dishwasher for a clean mug." He flipped his wrist in an odd, slow wave, threw a red cloth napkin over the basket, put it on the table.

Rachel said she was good, don't worry about her. She pulled a coffee cup from the dishwasher, filled it with coffee, sat at the kitchen table. She tore two packets of artificial sweetener, dropped them into the cup, poured some cream. Julianne said, "Lettie and them should be getting in soon. Had a crack-O'-the-dawn flight this morning."

James said, "They left on the six o'clock." He looked at his watch. "Should land in another few minutes, I'm guessing."

Rachel looked up at the *Home Sweet Home* clock over the front window. It was half past eight.

Julianne shook her head. "Don't know why you all didn't come on the same plane."

Rachel said, "We tried, but Michael had a cap or something fall out. Dental nine-one-one. Changed their flight at the last minute."

Hadley looked up. "When Aaron gets here, Mom, you have to sleep with Dad."

Rachel said, "Yes, baby," pointed to Hadley's cereal bowl. James smiled, nodded eagerly at Rachel. Julianne said, "Oh God," and walked over to the sink.

Julianne said, "Sammy and Cliff should be getting here sometime tomorrow afternoon. They're driving up after Sammy gets off work. I think she's only doing half a day."

James said, "I have to get that guy in shape before he keels over."

Rachel glanced at James, took a sip of coffee. "Cliff is not in bad shape. You don't have to run eight hundred miles a week to be in shape."

Julianne said, "Take him on your runs anyway. It'll be good for him." She turned a knob, shut the stove off. Pushed the eggs onto an oversized plate with a spatula. She stuck her hand in a bag of shredded cheese, sprinkled a handful over the eggs. She said, "All of us should try and sweat some. Get the blood pumping, all the goodies going to clog our arteries the next month."

Once Julianne sat down everyone dug in. When they finished, Harvey and Julianne did the dishes, Harvey scrubbing, Julianne dipping the plates in warm water, Rachel organizing everything on the dish rack to dry. James read Hadley a Harry Potter book, the both of them snuggled up by the fire, Hadley staring at the pages, grabbing James' hand, looking up at her father when something got good. Hadley said she liked Hedwig the owl best. James said him too. She's soooo cute, she said.

James' BlackBerry buzzed on the table, and his body tensed, as if he were going to move. Hadley said, *Dad*, and James said, *Hadley*, but Rachel was already unlocking the BlackBerry, scrolling around. Rachel looked at James, shook her head no. Nothing. Hadley grabbed her father's head on both sides, pulled it back towards the tome resting in his lap. Harry Potter, she said now in what was her version of an English accent, deepening her voice, pursing her lips. *Continue, kind Sir.*

It was after one and Hadley was taking a nap on the couch. Julianne lay a CoCaLo sweater knit blanket over her, brought Rachel some chamomile tea. She sat on the recliner, pulled her legs up to one side. The telephone rang and Harvey picked it up, said, Okay, see you then. He looked at the receiver in his hand, put it back next to the charger. "They should be here in another hour or so. Stopped at the Underground in Atlanta." He picked the phone back up, put it on the charger. Jiggled it until it beeped. He said, "James and I are going to go for a walk, get the paper. Be back in a bit." He leaned over, kissed Julianne on the cheek. "See ya," she said. She watched him make his way to the front door, scratch his head, and depart.

The road to downtown Helen was still wet, the asphalt glistening under light fog. They were careful not to step where you could slip; careful to maneuver the little inclines here and there, the ankle-busters, the knee-scrapers. The wind was up a little, rattling the leaves in the trees, but it was not cold, barely chilly, really, and James had his windbreaker open at the neck. Harvey wore an olive drab Allegheny Upland coat, which James admired; James had almost bought the same coat, from a higher-end retailer. James knew Harvey was a university guy, a practical shopper, bought everything discount, Army Navy surplus hole-in-the-walls where everyone wore camouflage and corny T-shirts that said *From My Cold Dead Hands* or *Lock & Load* or *Come and Take It*, pictures of assault rifles below the writing. If you couldn't give it a test drive, what's the use, Harvey said. He was referring to buying stuff online, from catalogs. James told Harvey he liked the jacket; Harvey told him how little he paid for it. Good deal, James said. James looked at his BlackBerry, put it back into his pocket. He didn't want to seem a nervous Nelly, but he couldn't feel the phone vibrate when he was walking, and he didn't want to miss any calls.

Harvey said, "Pretty antsy about that house, huh? Must be some house." James looked at Harvey. Harvey had a look on his face, like I'm not going to ask if you don't offer. And James knew the jig was up. There was no point in keeping on with the whole house story, poorly thought out as it was. He said, "I'm waiting on an e-mail about a job. It's a pretty big move."

Harvey said, "Figured it was something like that. I didn't think you were one to get all excited about a vacation rental. Not that titillated, anyway." Harvey put his hands in his jacket pockets, smiled. "Same company?"

"Yep. Same company." James thought, *titillated*.

"You're pretty high up in that organization already, aren't you?"

"Just one place to go. CEO isn't going anywhere."

"Would you have to move?"

"No. I'd stay at corporate. Different office, same building."

"Mind my asking what the title is?"

"President. And COO."

Harvey said, "Well, that's something." He put his hand on James' forearm. "Congratulations are definitely in order, aren't they? That's a very big deal, James."

James gripped the BlackBerry in his pocket, let it go. He said, "It's just taking them a long time to get back to me. They have me on pins and needles."

They walked down a street that ran parallel to Main Street, turned on Munich Strasse. They walked past *Pirates Cove Adventure Golf*. James looked at the dried up waterfalls, the fading putting greens. The black matting curled at the corners. "Maybe we can take the kids here again if they're open." Harvey said sure, they can call, check their winter hours. Harvey scanned a sign with a pirate's face on it, beard and earring, black eye patch. He said, "Winter they have different hours. Just gotta check, see what's what." Harvey seemed to stare for a long time at the putting greens, the walking path, the rocks where the waterfalls came to life, where children would stick their tongues to catch the cool water spraying down. He heard the children's laughter from the previous summer, walking, whispering along the wet concrete, the curves of the miniature buildings. Echoing all around him.

They walked for a block in silence, the breeze on their faces, and then, for apparently no reason, James clapped his hands loud, pumped himself up like it was the fourth quarter and the score was tied, a minute left on the clock. The claps reverberated around them, down an alley, up the mulchy hills they'd descended. He said, "Come on now!," smiled a big smile at Harvey, like Harvey was on the same team, like they were getting ready to sack the QB and win the game. Harvey fell back some, checked something in his pockets. Stood there, blinking. James watched a young boy run into a pile of leaves. Harvey was shaking his head, rocking it to one side, dislodging something. He said, "I'm sure you'll get it. From what I've seen, it's pretty clear you're the bee's knees." Harvey took a minute. James watched the boy. Harvey said something but James could not hear what he'd said, brushed it aside. He lost himself in thoughts of the new job, what it would be like to be damn near king.

James said, "Objectively, I can't think of anyone else. Sales have been up every year. Last year we had record quarters. Our EBITDA was impressive, if I do say so myself. If I don't get this, it better be Steve Jobs walking in that door."

Harvey said, "How long you been at that company?"

"Twelve years. Good numbers every year. Time-wise, only the CEO has me beat."

"You'll get it," Harvey said. "I'm sure they're just figuring the details."

"I'm sure. But they take too long, maybe I do talk to that headhunter's been calling."

"Keep the options open," said Harvey.

"Exactly," said James. But it was smoke and both of them knew it.

On the way back, James popped into a gift shop, bought Hadley an Oktoberfest teddy bear. Harvey was scanning the classifieds section of the paper, bending a page, straightening the newspaper out, the wind crumpling it over, bending it back again. When they were cutting through a parking lot a car pulled up behind them and honked. They saw Lettie and Michael, Aaron squinting from the back seat of a black Suburban. Lettie shook her head, said, "The riff raff Helen's putting out these days," and swung the back doors open.

Aaron burst through the door, squealing and hollering and loud as usual. "We're here! We're here!" he said, running through the kitchen, bumping into everything like a madman, disappearing behind walls, footsteps clopping out of sight, turning a corner, hands flailing in the air. He stumbled into Julianne's arms, let himself droop, played dead. Julianne bent over, squeezed Aaron tight, kissed him over and over on the forehead and cheeks. Hadley dropped the sheet of red construction paper she was cutting with her plastic scissors, stood beside Aaron and her grandmother. Julianne let Aaron go, and Aaron and Hadley ran off, holding hands, Hadley reminding Aaron about the bunk beds, how hers was on the bottom and he could have the top bunk, Aaron saying something about how he was older, and Hadley saying she wanted the bottom bunk anyway, in case she had to go to the bathroom.

Lettie came walking in, light on her feet as always (the runt of the litter as her father used to call her), thumping the wheels of her suitcase against the steps. Julianne said, "Let me get that, dear," but Lettie said she had it, kissed her mother on the lips. She dropped a notebook; Julianne picked it right up. Michael walked in behind Lettie, pointed with his head to Harvey and James. He said, "We found some hitchhikers down on the slopes. I was going to leave them, but Lettie said, No, they might be handy round these parts."

Julianne gave Michael a quick squeeze on the neck, said, "No country accents from you, Mister." She glanced at Harvey, who was carrying one of her daughter's duffel bags, which she remembered from the last time they had vacationed together, down on the Redneck Riviera, which is what Lettie called Pensacola. Michael said, "Aw, Jules," but kept walking down the hall. He dropped the duffel bag, slipped into the bathroom and locked the door behind him.

Rachel said, "Hey, sis," brushed her cheek up against Lettie's. Rachel closed the door behind everyone, followed Lettie back to her room. Lettie made an exaggerated display of letting the suitcase fall to the floor. She swiveled around on her foot, let herself fall straight back onto the bed as graceful as an old film star fainting. Rachel said, "That good, huh?"

"Michael let Aaron have a super-size Coke at Mickey D's." She made castanets out of her fingers, said, "Bla bla bla bla bla," put her palms to her eyes. Grunted what sounded like "Alacazam." Rachel said, "What?" And Lettie said, "Xanax. I need a hundred Xanax, stat!" And they laughed.

Aaron and Hadley came running in the room. Before they spoke, Lettie said, "For the love of god!" but she was smiling, and Aaron said, "Mom, can we go outside?"

Lettie waved her hands. "Go. Flee. Run away!" Rachel said, "Stay in the driveway, kiddos."

Aaron and Hadley ran back down the hall, slammed the front door behind them. Rachel said, "James," and James said, "I can see them fine from where I'm sitting, *dear*," with a little wee bit of annoyance.

Lettie was the youngest of the three, the smallest of the three, but she hit her stride after meeting Michael, after graduating summa cum laude and getting an MBA, but giving up her career to stay at home with Aaron. Or not giving it up but switching; she was a reporter now, freelancing part-time for the *Herald* and the *L.I. Times* while she wrote the great American novel or her short story cycle or whatever she was working on, because she was always working on something no one ever got to see. Lettie's void, James called it. Michael called her the most educated housewife in East Islip, and she'd said, Not even close, which was true. Some of the wives collected diplomas like people collected butterflies, displaying their degrees from Columbia and Harvard and Yale behind glass in their offices at home, where they sat behind computer screens, stared out at the sailboats undulating on the break, and shopped for everything on Amazon or Bed, Bath, and Beyond. Their house (and many of the others in their neighborhood) seemed like refueling stations for UPS and Federal Express, and some days their entire street looked like a recycling drop, cardboard boxes sitting before all the door fronts, waiting for their owners to come home from work and claim them.

But Lettie and Michael pretended they were not pretentious like some of their neighbors, did not flaunt their blessings like some of their neighbors. Rachel remembered a barbecue at her house the previous year. She and Lettie had been watching the kids running around, jumping in the pool, falling all over the place.

Aaron had knocked over a plate of seafood that was sitting on a table, waiting to be grilled, onto the grass. Just ran by it, looked back, yelled sorry or something and cannonballed into the water where Hadley had been lying on an orange raft in the middle of the pool. They were talking about how much or how little they participated in their local church, and she had said, *You're just like us*, as she dropped what must have been four pounds of shrimp and lobster and crab into the trash. And Lettie, apparently horrified, had said, *No, not really*, and watched her walk back into the house to fetch a new plate of seafood from the basement fridge. She had come out with a large bowl, freshly defrosted, of crab legs and lobster tails, shrimp, stone crab claws. As if to substantiate what Lettie was still rolling around in her brain, a stone crab claw slipped out of the bowl onto the grass, and she'd bent at the knees, dropped that into the trash as well. She said, the boys will be back from golf in a bit, and Lettie said, How can I help? But she was looking at the trash can, the flies zooming in, hovering over the discarded shellfish. Rachel was looking at her now, saying something about what Lettie was saying right before she'd walked inside? And Lettie said, *Nothing*, but Rachel had heard her and believed she'd known what she had been implying. But she dropped the subject. When Aaron had cannonballed again and Hadley had nearly been thrown out of the pool by the waves and began crying, they had rushed over to make sure she was okay.

Only later did Rachel convince herself that yes, Lettie *was*, in fact, judging her. When James reminded her that Lettie, the previous summer, had written a two-column guest piece on domestic waste for the *Sentinel*, bashing how much food not only Americans in general but Strong Islanders wasted each summer, she just nodded. Totally forgot about that, she'd said. Because she had. Wrote it off as another one of Lettie's bleeding heart, liberal, hypocritical Lefty rants about the end of the world, the end of freedom, all that Enron and Blackwater and Dick Cheney is the Devil stuff. Was it a good article? Sure. Great statistics, impressive research on how many burgers got tossed like hockey pucks to the trash, sitting alongside miles of Wisconsin brats at barbecues every summer. Even guesstimated how many pounds of red potato salad and coleslaw got trashed per Strong Island town, from Mineola to Montauk. But a good article did not a hypocrite absolve. Lettie was just Lettie. She could pretend to be better than everyone, even casually, but pretending didn't make it so. The fact was that Lettie was her sister like Sammy was her sister. You got over the little things.

Normally, James loved Georgia. Not every year but the past few except one, they had flown down for Thanksgiving or for Christmas, hiked and jogged the trails around North Georgia, around Helen. *Acclimated.* Sometimes they'd stay the first night in Atlanta, or maybe the last night in Atlanta before they flew back home, checked out the restaurants in Buckhead or Midtown, maybe walked around the Highlands, did some shopping, ate at some chic restaurant whose proprietor had won or been a finalist on Iron Chef. But this year they'd landed, saddled up, driven straight to Helen. This year he was incapable of relaxing.

He watched Aaron and Hadley running around outside, collecting pine cones, pushing something (a dead squirrel? an opossum?) around with bent mockernut branches. To relax, he pulled out his laptop, let *Messenger* pop up in case someone was on, in case maybe the servers were down and e-mails weren't being sent out. But no one was on. Not Thorpe, not Raney, no one. He pulled up his calendar, his list of *To Do's*, started typing. E-mails to clients. E-mails to reporters. E-mails to old friends he hadn't talked to in a while, who were off living their lives, flying around the world like he flew around the world, leading merger meetings, raising capital, executing mass layoffs, coddling inquisitive boards. Friends from college who had made it like he had, who were pulling in beaucoup bucks, building log cabin estates in Jackson Hole and winter getaways with floor-to-ceiling windows along the waters of West Palm Beach. He closed the laptop, picked up Aaron's Game Boy. Started playing Pokémon.

Rachel walked over, sat beside him. She said, "You'll never beat my score," and he said, "Go away, you're messing me up." Rachel watched Hadley chase Aaron around the Tahoe, get frustrated, give up. Saw Aaron throw up his hands, say *okay, okay,* when he saw Hadley making to go back inside. Now Aaron was chasing Hadley, letting her stay one step ahead. Rachel said, "My turn," when she saw James restarting a new game. James said, "Get your own," whiney like Hadley would say it when she was talking to one of her friends back home. Rachel said, "I married a five-year-old," and walked away. "I'm going to erase every one of your scores," James called after her. And he meant it. Later, when James was outside trying to fix the grill, she would sit on the couch, her turn now, and she would do her best to push *JAM01* off the High Score list, replace them all over again with her cyber moniker: RrulesYa.

Rachel asked where Harvey was, and Julianne told him probably reading a textbook somewhere. Julianne and Lettie were making pistachio linzertortes with cherry jam, shaped like stars. Lettie said, "Make yourself useful." Rachel said, "Hit me," and Lettie said, "Mom, tell your daughter where she can find cooling racks and a big Tupperware." Julianne scraped cherry jam from one linzertorte, spread it into another. She said, "Okay, Julia Child."

Julianne kicked the cabinet door below where she was punching star-shaped cookies out with her cookie cutter. "Everything should be down here," she said. She scooted her mess of dough and flour to one side, let Rachel bend down below her, rummage through the tangle of aluminum and wood and Tupperware that was thrown in there haphazardly over the course of the year. Rachel said, *Jeez*, but found what she was looking for. She said, "Looks like you two got it under control," and walked out of the kitchen. "Lazy Lizzy," said Lettie, but Rachel was already closing the back door behind her, standing out on the deck against the warmth of the Jacuzzi, steam bleeding into the cool air. She picked up the grill brush someone had knocked down but never picked back up. She wiped her hand on her backside, looked out at the trees, the few yellow and orange leaves clinging for dear life to the naked branches. She took a deep breath, let it out. She lifted the Jacuzzi cover, stuck her face in, let the huff of heat press up against her. The steam whooshed out, hit her face. When she pulled back her neck was clammy and cold. Chlorine filled her nostrils. She wiped moisture off her cheeks with the back of her hand.

And she thought about where they would celebrate in Helen when James got the call, what the best bottle one of the little restaurants in town would have hidden away in whatever room they called a wine cellar. She saw James saying, "Bring us the best," to the waitress, who she imagined would be some plain Russian girl named Ekaterina with thick calves and an accent, doing a summer abroad or maybe passing time until one of Helen's Jimmy Bobs or Bobby Joes or Bucepheluses fell in love and proposed, got her the green card she'd always dreamed about. And she saw James smiling his big pearly whites, not making fun of Ekaterina directly, because he wasn't like that, but ribbing her in his way when she warned him, in her thick accent, *I must inform you, eet's eighty-five doh-larz for bottle.* And James, of course, pretending to think long and hard about it, like maybe, just maybe, eighty-five dollars was a little extravagant. She realized, or not realized but was reminded, again, that everything was no longer about them but about *him*, about James. About where his career was going to take them and about what they would do when *he* got that bonus or *he* had time off. But again she brushed it aside, because she had always agreed with it. She knew that the only reason she thought of these things now was because of materfamilias Julianne and because of crusader for the righteous Lettie and her little writing thing, because once Sammy was here any of these pinprick feelings she was having would simply vanish, and her place was her place. And it was a place of power, not a place of submission. Not that she didn't want to be here, because she did. But back home, home was home. Back home women like her made sense. Back home she had an identity. *Her* identity. An identity that was a secure identity. An identity that did not have to relentlessly prove, over and again, that it was an identity of value, and not some frivolous and cutesy rationalization of one, as she knew the rest of them, all of them, probably thought.

If they got the call, or rather when they got it, because they had *always* gotten it, maybe they would finally start working on that second child. Hadley was already past five, and five had been the magic number for so long that now she had to ponder, now she had to consider, at least for a second, what one child and only one child meant. Two children, a few years apart, that was good. That was one child protecting the other. That was one child roughing it out, excelling at school both academically as well as socially, clearing a path for her little brother or sister. Sanding down the sides so that they didn't get any splinters. Only children, that was something else. Only children were a different breed, a sad strain of child, a knock with no echo. She did not see herself, did not imagine her family, her home, as an only-child home. That was not the home she lived in. That was not the home she saw in her dreams. Her home was one filled with children, storming up and down stairs, dressing up for Halloween, playing soccer in little blue Umbro shorts and knee-highs and rubber cleats. As soon as James gave her that smile, they could let the party begin. As soon as he put his palm out to Hadley for her to give him five, baby number two could start packing his bags (she always imagined a boy), and he could start getting ready to join them in their world, the world outside her womb.

She thought of this second child more and more these days, expecting him to come running through the doors, like Aaron but not like Aaron, because, well, Aaron was odd somehow, a little too rambunctious, a little too *free*. Lettie let him get away with murder, day in day out, let him be too loud too often, let him coast over the important things like math and science and computers so he could pretend he was Peter Pan, running around stretching her good pantyhose, reading his fantasy books and remaining immersed, all day and all night, in his made up worlds like life was forever Neverland, always reciting not the more typical lines like "I'll teach you to jump on the wind's back, and away we go!" but the more peculiar ones, like "Who and what art though? . . . I'm youth, I'm joy!" and "Do you know why swallows build in the eaves of houses? To listen to the stories!" Not at all behaving as her son would behave. Too much, she thought, that boy of Lettie's, even if Hadley was crazy about him.

When Rachel went back inside for a cup of tea, Julianne and Lettie were in the middle of what looked like a heavy discussion they were trying to keep secret. Julianne looked over her shoulder when she heard footsteps, said, "We're talking about Sammy and Cliff." Rachel said, "Oh, what about?" And Julianne said, "Sammy did not want Cliff to come."

"Why not?"

Lettie shushed her. Rachel said, "Uh-oh."

Julianne stuck her head down the hall, walked over to check on James in the living room. She saw Hadley whispering in Aaron's ear, both of them sitting on the bumper of one of the trucks. She said, "I think Sammy's done. I think she's going to leave him."

Rachel raised her eyebrows, bobbed her head back like a hen. She looked like an exaggerated character from a bad TV show, maybe Don Knotts catching something fishy going on between Jack and Chrissy, his eyes bulging wide like a pug's, that too-surprised look that killed his chances of ever being taken seriously. She said, "If that's so, why is she bringing him then?"

Lettie said, "She wasn't going to. He begged her."

"Shocker, USA." Rachel shook her head in disbelief. Lettie couldn't tell if she was truly shocked or just pretending to be. Rachel said, "They've been together longer than Mom and Dad here."

"Funny," said Julianne.

Rachel said, "The booze?"

"Apparently not," said Lettie.

"She doesn't know," said Julianne. "You'd think. But I think she's just bored and sick and tired of struggling to make it. Who can blame her?"

Rachel said, "She should have stayed in school. She was always smart."

Lettie thought about it and said, "To do what? Meet a James or Michael?"

Rachel said, "Huh?" and Lettie said, "You and I have worked a total of twelve minutes combined since we got married."

Rachel gave Lettie a look. "You know what I mean. And the work comment? No one's forcing you to stay at home."

Julianne said, "Girls, girls."

Rachel said, "I'd like to say good for her, but I don't know."

Lettie stood up, looked out the window. James was out there now, helping the kids climb a tree. She wanted to bang on the window, tell James to be careful, but didn't. She didn't want to distract him with both of the kids already barely hanging on,

kicking their feet like they were running on air. She said, "I have
to agree with Rachel. Cliff's been there for her bar none. Through
the ups and downs, that guy hasn't gone anywhere. And I *know* it
hasn't been easy." She did not say that Sammy had had her own
issues, because all of them already knew. There were drugs and
drink, and if any of them had ever had a temper, it was Sammy.
She had even been thrown in jail for beating someone up. Actually
physically *beating* someone up.

Julianne was already pretty over the topic when Michael
walked in. She said, "It is what it is," and Rachel and Lettie knew
to change the subject. Michael said, "What is what it is?" and
Lettie said, "The tea in China," and Michael got the hint. He was
about to say, Where are the kids? But he saw them dangling like
fruit from the tree and heard them yelling at James. Michael said,
"I love it here." Rachel said, "I'm sure you do. Built-in babysitters
everywhere." And Michael said, "Praise Jesus! The clouds have
parted, the sun is shining, and God said, Children, play outside
and be free like lambs!"

Julianne said, "I don't think that's how it goes, preacher
man."

Rachel put an oven mitt into a drawer. "I don't think
preacher man cares," she said.

Aaron and Hadley came running into the kitchen. They
left the front door open, James lying across the top of Harvey and
Julianne's car hood. Aaron said, "We want water!" and Lettie said,
"We want water what?" and Aaron said, *Pleeeeze!*

Julianne poured tap water into two glasses, gave them to
the kids. Rachel said, *Mom*, but Julianne quickly cut her off. "The
water here is fine, prima donna. I promise. Your precious angel
doesn't have to pee Evian."

Hadley said, "Mom says I pee Capri Suns."

Julianne said, "More like choco-machiatto-yoohoo Suns,"
and tickled Hadley's sides.

Hadley said, "That doesn't make sense, Grandma," and
ran off right behind Aaron.

Rachel said, "Don't run!" and both children stopped
running and sat down by the television, which Harvey was just

turning on, hoping to watch a documentary; but once the kids were there lying at his feet, searching for a cartoon channel. Lettie listened to Harvey talking to the kids, asking them if this channel or that channel was better (there were only three channels), did they want to watch a movie instead. When Harvey pulled out a VHS tape, the kids went silent, but then Harvey said, "It's like a DVD but better," the kids said, *Yea yea yea*! Harvey put a tape in, sat down in his recliner, pulled the leg rest up. He asked the kids if they wanted to see his pictures from Spain, the castle Christopher Columbus visited before sailing to America. Hadley said, I do, I do, and Harvey got back up, went to fetch his albums from the office. He lowered the volume on the remote, crossed his legs, and Hadley sat scrunched beside him on the recliner, wiggling every so often to get comfortable and a little un-scrunched. Aaron kept watching TV, laughing at cartoons that were probably around when Harvey was a kid, but Hadley and Harvey were soon lost in the pictures of bulls and capes and Moorish artifacts, Harvey pointing at this or that, happy someone her age was so interested not only in other cultures and history but in learning more about her Grandpa's past, the things that made him smile and that were important to him.

In the abrupt stillness that had overtaken the cabin, Michael walked by the kitchen light as a feather, careful to not let the kids see him walk by. He caught Lettie's eye, mouthed something, pointed outside, and she knew he and James were going to go for a walk, that maybe they would talk shop. Lettie said, "The boys are going to bond." Rachel looked out the window, watched James and Michael heading up the hill.

Rachel had always liked Michael. When one day James came home from work and told her that he'd made Michael an offer to a senior position at his company, Rachel had kissed him, held their foreheads together for a brief but genuinely tender moment. She did not know much about Michael's previous employment or accomplishments, only that he seemed to be doing well enough to have the nice house, to take nice vacations, enough that Lettie did not have to work and they could talk to each other during the day when both of them were preparing supper (Lettie chopping and dicing and boiling, Rachel running her fingers along the alphabetized delivery menus or browsing them online). Thank you, she had said. And she meant it. Having Lettie nearby, well, she couldn't ask for more. But James had said, "The guy's qualified." He'd been eating an apple, sitting on the island in the kitchen, which he rarely did. It was another reason the memory stuck with her as it had. "Michael's a bargain, if you want to know the truth." And that was that. Michael working for James, Lettie and her family moving twenty minutes away. One big happy family living on Long Island. Everything coming more and more together how Rachel had always pictured it coming together.

It was still pretty warm out and his heart was still pumping from holding the kids up, but James was feeling good even though he was still thinking about the job. After he'd mentioned the whole deal to Harvey, he promised himself to forget about it, to not bring it up again, to let it just happen. If Michael brought it up he could talk to him about it, because he probably already knew what was going on. Though Michael no longer reported to him, he had to have heard chatter going around the office. Maybe he was in on the pre-celebration party planning that was surely already underway. Instead of letting the silence lead him to shop talk, James said, "Maybe we do something nice for Harvey and Jules for their anniversary, what say ye?"

James looked at Michael, who was nodding. Michael seemed relieved somehow, like he'd tensed up and released. Michael didn't like to talk about work all the time, at least not when he was on vacation. It had been a conversation they had had, because James, while being an ignoramus about a lot of things, was not ignorant about how people felt around the boss outside of work, even if he was no longer really his boss, even if he couldn't help but talk about work more often than not. James knew what he was. He'd been who he was for too long. But the moment passed. Michael cracked his neck to the left, to the right, stretched his back. James said, "What do you have in mind?"

Their wives had tried planning something out previously, but nothing ever came to fruition. What did you buy a couple in their late sixties who had been married ten years? Sure, you could go the traditional aluminum gift theme route, but none of them had been able to decide what they, Harvey and Julianne, would actually use that was made from aluminum. If it wasn't practical, it would sit in a closet except once a year, when they'd pull it out so no one got offended, though none of them probably would have ever gotten offended anyway.

Michael said, "My thought was a trip somewhere, but they'd never accept it and if you surprised them with it they'd probably never go anyway."

"I'm thinking we just do something for them while we're here. Maybe hire someone to redo the deck or something." James reached down, picked up a flat gray rock, seemed to study it in his hands. "Either that or just give them some cash to do what they want to do."

"I'm down with the deck idea."

"That's what I'm thinking. Just have some guys come out here while we take them hiking or something, come back to a new deck." James zipped the rock into the trees, heard it knock up against a trunk.

Michael said he would look up some numbers when they got back to the cabin, and James said No, I got it, and Michael did not push. He said, "Just let me know how much it is and I'll write you a check."

"Cool. Deck it is."

"Deck it be," said Michael, and they cut through a narrow path that ran alongside one of the holes of the golf course, Michael high-stepping, working his glutes, while James swung an imaginary 9-Iron.

Later that afternoon James hollered, "Who wants to go rappelling?" but neither of the kids responded. Everyone was gathered around the television, and James could see they were watching the Grinch steal Christmas. Hadley lay on her stomach beside Aaron, their feet up in the air, their sneakers like pendulum balls at the ends of their legs, kicking the floor, bouncing back up. James saw an equation in his head, $T = 2\pi\sqrt{L/g}$. Everyone but Rachel turned back to the television, back to Jim Carrey running around like a madman. Rachel gave him a look, like why are you riling everyone up? But he ignored her. James said, "Tough crowd." So he lowered his voice, still pretending to holler, said, "Okay. Who wants to climb down a mountain hanging from a rope?" and Aaron jumped up yelling that he did. Lettie said, *James*, but Michael was up out of his seat now. He said, "Let's do it," and headed down the hall to change.

James left his BlackBerry on the dining room table. Rachel pursed her lips like *Wow*, really, can you handle it? "Michael's got his, if you need us," he said. He kissed her goodbye and off they went, he, Michael and the kids, Harvey deciding to stay back with the women, though only at the last minute when Julianne reminded him of his back, what happened the last time he tried to go spelunking with his children years ago. Lettie, hearing that, reminded that he had children, said, "How are they, Harv?"

Harvey Lipscomb had married their mother in what, at the time, seemed an impulse. Julianne had mentioned Harvey to them over the phone, dropped his name casually one evening on a three-way call, probably twenty minutes in. He's a professor, she'd said. "And I think he's keen on me." Lettie had said, "Keen?" and Lettie and Rachel knew maybe it was the other way around. Rachel said, "Is Harvey *keen* on you?" and their mother had said, "Yes, I believe he is," and that was how Harvey Lipscomb came into their lives. Apparently it had been going on for some months, Julianne dining with Harvey's family, going on weekend trips to Hilton Head, where one of Harvey's sons, EK, which was short for Edward King, had a vacation home. Nothing ostentatious, a three/three and a half, harbor views, on a golf course, somewhere to escape for a long weekend. Julianne had mentioned EK paying almost twelve thousand a year HOA, which she thought was outrageous, which it was. But when she'd said it, when she'd waited for her daughters to agree and they hadn't, it was clear they did not seem to understand what the big deal was. Julianne had said, *Well well*, but that was it.

But once they had been married, once Julianne was Mrs. Lipscomb, Hilton Head was no more. To Harvey's children, there was only one Mrs. Lipscomb, and she hadn't passed away and she hadn't left their father—their father had left her. They had not attended the wedding. EK was still friendly, still called his father, and his father still called him, but Grace, Emily Grace, Harvey's youngest (though still in her mid-thirties), she still believed in reconciliation. She still thought Harvey was going to go back to Jean, which was Harvey's ex-wife's name. She thought they would get back together like she and her ex, Jose, would get back together, maybe not tomorrow but soon enough. How could you not when there were children in the mix. Even after Harvey had told her over the phone, on Julianne's and his five-year, that while he was sorry, No, he wouldn't be going back. All this Julianne had told them, and they had simply nodded. No questions, no prodding. Just nodded, like they knew the story, like it was really not so uncommon, these family imbroglios, these pickled to-do's. It was then that Julianne understood that they, Harvey's kids, thought she was just another girlfriend of their father's, a fly-by-night little floozy or whatever.

Harvey just smiled, said, "Good. Thanks for asking," and trailed away, not wanting to discuss this other life of his, which remained hidden from them except for the bits and pieces Julianne shared with them when he shared them with her, when he shook his head slowly and said, What am I supposed to do here? with every little row?

They listened to Harvey go outside now, open the garage, push something against something else. They watched him rake the leaves off the small patch of grass dividing the driveway and the road. It was odd, him scratching a leaf from one side, a branch from another; most of the grass was blocked by dividing boulders, and you could barely see what he was digging at. Rachel said, "Now look what you've done," referring to Harvey, who was on his hands and knees picking at something. She said, "You've flustered the poor guy," and Julianne said, "He'll do that for a few minutes and then he'll start turning a bowl in his shop."

Lettie said, "Jesus." Julianne looked up at the stained bowls running along the tops of her cabinets. "You didn't think we bought all those bowls, did you?" And they laughed.

When Aaron and Hadley were younger, James brought Hadley to Mount Yonah and they had rappelled while their wives had stayed back at the cabin. Michael had never rappelled, but after that first day he'd become addicted to it, and back home had even built himself a climbing wall in the backyard. Now it was exciting to take their kids, but they would not get to do the climbing they had done then, when they would swing around like monkeys, see who had the biggest cojones. Now they would have to assuage the kids' fears, and they both knew Aaron would be the one scared if either of them showed fear. Michael carried the equipment while James carried the backpack of snacks and juices and water, the first aid kit Julianne had thrown in there on their way out. They drove up Chambers Road and parked. They hiked the mile and a half up to the campsite the Army sometimes used, neither Hadley nor Aaron making a peep. When they saw the granite slab and cliff, Aaron said *Whoa*, and James could see an expression on Hadley's face, like, *We're* supposed to climb *that?*

James dropped his backpack on the ground, and Michael started pulling out different colored ropes, harnesses, belay gear. Normally they would plan it out a little, but they were familiar with Mount Yonah and knew it was a relatively straight shot. The only thing they had to be careful of was up at the very top, where they would connect to the cables and bolts. Up there, before you were hooked in, you had to maneuver an exposed slab of sloping granite, and for the kids that could be tricky. They would have to keep them close before clipping them in. All Michael could see, for a time, was everyone falling.

James grabbed a fifty-meter rope, threw it over his shoulder. Michael said he would wait down below and guide them. When Aaron said he wanted to wait with his father, James said, "Good idea. We'll go in pairs," and Hadley said "See ya!" and they headed up, Hadley lugging the rest of the equipment in the backpack her father had been carrying, heavy as it was.

For a few minutes Michael and Aaron could hear them up there, Hadley protesting something loudly, and then James peeked his head over the ledge and said, "I'm throwing the rope," and Michael said, "Roger." Michael said, "A, *over here*," and Aaron jogged goofily over to where his father stood, off to the side, squatting on a jutting rock formation. He squatted beside him and they watched the rope tumble over the side, get stuck in a tree. Michael said, "Try again!" and James peeked over again and shook his head and soon the rope was inching its way back up the side of the cliff. The second time the rope came all the way down and hit the ground at the bottom of the rock wall. James yelled, "Good?" and Michael yelled, "Roger," again, and James said he was sending Hadley down first, the first time on the left side. He yelled, "On your *right*, Mike."

Michael said, "You have to help me guide your cousin down, okay?" And Aaron said okay.

They craned their necks up and they could see James and Hadley clearly now to one side of the cliff, James holding onto the rope as Hadley dangled a little until her feet met the side of the rock face. Aaron yelled, "That way more," and Michael said, "A little to your left," and James tugged Hadley to his left until Hadley was walking solidly along one side. Hadley was tentative for a minute or so, but once she was comfortable she turned and looked down past her legs and said, "Aaron, I'm coming down!" and Aaron yelled "Duh!" and said "You're so high, Hadley!"

James let the rope some give, and Hadley continued down, holding onto the rope as if she were controlling her descent, but Michael knew James was controlling the whole show. Soon Hadley was on the ground and when Michael had pulled Hadley to the side James came storming down like some Airborne Rappel Master, zipping down the line faster than Michael thought safe, faster than he'd ever zip down ever. Hadley watched her father zoom down the line, bump against the side of the rock face, and land in front of them like Spiderman. "Cool," said Aaron, but Michael just shook his head. "Easy," Michael said. James gave Hadley a high five.

Michael said, "You ready, Tiger?" and Aaron said, "I think so." But when they were walking up the right side of the rock face to where the cliff jutted out, Aaron looked up and with a little quaver in his voice said, "That looks high, Dad" and stopped. Michael wanted to squeeze his son, tell him he wasn't going to let his cousin Hadley outdo him, was he? But instead he just winked.

"If the rope breaks I'm dead, huh?" and Michael said, "I would never let the rope break, A. Never." And that was enough for Aaron.

Michael strapped him in and gave him another wink, and then Aaron put on the bravest face he could. When he reached the bottom, when James grabbed him out of the air and put him down and lifted him out of the harness, he looked up at his father and yelled, "I want to do it *again!*" and soon he was doing it again. James smiled. He looked at Hadley, who just said, "As do I, father," which made him laugh. He wondered where she picked up such things.

Sometimes he could look at her and see her mother, and sometimes he could look at her and see himself. But there were times when he looked at Hadley, with her beautiful hair and her heartbreaking smile, and thought, who is this little person? Which was something he had done a lot more earlier in her life, when she was more baby and less person. Because at first Hadley had not been invited to the party. Or she had barged in a little early and, for him anyway, unexpectedly so. Right as he was moving into the EVP role at Microzoot. Right when he would have to be away a lot more, which he knew (and which turned out to be pretty true, regardless of what she said now) would cause problems between him and Rachel. Because she could talk the talk, but when it came down to it, she had just as many womanly needs as the next woman. Which was fine—no problem at all, if she would just own up to it and not try to project that she wasn't. For a time, it had been rough.

Divorce had been mentioned, and it had been mentioned more than once, and for a bit there it had gotten a little too personal, he knew, knows now. The arguments had gotten a little out of hand. A little too mean-spirited. He never understood what she was going through; he never appreciated her; he didn't show her enough affection; he never kissed her anymore; he never never *never* [insert this or that travesty here that he never did or didn't do anymore]. And could be he didn't. Could be she was right. Hadn't always been that way, but could be that after a while he just said to hell with it, what's the point? Bust your butt all day, put the roof over her head, fill the fancy refrigerator with the french-door bottom freezer that cost more than any refrigerator should; surprise her with first a BMW 6 Series, then the CLS550 Coupe, metallic obsidian, black leather, red bow, sitting in the driveway of a house with a mortgage payment large enough to buy the first house they'd lived in after college.

What he hated most, out of all of it, was paying some useless, whiney counselor or psych or whatever she was, all that money. That's what irked him the most. Not the yelling, not the slammed doors, not the idle threats (because where was she going to go? Really?). He couldn't stand the voice in which that woman, therapist or whatever it was she called herself, spoke. Like she did it on purpose. Like it was part of her technique. Talk as soft as you can, look like a puppy, and men will hate you so much that they'll look at their wives and just give up, say, you know, you're right, you're nothing like this lady, who's driving me more batty than anything I've ever experienced in my life. Let's get out of here. You win!

Which was, in a way, what happened. He just couldn't stand their therapist for one more second. And so he listened to everything she said, and then listened to everything Rachel said, and made the changes he needed to make. Opened his eyes to the beauty around him—in his wife, in the bump in her belly that was going to be their daughter; in the goals he had and was achieving for himself, not only professionally but personally, which was something, he knew, his father had never achieved. And everything got better. He appreciated the house and he appreciated the material things he could buy, and the places they could go around the world that they had always dreamed about back in college, when the best they had been able to afford was a week in Syracuse or once, when they'd saved enough, Daytona.

It was the tunnel vision that was his problem. His inability to see beyond the immediate goals he'd had for himself. That was the one and only line that stuck with him after one of their sessions. You have a narcissistic tunnel vision that impairs your ability to appreciate what you have because you're too focused on what you want. That's what the therapist had said, and also the moment it all clicked. Because she was right. He loved that line. *Narcissistic tunnel vision.* Probably not a clinical term, but it got the point across. And she was on the money.

That night, the night of his awakening, the evening after their last whiney session, James took her on a shopping spree and then to Peter Luger's for dinner, where he told her he would never take her for granted again, which she did not believe. But it was okay, she told him, because at least he was making the effort she needed him to make, and that was all she had ever wanted. To see him make the effort for them, not just for him, but also for his career. And since then, it was all he ever needed to do. The layer of doubt that had crept below the surface for Rachel was gone, and they could go on living. Everything would be okay.

They ate lunch—low-fat ham sandwiches on wheat with light mayo, Bugles, apple juice—sitting around the campsite at the base of the rock face. Hadley and Aaron ate Oreos and a banana for dessert while James and Michael drank coffee, black and bitter, from a thermos. A couple of college kids were rappelling now, Aaron and Hadley watching, their little legs and arms and butts tired from where the harnesses pinched their backsides. The college kids were good climbers, had the long stringy look in their muscles like they'd been doing this for years, bouncing around cliffs and ledges, dangling fearlessly in the mountain air. On the ground, when they were done, they asked Hadley and Aaron if they liked Power Bars, and when they looked at James and Michael and their dads had nodded, they told the college kids, yea, they liked them, and were rewarded with gold-wrapped peanut butter bars, which neither of them liked once they'd torn the wrappers and taken bites.

Aaron led Hadley to a fire pit campers had left behind, and they began carrying twigs and branches and dried leaves to the pit, searching all over for anything dry or that looked like it would catch easily on fire. Hadley said, "Dad, can we have a campfire," and James said, "We'll see."

Michael was winding up the ropes, stuffing a harness into the bottom of James' backpack. James was making brass knuckles out of the Super 8 rappel device. Michael watched James jab at the air, jab, half-jab, uppercut. Michael said, "I think we're done here, Rocky." He coiled a rope on the ground, stuffed it into the bag. "Rappelling one-o-one is done for these monkeys."

James looked over at the kids—Hadley pulling out a wedgie, Aaron walking with a slight limp, his arms full of kindling, rolling the twigs and sticks down his dainty arms into the pit— and said, "I think you be right."

They packed the backpacks and looked around, told the kids to say bye to the mountain. They headed back down the trail, Hadley and Aaron walking slow, Michael waiting for Aaron to say he wanted to rest, his legs were all beat up, he was tired. James said, "You're doing good, baby," when he saw Hadley doing that thing she did when she didn't want to walk anymore, bumping her body side to side, swaying like choppy waters. But they made it all the way down, no problems, and when James backed the Tahoe up and started rolling down the road, the kids leaned against opposite sides inside the car and remained there, eyes closed, until they pulled back up to the cabin.

James carried Hadley in, laid her on the couch next to her mother. Rachel was knitting a scarf or the first row of a throw blanket (she couldn't decide), and Hadley fussed for a second and then fell asleep with her mouth open. Michael walked in behind Aaron. Michael told him to go lie down, but Aaron said he wanted cereal, and Lettie asked him what kind, began looking through the pantry. Rachel listened to James walk over to the dining room table, linger for a minute, put the BlackBerry back down, and walk off. A few minutes later she heard him taking a shower, and soon Michael was also taking a shower, and from what Rachel could tell Lettie had jumped in there with him. She remembered when she would do that, casual-like, pretend she was just using the bathroom while James took a shower. Lettie, she thought. Of all three sisters.

It was quiet now, everyone off in their own little hideaways, the water running on opposite sides of the cabin, the television humming through an infomercial, Aaron playing video games in his room, half falling asleep, Julianne outside with Harvey, dropping compost and soil conditioner into their flowerbeds, figuring out what precisely they would need to buy in-town and what they would need to order, if they wanted seeds of nicotiana, cleome, or other summer flowers sprouting in the months ahead. Rachel squished the skein of yarn, *Worsted Merino* it was called, let the needles fall from her cramped hands. She stretched her palms, her fingers. Listened to her daughter breathe heavily in, out. She listened to the hum of the BlackBerry in the dining room, buzzing away on one of the thick cotton placemats with the quilt snowflake pattern. She did not think to get up and look, scroll through, find more spam, let herself be disappointed all over again. Go through the mini heartbreak, or mini letdown, or mini whatever it was she went through each time no news came. *No, Gary. No news is not good news with you, Mr. Gnews.* She heard the water turn off, heard Michael and Lettie shuffle into their room, past Aaron's open door. She heard James turn off the water, turn on his electric shaver, turn on the blow dryer, turn on the Waterpik, which she liked but rarely used. And then it was quiet again, and she closed her eyes, and waited for James to check his BlackBerry.

Michael told Lettie what they were going to do, he and James, hiring some guys to rebuild the deck out back. Lettie said, "Cliff is a carpenter. Maybe you guys should wait until he gets here." Michael said he would, said he'd mention it to James. Of course, James looked at Michael like he was crazy. "I'm sure he's good," he said, "but I'm not going to ask the guy to work on his vacation. Let's just do it and have him oversee everything."

They searched online for handymen, came across a number for *Two Guys & Their Tools*, which had a 770 area code. James walked along the driveway as he told one of the two guys about the deck, which the guy said was no problem. When the guy told him it would be a few weeks, James told him he'd pay him double, so long as they got to it sometime this week. The guy said he'd call James back.

When he hung up, his phone vibrated. Mitch Bloom, an old college friend he'd e-mailed, writing back. All is well. Having another boy. Going to Machu Picchu over the holidays. Great hearing from him, let's plan something. Another e-mail, from Chase, your bank statements are ready. Nothing else. Now it was all just bordering on inconsiderate. He typed a quick e-mail to Mr. Oggy, checking in, down in Georgia, doing some hiking, just wanted to see where we were at with the whole President/COO thing. *Happy Holidays,* Oggster.

That evening, after the kids have gone to sleep, Harvey pours James and Michael tawny port in port glasses, the women Riesling. He slices some Raclette cheese, lays it all out on a plate with some figs. He sits in his recliner, staring at the fire he has started in the fireplace. The room is warm and Julianne has left a few corner lights on. Flames from the fireplace throw shadows against the log walls. Julianne says, "Sammy and Cliff will be here early afternoon. She called earlier."

Harvey says, "Splendid."

Rachel says, "Still bringing Cliff, huh?"

Julianne gives Rachel a quick look, which does not go unnoticed.

James bites into a fig, puts the stem on the edge of the plate. "Not all roses in Texas?"

Lettie is staring at Rachel. She says, "You know them kids." She lifts her chin to the television. "Why don't we see what's on the boob tube," she says. "I think *The Bishop's Wife* is supposed to be on this week."

Michael is curious, but just watches them all in silence. He sits back, prepares for whatever it is that's about to begin.

"Only fair we know what to expect," James says.

Rachel looks at Julianne, at Harvey (who is no longer paying attention because he is nodding off), back at Julianne. Julianne says, "Go on then, if you must."

She had not wanted to upset her mother, but in truth she also did not know what the big deal was, discussing family issues as a family. Everyone had their issues, although sure, Sammy and Clifford had more than their share. Always had.

Lettie shook her head, but she wasn't going to leave the room or anything. She said, "Be nice, please." She was talking to Rachel.

Rachel says, "Mom thinks Sammy is going to leave Cliff."

"Never happen," says James. "They're codependent."

"Codependent or not." Rachel looks at her mother, says, "Tell them what you told me and Lettie. About down in Gainesville."

Julianne gives Rachel a face. "I guess I know who not to open my mouth to again," she says.

"It was going to get out eventually, Mother."

"Some things you don't have to tell the whole world," Julianne says.

James says, "Come on, Jules. Now you got us on edge." James looks at Michael, who is thinking it's probably a good time to go read, go take a shower, go do anything else. James says, "Michael is *dying* to know what happened in Gainesville."

Michael shakes his head no. He's not.

Julianne looks out the window. "He says she says. But I'm sure the truth is somewhere down the middle."

"Michael will be the judge of that," James says.

Lettie says, "Oh God. Just go, Mom. Get it over with."

Rachel says, "Well, Samantha says they both relapsed last year. After they left here. Drinking and their other little things, I guess. Went up to Gainesville and got themselves arrested, thrown behind bars. *Again,* if you can believe that." Julianne never says *pot.* Never says pills, cocaine, nothing like that. As if saying it out loud makes it worse. "Little things," she calls it all—all of it, whatever it is, all the time.

James shakes his head. He remembers last year, Sammy and Cliff having their usual fights. Last year they'd spent five days over the summer at the cabin. Cats and dogs all five days. He says, "What for this time?"

"Apparently Cliff jumped on someone's back. Split the guy's head open or something."

James says, "The guy sue him?"

"No," says Julianne. "Cliff was the one split his head."

"He's fine," says Lettie. "In case you were wondering."

"Of course I was," says James. He has his sarcastic smile on, which Lettie finds disgusting. Head trauma is not something to take lightly. This is something James should know, considering how many times they'd had to drive girls from Hadley's soccer practice to the hospital, the soccer moms always freaking out when one of their princesses smashes into another one or takes what looks like a fast header.

"Anyway, they both got arrested. Sam started scratching the guy's face. Cops came. Took them both in after taking Cliff to the hospital. Disorderly conduct. Public intoxication. Something else they got charged with, wasn't there?" Julianne looks over to Harvey, but Harvey is fast asleep, curled in the fetal position on his recliner.

James says, "No hard time?" He is clearly enjoying this, but it's hard to tell if it's the humor of the situation or the suffering someone else has had to go through.

"They had to do community service," Julianne says. "A hundred hours of picking up trash or some such thing. Had to pay a fine."

"That's too bad," says Michael now, turning serious what James has clearly made a distasteful joke. "Sounds like they were a team on that one." He scrunches his eyes, like he's thinking. "She trying to distance herself from him, or *him* from her?"

Rachel says, "That's not the whole story." Again, a look from Julianne to Rachel.

Julianne says, "There were indiscretions." Substituting words again. "They went their ways for a few days until they found each other again. Like Gainesville's Manhattan or something. Samantha got out first, apparently. Had to wait a day until Cliff got out. She went drinking. One thing led to another. Who knows."

Michael says, "I think this is more information than either of us needs to know."

James says, "Mikey maybe no likey, but I like indiscretions." He leans over, puts his hand over Michael's mouth. He says, "My lips are zipped, Jules. I swear."

It was uglier than even he could have imagined. While maybe Sammy was as much responsible for their tumultuous relationship, James' view of Cliff stopped being one of condescension and superciliousness. Now that it was all out, now that Julianne let them know what was what. Now James understood why his wife and why Lettie and Julianne had been so serious. "I'm sorry," he tells Julianne. "I didn't mean to make light of it."

"I know you didn't," she says. "You just saw the tip of the iceberg. It's okay."

Now James feels bad. Feels like they've allowed him to be an unfeeling ass. He says, "Why is she bringing him? I don't get it?"

"In your jerk-ness," Rachel says, "you said it yourself. They're dependent on each other."

"Dependent is one thing," James says. "Violence is something else."

Lettie says, "They've been together since the dawn of time. That's why."

Julianne says, "Sammy has to deal with their relationship how she sees fit. All I ask is that my children support their sister. That's all."

Lettie is holding Michael's arm now, looping hers around his, as if she's holding tight to the one man she knows will never be Cliff. She says, "Of course, Mom." She shakes her head. "But I can't promise I won't be honest."

"I'm not asking you not to," Julianne says. "All I'm asking is that you be supportive. All I'm asking is that you all understand that any of us could be any of us at any time."

"Maybe James and I can talk to him," Michael says. "Not confront him or anything like that. Just talk. Feel him out."

"I can't say as that would be a good idea," says Julianne. "God knows Harvey and I have tried."

"I don't mean an intervention or anything. Just—I don't know, maybe keep him out and about. Get him thinking about other things."

Rachel is flipping through a magazine, *Elle* or *Cosmo*, maybe *Vogue*. Lettie says, "Maybe me and Rachel hit Sammy and you guys hit Cliff."

Julianne stands up, starts collecting the port glasses the men have left scattered around the room. She says, "Just take it easy. On both of them. They're not naïve. Before you all go kumbaya-ing all over the place, just keep that in mind."

Rachel says, "Says Mrs. kumbaya."

"They'll walk away from you in three seconds flat, they think you're trying to meddle in their kerfuffle. That's all I'm saying."

"We won't mess in their *kerfuffle*," Lettie says, smiling.

"Make fun all you want," Julianne says, pointing a finger. "I'll put laxative in your Jell-O. See how funny you find kerfuffle then."

Rachel had known Sammy and Cliff had problems, but never had she thought Sammy would put up with being abused physically, taking any type of violence from Cliff. She had never viewed him as being that sort of man. He was not small, Cliff, not the type of guy you would expect anyone to tango with, but she had never viewed him as raising a fist to anyone, much less a woman. He wasn't that type of guy, or she thought he wasn't. But now, from what her mother had said, he was. Who ever knew anyone, really? And Sammy, she couldn't be lying. Not about that. Not about something so serious. Not to their mother. Could she?

She thought about their trips together over the years, or not trips but vacations, because they, the two of them, had never gone anywhere together, not alone. Not like she and Lettie had. Her relationship, hers and Sammy's, was not the same as hers and Lettie's, though you would think daughters one and two would have formed a bond faster than two and three. Or first, anyway. But it had never been like that. Rachel and Lettie were the pair, and Sammy—Sammy did her own thing. Sammy put the sails out earliest, being daughter number one. Sammy let herself fall into the grip of peer pressure, drinking and staying out late, worrying their mother like no one's business. Later their mother knew that it wasn't her fault, not completely. Said so in passing more than once. There were ingredients in children like there were ingredients in pies, in cakes. And Rachel knew it, too, because she had a child and because she watched Lettie's child as well. And because she had more than once thought about it, how she was her and Lettie was Lettie and Sammy, well, she had always been who she was. Sure, Sammy's mother was not the same mother that either Rachel or Lettie had. Sammy's mother was still a work in progress, still a child in her own right, figuring things out, making mistakes, getting knocked down and then back up. And that was the most important part—the getting back up. It was Lettie who made her understand that. Her always sending books, and then when they'd moved to East Islip, leaving them behind after she'd read them. Her mother had said it more than once, but it hadn't hit home until Lettie, the youngest, had said it. It's one thing to have a kid when you're twenty, Lettie had said. Think about it. Rachel did. And then she thought about Hadley, having her in her mid-thirties, the little tornado that that had been. The disruption to their lives, hers and James'. A good disruption, no question. But would she have had the patience ten, fifteen years earlier? Would she have been able to go to college? Would she have been able to put up with a baby crying every night at three in the morning without wanting to throw her against the wall? She tried not to think about it. But yes, the thoughts were there, hidden behind the thoughts that she could tell people without them thinking she was completely nuts. And Hadley's ingredients came from her, from James. Sammy, she got her ingredients from their father, more than she got them from their mother. Or she got certain ones from both of their crazy drawers.

She saw the ingredients before her, or saw her mother's and father's bodies, split in half, the both of them, like a dissected frog's. There was a crazy side and then a normal side in each of them, though maybe the parts weren't exactly equal. Julianne—fifty percent crazy, fifty percent normal. Joseph Beasley—fifty . . . no, make that seventy-five percent crazy, twenty-five percent not. Sammy got fifty percent from Mom, and then fifty percent from Jo. But the fifty from Jo was all crazy. And then she, Rachel, got sixty percent from Mom, forty from Dad. And Lettie, she had to have gotten the entire one hundred percent from Julianne, and only from the normal side. Or maybe ninety-nine percent, because she still had a long life ahead of her to prove otherwise. And she had to admit it too, the writer in Lettie, the dreams of one day being George Eliot or Margaret Atwood. There was a little insanity in wanting to do that, lock yourself in a room all day, making things up, putting lies and half-truths on paper.

Maybe that's why her life was like that, Sammy's. Because she could see Joseph Beasley living that sort of life. Beating up on people, getting beat up. Boozing it up, going crazy all the time, doing things no sane person could do and be all right with the next morning. Or afternoon or evening, or whenever they actually got up. Maybe she never grew out of the rebelliousness phase. Maybe it was what she had to do to feel like she had a dad somehow; keep the craziness going and it's like Measly Beasley was still around. But it wasn't right, of course. It didn't make it right, anyone hitting anyone. Sammy didn't deserve it, and if she was hitting Cliff, he didn't deserve it. Neither of them did. Just because they were grown up didn't mean they weren't still children in some way. Just because they lived alone didn't mean that that was a good idea. Not given who they were. Not given how damaged they'd become.

When Sammy and Cliff arrive, when they all hear their rental pull up, everyone is sitting around the living room, writing out lists: List 1: Restaurants to celebrate Julianne's and Harvey's and Michael's and Lettie's anniversaries, and 2: What to buy and bring back if we celebrate at home. James looks outside, sees the Chevrolet Cobalt in the driveway, hiding behind Michael's Suburban. He knows Cliff will ask him or Michael to drive him over to the local rental place like he has in the past, that he's only rented the compact two-door for the drive up, no way he's rented it for the whole time they're up there if everyone's already got cars. And sure enough, ten minutes in, after hellos and awkward silences, Michael drives Cliff down to Cleveland, drops the little red compact off at Enterprise.

James sees Julianne talking to Sammy outside, and though the thought occurs to him to go out there and say something, he doesn't. Not yet. There will be plenty of time, and he isn't really the one to be a shoulder for Sammy to lean on. Never has been that way between them, which he knows is probably a good thing. Lettie joins them outside. After a few minutes they're all smiles, laughing and standing close to each other, interlocked arms, soft bumps, shoulder to shoulder. James looks at his BlackBerry, shuts it off. Puts it in their room, in a drawer. It feels like he's severed an appendage or lost a lung.

The next day everyone is settled in, but it's cold now in the house. The temperature has dropped now that Sammy and Cliff are here, as if just their presence, their baggage, could do this. There is a silence in the halls, the bedrooms, and more than one of them is sure there's lots of whispering going on. James asks Michael if he wants to go for a run. He doesn't ask Cliff, who is already bickering with Sammy behind their closed door. No one can hear precisely what the argument is about, but it's clear what's going on. Michael says sure, give him a few minutes to change.

Soon all of the women and the kids are dressed, heading to town to do some shopping. James and Michael are out in the driveway, stretching. They wave as the women and kids rumble away in the Suburban. Michael says, "Let's do the loop then head down into town. I wouldn't mind jogging along the river."

"Sounds good."

"Maybe head down to the peanut farm and loop back. That's a good few miles."

James says, "I'd say that's more than a good few. Looking to get out of here, huh?" He laughs. "I need airing out myself."

Michael looks through the window, sees Cliff talking to Harvey out back by the Jacuzzi. Says, "Let's do it," and off they go, up the hill, calves flexed, feet crunching gravel.

Normally they are men of few words on their jogs. Their jogs are a form of decompression. Run themselves loose, get out the knots and kinks. Work out the unbridled aggression, the stress. At work, when they're both in town, they jog during lunch, around Heckscher State Park, the Bayard Cutting Arboretum. Sometimes on Fridays they park at Friendly's on Main, between Secatogue and Wyandanch, jog down to Orowoc Lake, jog back, eat Fra Diavolo or Zuppa di Pesce at Vinnie's Mulberry Street. Other times they just hit the gym, lift weights, do the 6:30 – 7:30 spin class at E.I. Health & Fitness before work so they can be home early, spend time with their wives, their kids. James has enjoyed his time with Michael, whom he sees as a young him though they are just a few years apart. He's always liked Michael, always pictured him as the clean-cut version of himself, a little less edge perhaps, maybe a little less abrasive in his comments and definitely a lot less selfish with his time. And absolutely a great deal more capable of handling the monotonous aspects of their shared lives, the shared family they have married into.

When they first met, James had called Michael *Softy*, not to his face but to Rachel, who said that's what Lettie was attracted to. Nice guys. Thoughtful guys. Not jerks like you, she'd said. Michael was always making sure everyone had drinks in their hands, making sure Lettie didn't have to handle all of the domestic duties herself when they had company. Michael just as good at heating up hors d'oeuvres as Lettie was, probably better. Or at least more expedient in certain tasks, like engineering the tawdry black olive and carrot and cream cheese penguin appetizers they always put out next to the caviar, like black canapés belonged in the same general vicinity as other black canapés. Michael thought of others naturally, which was not true of James, or at least not with him having to plan it all out, which he would do, but only for certain reasons—reasons, of course, that likely paid in dividends somehow. But they all knew what he was just as he knew what everyone else was, and you didn't have to let everything bring you down all the time. You just lived.

James slows down, jogs alongside Michael. Pulls his earplug out of his ear. He motions for Michael to do the same. "Let's switch," he says, meaning switch MP3 players. "I can't take Fifty and Taylor Swift."

"Taylor Swift?"

"*Hadley.* Don't ask."

Michael keeps jogging. He pulls his MP3 free, does the pass, the grab, like they're baton runners. "As long as I'm not listening to baby bop the next hour."

"Not all baby bop. She got like thirty songs on before I got it back."

Michael says, "There's everything on there. Neil Young. Billy Joel. Classics." He says this as he jogs, pulling breaths.

James says, "Good." After he plugs the MP3 in and secures it, he takes off again, ten steps ahead of Michael, as he always does when they jog, looking back every now and then to make sure he's either still back there or that the distance he wants to maintain between them is maintained.

He says, "Forgot to mention. The guy called. They're coming in the morning."

Michael mouths, "I can't hear you," when James looks back at him. James turns around, jogs backwards. Hits pause on his MP3 player. He says, "I said, the guy is coming tomorrow. To work on the deck. We have to get Harv and Jules out early. Like eight A.M. early."

Michael says, "Roger. Any ideas?"

"No. We'll think of something. Maybe ask the girls. They'll figure it out."

"You tell Cliff?"

"No. Forgot. Remind me back at the cabin. Maybe it'll give him something to do. Keep the peace for a while."

Michael says, "Maybe." He puts a hand out, scrunches his face, like he's got a question or doesn't believe something. "One guy can't rebuild that deck in a few hours. It's impossible."

"I told him that. He says he's bringing a crew. Says it's not a complete rebuild anyway. Said he was just out here a month ago."

"Still."

James says, "I told him that. He said he knew the place. Says the deck is in two parts—he can have part of it done by five. Enough that they'll see a difference."

Michael says, "I'll believe that when I see it." He takes a deep breath, gets his second wind. "A month ago? Hell of a coincidence, no?"

"Timely," says James. "I gotta think it's a money thing."

Michael puts his earphone back in and James puts his back in and they jog and run through town and out past the town, and now they're sprinting back towards town, having looped back around Fred's Famous Peanuts and past Woody's Mountain Bikes, tearing down the Unicoi Turnpike at full speed, calves and thighs pumping, arms swaying, pushing themselves until they are out of breath, the Skylake Realty Office their finish line, where they nearly run over two old ladies peeking at the glossy MLS printouts pasted on the windows.

After they shower and dinner is cooking and everyone is getting ready to eat, Rachel comes out of Sammy's room, asks James to go look for Cliff. The A-hole left hours ago, and he isn't going to ruin dinner, she says. James shakes his head. He pulls on a pair of slacks, grabs his jacket and keys, heads out alone. He figures he can spit across Helen he can find Cliff.

James parks his car on a side road, peeks his head in all of the places he figures he'll find Cliff: by Paul's and the Troll Tavern, the Over The Top and the Hofbrau River Hotel bar. He goes into the Hans Restaurant & Lounge, by the Nacoochee Grill. It is not until he's about to give up, figuring Cliff maybe caught a ride to Cleveland or somewhere, or worse—passed out in a ditch on the side of the road, that he realizes he's missed the most obvious place—the Southside Bar & Grill, off Waldheim, right near the cabin. If he hadn't gone down Edelweiss the Southside would have been the first place he'd have checked.

A cook is standing outside, smoking a cigarette. Eating what looks like a hot wing. James puts the car in park, shuts the engine. Gets out and clicks the door closed. He says, "You know if there's a guy sitting at the bar? About my age?"

The young cook takes a pull from his cigarette, smiles. He says, "There's always a guy sitting at the bar about your age."

"Right."

The cook flicks his cigarette into a small pool of dirty water coming from a pipe in the wall on the side of the building, goes back inside, slams the big metal door behind him.

It takes a moment for his eyes to acclimate to the darkness, but there's Cliff, leaning over the bar smoking a cigarette, empty glasses on the bar in front of him, staring googly-eyed at a bartender who looks like she's had a tough life and a hundred too many. In the light coming in from outside, James is repulsed by the weathered skin, the gray bags under her eyes, the sagging lobes of her ears, dangling some version of what's supposed to be Native American earrings. She asks what she can get him. He tells her Cliff's check. Cliff's done, he says. Cliff, staring at him like he's got six heads.

In the car, James says, "Do what you have to do, man. I don't care. But you know better than anyone you can't go get hammered the whole day and not be home for dinner." Cliff stinks of cigarettes and alcohol. His knees are leaning against the car door, his head wobbly on his neck. His eyes are watered and he is slurring, not bad slurring but enough. James pulls over, says, "Cliff. Please take a shower when we get to the cabin." Cliff says fine. He will. He says something about everyone being against him. James ignores him. Tells Cliff to get over it.

After they get to the cabin, James makes sure Cliff goes straight to his room to clean up. When Cliff joins them at the dinner table, smelling of green apple body wash and Listerine, too much Old Spice or whatever he found in the medicine cabinet, only James and Sammy look up.

Though he has never told, not even Rachel, James's father was an alcoholic. Ten times worse than Cliff. Died before James was out of high school. Cirrhosis of the liver. Throat cancer too, but the doctors said it was the cirrhosis that killed him. Half dozen of one, he'd said. If the cirrhosis didn't get him, the throat cancer would have done the trick.

For a long time, James thought his father worked a lot, because he was always sleeping when James was a child. But later it was clear to him that his father wasn't sleeping—his father was passed out. The last time he visited his mother in Connecticut, where she lived with a friend, he had gone through picture albums with her, reminiscing about the good old days that he later realized, at least from his mother's perspective, weren't so good. His mother had shown him all of the pictures she had, many of them new to James. Now that James was a man she had consolidated all of the pictures into a set of albums, rather than keeping certain albums hidden from him. She said she knew if James saw his father like that, slumped in chairs, lying across sofas half on, half off, drooling all over his chest, his body all discombobulated because the booze turned it to Silly Putty, it would have caused problems for James, even though he probably would have thought it was funny for a while. For while his father was an alcoholic, his father was always a good friend and buddy to James. A kind friend to him and to his friends, who were always around, lifting weights in their yard, watching Tuesday night boxing, playing cards on fold-out tables. His father had not been a mean alcoholic, as many alcoholics tended to be. His father was a happy alcoholic. Hugs and kisses, gifts, happy hollering and rah-rah'ing when he had money. Stuff like that. But after his death, the truth of who he was came out. An ordinary man who kept a steady job at a factory but was drunk all the time, and about as irresponsible as anyone ever could have been. Too many times I had to beg the landlord for us not to get kicked out onto the street, his mother told him years later, after his father had been dead a while. I loved him, your father. But he was sick, that poor man. Bad-sick.

He told himself never would he be like his father. Watching Cliff was like watching his own father again. Death by vice. Rachel's father, her "sperm donor," as she called him, was like that too, from what Rachel told him. Two families full of alcos. You couldn't get away from them. He figured they were worse than those websites where you punched in your zip code and a map lit up bright red with all the sexual predators in your neighborhood. He figured if he could superimpose the alcoholics in the same neighborhoods, their little brown and martini-colored dots would drown out the perverts.

The day his father died he swore he would never be like him. Swore he would succeed in places his father never dreamed about. Told his mother I will never work in a factory unless I'm going to own the factory. Period. And he made sure of it. Made sure he studied while his friends drank and fought other neighborhood kids, skipped school and started falling away to their own blue-collar jobs. Jobs working as mechanics at Aurelio's Auto Center, cooking at Von's Wings n Things, tossing pizzas at Buseto's. Signing up at the local union to get on their job lists. His friend Sal started working as a garbage man a few towns over, dropping out at sixteen, never getting even his GED. And then one day who shows up picking up his trash? To see Sal outside hanging off the back of that truck was heartbreaking. You done well for yourself was all Sal said. After that he must have switched with someone, because though James made sure to avoid being outside whenever he was home on garbage day, he never saw Sal on the back of that truck again. He could see Sal at a bar with his other buddies, telling them all about this big *mansion* James was living in. *Sellout.* That's what they'd call him. He's one of *them*, they'd say. Fucking high and mighty motherfuckers. Mucky Mucks. And sure, he understood that. He knows that mentality. Because he *was* a sellout. The difference was, he'd chosen to be a sellout. He'd choose to be a sellout any day of the week rather than doing any of those other things which everyone in his family, every single one of his friends, had always ended up doing.

He got in to BU, full scholarship. Then Duke. Not top of his class, but top three, depending on how you calculated everything. Recruited before he'd graduated. All the best connections, thanks to some alumni, some professors took a liking to him. Failure was never an option—he'd already had too much of that in his family. He wasn't going to be one of them. No way. He worked the long hours, put in the time. Not only had it paid off—it was looking like it would pay off even more. Pay off beyond anything he could ever imagine.

He stood by the drawer where he had stuffed his BlackBerry and waited for it to buzz, for it to say, Hey, unlock me, check out the e-mail someone just sent you. But it didn't. He walked into the kitchen, grabbed Hadley, carried her like a suitcase to the living room. Asked her if she wanted to read with him. No, she said. "When Aaron is done brushing his teeth Aunt Lettie said we could play one last game of Connect Four. And then Grandpa Superfly is going to help me build a model of a bullring from Spain he got me. With little itty bitty bulls, Dada!" James points to his cheek; Hadley gives him a peck, runs off. He stretches his arms, laces his fingers over his head, stares at a small painting of a ship at sea over the fireplace he has never noticed before. The boat is all white, the water blue, white puffy clouds in the sky. No waves, no people, nothing. Just the boat in the water.

Rachel tucks Hadley into bed. Lettie pulls out a deck of cards, challenges Rachel to a game of Crazy Eights. I've been practicing, she says. Bring it on, Rachel says. "I believe I'm up like fifty to one or something from last year, no?"

Lettie says, "Don't get cocky." She puts a notebook on the empty chair next to her. "Scribbles" is written in red ink on the worn cover.

Rachel sits down, rearranges the cards that Lettie has dealt her. She looks over at James, who is slumped in his chair like he's depressed. He's watching the news and not watching the news, staring out the window, tapping his finger slowly on his armrest. She thinks, my husband is not good at patience. She says, "James?" and when he looks over, she pushes the air in front of her down, down, down. "Read a book. Watch a movie. Go sit in the Jacuzzi." She takes an exaggerated breath, lets it out. "*Re-lax*," she says.

"I'm fine," he says. "I'm relaxed. I'm *relaxed*."

Lettie looks over at him, back at her cards. When James begins flipping through the channels, Rachel whispers, "You can't say anything, but I can't keep shut any longer."

Rachel turns over the card by the deck. Lettie says, "Your move."

"I don't know what Michael's told you, but James is up for a promotion." Lettie looks up at Rachel, back down at her cards. Rachel says, "*President*, Let. And COO!"

Lettie raises her eyebrows.

Rachel says, "How cool is that?" but Lettie just nods. No excitement. No nothing.

Rachel says, "Well, *I* thought it was cool. It means a lot to him. He's worked all his life for this. Rachel throws down a card on top of Lettie's. Lettie says, "One can only hope." It is a line she has picked up from their mother, which she has been saying since they were children. A dismissal, kind as it is.

Lettie nods again, throws down a card on top of Rachel's. "Let me go check on Aaron," she says. "Make sure he took his allergy medicine." She puts her cards down on the table, walks off. Rachel looks back at James, who is apparently finally interested in what he's watching. Rachel wonders what medicine Lettie is talking about. She is deflated, although not completely so, by Lettie's indifference. If anyone would understand, it's her.

Ten minutes go by but no Lettie, and Rachel walks over to her room. The door is closed now, and she can hear Michael and Lettie arguing about something, though it's clear they're trying not to make too much noise. She can't hear what they're talking about, but she can hear Lettie repeating, "I can't. I can't," over and over. When Harvey comes walking out of his room, Rachel says, "Hey, Harv," and walks back to the living room, sits down on the love seat by James. James throws a blanket over Rachel's legs. "I thought you were playing cards?"

"So did I," she says. She looks to see where Harvey is, but Harvey has gone back to bed. Rachel mouths, "Lettie and Mike are fighting."

James raises his hands why? Rachel lifts her shoulders. "Don't know," she says. "I'm sure we'll hear about it tomorrow." She pulls the blanket up a bit, tucks an edge under a sofa cushion. "I'm sure it's nothing," she says. "Mr. and Mrs. Perfect, for heaven's sake. What could they have to argue about?"

They drove to Atlanta, Michael following James, both SUV's rolling down US-129 and then down I-985. Michael had wanted to let Cliff hang back, wait for the workers to show, put up the deck. But Julianne said no one was staying behind. She wanted everyone as a family, especially since they were going to be gone all day. Problems or not, she wasn't going to put Cliff on time out after trudging all the way there for the holidays. If we're going anywhere, she said, it's as a family. "Damn it, I'm putting my foot down, once and for all." She is laughing, but in the laughter, in the cacophony of it, it wasn't hard to hear the hurt. It wasn't hard to hear the hurt at all.

Me and Sammy

This is what I was thinking: There's a kid, small, like a fetus. A catchy title that's two words max, maybe a book that they make into a movie, a play off Broadway or out in London somewhere, a pseudo-horror flick of some sort, something with eerie organ music, a cherubic, angel-looking fetus in a Victorian getup—all black. The kid's giving a monologue, pacing back and forth on stage, a little itty bitty solemn-looking character, tough like a Dickens' orphan tough, but a little uh-*oh*-scary a-la *The Shining* or *The Ring*, the original version of it, the *Ringu* version with subtitles. Something like that. Maybe I tell Lettie, Sammy's sister, about it, let her write it all up, give her a good story to really write about, just in case she doesn't have any good ideas already.

I couldn't help thinking it. I thought it all the time. A boy and a girl, crawling on Berber carpet, riding Big Wheels, kneading too-wet dough to bake bread in Easy Bake ovens. Not never-born kids, I guess, but definitely never happened ones—aborted ones, snuffed out by Sammy and me before we got married, before we wanted children.

Now that we're older, not being able to have what you want, not having what your friends have, kills us. Especially when before you didn't think twice about driving to a clinic, filling out some forms—her laying down for a bit, me reading about bone fishing in the Keys, her crying—not sobbing crying, but enough, distant for a few hours, thinking of what could have been.

The first abortion we had (you have to say "we," or you come off like a big jerk) felt like dodging a bullet. Like the gun went off and we ducked, looked back, and phew! Close one. That simple. The second one was a little more depressing. The only way

I can describe it is like the feeling you get when you realize that your numbers didn't come up, that you didn't win Powerball when you knew, deep down in that revved-up holy ball optimistic pit in your gut, that you had picked the right numbers, no question. Only, of course, to be let down one more time, to watch Arjan Rawalpindi of Cumming, Georgia, win the big one on his first try, having played two bucks on a whim.

It was not Sammy's idea to have Christmas at her parents' house. Not with me there. But I begged. I sat her down and we talked and I held her hand. I had been proactive about it. I had made arrangements. Gotten another carpenter to take over my job at the site. This year vacation meant a little more, multiple anniversaries (theirs, not ours), and Sammy's family, all of them, were taking an entire month off. If they could do it, we could do it. Three weeks, anyway. Longer than either of us had ever taken off ever. Even in good times, three weeks—that was an eternity in work years.

I guess I wanted to save what there was of us. Sammy felt there was very little at best. I told myself that she was just upset, told myself (and her) that it was the meds, or actually the lack of meds, that she had been on the birth control pills for so long her body didn't know how not to be on them. It was an easy ruse, because it wasn't a ruse. We both knew to some extent that it was true, that if you stopped taking them that it messed with your head, made you upset and irrational and who knows what else. We'd seen it before—her on other pills, loopy, barking for no reason, making her not her. How could you expect anything different, messing with the body like that for so long, upping this, lowering that, rocking the little test tubes inside like you were God.

Anyways, I always enjoyed going to Georgia. First Atlanta, but then Helen especially, where Sammy's folks moved when they retired. A little alpine village in the Blue Ridge Mountains. I guess Helen also held a little irony as well, so close to Cleveland and *BabyLand* General Hospital, the "birthplace" of the Cabbage Patch Kids. But really it was the Chattahoochee River and Sammy's parents' cabin that I loved the most. From the deck, overlooking the mini forest, you could have been in Wyoming. Montana, maybe, which is what Harvey always said. Someplace far away and distant. Someplace where you could just go and vanish.

On the way up from the airport we had plenty of time to not talk. Of course, I should have stayed quiet, but when she has the upper hand I always melt. Turn into a blubbering, pathetic moron. And she turns into Stalin. Or I feel that way anyway, like she turns it up a notch, makes sure there's no doubt who's ruling the roost, who's winning, who's losing.

"Let's be civil," she says.

"I am being civil."

"No. You're not," she says.

"Defending myself does not mean I'm not being civil, Sammy."

"You're not defending yourself," she says, "because I'm not attacking you." Always the smart one, my Samantha.

We met after high school, but not in college, because neither of us went. She went to ABC Esthetician Academy in Carbondale, Illinois, her big trip away from home when she was nineteen. When we first met, after we'd slept with each other a few times and I was comfortable and didn't have to pretend anymore to get into her pants, I'd said, "Dreamed big, huh?" and she'd put on a serious face like she was mad. But then she'd cracked up, like finally someone had voiced what she'd always felt. "Yeah," she'd said. "Not going to get rich, but always look like a million bucks."

Sammy was neither the prettiest nor the most athletic nor obviously the most educated out of her friends, but there was something that made her more appealing than all of them. Something you couldn't touch, which is probably what I saw day one. Meeting her friends was validation I suppose, that if my life were a big crap shoot and she and her friends were the prize, I'd hit the jackpot my first try. I think her confidence was the clincher, but that she was direct, that she was fearless in what she wanted, that was what stuck a fork in me. I was done before I began. I was a kid, twenty at the time, but even later she still had that thing that drove you wild wanting her. Something my friends saw just like I saw, something dangerous but alluring, something you knew would either save you or, more likely, destroy you twice over. She had walked right over to me on that day, looked me in the eyes, and said, C'mon. You're with me. And that was it. I was.

Sammy is outside now, sweeping the wooden deck, talking to her mother. Her mother, Julianne, is like an older version of Sammy, free-spirited, long patterned dresses, a couple braids in her hair like she never left the sixties. Julianne met Harvey Lipscomb, her second husband and a professor, at a sexuality conference in Ypsilanti, which has always seemed more than appropriate to me, though I don't know why. Mostly they sit around over cups of decaffeinated English breakfast tea, criticizing sitcoms and debating Fox News panelists, going back and forth about second-wave feminism something-or-other, which none of us know anything about. Harvey has always seemed somewhat effeminate to me, but he's nice enough and has always been the peacemaker of the house, which I respect. Has a casual, aloof demeanor, like he's not taking anything in but in reality he is taking everything in, all at once, digesting what needs digesting. Then his responses trickle out like drops of melting ice. The answers come, even if it's three days later. It's Harvey's way, I suppose.

I watch Sammy and Julianne go back and forth, Sammy pausing every now and then, Julianne shaking her head, like *tsk tsk*, me thinking, What lies is Sammy telling her about me now?

Since day one, everyone has treated me like a leper, and all I can think is that everyone knows what's going on, that Sammy spilled the beans to everyone here (mostly family, but there are a couple saps like myself who've married in), that I'm this big loser who everyone just wants to go away. But no one says a word. I'm small-talk guy. Even Harvey seems to shy away, like they've all sat him down, told him this is how it's going to be, if you're not in then you're out. But day two, when the ladies of the house have taken the kids and gone out to Betty's Country Store for Gundelsheim sauerkraut and apple butter, I ambush Harvey in the Jacuzzi.

Harvey walked out on the deck while the women got ready, still in his oversized jeans and sweater, turned on the heat in the Jacuzzi. He'd taken off the brown pleather cover, pulled out a couple leaves from the filter. Just as he's slinking himself down into the bubbling water, I come out in my shorts, ask him does he mind if I join him. Come on in, he says. It's delicious.

He has always used words like that, like "delicious." Words I would never use other than to describe food, and only if I were making an extra attempt at buttering someone up.

The cabin is huge, six bedrooms, bunk beds for the kids, a long driveway for multiple cars. The cabin is perched higher than the town, sits beside other large log cabin rentals. There is a security gate down at the bottom of the hill, and I imagine that for others it's a great place to go for a honeymoon if you're from Valdosta or Macon and can't get away to a real Bavarian town. People like me and Sammy. Not people like Michael and Lettie. Definitely not people like James and Rachel.

Harvey tilts his head back, rests it on the edge of the Jacuzzi. His face is pale in spots, and his nose hairs stick out like toothbrush bristles. I put my foot in, pull it back out. I go back inside, come out with a bottle of Chardonnay (not my favorite) and two glasses—for red, not white, but that's all I can find in the cabinets. The glasses say *Georgia on My Mind*. I look out towards downtown Helen. I open the bottle, pour two glasses three quarters full. I hold one out, say, Harvey, and he opens his eyes, his head still tilted back. He looks at me for what feels like thirty seconds but is probably two. He says, "It's ten in the morning, Cliff."

I've never really liked my name, and when someone says it like Harvey says it, with disdain, with some feeble attempt at condescension, I like it even less. But I like Cliff more than Clifford, which for as long as I can remember reminds me of a big red dog.

Harvey closes his eyes, dunks his head. Comes back up slowly. Wipes the water from his face. He says, "Ask me again at noon," which is his attempt to smooth the moment over. His charity to me. He knows it can't be easy, being me, surrounded by all of *them*, which is what it's felt like since the moment they all came out to greet Sammy and I. I tell him, Will do.

When I first started hating my name, I looked it up in books, stumbled on it in documents in the library. Source: U.S. Census Bureau, Population Division, Population Analysis & Evaluation Staff. The Census people said my name was 149 out of the 300 most common male names in the United States. % Frequency: 0.123. Approx. Number: 179,452. When I first saw that number, 179,452, I thought, fitting. There's 179,451 other Cliffords out there. I'm a reproduction, model # too many.

I start drinking anyway, not wanting to waste the Chardonnay I've opened. I don't want to be blamed for wasting the precious Chardonnay. It's just me and him in the house now, me and Gender Sexy professor Harvey. X and Y's fathers have gone out jogging, PDA's on their elastic jogging shorts, MP3 players velcro'ed on their biceps. I saw them warming up in the driveway, Michael stretching his calves against a tire, James T. reaching for the sky, his abs freakishly defined, like they're chiseled in stone. It's always baffled me, these perfect men Sammy's sisters have married, built like underwear models, each pulling in bonuses larger than my entire year's salary. Too perfect, really. But I've learned to live with it. Even now, it doesn't bother me, because perfect or not, I'd never want to be like them. And it gives me pleasure giving them names like James T.—"T" for Titties, though that's not what I tell them.

Harvey is doing breathing exercises, inhaling and exhaling in jerky puffs, like he's trying not to vomit. When he stops the ridiculousness, I put my glass of Chardonnay on the deck, stretch out my legs. I say, "Mind if I ask your opinion on some things, Harv?"

It's pretty clear it's the last thing Harvey wanted to hear, which pisses me off a little, him being this totally understanding guy except now, when it's me that he has to understand.

"Sure," he says. "Lay it on me."

And though I should have prepared for this, I haven't. Though I have my questions, he plays for Sammy's team, which means I need to be careful. I need to think like him, think like they do. Play by rules I would not ordinarily play by. When you're not holding any cards, when the game's rules don't allow bluffing, you just have to be honest. You have to be humble. Have to allow yourself to be at the mercy of the dealer, or in this case, the entire house.

"Just some advice, Harv. That's all. I don't want to put you on the spot."

Harvey smiles. "Don't worry," he says. "I have a dog in this fight, but I like muzzles." He contemplates what he has said, shakes his head. "Doesn't make sense, but you get my drift."

"Got it." I take a quick slug of Chardonnay. I say, "I love my wife, Harvey. I do. But I feel like I'm on a sinking ship here."

Harvey nods, dips his mouth into the water, blows some bubbles. He says, "I think that ship's already sunk, Cliff. I mean, I'm obviously no authority, but, well . . ."

Harvey looks for something, anything, to look at, as long as it's not me. He grabs the side of the Jacuzzi, skids the water off the edge, down onto the deck. He says, "Look, Cliff. Sometimes you have to go where life takes you. You can still love, but sometimes you're no longer in love."

He means Sammy, not me, and he knows he's let out too much. But it's okay. It doesn't hurt. I have already come to that piece of information. Or Sammy has let me come to know it. She has never tried to hurt me, not intentionally, but she's never been one to sugarcoat anything. Never been one to not say what she means. And those words, she's already used them.

"I won't pretend I'm oblivious, Harvey. You don't have to worry about hurting my feelings. I know where Sammy and I stand. Clearly everyone here knows where we stand."

"Okay," he says. "Deal. I won't pretend either."

I feel good. Like maybe we just made some progress, maybe I can actually have someone straight-shooting with me, at least a little bit, at least *something*.

"Okay," he says. "Now that we're here, where do we go?"

A car rumbles over the rocks in the driveway, and I know the women have returned. Like it took them literally three minutes. We can hear the voices of Michael and James T.

roughhousing with X and Y, and X and Y yelling and screeching as if tickled by giant feathers. They must have passed them jogging along the road, which is not hard to do on a one-lane road. Harvey and I look through the glass doors. We can see everyone pulling bags out of the trunk of the car, X and Y running in circles around the adults, Julianne struggling with paper bags. Harvey says, Hold that thought, wraps a towel around his waist, hastily makes for the grocery bags. In a second he's relieving Julianne, taking the heaviest bag from her. I get up, realize I have forgotten to bring a towel with me out on the deck. If I walk through the living room, everything will get wet. I can see Sammy's eyes on me, three bags juggling in her arms, and I know what she's thinking. She's thinking, *Thanks*, Cliff. Enjoy the Jacuzzi while everyone else helps out. I push the bottle of Chardonnay behind the Jacuzzi, but it's never worked in the past, and I don't expect it will now.

Harvey passes me a towel through the door, gives me a wink. Julianne and Sammy and the girls and X and Y are still unloading the groceries when I enter the kitchen. X opens a bag of sunflower bread from Hofer's, pulls off a nibble, and Julianne says, Hey, but let's her keep eating. Y pulls a menorah out of a sac, which I can only imagine they found at *Christmas & More* or one of the little trinket places in the Alpine Village Shoppes. No one here is Jewish, but X or Y probably has a friend that is, and Julianne, ever the tolerant matriarch, probably said, Well, go on and get it, there's room enough for everyone! Which, of course I'm thinking, everyone except me.

Rachel, Sammy's sister, tells X and Y to go take showers with their fathers. X and Y are a year and two months apart, and though they all say it wasn't planned, I can't help but think that it was planned, that all the husbands and wives got together and said, Hey, let's have children *Now*, and let's not tell Sammy or Cliff.

X and Y protest, but their fathers swoop in, barefoot but still clothed, and race them off in little make believe planes, close the bedroom doors behind them. I can hear them talking, hear the showers turning on, and then just the fading hum of plumbing rattling throughout the house. I empty a bag on the table, the bag of staples: orange juice, toilet paper, salt and pepper in little cardboard cylinders. Julianne says, Don't worry about it, go back out and enjoy the hot tub. I tell her, No, I'm done, I don't mind. Sammy tells me I'm dripping water all over the floor. *Please*, Cliff. *Jesus.*

It was easy, telling them I was going for a walk, that I would be back way before dinner, that I could get the barbecue started. It was something I said just to say it, like I was telling them I wasn't useless, I had the grill outside under control. Sure, I could keep taking the abuse, but I'm also human and not so dense that I don't know when to take a break. Harvey asked if I could grab a paper for him, *White County News* or whatever I could get my hands on. Sure, I said. Anything else? Nada.

Helen's a quaint town that feels cozy and aged until you open your eyes and look around at the Disneyland buildings with the Disneyland tourists walking around, staring at the sleeveless, tattooed locals, driving their General Lee replicas. I've been here twice before, in better times, and I've always enjoyed the funny plasticity of it all, because buried in there under all of the Schweinbraten and Nacoochee Valley Bauernpfannle, there are real people. Retirees like Julianne and Harvey who have made it in the outside world, the *real* world, and decided you know what, forget it. I want a city that makes me feel good. I want to live in a town where I can walk on Main Street and know who I'm looking at. And I can't blame them. I want what they have. I want it right here and right now.

I walk down Brucken Strasse onto Edelweiss, head down Main Street. There's a plastic magazine/newspaper stand in front of Southside Bar & Grill, but when I open it there's no *White County News*. I head inside and figure what the hell, no one's going to miss me anyway. I order a Cuba Libre, and when the bartender says, What? I tell her a rum and Coke with a lime.

There's no one in the bar except me and a table full of old men wearing overalls. I can't hear what they're saying, and really I don't care to. I'm feeling a whole lot of self-pity right now, and I just want to take the edge off. It hits me that I've already had a few sips of Chardonnay, and that right about now Sammy is probably staring at the bottle and the glasses, wondering if I thought I was being sneaky, like she wouldn't find them outside by the Jacuzzi. I imagine her leaving them there, or better, putting the cover back on the Jacuzzi and putting the two glasses and the bottle on top, maybe verifying with Harvey that yes, it was me put them there. And Harvey being Harvey, not saying yes but saying yes by not saying no, because he won't lie. And then I think, I bet that damn bottle of Chardonnay is like some twenty-year-old bottle that they were saving for Christmas dinner.

The rum and Coke goes down way too easy. The bartender raises her eyebrows and I nod yes, but I also ask her for a menu. She says I can get fried stuff, but anything other than that I have to wait until the cook comes in at noon. When I tell her it's already past noon, she laughs. I meant the cook's noon, she says.

I tell the bartender I'll have the onion petals and celery and blue cheese. She says they aren't fried, but she thinks she can help me out. I tell her thanks. I tell her I'll make it worth her while. Right, she says. She says, I'm Val. Holler if you need me. I do Tarzan's little call, but she just looks at me like, Come on, pal. It's too early for this shit.

It's a decent sized bar. Streamers of beer pictures dangling from the ceiling, white plastic chairs, black plastic ashtrays, an electronic dartboard, a pool table. I look over at the old guys at the end of the bar. They're playing cards, gathered around one corner of the place. Empty mugs of beer, upturned shot glasses. Val comes back with an empty bowl filled with napkins and plastic ware, another bowl with the celery, the blue cheese. I ask her if they have a cigarette machine. I haven't smoked in years, but I figure I deserve it, deserve to be bad, given the circumstances. She tells me the machine is broken, but I can smoke hers. She reaches under the counter, pulls out a soft pack of Basic Full Flavor 100s, pushes an ashtray in front of me. I say thanks. Val heads back to the kitchen.

I light a cigarette and get that little queasy lightheadedness I always get when I haven't smoked in a long time. But the smoke in my lungs, the taste of the cigarette with the rum and Coke, tastes real good. Now I'm cooking. Now I'm feeling good and relaxed. Now Sammy and Julianne and Michael and James T. and their bonuses go bye-bye.

Val comes back, puts the onion petals down. She says is there anything else she can get me.

"No," I Say. "Sorry about the Tarzan thing. Rough year."

Val says, "You're telling me. No worries, sugar. This is the place for it."

"I'm Cliff," I say. "I guess I'll be your first tourist of the day."

Val says, "Cliff, you're an okay tourist." She looks up and down, like she can see my legs under the bar. She says, "At least you don't have on a Hawaii Five-O shirt." She grabs a rag from a metal container in the metal sink. "I have to do a little prepping for cook boy. You mind hollering if anyone comes in?"

"Sure," I say. "No problem."

"Just no Tarzan."

"No Tarzan," I say. Val heads back to the kitchen.

In Hawaii, we almost did buy me one of those flower shirts. A red one with white flowers. Sammy thought it would be cute, or maybe she just wanted to think she was with Tom Selleck, but once I told her I wasn't growing a moustache, and I pointed out I would need four times the amount of hair on my chest, she said, Ugh, I guess no Magnum for me, and gave it up.

We had gone on a lot of trips in the beginning. Especially after the two abortions. Like she wanted to get away from it all, even though she was all for both of them as much if not more than I was. Terminating lives, or terminating the possibility of lives, is never an easy decision to make, and it was not easy for either of us, though we had never once considered not having the abortions. We were too young. We were just kids. The pregnancies weren't planned. We couldn't afford to pay our own rent, much less feed another mouth. We had dozens of reasons why not. Now, over the last few years, trying had become an impossible task. We both wondered if this was our punishment, our payback, from A and B, our aborted children. We'd even imagined them sitting around in heaven, talking to each other, like they had grown up in the clouds, matured, learned how to speak, found each other up there, formed an aborted kids support group, and put their heads together on how to fuck us.

Two years and nothing. Zippo. No kids. No almosts. No nothings.

Val comes back out of the kitchen, lights a cigarette, tells me thanks, the next one is on the house. She walks over to the old men, refills their shots, their beers. One of them, white-haired and pot-bellied, wearing a striped shirt, gets up, dances a little, waves for Val to come join him. She's not having it, says she shakes even a little and he'll have a heart attack and she ain't doing mouth to mouth.

The front door opens and in comes a young guy with long black hair and a few whiskers on his face. Val says *W-T-F*, but young guy just says not now, Val, and walks to the back. Val shakes her head, pulls out a newspaper, starts circling something at the back of the paper with a pencil, biting the inside of her cheek.

When I first met Julianne she was great. Later she told me that she thought I was just passing through, but that she didn't mind when it seemed I'd parked my car. She always had a way with words, Julianne, and was always fun to be around, until, of course, she wasn't fun to be around. Like a light got switched off. But in the beginning it was fun. In the beginning Sammy was always all over me, kissing me, hooking my elbows with hers, nudging up against me like if she didn't someone else would come in and yank me away. Julianne didn't like it, thought it was too much, and she told Sammy to lower the flame before it burnt out. She didn't like Sammy being so clingy, so dependent on one person, especially a guy. But Sammy didn't listen. Sammy was headstrong, like her mom, and Julianne knew you could do and say so much, but in the end everyone did what everyone wanted to do. Everyone had their own priorities.

Sammy's father left them when Sammy was a baby. Just up and left, no fight, no note. No phone call. Julianne slipped for a few months, smoked a little weed, hung out with some bikers, but that was it. I caught myself, she said. I had daughters that needed me, and damn if I was going to be a bad mother. Never ever let a man tear you down, she told Sammy one day in front of me. *Ever.* But she'd also winked at me, like, not you, Cliff. I mean other guys. Me of course thinking, other guys? But she was cool about it, just general chit-chat about it, so it didn't really bother me. But now? Now I wondered. Now was it general any-guy chit-chat, or was it me chit-chat, Sammy, run for the hills, leave this guy now, you've wasted half your life with him, and for what? I didn't know. I wasn't sure.

Val brought me another rum and Coke. She forgot the lime, so I reached down and got one from her little citrus/olive/cherry bin. She looked at me, shook her finger, like I got caught in the cookie jar. She said, Sorry, darling.

The front door opened and the sunlight tore through the bar like a spotlight, like someone shining a light in your face when you're sleeping. And then James T. is standing there next to me, looking like someone killed his cat. He's wearing khakis and a white Polo, a beige jacket. Val says, What can I get you? And James T. says, His check, and puts his hand on my shoulder. He says, "Time to go, Cliff. Dinner's ready." And that was the end of the Southside for me.

On the way back up the hill to the cabin, James T. wants to know why I would do that, disappear to a bar for eight hours. I look at my watch. It's almost seven.

"Didn't realize it," I say. "Didn't figure anyone would miss me."

James T. says, "It's not cute, man. Come on. Just a few more days and you're good."

I want to say, Really, James? Good? But I say, "Look. I feel like I have a polka-dotted dick on my forehead. I feel like I have to beg for everyone to spit on me."

James T. pulls over next to a small water park. I can see the slides emptying into a pool, a pink bus parked in the parking lot. The bus says the park has four waterslides. It also says "Lazy River" and has a phone number with the word "Pink" in the number for the last four numbers. There are discarded inner tubes sitting beside a trash can, and the fence is locked up tight for the winter.

James T. says, "Look, Cliff. No one forced you to come. Just try to make the best of it. There's kids here, and you know

Harv and Jules. There's no point in upsetting everyone. You're just going to come off as an asshole."

Harv and Jules. I've never called Julianne Jules, and I've known her longer than any of the other husbands. And kids? X and Y? I want to say, *And there's kids that aren't here too, you know.* But I don't.

James T. says, "When we get to the cabin, just jump in the shower. Clean yourself up a little. You smell like a brewery. I'll keep everyone busy until you're done."

"Haven't had a beer all day," I tell him. "Maybe I smell like a distillery."

He says, "Whatever, man. Just do this solid for me and I won't ask you for shit again."

It's the first time I think I've ever heard James T. curse. Michael, sure, every now and then, even if it's mostly *Frick*, or *Freakin*, or some other form of a cussword that's almost a cussword, but not James T. James T. has always been too proper for that. Too corporate on-my-toes man.

"Fine," I say. "Shower it is."

And I pull through. I do a "solid" for James T. Jump in and out, clean up, put on fresh clothes. I even drop some of Sammy's Visine in my eyes. But it's clear as soon as I sit down at the table that none of it matters. Everyone's going to be mad at me no matter what I do.

There's plenty of food on the table. There's a cornucopia with plastic grapes and apples and squash. Around the cornucopia are plates and bowls, enough to feed two times the number of people sitting at the table. There's spinach salad, and apricot almond dressing, twice-baked potatoes and deep-fried turkey, which someone must have cooked outside somewhere while I was at the bar. Harv, no doubt, because neither James T. nor Michael can cook.

Julianne is on one side of me and Sammy is on the other. Lettie, Michael's wife, passes Julianne the Asian broccoli slaw, which she immediately passes to me. She looks at me, but it's a cold look, like I'll look at you, but only because I don't want you to drop the slaw. I put some on my plate, pass it to Sammy, who takes a spoonful, passes it on down. For some reason, Harv is sitting by Michael and James T. I want to make a joke, something about a Julianne Sammy sandwich, but I don't. I'm buzzing, but I've not lost all of my senses yet.

X and Y start complaining about having to eat the vegetables on their plates, and everyone jumps into a discussion with them about why they need their veggies. Sammy leans a little towards me, says, "Did you have to embarrass me like that?"

I didn't realize I had been gone that long, but still. What did she expect, treating me like she had been, everyone treating me like a criminal. I say, "I'm sorry. I am. But what did you expect?"

"I expect you to act like an adult. That's what I expect."

"And I am. But you can't treat me like shit all day and expect me to be happy about it."

Julianne passes me a basket of bread, and when I pull at it it's clear she's holding a bit tightly to it, making a point somehow by preventing me from passing the focaccia to Sammy. She lets the bread go, and I pass it to Sammy without taking a piece.

"Look," I tell Sammy. "I'm sorry. Just be nice and I'll be nice, and we can all get along."

"Stop repeating yourself. Stop saying you're sorry."

"Stop being like you're being, and I will. It's that easy."

Sammy takes a bite of bread, pours herself some Chardonnay. I can't tell if it's the same bottle I left outside by the Jacuzzi. She says, "Helen's tiny. I don't know where you could have gone for eight hours. Seriously, Cliff."

We've had this fight before. And like now, we've had it in front of other people, but maybe not sitting around at the dinner table with kids. But back then, the roles were reversed. Back then, it was me asking Sammy where she'd been all day. Back then, it was me with the leg to stand on and the high moral authority or whatever it is that she's holding over my head right now.

Two days before Christmas I walk out into the living room and I can see, by the foyer, a bunch of packed lunches in paper bags with everyone's names on them, mine included. I feel like a kid, like mom's packed our lunches, is about to send us off to school. Julianne drops a banana into one of the bags, looks up at me standing in the doorway, says, Morning, heads back to the kitchen. She's wearing her Christmas bathrobe, reindeer and mistletoe all over, her Asian fish slippers that look like fish, all the way down to the caudal fins. She looks ridiculous, but I can't imagine Julianne dressed any other way in the morning, unless she has her long johns on (no underwear of course), which is another odd and somewhat unnerving sight, especially if Sammy or Harv are around. She's old, but she isn't bad looking.

It's early. The sun isn't out yet, the clouds are heavy and low, just over the cabin, and the dew is frozen on the grass outside and has frosted the deck, the barbecue grill, the few cabin roofs I can see down the hill. Steam rises from under the pleather Jacuzzi top. It's just me and Julianne. Harvey, who is usually up with Julianne, is still in bed. James T. and Michael and their families stayed up late, playing Scrabble and Cranium and, I guess for the kids, the Christmas Story edition of Monopoly. I pour myself a cup of coffee, sit at the kitchen table while Julianne empties the dishwasher, trying to stay quiet.

We've had plenty of mornings like this through the years, well before Harvey was around. This year, though, it's clear that things have changed. Back east, as Julianne, for some reason, calls Florida, we were all family. Julianne and I and—when her almost-second husband was around—Jasper, would sit around their pool under the screen, drinking coffee and eating bagels, waiting for Princess Sammy to wake up. We'd be getting ready for lunch and Sammy, like she'd run a marathon overnight, would come out grumpy and puffy-cheeked, mumbling *Coffee*, please. *Shh . . . Coffee.* And we'd have to lower the volume. I remember never feeling that those times were special, but looking back, they were what I wish we had now.

Julianne puts a toaster strudel with icing in front of me, starts pulling out disposable cutlery from a cabinet. The pastry is an early show of kindness. I tell her thanks. I ask her if I can help. No, she says. I got it. She pulls on the edge of a shelf liner to get at a metal espresso maker, and I know, from her height, she can't see the glass butter container right behind it. I get up, grab the espresso maker, hand it to her. I push the butter container back, put the liner back in place.

"Thanks," she says.

"No problem," I say. "Sorry about yesterday, Julianne. I messed up."

"You did," she says. "Let's just have a new day, huh?"

"Good idea." I say, "Julianne . . ." but I chicken out. I don't want to be the pathetic son-in-law, harassing Julianne the day after trying to interrogate Harvey, especially when I'm sure they've already spoken about our Jacuzzi chat, short as it was.

Julianne looks at me, goes back to filling the espresso maker with water. Normally she would say, Yes, Cliff? What is it? But not this time. This time she doesn't say peep.

"I want to make everything right," I say. I can't help myself. I'm so lost, so overwhelmed with what I should do or not do. I can't stop my mouth from trying to make things better, when most of the time I know I'm making things worse. I say, "I don't know how we got here."

Someone flushes a toilet on one side of the cabin, the side where everyone but Sammy and I sleep. We can hear whoever it is get back in bed, shuffle around.

Julianne says, "Hmm," screws the espresso top back on. She puts it on the smallest burner on the stove, wipes her hands on a dish rag. She looks at me. She says, "Life is work, Cliff. No way around it."

Like I don't know that.

She says, "I'm no one to talk about successful marriages and compromise and la-di-da. Far from it. But from what I can tell, your head's not on straight when it comes to certain things."

Certain things. I run through what I know, or what I think, those certain things may be. They are all things that Sammy discovered one day were about me, not about her, not about us. Things she has become too high and mighty to acknowledge in herself. Sure, there's the kid thing. But we've always been on that. That's been a topic of discussion for a few years. No one's fault. No clue if it's her or me, so can't put that on my shoulders. And the job? That's the economy. Ups and downs. It's not all me—it's definitely us. Both of us getting laid off, then one of us getting a good paying job, then both of us. Then one of us getting laid off again. The luck of the draw.

We haven't missed a mortgage payment yet. But I admit it hasn't been easy. It's been a bumpy road for a long time, and sometimes I know it's me, but sometimes it really is her. But I can't say that. I can't say, Julianne, your daughter changes the rules without telling the other guy playing. Because I know what she'll say. She'll say, Well, Cliff, it ain't a game.

I say, "I'm working on me, Julianne. I am." I know when I say it like that, that it makes sense to her. Actually, I think it's her line I'm stealing. "I'm working on me," I repeat. And then I say, "And I do. I ask Sammy to help me so that I'm the me that's good for her too."

Julianne nods, like she agrees with me. But at this point I just don't know. Maybe she thinks I'm sincere (which I am), or maybe she just thinks I'm trying to come off sincere, like I have some hidden agenda. Like I'm going to play the nice guy to win everyone over now that Sammy has made me the antagonist of her story, a story in which she is clearly, conveniently, the only victim.

Julianne says, "Cliff. That's noble. It is. But listen to yourself. Listen to what you just said. Focus on what you just said. You said you had to work on *you*. And you're right. But then you added Sammy into the equation. Like you're codependent. And I'm sure you are. You both are. But you need to focus on the first part—on you. That's the only thing you really need to work on. *You*."

Julianne bends down, rummages through the oven drawers, comes out with a dented cookie sheet. "After that? After you've taken care of you, then you can start thinking about others. About Sammy. But there's an honesty you need to have within yourself before you open up to others."

Truly, I want to vomit. All this talk, all these things Julianne is talking about, makes my skin crawl. I feel like I'm on an episode of Oprah, or worse, Dr. Phil or Maury, or Sally Jessie or whatever. Like we all need to have a big corny huddle, a pity-the-bad-husband, make-him-well-and-then-send-him-on-his-way moment. And I know that's what is going through my mind, what my greatest fear is. The fear that I'll be abandoned. That after all of it is said and done I'll be alone, sent on my way, and Sammy will go on with her life, have thirty beautiful kids, a storybook life, some giant castle-ranch out in Montana with horse and bison. And me, I'll be a shunned hermit living in a studio somewhere in Poughkeepsie watching a bridge rust, collecting unemployment until it runs out and I have to go to classes to learn how to put computers back together.

"I get that," I tell Julianne. But I want to say, just tell me. Tell me what you're referring to because, goddamn it, I'm not a mind reader. What I think is wrong may not be what Sammy thinks is wrong. What they all think is wrong.

Julianne looks at me, cracks half a smile. I say, "Can you help a brother out?" and smile back.

She says, "I have two words of advice that ain't two words. Clean yourself up, and *listen*. That's all I'm saying. Just listen."

I say, "Okay. Sure. Absolutely." And I'm about to ask what she means, because I thought I'd been doing both for a long time now, and maybe I'm dense, and maybe a thousand other things. But Harvey walks in in his flannel pajamas, and then James T. and Michael and Rachel and X and Y all come walking in, like they said hey, everyone, rise and shine. X walks over and brushes against me, sits down in the chair by me and Y sits on the other side of me and everyone says Good Morning to everyone else, and by some miracle I'm back in the family. Sort of.

In the breakfast table commotion Julianne sneaks a peek at me and winks, and then so does Harvey, like they planned it, but I know they haven't. Then, feeling the best I have since we pulled up in the driveway, I feel like I've won Sammy's parents over. Not that they're completely with me, but the wall that was there yesterday, maybe it's a little shorter.

Everyone heads out in their own little groups, the men with the backpacks full of the paper bag lunches, the bottles of water and hot cocoa thermoses. X and Y and their parents, me and Sammy, Harvey and Julianne. X and Y require a lot more stopping and pausing, and Julianne and Sammy want to make sure they get the cardio in. The roads in the little community are pretty steep, run along a golf course, and there are plenty of places to slide on rock and pebble.

At first, it's me and Sammy side by side and Harvey and Julianne a few feet ahead of us. We're all wearing warm pullovers and hiking boots, but Sammy and I have on jeans and Julianne and Harvey are wearing North Face hiking pants, making swoosh noises with their legs. James T., Michael and their families start out behind us, yell that they're going to have to go downhill with the kids. They're already dipping into their lunch sacs, sipping cocoa from plastic thermos cups. We wave to them, walking backwards up the hill, then turn around and pick up speed. The three of them, tilting forward, seem just fine, but my lungs feel like they're going to catch fire, jump out of my throat.

Harvey jogs up a little ahead of us, unzips his pant legs, tosses the sleeves into his backpack, makes sure he doesn't fall out of stride with Julianne. The shorts seem a little too short, like short shorts or Daisy Dukes, and Sammy gets a smirk on her face and shakes her head, looks away like *eesh*. It's hard not to laugh. For a man his age, Harvey's calves are probably twice the size of mine. They look like a football player's calves.

Julianne says, "Let's do the whole loop once fast and then one more time after that."

I say, "You sure? Maybe we do it five times fast and then once backwards." I can barely catch my breath. My stomach feels like someone's stepping down on it.

Sammy says, "You don't have to do it. You can go back to the house."

Harvey turns around, keeps walking backwards, smiles. "Now now," he says. "We're all making this walk if we have to crawl. Every single one of us. It'll get the blood pumping." He turns around, puts his arm around Julianne. Says, "Smell the air. Inhale the beauty." Julianne pecks him on the cheek, pushes his arm off of her. The peacemaker, she says.

"I can make it fine," I say. "It's no problem."

Sammy looks at me. She mouths, "You don't have to if you don't want to." And I mouth back, "No, I'm good," and I mean it. I am.

Harvey says, "We'll take a break at the overlook." He says it as if he's been listening the entire time.

We've walked this road before, the slippery, pot-holed vacation road that leads to all of the cabins. Our first trip here, Julianne and Harvey gave us the rundown of who lives here year-round, who rents out their cabins to tourists through the rental office down in Sautee. They tell us about eighty percent are rentals, which is good and bad. Most of the time they feel like they have their own mountain. But sometimes, especially when the weather is bad or something's going on in another town, it gets lonely.

The overlook is a small area where you can look at one of the holes on the golf course. It's a pretty course, the Innsbruck, but Harvey has never played it. He's probably never played a sport in his life. Harvey is from Oregon, somewhere outside Portland, and besides hiking the only things he's ever done outside are camping and biking. For some reason he's always reminded me of an ex love guru, like he's got some hippie past, running around naked with girls with underarm hair. But who knows. Out here, the few times we've been out here together, we've never seen a single person playing. Probably because we come out when it's cold and rainy, but the grass is always green, and it seems like someone should be out here, hitting balls around.

We go around the loop one time and Sammy asks me if I don't want to call it quits. I tell her no, I'm fine, I just need a quick drink of water. That I just need to recalibrate my insides. Harvey and Julianne have a bit more of a lead on us now and Sammy waves them on, tells them we'll catch up. She pulls her sweater over her head, ties it around her waist, pulls her socks up. She says, "Let's go, Jack Lalanne."

"Funny," I say. "I'm right behind you. Just keep on."

She starts walking again, sees something in the bushes, checks it out, gets back on track. She says, "I'm thinking about going back to school. In the fall."

She's mentioned this before, going back to school. For what, she still hasn't decided. But she's considered a few different subjects, completely unrelated to each other, which makes me think she just wants a change, maybe something other to do than watch reruns of *Night Court*. Some sort of brightness to a future she apparently thinks, has thought, was maybe not so promising. Communication. Psychology. Ethnic Studies. General. And Gay and Lesbian Studies. The last one is a little confusing to me, but these days nothing surprises me. And with Harvey I'm sure she's got some sort of in.

"Cool," I say. "Can you get good jobs with those degrees?"

And I can see that was maybe not the right question to ask. She says, "I don't have the fucking slightest," and keeps walking.

I say, "Sam, I didn't mean that like it came out. I was curious. I know what a psychologist does, but I don't know what any of the other ones do."

She seems to believe me. She slows down, let's me catch up to her. For a second she allows herself to smile. She looks at me, says, "I don't know either," and laughs. She says, "What's the difference between a psychologist and a psychiatrist?" And I say, "Yea right."

At the top of the hill Sammy pulls out the thermos from her pack, sits down on a boulder off to the side of the road. I let the only car we see all day pass by. I sit down beside her on the boulder. Julianne and Harvey are nowhere in sight, and we can't hear them talking if they're close by. She takes a sip of cocoa, hands the mug to me. She sticks her hand into the backpack, pulls out a gold bandana, ties her hair up into a ponytail.

"It's good," I say.

"Mom put real cocoa in it. Harvey taught her. Tastes way better, huh?"

I tell her yes, it tastes way better. I say, "It's nice out here, all the quiet. You can smell the air. No mosquitoes."

"There's mosquitoes. Just not now. It's too cold."

"I guess." I look at her, down at the sweat on the backs of my hands, my arms. I say, "Sammy?"

And Sammy says, "Yes?" knowing what's coming. I can hear she knows what's coming just in how she says it.

"What can I do here? Just tell me and I'll do it. I will."

Sammy looks away. I know the look. It's a look that says, Look, it's too late. It's done. We're done. Just go away. But it's not a definitive No look. It's a conditional No look. It's a No that says, If you walk away, I won't chase you. If you walk away and disappear for good, I'm fine with that. I'll start a new life with someone new, someplace new, and start everything new. But it's also a No that tells me, or that I think tells me, If you try, If you really, *really* try, maybe, just maybe, we can run through this ugly a little bit longer and maybe, just maybe, you'll wear me down enough that I can get over it all, get over this funk I've been in for so long. Get through this, whatever *this* is, again.

Sammy takes the mug from me, pours more cocoa into it, takes a sip. She crosses her legs underneath her, the thermos on the ground, the backpack in her lap. She fumbles with the zipper pocket, pulls it up, down. She says, "Cliff, I need a life. I need my life. You already have yours. You have it. Or you have what you want it to be, anyway. I need mine."

I say, "What do you mean, my life? What life do I have that's not our life?"

"There you go," she says. "You just said it. You just proved my point."

Instantly, I think, *that's* Julianne. That's her speaking. That's not Sammy.

Sammy says, "The first thing out of your mouth when I tell you I need a life is about you. I tell you I need a life, and you attack me with a question that revolves around you. Around your life, like you're the only one that's made sacrifices."

"I was just asking a question, Sam. Don't say I was attacking, because I wasn't."

"But you were. You didn't say, 'Tell me what you mean, *Sam*.' You didn't say, 'You know, you're right. You do need more in your life.' You said, 'What do you mean, my life?' You said, 'What life do I have that's not our life?' That's the problem, Cliff. We don't have lives. We share one, and it's one that leans one way. We have a life that leans your way. And I'm just so over it."

Every time she says it's over, my heart sinks. It feels like I can't get my head out from under the water, like there's a fist pressed to my skull, and it's just a matter of time before I drown.

"You can't just pull this out of the air on me like that, Sam. It's not fair."

"Fair has nothing to do with anything. And it's not anything I'm pulling out of the air. Don't do that. Don't. Because I won't have this conversation if you do that. I'll get up and that'll be that. I mean it."

I know she does. She's a lot more hardheaded and hardhearted than me. Always has been. I can bark and yell and scream and be mean as hell, but she can just get up and walk away and the hurt from that, the coldness, kills anything all my hooting and hollering could ever do. She says there's no point in arguing, that's why she does that. But there's a detachment in it, in the walking away, an aloofness that always makes me feel like she doesn't care as much as I do. My yelling, my cursing, all of it makes me feel like it's all because I care, maybe too much. When she walks away, it's worse than if she told me she never wanted to see me again. At least in the words she's telling me something, even if it's not what I want to hear. When she walks away, I don't know what to do.

"Okay. Okay." I put my hands up, put my head down, like I'm bowing to the power that is the great Sammy. "Truce," I say. I pretend like I'm a puppy, like I'm a whimpering bag of bones, she's the big dog. "Sorry," I say. "Go. Go ahead."

"Go ahead, what?" she says. "I don't have anything to say. From now on I'm just going to do. I am going to do what I want to do. I am going to make something of myself. Period."

"That's good," I say. "I support you doing what you want to do one hundred percent."

"You support me," she says. There's more than a little something in how she says it, though it's not really sarcasm exactly. I'm not sure what it is. She says, "Support me or not, I'm doing it. *I* am doing it."

Again, it seems no matter what I say, I can't win. No matter what comes out of my mouth, it's the wrong thing. "You've always been able to do what you've wanted to do. I've never said No, Sam, you can't do that." I'm feeling a little tired of being the punching bag, but nevertheless my goal isn't to stand up for myself just yet. If I can convince her, or at least lay the cards out some, maybe she'll realize that I've never been the enemy. I've never been the bad, self-centered husband she's making me out to be. Not perfect, I know. But if a stranger walked by us right now they'd think I was Ceaușescu.

"You haven't? Really, Cliff?"

I shrug, suck in my lips. I raise my hands again, but this time I'm saying, Show me. Tell me. *Prove* to me I'm this guy you're saying I am. Give me some examples. *Please.*

Sammy says, "You want me to run down my list?"

For a second I'm thinking, maybe she thinks I'm bluffing. Maybe she thinks I'm looking for an argument. But then I think, maybe *she's* bluffing. Maybe she's making mountains out of molehills. Then I look at her. She isn't bluffing. Or she feels she's not. She says, "Okay. Here goes." She stretches her hand out for me, fingers out, starts ticking down her little list.

"Cliff's list of *No*s. No, wait, wait. Even better; Cliff's list of *absolute No*s." She gives me a quick courtesy look, like, you have half a second before I lay it all out. She says, "Okay, studio audience, Cliff wants to play, so let's play. Number one: Jamaica."

And it begins. Jamaica. This tiny Caribbean island that's become like the iceberg that sunk the Titanic. That's all she has to say for me to know what kinds of *No*s she talking about. Not No, you can't go study to get your degree. Not No, you can't buy a car. Not those kind of *No*s. No, Sammy's *No*s are the *No*s that if her friends' husbands had offered their wives, maybe they would all still be married, because certain things would never have happened.

Before she continues, I have my own one word zinger to add to her Jamaica. But she wasn't going to continue anyway. Jamaica is a big deal for her, and she just sits there, waiting on anything I have to say, which I assume she thinks my tool chest is empty. But it's not.

"Tell me how Jamaica was a good thing for, what, half your girlfriends that went?"

She knows where this will go. But she's not backing down. Clearly she wants to have this argument. Clearly she doesn't care.

"I give a shit," she says. "I don't care about Marie and Jimmy. I don't care how many guys Ivy slept with. I don't care if she slept with ten guys at once. That argument holds no water."

"It's where people go to shack up with other people," I say. "I mean, come on, Sam. Seriously."

"No," she says. "Come on nothing. My friends went to have a good time. They went to have, for once in their lives, some time on their own, without a bunch of meatheads calling the shots. Would I have slept with anyone? No. Gross. But Marie and Ivy, they were done anyway. They were married to assholes, and I'm glad they did that. I am."

Of course Jimmy, Marie's husband, and Ivy's husband, Roly, are my friends, but they aren't angels, and I'm not going to bring them up. Like an attorney, there's certain people you don't put on the stand. If I were defending myself, Jimmy and Roly would never testify.

"Then get divorced. Don't go sleep with a bunch of guys saying you're on vacation."

Sammy is untying her laces, pulling them tighter, tying them back up. I can see it in her face, she's listening, but she's doing it in a way that's not really listening. We've already been down this path. Right now it's about her list, and I need to let her run through it. I don't, I'm sure she'll use it to substantiate her point, to back up the fact that I just don't listen.

"You done?" she says. "Because if you're not . . ."

"I'm done," I say.

"Anyway, they slept with one guy each, one time, and they were well beyond shitfaced. But anyway." Sammy pulls out number two, both her fingers out, making either a peace sign or V for victory, although I'm sure she probably isn't thinking either one of those things.

"Number two," she says, glancing over at me to make sure I'm paying attention. "New York." She pauses for a second, waiting to see if I am going to interject again, but I don't. I let her do her thing, because in all fairness, I know I need to let her go on without interruption. This is her time, and she's always been fair about letting me have mine.

"We've watched football every year since the dawn of time. Every year, Super Bowl Sunday, our house, all your drunk friends, dirtying the carpet, pissing all over the bathroom floor. Vomiting. What, twenty years now?"

I nod.

"But heaven forbid, heaven forbid, I have one dream trip I've always wanted, one three-hour flight away that can finally happen, and it's *covered*, we don't have to borrow no money, and we can't go because of the damn Super Bowl."

I don't say, Well, you could have gone without me, because though I can't remember it all that well, I'm sure she'd remind me I had a problem with letting someone else go in my place, especially one of her "girlfriends." Instead, I say, "That was wrong. I know it. And I'm sorry."

Sammy shakes her head. "Right," she says. "Do you even remember *why* I wanted to go? Do you even remember *how* we got those tickets?"

I don't remember either. Before I can fake a *Yes*, of course I remember, she's already asking the next question, which she knows I'll know. She says, "Who won the Super Bowl that year?"

"'Ninety-eight? Denver."

"Who was the leading rusher?"

"Terrell Davis."

"How many yards did he rush?"

"*Sammy.*"

"No. How many?"

"One hundred and fifty-seven."

"Who scored the most touchdowns?"

"T.D."

"Anything else special about that game?"

"The AFC broke the NFC's streak of Bowl wins."

"How many?"

"Sammy."

"How many?"

"Thirteen."

"How did I get the tickets to New York?"

"Sammy, *please.*"

"I worked double shifts for a month, Cliff. That's how."

I nod.

"Why did I want to go to New York, Cliff?"

"To see the Rockettes?"

"No. Not to see the fucking Rockettes, Cliff. I wanted to go to renew our vows on our ten year in Times Square. I thought that would be fun. I thought it would be romantic. Instead, I busted my ass for us and what did you do? You took a shit on it. That's what you did. You destroyed it."

Now it rings a bell. We've had this argument before too. Not in the same way, because now it all looks a little clearer. Now I see her point some, because only now do I see all she went through to do that—and it was for us, not just her. For *us.*

"I'm sorry," I say. "I was an asshole."

"I had a goddamned priest and everything, Cliff. Do you know what I had to do to get a priest to do that in Times Square in January? I mean, *Jesus.*"

"I'm sorry," I say again. I don't know what else to say. I can't argue with her. Everything she's said makes sense. All of a sudden I'm thirsty. I take a bottle of water out of her backpack, take a long drink. I want a beer, but somehow that doesn't sound like a good idea. I say, "There's nothing I can say right now, huh?"

Sammy says, "No, Cliff. Not really. She puts her hand back out, pulls number three finger out, and I know it's just going to get worse.

In the evening, after supper, Julianne and Harvey and X and Y sit down by the fireplace with big cardboard boxes and plastic containers of Christmas decorations. Lettie and Rachel are already in their pajamas, and I notice Lettie's have feet, which I didn't know adult pajamas could have. It makes her look like a big kid, like one of the characters from *Saturday Night Live.* She walks over and grabs Y, puts Y on her lap. Julianne passes them a small white box full of little red figurines—Rudolph, Frosty the Snowman, a bunch of elves. James T. and Michael go outside, come back in with a big Douglas-fir they must have picked up and hidden in the garage, because I don't remember them ever leaving in their cars.

The tree is full and perfect, no straggling limbs, no bare spots, the mesh long-gone. When they're carrying it in the needles and branches scrape along the wall, knocking down an old watercolor of a lake and deer. James T. and Michael are making a big hullabaloo for the kids, loud voices and Oh Boys, and then X and Y are picking up fallen branches off the hardwood. Rachel gets up and gets a broom, picks up the water color, starts sweeping the pine needles. The whole cabin smells like Doublemint.

Julianne and Harvey clear a space by the window, just to the left of the fireplace. Harvey says, Hold on, hold on, as he frantically twists the screws that will stab into the tree to keep it standing. Julianne says, Let me get some water before you put that tree up, and hustles to the kitchen. Sammy passes the little packet of Christmas tree preservation solution to Lettie, who tears it open with her teeth. She passes it to Julianne, who has returned with a glass pitcher of water. Julianne pours the solution into the pitcher, the pitcher into the stand, and then James T. and Michael put the tree over the stand and let Harvey guide it into place. After a few twists, the tree is standing straight up, and the kids are hugging the tree like it's a person, they're so happy.

Harvey says, "Great teamwork." I can't help but think I'm the only one who didn't lift a finger in the whole process.

X announces that she wants her uncle Cliff to help pick out the ornaments. For a second, I look at the adults, who I can see are about as shocked as I am. Not that I don't enjoy hanging out with X and Y—I do. But it's normally someone else they're looking to hang out with.

"Let's pick out the ornaments!" I say, in grandiose fashion, a bit of sing-song in it. I sit down beside X, pull her close, and we begin digging through the box, me saying, "Nope, nope, this won't do," X repeating everything, cheeks high on her face, checking out her mom every few seconds, hungry for assurance or permission or something.

Soon everyone is pulling out ornaments and laying them on the floor, figuring out how much garland to put up. Harvey has turned on the tape deck with the Christmas mix—Julio Iglesias, Bing Crosby, Jose Feliciano. Julianne's mix, I'm sure. Everyone is walking around the tree, cozying up to the fire, drinking virgin eggnog, humming Feliz Navidad to the crackling of the embers. Sammy even brings me over a glass, which I sip, even though there's no rum in it, even though she makes clear there isn't going to be any rum.

"Just a drop?" I plead.

"Not a chance," she says. I pretend to be hurt by her cruelty.

Later that night, when the tree is heavy with Christmas lights and glitter ice finials, candy snowflakes and too many green and white candy canes, I help Michael carry X and Y to their bunk beds. Julianne has lowered the music, David Gray singing *Babylon*, and everyone is sitting around the television, watching *Dateline Mysteries*. Keith Morrison is reporting the story of a doctor trying to save the life of one of his patients by speeding up the death of another one. Everything I see, eat, touch, watch, hear, all of it has something to do with me and Sammy, this thing we're going through, and I find myself shaking my head. But no one looks at me. No one smirks. No *Hmms*. No comments at all, they're so engrossed. Sammy is sitting on a chair; everyone else is snuggled up under blankets, on love seats, the couch. Julianne and Harvey are sitting together, squished but comfortable, on the recliner. Lettie has her head leaning up against Michael's shoulder, tucking her feet in between the cushions. I want to say, Well, I guess there's no room, I'm hitting the hay, but instead I grab a pillow from the dining room table, lie down on the floor by Sammy's feet.

That night, when I slip into bed after brushing my teeth, Sammy nestles up against me. At first I think it's just her showing affection. Passing the peace pipe. But soon it's clear Sammy's got other motives. Something has tickled her today, and though I'm sure it's not me, I am rarely one to shy away from anything ever. I have needs, I know, and she has needs, I know, and sometimes, or most times, they don't arise at the same time. Now is one of those occasions, but it's been months since we've done anything (I try to recall the last time and can't), and I know what it's like to be turned down, what it's like to have to flip that switch, turn it off when it's revving at a zillion RPMs.

Sammy doesn't say anything, just follows a pattern we created years and years ago, a step-by-step that gets us both to where we want to be in the least amount of time. There's none of the giggles, the playful remarks that existed even a few years ago. None of the foreplay. She's all business, which works on me, and then I'm all business, which works on her, and then she's sound asleep next to me, sleeping on her side, facing the wall, breathing heavy, deeply. It's been so long since I have had a one night stand that I don't really remember the awkwardness after, but I imagine it's pretty close to how I'm feeling right then. She tussles a little under the covers, and I'm afraid to move, because I don't want to wake her, have her look at me, relive the mistake she's just made.

But neither of us has had much experience outside of "us," anyway. I'd like to say that I have had more, way more, but that's just not true. Sammy says it's true, always sticks to her guns on that one, but I know it's probably not true; I know she's probably a little more experienced than me, has probably even had more steady relationships than me, even though that's not that big an accomplishment. But she never budges. She can't admit that she's ever lied, not about that. Especially about that. Even now.

Nine is the magic number. Her magic number. Clearly not into the double digits, but I've always thought, Yea right. *Nine.* How convenient. At first, sure, we were young. I thought, yea, I guess that's about right. I guess nine is a good number for someone in their early twenties. And in your early twenties, nine isn't so bad. It's not in double digits, which does something to a guy when you hear a number like that on a woman you love. Like you expect she knew you were going to come along one day and anything higher than nine was going to be unacceptable to you. Not a deal breaker, of course, just unacceptable. A point of contention. Enough to drive you crazy and, eventually, her crazy as well.

Me? Yea, double digits. But they didn't mean anything, which I guess is what bothers me more than the actual number on Sammy. That there's more than a few guys out there who, fifteen-plus years or not, probably still think of Sammy as their true love or whatever. Guys who probably still think high school should have some sort of influence on how people view them now, years later, if they're a bum or not, rolling in it or not.

In the morning, James T. and Michael are all geared up for a "man hike." There's some hesitancy in how they look at me, but we're the only ones up and they invite me to go with them. When I tell Sammy she says, Go. It'll be good for you.

She says, "Where you going?"

"Anna Ruby Falls."

She says, "That's not a man-hike. That's a moderate hike. X and Y can do that hike backwards."

I say, "Maybe that's a man hike for Hans and Franz and their BlackBerrys."

"They all man-hike dressed?"

"Totally man-hiked dressed."

Which they are. They look like they bought out REI's camping and hiking section. It's sad how badly they don't get it. They look like twins, both of them barely able to move about without knocking something over or dropping something. Headlights and flashlights, water bottles, Gerber knives, fire starting gear, GPS's, health and safety equipment, Power Bar gels, Clif Luna Bars. The worst part, of course, is that everything is brand spanking new.

I pull a tag off of Michael's Synchilla Snap-T, remind them that it's a day hike at best, they may not want to overdo it.

James T. says, "Trailhead and parking location. Longitude -83.71, Latitude 34.7579." He says the numbers one at a time, like he's giving coordinates to Audie Murphy.

He says, "Overall rating, four. Scenic rating, five. Difficulty rating, three." He's looking at his BlackBerry. He looks at Michael, who nods, like the numbers mean something.

I tell them their ratings don't hold.

"What do you mean?"

"Scroll down."

"Oh," he says. He smiles. "Two thousand four, huh. Why don't they erase those?"

I look over at Michael. Michael is tightening the straps on his CamelBak. He has the bite valve in his mouth, sucking what looks to be red Gatorade or cranberry juice, but knowing him, probably some sort of vitamin water drowning in electrolytes.

James T. says, "This rating was added on November eighteenth," and gives us new numbers.

Michael says, "What are you bringing?"

I point to a bottle of water and some homemade trail mix, almonds, raisins, granola.

James T. says, "That's it?"

"That's it."

It doesn't take us long to get to the trailhead. James T. cuts up GA 75, gets off on GA 356, makes a left onto the entrance road to the falls. We park the car. After they've gone through all their little checks, pulling straps and satellite-ing their coordinates, securing knives and tying and retying their waterproof Merrells, we're finally on the trailhead. I'm feeling okay after the few walks Sammy and I have gone on over the past few days. My legs are a little sore, but I'm not as handicapped as I thought I'd be. There's only one other car, a green Subaru Outback, parked in the lot, and when James T. looks at us I tell him, "Go ahead, man. We'll hold up the rear." I think: If either of them starts yelling *Hey, Bear*, I may have to kill them.

Things have only recently been this way with me, James T. and Michael. Usually I just kid them about all of their corporate America quirks, their power-driven lives, their responsible-men, dog-and-pony shows. But somewhere, in their church-going views, I've crossed a line. Gone to the dark side. Lost whatever respect they may have had for me. I can't help but think, deep down, that they don't know anything. They've been around what, ten minutes in the scheme of things? But I can't say that. I can't say, Hey, tight asses, while you guys were going to Duke and Brown or wherever, doing elephant walks with your fraternity brothers, I was mowing Julianne's half acre in ninety-degree weather, a hundred percent humidity. While you guys were getting hand jobs by the girls at Theta Nu, I was carrying buckets of shit water out of their kitchen every damn hurricane season.

I can't say any of that because none of it would matter. I would just look like I'd been keeping tabs. And they wouldn't care.

The switchbacks take their toll on Michael. Even though he's not saying anything, I suggest we take a break at the next switchback. I want to hike off the trail, maybe get some little feeling like we're actually out in nature and not on a paved path, but I know they would never go for it. Stepping on flora or whatever. Killing endangered something-or-other. But if we just sit down for a while, I can actually enjoy where we're at, take a breath, run my fingers over some dirt, some bark. Listen to the wind. Think about what I can say to Sammy to fix us some.

James T. looks back, smiles. He can see Michael is struggling too, even if he'll never admit it. He isn't a marathoner like James T. He's more a swimmer, and it's a different sort of workout for him. When we hit the switchback, I sit back against a white pine, watch Michael and James T. strip their bodies of their armor. James T. helps Michael take off this CamelBak, which is stuck on either his MP3 player or the heart rate monitor strapped across his chest, I can't tell. James T. sits on an upturned stump, bites into a vanilla almond Clif Bar. Michael finally sits down on some brush, just off the path, slurping from the blue CamelBak hose dangling from his teeth.

James T. says, "It's definitely pretty out here." He's still chewing, letting his lips smack, like that's the way you're supposed to eat Clif Bars out on the trail, his arms dangling over his knees, looking mountain-man-y.

Michael says, "Absolutely." He is unzipping his pants pocket. He pulls out a little red box of raisins, shakes a half a handful into his palm, slaps them into his mouth.

"Gotta have our man time out here," I say, knowing how stupid I sound. Michael grunts like a caveman. James T. takes another bite of his Clif bar, stomps his boots, one at a time. His giant man stomp/walk, I'm guessing.

James T. says, "I wish I could do this every day. I'd give up the desk job to be a ranger tomorrow."

Michael says, "Sure you would," and snickers. "You'd die without your intranet access."

"I could take it or leave it," he says. "Really."

"You could take it or leave it like I could take it or leave it," Michael says. "And I can't have it. You? Never happened."

"I don't think either of you could survive a weekend," I say. "It is what it is, isn't it?"

James T. finishes the last of his Clif Bar. He crumples up the wrapper, puts it into his pocket, pulls it back out, puts it into the elastic meshing on the side of Michael's CamelBak. He says, "You never know," and laughs. I can tell he's thinking about the bears out here, though I doubt we'll see any.

James T. says, "So, Cliff, any elephants in the room?" Michael shakes his head.

"No," I say. "None I can think of off the top of my head. You?"

Michael says, "Guys," and looks at us with a sort of pleading expression, his eyes sincere, his eyebrows at the top of his forehead, like let's just enjoy the hike, forget about anything else.

"It's fine," I say. "Seriously."

Michael crosses his ankles, leans up against a poplar. He looks up the trail a bit, where something—a tree limb, an animal—has made a cracking sound.

James T. says, "I'm just messing with you, Cliff. It sucks, I'm sure. I just don't want to spend my one and only big vacation dodging drive-bys."

"Trust me. It's not a picnic for me either."

Michael says, "No offense, man, but getting tanked on day two?"

I tell him I know. "I need a mulligan on that one. I don't know what happened there."

And I feel like yes, maybe these guys aren't so bad. Maybe we can get back to the civility we had before, when we were the vacation boys, the men of the house, the three of us, and sometimes the four of us, if Harvey ventured out and away from Julianne. The Three Musketeers or Four Musketeers or whatever. Maybe I just need to crack them, crack everyone back at the house, little by little, make my way back into everyone's good graces, even though I'm not one hundred percent clear on why I've fallen out of their graces so fast.

"It's like I've hit a wall with her," I say. "Believe me, I'm trying. I'm trying my best."

James T. says, "Far from me to criticize, god knows I've got my demons, but you shouldn't be averse to seeking outside help, Cliff. There's nothing wrong with that."

Demons. I'm thinking, what the hell is this guy talking about? *Outside help?* Again I feel like I'm a spectator in my own life, like everyone has already had some sort of powwow, and I'm just getting wind. I say, "Man, I have to be honest here. Just level with me. It seems like I'm the only one here that doesn't know the whole story of why my marriage is shit."

Michael starts to say something, changes his mind. He's always been like that, the follower to James T.'s leader. I can't help but think it's some sort of understood rank thing, like the guy with the higher rank in the corporate world, in their corporate world, rules the roost, and Michael knows he's made his little faux pas by trying to speak before James T.

James T. says, "Come on, Cliff. Really?"

And I say, "Really, man."

Michael says, "Just be cool, James."

James T. says, "I can give it to him straight or I can baby it. Either way, I'm going to tell it like it is. He doesn't want to hear it, that's his decision."

"I'm right here," I say. "Right here, fellas."

"You're a drunk, Cliff. You're a clueless ass, and you're a drunk. You're an alcoholic. Everything stems from that. Everything, Cliff. You fix that, maybe you'll have a chance at fixing everything else." James T. claps his hands, rubs them together, looks at Michael, back at me. "There you go. Finito. End of story."

Michael says, "Geez," but that's it. He picks up a few leaves, pretends like he's studying them. It's an odd moment, and

I can't blame him for wanting to disappear. James T. is staring at me, his face saying, Well, pal, there it is. What are you going to do with that?

"Wow."

James T. raises his hands. "You wanted it, you got it, Cliff."

I take a second, nod like I'm agreeing, I'm considering. I say, "That's what Sammy told you? That I'm a drunk?"

"No. That's what I'm saying."

"You?"

"Yeah. *Me.*" He pauses for a second, lets it sink in that he's accusing me of being an alcoholic. Not that I occasionally drink too much, that I need to slow down, none of that. He says, "Sammy, Julianne, they think you're having some sort of early midlife crisis or something. I mean, I think they think you have one too many on occasion, sure. I don't think they believe you have a problem. But I know you do. I've known it for years."

Michael says, "I think your point's made, James."

"No," I say. "It's fine, Michael. I asked for it. I want to hear everyone's opinions. I want to hear yours too."

James T. says, "It's not an opinion, Cliff."

The James T. floodgates are open now, like James T. has been holding in a bunch of things he's wanted to lay out for a long time. For a minute I just nod. All I can think is, What have I done to this guy for him to have such a strong opinion or whatever it is he has of me? I try and remember all of the holidays we've had together, the two other Helen Christmases, the one we spent at their vacation home on the water in Hull, when all we did was eat seafood and play touch football during the day, stare out across the water to the twinkling lights of Boston. I run back through the Thanksgiving at Michael's and Lettie's, where we spent hours listening to the water splash against the dock. I don't remember alcohol ever being a factor. Clearly James T.'s memories don't jibe with mine. Clearly he has a different definition of vacation than I do.

"I've gotta tell you, James. I'll admit I throw down a few, but alcoholic?"

"Hundred percent," he says. "It's like looking at my father."

I had forgotten about his father, though Sammy mentioned it the first time I met James T. I've made some Irish jokes through the years, but it's never occurred to me that they've ever penetrated. He doesn't seem like that kind of guy. Sensitive, sure. But in an "aware" type of way, not in an "I'm hurt" type of way.

I say, "Okay. Shoot. Seriously, my goal is to fix my marriage. Clue me in."

"It's not like that," he says. "You're acting like I'm telling you something, like I'm pointing something out that you've never considered. Like this is news to you."

"It is news," I say.

"Maybe we just take a little break here," Michael is saying. "I think this is getting a little bit intense. It's too early for this stuff, guys."

"No," I say. I ease my shoulders, let my body say everything is cool. "It's all good. Don't worry, Mike. I start crying I'll either rest my head on your fleece or run off into the woods."

"Funny," he says.

James T. says, "Just give it up if you can, Cliff. Cold Turkey. If not, just go to a meeting. I can help you if you want help. Totally fine with it."

I'm not sure how we got here, ten in the morning and I'm at an intervention with Hans and Franz on the side of a hill. My fingertips are cold and my nose is running and I'm an out-of-shape alcoholic on a trail in north Georgia being counseled by one guy who I'm sure sleeps with his wife missionary in the dark while his partner, Opie, plays mediator. I'm wondering when the transformation happened, when good old handyman Cliff became the bum and these two pretty boys became Tonto and the Lone Ranger.

"Look," I say, not without a tinge of defensiveness in my words. "I'm not saying I'm not, okay. I'm not. But there's a big difference in being an alcoholic and having a few drinks on vacation. If I'm an alcoholic, half the world's an alcoholic."

"Maybe it is," he says. "But half the world isn't hurting the people they're supposed to be loving."

And now it's personal. Now he's hit the low blow, and my reaction is definitely instant, but I do keep it under control. I don't say anything that's going to get me and James T. face to face, because I know he's trying, in his way, to help. Besides, I'm pretty sure I get up and in his face, if we did get to going at it, he's probably the local sensei in the *Hull School of TaeKwan-Do*, and I don't want to get a foot in the face from muscle boy.

Michael says, "Guys, please," and for a second he sounds a little like a woman, like he's walked up on a tough-man contest and it's gotten a little too hairy for his delicate self and it's time to go home.

"Let's just cool down some," he says. "Let's get to the top. You want to continue with this up there, I'll just jump off the cliff and you two can go at it."

Michael's remark breaks up the tension that's been building. James T. puts his hand out. We shake. I punch him lightly in the stomach with my other fist. When they get their packs back on and they've gathered their wrappers and made sure they're leaving the place with everything they've brought, when we're back on the trail and heading around another switchback, I say, "Hey, Mike, you still got that hotel bottle of Grey Goose on you? Or did I drink it already?" James T. says, "Laugh it up, loser. Go on and laugh it up."

Breathing heavily, the three of us find daylight at the end of the trail. There's an older couple at the summit of Tray Mountain, probably the owners of the Subaru we saw back at the parking lot. Though I'm yearning to get back into it with James T., want to dive deeper into the whole alcoholic thing and every little detail Sammy and Julianne and whoever have let him and Michael in on it, we don't. The circumstances aren't right. Not with the old man and his lady friend right there. The couple is too close to us, and after a few disappointing minutes, when it's clear they aren't going anywhere, I drop it. I tell myself I'll bring it back up on the way back down, and anyway Michael has us picking up pine cones to bring back to X and Y so they can put glitter on them and put them on the Christmas tree. Either way, it's a good pastime for them.

We sit down, stare out over the landscape, the trees and the birds hovering over the Front Range of the Appalachian Mountains, the shadows of the Blue Ridge Mountains to the east. You can see for miles, the bundles of dark green close up, the different shades of gray-blue fading off into the horizon.

Michael pulls what looks like something you would find in Starbucks out of his backpack. It's a Primus EtaExpress Stove, and in a few minutes he's cooking freeze dried Oriental style noodles. He says, "Serves two, but we don't want to ruin our dinner."

James T. says, "That thing's dynamite, isn't it?"

"Love it," Michael says. "Best hundred bucks I've ever spent."

The old man, who has been watching Michael the whole time, says, "We have one ourselves, but be careful. It's not as steady as it looks." The old man leans to one side, pretends like he's off balance.

Michael says, "Yes, sir. Found that out the hard way." He smiles at the old couple, stirs the little chicken pieces around in the water. You can hear the sound of the gas rushing out of the isobutane canister, a little fire trying to sound much larger than it is. Michael leans the spoon he's been stirring with on the edge of the pan, starts pulling out some sort of foldable plates and cutlery. When James T. asks Michael something about work, about a Mr. Oggy, Michael shrugs, starts talking again to the old guy. James T. stares for a second, hard, but says he'll be right back, heads off to go relieve himself away from us.

The old couple aren't really that old, mid-sixties maybe. They're both in good shape, like they hike these trails all of the time. They're wearing matching clothing, not exactly the same but pretty close, L.L. Bean rubber mocs, bright Torrentshell jackets, Lee jeans, UV sunglasses. Michael passes me red Christmas napkins, the same ones that are sitting on the kitchen counter back at the cabin.

I look at the couple. They're watching something from behind binoculars, following the crest of one of the mountains in the distance. I ask them if they're from Helen. It takes them a second to realize I'm talking to them. The old man says, "Not originally, but sure. Now we are." He doesn't ask if we're from Helen. He knows we aren't. He says, "You guys on vacation, huh?"

Michael nods. He says, "Our in-laws moved here a few years ago," but you can tell he doesn't have anything else to say. "Sorry," he says, looking at me. "I didn't mean to interrupt."

I say, "Where are you from? Originally?"

The old man is in full possession of the binoculars now, and his wife, wiping her face with her palms, says, "Idaho. Cliff is, anyway. I'm from a small town just next door in Utah. On the border. Just south of Preston."

"That's funny," I say. "Not that, but your name is Cliff. That's my name." I have no idea where Preston is, even though she says it like it's Vegas.

"Well," says Cliff. "What do you know." Cliff gives the binoculars back to his wife. He says, "Maybe I'm you later."

Michael glances at me.

"I hope so," I say. "If you are, things are looking up."

Cliff says, "Things are always looking up, son. Just look at that," and he points out to the mountains with his hiking stick. "How can anything be anyways else when that's all around?"

James T.'s voice comes from the trees and says, "Like what?"

And Michael says, "Like nothing, James," and passes him a third of the Oriental noodles in the Transformer plate. "Let's eat."

When we pull in the driveway Harvey's car is gone, and from outside it looks like the house is empty. James T. says they probably all drove down to walk around Helen. Maybe check out the Christmas lights, the guys dancing around in lederhosen. He says they better bring back some peanut brittle from that Hansel and Gretel place. James T. and Michael check their BlackBerrys, and I know they're both wondering how come they didn't get a text, didn't get a call. How can both of their families not have reported in? James T. hits some buttons, puts the BlackBerry up to his ear. Michael says, Ask them what time they'll be back.

James T. says Rachel wants to hike back up. Says she said it was too tight in the car, she wants him to jog on down and then walk back up with her. He says, Later, boys, and Michael and I watch him head back out, jog back down the road we just drove up. I want to sit down with Michael, ask him what all he's heard, is it really that bad. Am I really the Antichrist? Maybe bully him a little into giving me the dead honest scoop, the no-nonsense shebang. But he can sense it. He knows it's coming. He knows he wants no part in any of it.

He says, "I'm going to take a shower. I stink like poop."

"I guess it won't kill me either." I tell him I'll see him on the other side.

Michael takes off into the bedroom as if it's a race, stripping, jumping in the shower before I've even taken off my sneakers. He locks the door, which I find a little odd, especially considering no one is home but me. Like I'm going to accidentally walk in on him. Like I'm going to sit on the toilet while he showers, harass him for details. *Please* Michael, tell me. I know this is awkward, but it's awkward for both of us. What? Oh, sure. *Of course* I can pass you the soap.

I grab a beer from the fridge, put it back. Then I grab it again. I don't care what James T. said. I'm not an alcoholic. We've been here three days now, and I've had a grand total of one day drinking. One day, and only because Sammy was hammering me, making me feel lower than low. Making me feel like I crashed a party, ran over someone's Chihuahua, gleeked in the dip. I am not an alcoholic, and it's a ridiculous accusation. But I find myself hiding in the bathroom, drinking the beer as fast as I can, the water running like someone can hear me gulping. Maybe I'm showing James T. in some stupid, juvenile way. There you go, muscle boy. There you go. You don't have the slightest what you're talking about. Sorry about your dad, man, but that has *nothing* to do with me. Don't put your fucked-up, BS childhood on me, man.

I drain the bottle, put it in the trash, under some plastic bags, an empty cereal box. I don't need to hear it from James T. or anyone later. And when I think this, I think, goddamn it. Damn you, James T. You've officially got me paranoid. Who's next? Who's next to play the Grinch, mess my Christmas up more than it's already messed up?

Michael stays in the shower well after everyone gets back. Even James T. and Rachel have made it back by the time Michael is out of the shower, and he only gets out after Lettie bangs on the door a second time. When he finally emerges from behind a cloud of steam, he looks like a prune, and I hope he didn't stay in there all that time just to avoid me, because if he did, it's probably the dumbest thing that will happen this whole trip. Or at least the most cowardly. I can't imagine that's why he stayed in there, steaming up the mirrors, running through all the hot water. Instead, I give him the benefit of the doubt. Kid and wife, it's probably the first time he's been able to have alone time in forever.

For the first time since this morning I see Sammy. She's wearing jeans and a tight champagne sweater. She looks *good*. She gives me a quick smile (how can she not after last night), and heads to the kitchen, where her mother and sisters and X and Y are unloading everything they bought in town. James T. and Harvey are out on the deck now, getting the barbecue ready, which I thought was my job. Instead of arguing over it I go into the kitchen with the women and ask if I can help, that I'm not going to take no for an answer, I don't care what they say. Y is up on a chair, pulling rice cakes and Capri Suns out of a paper bag, and X is trying to climb up on a chair to be like Y. I grab X under her arms, lift her onto the chair, push the chair closer to the table so she doesn't split her lip if she falls.

Julianne tells X and Y what good little helper elves they are. Rachel says can I put these up on the highest shelf. She hands me Mallomars and Vanilla Wafers behind her back, away from X and Y, who will bellyache for them if they see them. X pulls a big box from its own bag, lays it on the table. X and Y start some sort of little screech session. Lettie tells them to calm down, get their dads if they want to build it. *It* is a Create-a-Treat Gingerbread House Kit, Deluxe Model, complete with snowman, Christmas tree, an overload of gumdrops and generic M&Ms. I tell the kids I can help, I'm a champion gingerbread home builder. X says No, you're not, runs off to get her father. Y just shakes his head, like, Thanks but no thanks, Uncle Cliff.

Rachel says, "You can help me with the sweet potato pie, if you want."

I say, "I want," and Sammy looks at me like don't talk like that please.

Rachel says, "Okay. Grab the sweet potatoes, the butter, sugar, etcetera."

I say, "Whoa, Nelly, let me get my bearings here. Okay. Step one. Sweet potatoes. Where do I look for them?"

Michael and James T. stay outside fussing with the grill, but Grandpa Harvey comes in with the kids, grabs the Gingerbread Kit box, says, C'mon, kids, time to show them adults how to build a house. X and Y follow him out to the dining room table. Harvey hands X a stack of nondenominational holiday cards with pictures of friends' kids and grandkids, gives Y a coffee cup someone's left on the table. "You guys put those in the kitchen and come on back and we'll get the foreman going." X says, What? And Harvey says, "Chop chop."

I push the coffee cup and the cards to one side of the table, away from the recipe book Rachel puts in front of me. She says it's the best pie I'll ever have in my life and Sammy looks at me again, shakes her head, telepathically telling me not to even think about it. I give her a smile like, What? Have a little faith in me. I'm not a *complete* pig.

The recipe book is a binder that Rachel has stuffed with printouts of her favorite recipes off the Internet. She turns to the sweet potato pie recipe we're making, which is apparently not the first sweet potato pie recipe she had me looking at, but the ingredients are the same:

- 1 (1 pound) sweet potato
- 1/2 cup butter, softened
- 1 cup white sugar

- 1/2 cup milk
- 2 eggs
- 1/2 teaspoon ground nutmeg
- 1/2 teaspoon ground cinnamon
- 1 teaspoon vanilla extract
- 1 (9 inch) unbaked pie crust

First thing I have to do is boil the sweet potatoes for fifty minutes. There's a pot on the stove and I ask Julianne if I can use it. If it's big enough, she says, Go for it. No look from Sammy this time, but I force myself to stop thinking like I'm ten.

There's a bottle of cheap Bordeaux by the stove Julianne uses for cooking and the thought crosses my mind—not that I want a drink but that if I were an alcoholic I just wouldn't be able to control myself. That I would be drinking rubbing alcohol in the bathroom, swallowing mouthwash. But I'm not. I don't even want a sip of the wine.

Lettie says, "Now you just have to wait." She's pushing the sugar and the nutmeg and the butter to a corner of the table. "Maybe you can go help Aaron and Hadley and Harvey."

I nod okay. Sammy pushes two half-filled plastic cups of sweet tea to my chest. She says, "Come back and I'll have some for you and Harv."

I look out to the deck. James T. and Michael are hovering over the barbecue. Michael is tilting the grill to one side while James T. is checking either the gas tank or the valve connection. I can hear Michael saying something, but can't make it out. Again it looks like James T. is pissed about something, Michael avoiding his stares, turning his back and not turning back, walking off. I sit down next to X, put the cups on the table in front of them, which they grab and guzzle down, like they knew it was coming.

Harvey says, "Let's team up. Me and Hadley, and Uncle Cliff and Aaron."

I look at Y. "I think we can take 'em," I tell him. I wait for Harvey to say something like, No, no. We aren't competing.

This is an everyone-have-fun type of thing. But he says, "Let's whoop some booty, patootie!"

X and Y are younger than A and B, or they're younger than what A and B would have been. A and B would have been their older cousins, by far. Not that they're substitutes, because they're not, but I tend to pair A and X and B and Y together, and when I think of A and B I do think of X and Y. I guess because they're related to Sammy they can pass for our kids. I like to think A and B would have been an improved version of these two—Y is a bit short and small for his age, and X can be a little insufferable if she doesn't get her way sometimes—but all in all A and B have become these invisible but ever-present non-people. Ghost kids, or something. Like when guys lose an arm in war and can still feel their hands. Here A and B in their black and white stockings and proper dress attire and pale skin just pace around, busy in their own worlds.

More than once I have imagined them, A and B, not only in our house but at school, visiting friends, walking door to door selling thirteen dollar tubs of chocolate chip cookies to raise money for school trips. Hiding in the backyard in a tree house we didn't build and that doesn't exist, peeking out the tree house windows at Sammy and me, telling us, No, we don't want to come in yet. Please. Please. *Please!* Just ten more minutes!

Y says, "Hey, Uncle Cliff." And I say, "Hey, Aaron," and he looks at me with his big eyes. "Well?"

"Well what?"

Harvey says, "Uncle Cliff just fell asleep for a second is all, Mr. Man. He's back now." Harvey doesn't miss a step. He says, "Here, Cliff," hands me a bag full of green and red sugared jelly candies. "Go ahead and put the icing on the roof. Your uncle will hand the jellies to you."

Y squeezes a white roof onto the gingerbread house, starts spreading it all down with a spoon. I tell him he better hurry up, I'm going to eat the snowman. X says, "You better not! I'll tell Mom!"

When the sweet potatoes are done Sammy calls from the kitchen, says, "Come finish your pie, you dirty old man," and Harvey looks at me. He says, "Oh boy." I tell X and Y finish without me, I'll come check up on everything when I'm done.

Lettie and Rachel are out on the deck now with their husbands, sitting around on chairs, watching the steaks cook on the grill. James T. and Rachel are drinking red wine. Michael and Lettie are sharing a beer, but no one is really talking. Julianne is in the kitchen helping Sammy put a basketball team of Cornish hens in the oven. Sammy says, You're sure that's enough, Mom? Julianne says, Yep. She says, neither Michael nor James eat fowl. Some cuckoo reason or another. And your sister Rachel has just sworn off meat altogether.

Sammy says, "I have an oddball family."

Julianne wipes up a wet spot from the floor, says, "Everyone's family is oddball." Hallelujah to that, I say.

"Get to cooking," says Sammy.

"Yes ma'am." I start measuring out everything into a bowl.

I put the butter in, smash it all up with the sweet potatoes. I put the sugar, the eggs, nutmeg, vanilla, cinnamon and milk in, mix it all up. Julianne takes the wrapper off two pie crusts, puts them next to the bowl, starts pressing down some of the crust. "The oven should be ready in five," she says. "Time for a little vino with my chickadees." She grabs a wine glass from the counter, a bottle of Cabernet screw top from a wooden wine rack, heads out to the deck.

I look at Sammy. "Looks like it's just me and you, kid."

Sammy says, "You want a beer?"

I tell her, No, I'm good.

She looks around like gunfire has erupted outside, like the earth is tearing at the seams.

"Really?" I say.

Sammy shrugs. "Never seen you turn down a beer, is all."

I hop onto the counter, lean on my hands. "Can I ask you something?"

"Shoot."

Softly, so that Harvey and the kids don't hear, I say, "Do you think I'm a drunk?"

She seems to ponder the question. She shrugs, pushes an oven mitt away from the stove. "Never gave it a thought. Why?"

"No reason. Just getting that impression."

"What impression?"

"That people think I'm a drunk."

Sammy takes a handful of peanuts from a bowl next to the microwave. "People?"

I tell her never mind.

"No," she says. "Who is people?"

I don't want to tell her, don't want any of this coming up later over dinner, or later in the Jacuzzi after everyone is nice and lubricated. Oh, by the way, I heard you called my husband a drunk. But I know Sammy won't let it pass. I know my only hope is that I get her to promise not to say anything, because it's clear the alcohol thing isn't an issue, or at least not *the* issue, with us. Not from her perspective.

She promises not to say peep, and I tell her, "James T. has it in his brain I need an intervention or something."

"He doesn't even know you," she says. I can see the fumes bubbling in her brain. She starts fixing everything in the kitchen, organizing the spice rack, wiping down the counters. It's what Sammy does when she's irked.

"Calm down," I say. "You promised."

"I'm not going to say a word," she says. "I just don't know how someone can say such a thing seeing someone on vacation once a year."

I want to say, My point exactly, but I don't. I say, "Maybe he's got a point. Maybe I'm a drunk."

Sammy says, "You're not a drunk. You like to drink. Who doesn't? I'm not married to a drunk."

I want to tell her to calm down again, but she's on my side for the moment. I don't want that to change. I don't want to transfer the anger she's feeling for James T. to me. I want her to stay on my team. I don't care how that happens.

Michael comes in for a rag. Someone's spilled something outside or dropped a steak. He grabs the roll of paper towels, a dishrag hanging off the oven door, sprints back outside.

Sammy says, "When did he say that? He just came out and said, Oh, by the way, Cliff, you're a drunk?"

"Pretty much just like that. He didn't really sugarcoat it."

Sammy is getting more steamed by the minute. I try to change the subject. The oven beeps; it's preheated. I start spooning the sweet potato filling into the pie crusts. I tell Sammy let's just drop it. We can talk about it later. We have pies to make.

Sammy says, "Pies. Fine." But I know she isn't fine. If she hadn't promised, she'd be out on the deck right now, pointing at the glass of wine in James T.'s hand, asking him can she fill it up some, maybe he can show her how much a man can drink and not be a drunk. She opens the freezer, pulls out the tub of Cool Whip. She says, "I'm going to take a shower. Let the pie cool a little and then put a smiley face on one of the pies for the kids."

"Hey," I say, and when she doesn't look at me I say, "Hey," again.

She looks at me now, her hand on her waist, leaning on her right leg, tilting her head. "It's okay. Really. Let's not make it a thing, okay?"

"Okay," she says, moving away now, heading for our room. "You already have my promise. What else do you want?"

"That's all." I smile at her. "Enjoy your shower, huh."

"Bla," she says.

I set the timer on the pies: fifty-five minutes, and realize that either Sammy wants the Cool Whip to be mush or she simply wasn't thinking about the pies at all, which I know to be the case. I put the Cool Whip in the fridge, next to a plastic tub of macaroni salad. I turn the oven light on, head back to the dining room, where X and Y and Harvey are putting the final touches on the gingerbread houses. Harvey has taken over for me. He's helping X put glittery sprinkles by the graham cracker chimney. I ask them what the sprinkles are and X says, sprinkles, like I'm asking a silly question. I say, "I mean, on the house, what are they?" and X says, *Sprinkles*, again, and I say, Oh, now I understand.

That first day, the day Sammy came over and swept me off my feet, I had actually been making out with her friend, Elena, whose name meant "shining light." Later, Sammy told me that if she knew not five minutes before I had my tongue down Elena's throat, she never would have approached me. Elena always went after the same guys as Sammy, and Elena had big boobs, so most of the time Elena got her man. Or boy, because most of the guys still had pimples and didn't know how to dress. I didn't tell Sammy that at the time I could have gone either way, but that she'd won only because she'd made it easy, taking charge like she did. And because Elena tasted like she'd just eaten pastrami. The truth was, I only thought about Elena once after that, and only because she showed up one night at a party, crashed it, made a big scene before we left, saying she made out with Sammy's man, which turned out to be a big mistake for her, what with Sammy's temper. When she left, Elena looked like a lynx tore into her.

Harvey tells the kids that they have to put the gingerbread houses up, that they can't eat them until after dinner, and only if their moms and dads say it's okay. X and Y groan, but Harvey lets them eat the remaining jellies and lick whatever frosting and sprinkles are left on the table. He tells them to come get some paper towels and wipe the table down, and when I see him looking around I tell him Michael took the roll outside. "Thanks," he says. "I would have been here till tomorrow."

Harvey goes under the sink, tears the plastic off the paper towel roll, wets a few sheets, hands them to X and Y, wipes X's cheek with his thumb a little queer-like, in my opinion, but tender, like a woman. We watch them smudge everything around, and Harvey says, Good job, guys, and they run out to the deck to beg for pre-dinner nibbles of their gingerbread homes.

Harvey is wiping down the table now with the wet paper towels. He says, "I used to love those things when I was a kid. Only they didn't come in boxes with instructions like they do now."

I tell him we used to build igloos out of fake snow they made from machines. "Eighty degrees outside and we're building igloos."

"What'll they think of next?" he says.

"What will they is right." I haven't spoken to Harvey since we had our little Jacuzzi thing, but he isn't the type of guy to weigh too many things for too long. He just *goes*, that man. I heard Julianne say it to Sammy one night, not that long ago. We'd been reading—me a book on Afghanistan, Sammy one of the *Dexter* books—and Sammy had gotten on the phone with Julianne and I could hear everything over the earpiece, it was so quiet. *It's like he can just turn everything off, like he's a robot. I love him to death, but sometimes I wonder if he's even human.* Sammy said, Mmm, but I think Julianne knew she wasn't paying attention. Soon after that they hung up and Sammy closed the book and went to bed.

"Sweet potato pies are going to be good," I tell Harvey.

"I bet," he says. "Can't wait." And that's it. That's all we have to say. Then he says, "Duty calls," and heads off to his room, leaves me alone in the kitchen. Everyone is still outside, and I can't imagine the steaks aren't done by now, but when I look out the window I can see they're all fussing with the grill again. James T. has the gas tank and Michael is twisting something, but you can tell everyone's sort of done with the whole thing. Julianne and Lettie come back in with a cookie sheet full of bloody-red, half cooked steaks that don't even have grill marks on them yet, just indentations. Julianne says, "Those pies still have a few minutes, Cliff?" and I say Yep. "Well," she says. "Just have to wait then."

Everyone comes inside when it starts raining. It's cooler out now than before, the clouds dark overhead, but it looks like it's going to be a pretty quick shower, nothing that's going to pound down for long. When it turns dark out and the pies are cooling on the kitchen counter and the steaks are back in the oven, Rachel tells X and Y to get ready for dinner. Sammy's back from her shower, chopping up vegetables to throw into the arugula and romaine. Rachel is standing beside her, throwing in handfuls of garlic salt croutons, sunflower seeds, homemade spicy pecans. She puts one of the pecans in Sammy's mouth, pops one into her own.

I touch one of the sweet potato pies, see if it's cooled down enough to put the Cool Whip on. Michael puts a split hose, the barbecue gauge on the counter by the telephone books. He says, "Probably go find a hardware store or something in the morning. Can't not have barbecue."

Harvey says, "One right down the hill, on Main."

Michael says, "Ace is the place."

Harvey says, "That's the one. Let me know. I need to pick up a roof rake."

And right then it hits me. Maybe there's something that can help this whole thing, make this train keep going down the nice train tracks it's been riding the past couple of days. Make everyone like Uncle Cliff again. Make Uncle Cliff one of the boys again. *Gifts.* Not just for X and Y and Sammy, but for everyone. For Lettie and Rachel, for Julianne and Harvey, even for Hans and Franz. Nothing over the top, just something *thoughtful*. Something they can't say I just picked up, running down the Christmas aisle at Walmart: Men get this, Women get this, Boy gets this, Girl gets this, etcetera. *Thoughtful.* If I can't get in by the grace of my wit, by submission to the powers that be, then maybe I can get in with a sucker punch. Maybe I can get in with material things, even if I end up going broke or looking like a complete sap. Even if everyone's thinking, God, how *pathetic* can Cliff get? At least they can't say I didn't try.

I say, "If you guys don't mind, maybe I can head down with you."

"Of course," says Michael. "I'd say let's walk, but probably have a carful of stuff, knowing us."

Sammy says, "What do you have to get from a hardware store?"

"Nothing," I say. "Just want to get some of that cream and butter fudge from that shop. Maybe pick up a book or something."

Sammy looks at me with that look, like what are you up to now? I wink at her. I say, "If anyone needs anything, just make a list. If you forgot anything or whatever."

Julianne says, "Maybe some of that creamer you guys use. I think we went through that container of it already. Other than that I think we're good."

James T. walks into the kitchen in shorts and a Duke T-shirt, wet hair, a towel over his shoulders. Sammy says, "You need any beer or anything? The boys are going shopping tomorrow." I shake my head and glance over at Sammy, head to the dining room with the salt and pepper grinders, Sammy right behind me on the way to our bedroom. She says, Sorry, but doesn't look at me, and closes the door behind her.

That night we lay in bed, listening to the rain, not being able to sleep. Neither of us bring up the booze comment she made to James T., which he didn't seem to pick up on. Instead we talk about how big X and Y are getting, how they're little versions of their parents, Y walking around with his own little iTouch, X using words like "income," strutting around in kid-size Uggs. Sammy doesn't say anything about leaving, about how when we get back home she's going to start packing up her stuff, looking for an apartment. Figuring stuff out. She knows if we really do go our own ways that I'll probably be the one moving out. I would never kick her out of the house and she knows it. The house is hers. If you went into the garage, then you'd know a guy lived in the house with her, but other than my clothing, there's nothing in the house that says Cliff and Sammy live here. Sammy says, "I can't believe they're still wearing reindeer costumes. They're too old for that, you ask me."

"They're pajamas."

"Still," she says. "You can't baby them forever. It's cute, but you have to admit they do look a little ridiculous. For heaven's sake, Y is going to be eight in April."

"I guess," I say. We're quiet for a bit. The rain is hitting the Jacuzzi cover, pelting the roof. It slows down and the wind scratches a branch against the window, bending a couple others together. Sounds like nails on a slip and slide.

Sammy says, "I can't sleep."

I moan. She elbows my ribs.

"Let's decorate the house," she says. "We'll surprise everyone."

"It's already decorated."

Sammy says, "Yea, right. That's half decorated, buddy. Mom's got an entire bin full of shit in the garage." She gets up out of bed, starts putting on her robe. "You in or you out?"

Everyone is asleep. When I pass by the hall clock on the way to the garage I see it's just after two in the morning. Everyone's on the other side of the house, so no one should hear us, even if we make a little noise. Sammy tells me to close the door behind me. She flicks a switch and the fluorescent garage lights start buzzing, turning the room a bluish-white. I want to ask Sammy about why we're in the master, don't Harvey and Julianne stay in there normally? But I don't. Sammy points to a big blue bin under some boxes. She says, "Start pulling those boxes off. I'll be right back." She heads back into the house.

On top of the blue bin are a few smaller cardboard boxes that aren't heavy but are definitely awkward to move. All three of the boxes are flimsy and damp from being in the garage, like they're going to tear if I don't grab all of the sides at the same time. They're all taped up, but once I put them down on the concrete they look like they're about to split wide open, spill whatever is inside of them all over the garage. Sammy comes back in, tip-toeing like she's about to spook someone. I can hear a clinking behind her back, and she says, "Here you go," and passes me a Corona. "For my alcoholic husband."

"Sammy."

She says, "Cliff. Fuck him. We're on vacation." We clink our beers.

From two-thirty until five Sammy and I go to town. She's in charge of everything that goes on the walls: garland and wreaths and plastic posters of Kris Kringle and some decorative thing called a kinara candleholder that she rests on the bookshelf besides Harvey's Noam Chomsky collection; I'm in charge of everything that doesn't require me possibly falling and waking everyone up: Santa's model steam locomotive, three lawn gnomes (including the mooning gnome Sammy won't let me leave out), and what's got to be a hundred glass figurines of angels and rabbits and snowflakes, which she wants me to scatter around everywhere. For a while we fly through some photo albums of Sammy and her sisters, her father, twenty-five, thirty years ago. Lettie and Rachel don't look like Lettie and Rachel, but Sammy, the pouty face she's got, the pictures could have been taken yesterday.

And then, like he's been waiting all night for us to finish, we hear Harvey shuffling to the bathroom in his sheepskin moccasins. Sammy puts the final glass figurine, a miniature nativity scene with Jesus, Mary, and Joseph all cut from glass, some figures standing behind them in a cave, on the TV. Takes the photo albums with her into our room. We hear the deep sound of Harvey urinating, and Sammy and I duck behind the bedroom door, careful not to knock into anything we've so carefully organized over the past few hours. When he flushes and washes his hands and walks to the living room, Sammy and I watch from a crack in the bedroom door Harvey checking out the Sammy and Cliff monsoon that's come in overnight, dropped a nuclear holiday bomb all over everything. Harvey just sits there, staring.

In the morning, Michael knocks on our door. He says, "Cliff, you still coming?" He knocks so low I can barely hear him, but I say, Yea, give me a minute. Sammy is sleeping soundly, hasn't moved an inch even when I'm dressed and closing the door behind me. I tell Michael give me another minute, I need a quick shot of coffee.

In the kitchen, Julianne and Harvey stare up from their bowls of oatmeal. Julianne says, "Must have taken you goofballs all night."

I smile, look around the corner at X and Y, who are just discovering Santa's playground. "I plead the fifth," I say, drop a packet of Splenda into my mug. "Believe it or not, not my idea." I raise the mug, ask Julianne if I can take it with me. Get out of here, she says.

Michael parks the car, and though I can see some hesitation in him after I tell him I'll catch up with them back at the house, he goes into the hardware store right after Harvey. I haven't been into town in a couple of days, but it looks like Helen has had a typhoon of its own come barreling into town. The light posts are covered in red ribbons and lighted chains of Christmas garland. All of the trees are stacked with blue and gold and silver ornaments, plastic red and white beads. A group of men wearing white shirts and black lederhosen are posing in front of a bench, surrounding a woman in a red and white dress. One of the men, an older gentleman with white hair, is holding an accordion; the other men have their instruments leaning against their legs. One of the men has his tuba sitting on the bench. A woman is taking a picture of them, everyone smiling their shiny whites as she says *One, Two, click*. I wait for a couple riding in a horse-drawn buggy to pass by before I cross the street, head over to the little concentration of shops on the other side. I figure I'll have another cup of coffee, plan out who's going to get what. Start laying out the credit card with one of the little old ladies' help from one of the stores.

I order a grande soy latte, and the lady says it's not Starbucks, darling, but a large soy latte is coming right up. Thanks, I say. I ask her if she has a pen, some paper I can borrow. She looks annoyed, but stops what she's doing, grabs a pen, looks around for something to write on. She holds out a cardboard coffee sleeve. Sorry, she says. That's all I have. It's all I need.

While she makes my latte I start working on my list. At the top I write: XMAS List. I write everyone's name—Sammy, X, Y, Harvey, Julianne, Rachel, Lettie, Hans, Franz. All the characters in my little Helen, Georgia, Christmas story. All of Sammy's family. I put a dash by each name. Not Starbuck's lady says, Here you go, darling, and puts the coffee on the little circular table I'm working on. I smile at her and she goes back behind the counter, starts talking on her pink cell phone.

Faced with the blank coffee sleeve, I'm blank. I have no clue what anyone wants, not even Sammy. Like I've met all these people for the first time yesterday. I tell myself to brainstorm a little, think, Cliff, think. How hard can this be? But it really is harder than I thought. I give Not Starbuck's lady her pen back, thank her again. I head outside, down some alley that takes me to a bunch of shops that are all decked out for Christmas. Frost at the corner of the windows, *Xmas Sale!* signs. Santa's sleigh and reindeers dashing through cotton clouds. I walk into HELEN *Jewelers* and UNIQUE *Gifts*. The lady behind the glass counter asks me if I can leave the coffee on the counter while I shop. Sorry, she says. No beverages allowed. No problem, I say. "But maybe you can help me. I need to buy gifts, and I'm about as clueless as they get."

"Sure," she says. She's smiling now, leaning a forearm on the glass counter. "What are you thinking?"

She looks like every sweet little old lady manning the counters in Helen. My guess is she either retired here with her husband, or she's White County born and bred. Maybe she watched Hodkinson, Wilkins, and Kollack transform the place from the small town nothing town it was into the Alpine village it's become.

"Well," she says, "Who are you looking to buy for?"

"You have all day?"

She says, "Oh, come on now. It can't be that bad." She puts her hand on the back of mine. Her hand is ice cold, but she's a sweetheart, the kind whose grandkids I can see running in here any minute, wrapping their arms around their sweaterred grandma's neck.

She says, "Okay, then," pulls a stool underneath her, sits down. "Let's get to work, sugar."

"I'm Cliff," I say.

"I'm Lou," she says. "Cliff, who are we talking about?"

I put my coffee sleeve list on the counter between us. She glances at it, says, "X and Y?"

"Girl and boy," I say. "My niece and nephew. They're seven and eight. The rest of them are my wife's sisters, their husbands, my wife's mom and step-dad."

Lou says, "Which one's your wife?"

"Sammy," I tell her. "Sammy's my wife."

"Got a man's name like me," she says. "I like that." She says, "Well, Cliff, let's start with Sammy."

I tell Lou I know I'm in a jewelry store, but Sammy just isn't one for jewelry. "She doesn't even wear the wedding ring I bought her."

"Not one for jewelry, huh? Okay. No biggie. We got other things." She says, "Does Sammy have any hobbies? Collect anything?" Lou looks around the store. "Helen is definitely the place for hobby people. Especially them little home and house statuettes. We have a few of them Hawthorne homes, with the John Deere and the Andy Griffith Village, I think it is. Has the Taylor home and Floyd's Barber Shop. We have some Thomas Kinkade Christmas Story ones too. All of'em with free figurines."

I give Lou a grin. "Sorry," I say. "You've just entered the I-don't-know zone."

"Okay. You think about what your wife might like. Let's just keep on down the list."

"Sounds like a plan."

"Okay. Y it is. Y is a boy, right?"

"Right."

"Does Y like sports? Is he a boy boy, like out running around, or is he one of these angels with the Game Boy and all that?"

I don't say what I'm really thinking, which is that he's a little effeminate in my book. So I say, "Game Boy. But they get him out there too. Soccer, I think. Tennis."

"Okay. Good." She says, "I hate when parents let their kids sit on their duffs all day."

"No. He's in shape. Dad's a brick house."

"Well, in here's probably not the place for him, but there's a shop called Jolly's. Sells toys and stuff that may be good for his sister too."

"Cousin."

Lou looks down at the coffee sleeve, says, "*Cousin.*"

"Yep. X. Different moms and dads."

"And they named their kids X and Y?"

"Long story," I say. Lou shakes her head.

She says, "Okay. Well, if the kids are into toys, Jolly's is where you want to go. If not, there's also ZuZu's. I think the full name is ZuZu's Petal Rock Shop or something. They have geodes, crystals, stuff like that. Kids usually like what they got over there."

I don't ask Lou to explain what a geode is. I say, "Great. That takes care of the kids." I don't want to walk out of here taking Lou's time, even though the place hasn't had a single person walk in the door since I've been there. I say, "You know. I think something in here will be good for Harvey and Julianne."

Lou says, "Yes, I saw the names on your list. Is Harvey and Julianne the Harvey and Julianne live up on the hill?"

I tell Lou Yes, I'm Julianne's son-in-law. "Sammy is Julianne's daughter."

Lou says, "Oh sure, sure. I thought so, but it didn't click. Sammy. Julianne's always called her Samantha. I knew something was ringing a bell."

"Well, this is great then. Sounds like you guys are pretty close."

"Lovely couple, them two. Me and Chance, that's my husband, we socialize with them pretty regularly. They told us y'all were coming up, but we couldn't plan on a date to meet y'all, what with all the schedules. She said maybe you guys would come down and pop in, but everyone's always so busy. I haven't seen either one of them all week."

"I'm guessing you'll meet us all in spurts."

"I guess so." She says, "Well, now that I know you're Julianne's family, I'll take you to the secret room." Lou winks.

But then Lou tells me she's just kidding, there is no secret room. She says, "I do know a few things Julianne *is* fond of, however. A little pricey some of it, but I know for a fact Harvey, he'd just as soon get Julianne what she wants anyway."

"He is a pretty simple needs kind of guy, huh."

"Just like Chance," she says. "They may as well be brothers, them two."

Soon Lou is wrapping up $493.57 worth of German steins and a five-piece set of hand-carved Matryoshka nesting dolls. She says Julianne will flip, and I hope she's right, because I'm down five hundred bucks and haven't even started. She says to leave everything here while I shop, come back when I'm done. "They're fragile. You don't want to take a chance."

I tell her, Thanks, I'll be back in a bit. Have fun, she says.

I go to Jolly's and pick up a *Hnefatafl* board game, which is some sort of Scandinavian board game. The objective is for a king to escape to the board's corners, while the greater force's objective is to capture him. That's what the kid behind the counter tells me. It's cool, he says. I get that for Y, get X a pair of moose dolls, the girl moose with a knitted bunad, the boy moose wearing a knitted sweater. It's almost noon and I start to get hungry. I can smell the bratwurst and the Robberspiess coming from the Hofbrau. The Hofbrau is a hotel and a restaurant overlooking the Chattahoochee. But they're not open. The sign says they're only open for lunch on the weekends. I walk over to the Troll Tavern, grab a table, order the Combo Wurst Platter. The waitress says it's Two-fers Hefe-Weizen, three bucks. Sure I say. But when I think about it, when I think, *Eighty-six that but thanks*, she's gone.

I put the moose dolls and the *Hnefatafl* board on a chair. On the big screen is an old basketball game, Lakers vs. Boston, Bird vs. Magic. Short shorts, and bad picture quality. A few guys wearing bandannas, cut-off shirts, biker boots, are sitting at another table, staring at some young girls at the bar, bottles of Icehouse sitting beside a half-eaten plate of nachos, a basket full of chicken wing bones. An old man with a white goatee sits in a corner playing Keno, coughing up a lung. An oxygen tank sits by his leg.

The waitress brings over two beers, some utensils, different kinds of mustard. Be right up, she says. She walks over to the bikers, says something, nudges one of their shoulders. The bikers put their hands up, like, what? What? They're all laughing. The waitress checks up on the old man, walks back to the kitchen. Soon the music is on and everything is easy.

The rest of the day is a blur. I find myself walking back towards the cabin with my bags, checking to make sure that I still have everything, looking back every now and then to make sure I haven't dropped anything, nothing's fallen out of any of the bags. I have the moose couple, and the board game and bags full of cuckoo clocks and smoked salmon, Russian carved reindeer, a "*Mac Daddy*" T-shirt with a picture of an Apple computer on it that's got Michael's name all over it. I'm about to turn up Brucken Strasse when I see the Southside, see Val smoking a cigarette out back, leaning against a trash bin, her legs a hundred feet long. And that's it. I say, Hey, stranger, and as soon as I start up with my *funny meeting you here* line, it's all over. Everything goes black. And black. And stays that way.

It's like the movies after that, when the camera comes into focus but stays somewhat blurred, and you're the guy that's waking up, the guy whose bed everyone's standing around in a too-white room. Only no one is in the room when I'm waking up. It's empty. At first I can hear people talking, a low buzz coming from an adjacent room, a grumbling drum roll I can't make heads or tails of. I don't even know I'm in a hospital until later, when the nurses come rushing in, telling me don't I dare pull that out, sweetie. The nurse standing there is this big heavy girl, probably in her mid-twenties, arms the size of legs. All I can think is, whatever happened, this is going to be the nail in the coffin. Whatever happened, it isn't going to be good. Sammy is just going to be gone. No fight. No ruffled feathers. *Gone.*

Big heavy girl says, "You've been in an accident, Clifford." She says it like we go way back, like she's an old high school girlfriend. "You're at Union General. In Blairsville."

I try to ask her where Blairsville is, how far away from Helen, but I can't talk. My mouth is dry as sawdust. Even breathing hurts. Something beeps behind me, and big heavy girl looks up, then back down at me. She puts her hand on the sheet that's covering me, touches my thigh. She says, "Some people here would like to see you." She goes back out the door, the other nurse following behind her.

A few minutes later, after some commotion of some sort just outside my room, Sammy comes walking in with Harvey, who whispers something. He stays standing awkwardly in the doorway. He waves at me, puts his hands behind his back, leans against the wall. I don't know what I expect, Sammy to have tears in her eyes or something, but she doesn't. She just smiles. She says, "I knew you weren't having a great time, but my family is not that bad."

She sees me trying to open my mouth, but instead I just grunt ha ha. She says, "The doctor says you'll be fine. You need some rest. Time to heal. He said you have to eat ice chips, that you can talk in another day or so." She sits down on the bed, touches my cheek. "You got a concussion. Your ankle is broken. But you're lucky, pal. The guy that hit you got arrested. Drunk and high, the asshole."

Behind Harvey I can see a nurse walk by wearing a Santa Claus hat. She hooks a chart onto a nail on the wall, says something to someone out of view. A hand with what looks like a cup of eggnog shows up, leaves the cup behind. The nurse raises the cup, takes a sip, puts the eggnog on the counter.

Sammy says, "Everyone was here yesterday. I told them not to come today. They're at home making you a special dinner." She bends over, kisses me on the forehead, wipes something off my cheek. "You've been here overnight, if the nurse didn't say. They gave you something to sleep."

"Hmm."

Sammy puts her hand in mine, squeezes. She says, "Harv drove us up." She turns to look at Harvey, who walks over, puts his hands on the bed railing. He says, "Hey, Cliff." He says, "Glad you're okay. For a bit there we thought we'd have to donate your huevos." He's smiling. "I kid, hombre, I kid." He pulls a chair up, and they talk and I listen, and finally I fall back asleep into the pillow.

On the way home Sammy is in the backseat with me while Harvey drives. She's feeding me ice chips from a Styrofoam cup, trying to keep my ankle from moving too much whenever we hit a bump or Harvey has to make a turn. I'm up to one syllable words, and soon I can talk, but I keep pretty much quiet the whole drive. Sammy tells me the gifts I bought, somehow none of any of it got messed up. Someone there, someone who saw what happened, she told the police that the bags just went up in the air with me but everything I was carrying landed in a bush across the street. Everything's in our room waiting for me to divvy it out, though obviously I shouldn't have spent so much money. "One of mom's friends, Louise, said you never came back to pick up what you bought at her store. She dropped off some mugs or something. It's in the closet. I hid everything until you could check it out."

I nod at her. I tell her I don't want to hear anything about how much I spent. Sammy says, "I promise," and when I glance at her she says, "Okay, Okay. I really, *really* promise," and chuckles.

When we get home everyone is sleeping. It's not even eleven, but the lights are out, a humidifier hums in one of the rooms. In the morning I can't sleep. I hobble over to the seat by the window in our bedroom. Sammy twists a little and mutters something unintelligible, settles down. It's snowing, nothing heavy, just enough that the tops of the trees are a little white, the birds have to flutter their powdered wings. It's barely light, maybe six or so, and it's about as quiet as it's been since I can remember. I can see myself in the window, a clear transparent me sitting in a chair, trees and rooftops and snowflakes fluttering over me, blending into me, putting me out there in the cold, cold air.

Down by one of the other cabins I can see a stream, maybe it's a brook, I'm not sure the difference, but I think, Maybe that's part of the big old Chattahoochee. Maybe it's one of the zillion little tributaries that feeds into the big boy, makes the Chattahoochee the Chattahoochee. Like, Thank you, little guy, I got you from here. I see A and B, maybe their shadows, playing in the water, us yelling at them to stop, they're going to catch a cold, don't drink that, it's not really clean, animals poop in there, you're going to catch giardia. B looking at A, shaking her head, like, It'll be all right, Dad, c'mon! We won't get sick. I promise you. We'll be *fine, Papa*.

I go back to that first night, James T. and Rachel telling the story of how they knew where they were going, even though they didn't know where they were at. They said they followed Polaris, the Pole Star, cut up 384 until they found 75 again. Voila! Helen, Georgia! Rachel said, That little light never steered us wrong. Lettie said, That's a cute story. James T. said, "Yea, but it's a true cute story."

I guess I'm pretty tired, maybe I've fallen asleep in the chair, because I don't hear all the footsteps. Everyone is there when I wake up, gathered right there in front of me, the sun bright though hidden behind the clouds. X and Y and Sammy are in their pajamas, kneeling on the floor, and Harvey and Julianne, James T. and Michael, their arms around their wives, are standing there in a corner of the room, under a pulled-up curtain, letting X and Y and Sammy do their thing. X is holding a bottle of what looks like cologne, wrapped in Grinch wrapping paper. She puts it into my lap, says, "I picked it out myself." Y leans quickly in, as if he doesn't want all of the praise or *thank yous* to go to X, says, "I picked mine out first." He hands me a big heavy box. I shake it, hear some liquid swishing around. Harvey says, "Y's present is a little more salutary." He laughs. "Let's just say you don't need to buy any Listerine for a while." I hug X and Y, and Michael tells the kids, Okay, that's enough, Uncle Cliff's in enough pain already.

The kids back up some, into their parent's legs, let Sammy get up and sit beside me on the chair, balancing her little butt on the armrest, careful not to bump into my ankle. She's holding what looks to be a book, wrapped in gold paper, maybe the size of a photo album, one of those big picture frames bound in leather that stand up on your desk, His and Her vanity shots staring at each other forever. Julianne hooks Harvey's elbow, tells everyone let's get out of here, give Sammy and Uncle Cliff some time alone. Y says, "But he hasn't opened my gift yet," and slumps his shoulders. "We'll come back," Rachel says. "Uncle Cliff will wait till then."

They all walk out, footsteps shuffling along the hardwood, Michael pulling the door behind them. Sammy sinks into my chair with me, careful not to hit my ankle, careful not to shake my concussed noggin. She doesn't say anything about why I got hit, what was I thinking, walking around drunk in the middle of the street. She doesn't say, James T. was right. She doesn't say anything about going anywhere anytime soon, that No, this doesn't change a thing, this little accident you got yourself into. Instead, we just sit there, staring out at the snow, which is falling heavier now. I grab her hand, wrap my heavy palm around it, just like she likes it, smothering her, keeping her thin fingers, her wrist, nice and toasty.

Sammy kisses my neck, inhales, exhales. She says, Let's go home, babe. She says, we can talk. For a second I hold my breath, like I don't want to jinx it, ruin anything by letting her know I still exist. I put my nose to her scalp, my arms around her small torso. I smell tangerine and Bergamot, a smell I haven't smelled, consciously, in a long time. I say, Sounds good. She has closed her eyes. I am about as happy as I have ever been. I'm thinking maybe, could be, the story of us, of Sammy and I, will have a happy ending. She lets go, and I let go, and she says, Okay, then. Let's hit the road, hubby. And I say, Happy New Year, Wifey. She smiles, says, And to you, dufus. And to you.

Aaron

Fifteen, sixteen years? later, and words still mattered. The callous words; the prying words. Pointed ones. In particular, the seemingly innocent ones. The ones you told sweethearts, your gaga'ing babies. Those words—*especially* those words—pricked him like razor wire. Dug under his flesh. Sliced his veins below the skin. They bled torturously throughout his body like rivers of fire. And they blinded him.

When someone's grandfather, someone's father, said, "Come here, baby, come sit on my lap," if they were fawning over some new mother's little bambino, made some proclamation like, "Well my, isn't *he* beautiful," the lights on the screens in his brain shut down, blackened. The light refracted, blurred, was sucked right out of his sky; generators powered-down, fuzzed-up in a cloud of squid ink, until he could see nothing but shimmering teeth in the blackness. Not sinister, pointed, vampire fangs (he did not live in Nosferatu-world), just dull, ivory molars and premolars, canines and central and lateral incisors with edges that bit like a vice and never let go. He fell into darkness. He could not escape the darkness.

He was not naïve to this, what it was; he understood that while everyone in a room might be all smiles, might be bubbling over with adoration, he was capable of only revulsion, that the triggers within him were not the same triggers in others, and that, conversely, the triggers in others were not the same triggers in him. His life had become a game; the rules, of course, being that he could never win, that to be successful he just had to not lose as bad as was possible.

He was a smart boy; he grew to be an intelligent man. *Eclectic and eccentric, my lads*; this how he liked to describe himself when he was out and about, running the social circuits, first in the big happening cities like San Francisco and L.A., New York and Miami, and then, eventually, the smaller, quainter, townie microcosms of Austin and Denver, Nashville. I'm Patrick Bateman sans le murderous impulses and without the tedious financial day job. I'm a boy of means, and I mean no harm. And a zillion other quaint one-liners that helped him get by. He thought of publishing a book of one-liners and adventures, and for a time he even took the project seriously. Walked around a la Oscar Wilde with flamboyant coats and umbrellas (the literary gene no doubt from his mother), pretending to lay idly around as his hero always did in the black and white pictures. Even had titles all lined up: *The Queer Well-Off Boy's Book of Pickup Lines*; *Lady Boys: A Dialogue*; *Back Doors of America (and the secret knocks to get in)*. Other craziness. But then he woke up one day and looked at himself and turned the page on all of that. Be. Who. You. Are, he told himself. Forget the ostentation; forget the martyrdom; martyrdom is pathetic. It's sad, dear boys. *Sad*-sad.

The isolation sometimes devastates him. He grew up with it, sure; it's always been there. Since the dawn of time it's been there. Yet once he was able to label it, once he put a name on it, it grew worse, when he'd hoped it would have grown better. The world they lived in, him, his mother, his father? A privileged world, for certain. But there was always a wizard behind the curtain, a Wicked Witch, and it seemed he was the only one who knew it. Or maybe he was the only one to admit it. Like his parents were either so stupid or ignorant, so good and pure in their thoughts, they were rendered blind. Though he wanted to, though there were times when he was so disgusted and distraught (a word he loved for its inherent drama, the bleakness it implied), he could never build the courage to even allude to anything, not to his mother, much less his father. Just couldn't do it. Couldn't wreck their world any more than their world was already wrecked—and it was certainly wrecked. They were wrecked in their way, even if the wreckage was below the surface and not flamboyantly out (as oh so many people would surely have loved) for everyone to gawk at. Just because they smiled; just because they played their tennis and had their toddies with their other obnoxiously wealthy friends; just because they laughed it up and went to premieres with the movie stars whose films they financed, donated shitloads of money to charity; just because all of it, it didn't mean they weren't secretly pained like him; because they were. He had gaydar, sure, but he also had paindar, which not everyone could say they had. But him? He had it. Always had. Sometimes, when it pushed on him and heated up and overloaded, when all he saw was other people's pain paraded before him, he wished he could just blink or nod his head like the Genie in that show his mother used to watch sometimes, the one with the astronaut, and it would just go away. All of it. G-O-N-E Gone.

Pain, though, at least in his family, you kept to yourself. You didn't share it even with shrinks. Everyone had it and no one spoke about it. Just like they were all Rh null, they were all depression positive. They just handled it in different ways. His mother retreated to her chapbooks and the note-jotting she'd done forever, preparing for her great American novel or whatever; his father bulked up and exercised until he was lean and mean, and when his freakish muscle growth was optimized, he switched it all up and got scary-ripped, jogging on his treadmill as if he were trying to wear the belt out. And then there was his little bar at home that wasn't little at all and had its own ginormous wine cellar attached to it, everything stacked to the max with obscenely expensive cognacs and wine from the year zero. Did his little business trips to who knows where for god knows what, though probably out there axing entire divisions of companies, destroying hundreds of lives. Wreaking havoc via collateral damage—*Sorry, son, Dad just got canned by his boss*—something about streamlining, but I'm sure you weren't ready for college anyway, overrated as it is. Go on, now. Go get some *practical* experience, lad!

He always knew when his father laid people off somewhere because when he returned he inevitably headed for the refuge of his wine cellar, and the smell of his expensive (and embargoed) cigars wafted up through the vents, filling certain parts of the house with a pungent (and telling) heaviness.

And he, Aaron, well, he was like Hadley, bopping around from here to there, but unlike her, the fear of crashing and burning, literally, grounded him. Kept him doing what she was doing but doing it by land, because, tough as he was, he just could not get himself back on an airplane. Saw it exploding, crashing down into a mountainside somewhere, him burning over ninety percent of his body but surviving, having to eat people knuckles and ankles to stay alive, keep himself nourished, like in that movie *Alive* where everyone was dead. And while he always saw the movie, it also reminded him of the true life version, where it was actually rugby players that were eating each other to stay alive, him thinking, *Yum*, short rugby shorts. And then, of course, thinking, Sick, sick, sick, I am! I am!

And here he found himself now, nearing the end of his lease, fattening himself up as best he could (which meant two or three pounds at best, all in the gut), eating thin crust and Chicago style, white and extra cheese pizzas and, occasionally, spinach and feta calzones—got to have your veggies! Drowning himself in lactose, revving up the heartburn with the garlic and tomato, as if eating himself heavy would change everything, make him normal-sized, puff out his cheeks, take away the skinny faggy look which, of course, it wouldn't. Instead, it just gave him a little paunch, not sexy, just the starving Ethiopian infant look, which was endearing in a way but ultimately, again, sad and pathetic. And the ulcers! Physical pain to match the psychological.

"You have to make a decision, honey. It's not that I don't love you, because I do, but Phil's having some medical issues, and I need to know rent's coming in." Aaron's landlady, sitting on the porch, smoking Aaron's cigarettes, drinking his Orange Crush. Him eating the gazillionth chewable cherry Rolaids, flossing with the metal wrapper, sliding his feet on the warm, sandy concrete.

"If I move out, I'll give you an extra month anyway, J. Don't worry."

"Honey, I don't care how much money you got in the bank, I'm not taking it if you ain't living here. Just come to a decision, sweetie. That's all I'm asking."

"You're asking a tree to bark," he said.

Jean said, "I wish I didn't understand you." She put a hand on his bony cheek. "Honey, I'm sure you're worse at something other than making decisions."

"See," he said. "Now how am I supposed to move away from that?"

Because, in a way, he didn't want to. Aaron had always loved his landlady. Jean was twice his girth, but not all that overweight. He liked to think of her heft as a giant pillow he could drown in. Her sarcasm—you couldn't beat it no matter what, and here, in heehaw, meeting her was the best thing that could have happened.

They never talked about *him*, probably because they didn't have to. The great, *unspoken*, purple, polka-dotted elephant. Instead, she took him under her ostrich wing and he pretended to take her under his chicken wing, and they got along well. She told him about Phil's health issues, and he told her about his other issues, whatever they were at the time, and they shook hands after each "session."

Thank you, sir.

Thank you, ma'am. Same time tomorrow?

Same time, kind sir.

Toodles.

Toodles.

Their psych sessions, beneficial for the both of them, always free of charge, always full of love, at least the kind you have with someone that would forever remain a stranger. Understanding love. Insightful love. Prescriptive love. Most importantly, love without baggage.

She, his surrogate mother; he, the sweet, doting son. He knows all of the terms for every little thing in his life, how he is supposed to act and react. What he's supposed to do at different stages of his fucked-up life. The crazier his life becomes, the less crazy it seems. He has new parents now, or a new parent, and somehow, with each move, he finds the next set of them. For the most part, he finds kindness. Only once has he put his neck out, risked throwing himself out into the hurricane. Sometimes he remembers that hurricane, out in Colorado. He'd loved the place. Three stories, super clean, three blocks from the Flat Irons, buffed-up boys from the university running around shirtless, full of Pabst Blue Ribbon and Coors. And he knew, putting down the deposit, that there was something about him, about the white-haired landlord that gave him the heebie jeebies. But he was retired, wouldn't be at the house but a few months out of the year to go hunting somewhere up in the mountains, so really the place would be completely his more than not.

And then the faggot and the nigger talk started happening after the first week he was there. Not at him, because the ignorant bastard didn't know he liked boys, and obviously the nigger talk wasn't directed him at all, but it was still there, out in the open, polluting the air with the vile, disgusting hatred. Even his sons, who rarely came over, asked how he could stand to be around someone with so much hate. Aaron had laughed, even going so far as to say, Well, clearly he's more bark than bite. As if that was an acceptable excuse for financing David Duke's lifestyle by renting his house. It was like living in a lion's den with a blind and handicapped jungle king, guns and rifles everywhere but nothing to shoot.

But true to his word, he was gone most of the time. Besides hunting, the old man disappeared to South America, chasing girls a third his age, returning only when elk season came around. So the rest of the year was good, and it was good for those two years. He'd loved that home, but then the ants in his pants kicked in and he'd packed and gone away. He fretted having to do it all over again.

Most times the happy times had to do with his mother. Aaron's father had tried, but his mother was always there, always understanding, always the lighthouse. His father had his own life, had for a long time. In the beginning, Aaron remembers, his father had tried, but once his father had started being the big man on campus, everyone in the family knew that meant that he would have to fade away some. That he would miss a lot of the little things and probably a good many of the big things as well. So he turned, naturally, to his mother, and when she started considering her own life, what she had missed out on, what happened in her own relationships and the things she'd given up, stuff like that, *well*. She had to take care of herself too.

Jean was feeding him pistachio pudding she made from scratch. Phil was at the hospital, staying overnight again, going through this test or that test, and Jean did not want to be alone. She said she'd be alone plenty once Phil was gone, and who knew who would be moving in after Aaron abandoned her. Funny, he had said. I know, she had said. And then she had followed it up with *Not!* Which always made him laugh.

"You know that went out like before I was born, right?"

"What?"

"The whole 'Not' thing. Maybe even before then. You saying it? The opposite of cool."

"Pipsqueak, at my age there's no such this as cool or not cool. There's just ways to make you smile."

"How depressing," he said. "Excuse me while I slit my wrists."

He was kidding, but she didn't like him ever saying things like that. You never knew how kidding someone was until they weren't kidding any more. "Honey," she said, "do me a favor, will you? Don't talk that way. It's not funny. I've done lost too many people already in my shitty life."

"It's words, Jeannie. Just words."

"It is until it isn't," she said, and her eyes were filled and shimmering. They were words, sure, but he knew all about words.

"Whoa," he said. "What's this all about?" He scooted himself closer to her, put his arm around her shoulder. He thought maybe she would say something about Phil, the doctors found something else wrong with him, he had a couple weeks left at best, something along those lines.

"Not sure," she said. "I'm sure it has to do with everything, but when I talk to you sometimes I feel like I'm talking to someone—I don't know, like you're a spark or something that's just going to burst into flames, disintegrate in my arms in a puff."

He hugged her even closer now. After a minute he let go. She pulled her head away and he was smiling at her with his pretty eyes and long lashes. "Wow," he said. "You're half right on the flame thing, anyway."

"I'm serious," she said. "Can't you not joke for even ten seconds?"

He said, "I have a little experience with landlords, Jean, and this is way beyond call of duty shit. But yes, I can be serious."

"Then let's be serious, okay? Humor me. For a few minutes?"

"Deal," he said. He put on a serious face. "Let's do it."

"Promise me you will call me anytime anywhere if you ever feel you need a session." She raised her eyebrows, put out her pinky.

"Anytime?" he said, hesitating to meet her pinky with his.

"Yes, mister. Anytime."

"This is so a moment where I'm supposed to be jokey."

Jean looked at him like, Come on, honey, be serious for once in your life.

"Okay," he said. "Okay." He hooked his pinky around hers and they pinky shook. She said, "That's a promise, honey, and I take promises very seriously."

"Okay," he said. He sat back on the couch, took the pistachio pudding from her, began scooping half-spoons of it into his mouth. He said, "Are we done with all of the tele-novela stuff?"

"Nope." She turned to face him more directly on the couch. "I want to know that you're going to be okay, Aaron. I mean really okay. I don't want you to go on and disappear and not have someone like me watching out for you. You need watching out for."

He took a last scoop of the green pudding, put the bowl and spoon on the coffee table. "I've done pretty well on my own for a while, Jeannie. You know that. I'm not telling you anything new."

"I know, honey. I'm not trying to baby you. I just worry."

"Worrying is fine. I won't pretend that that's not normal. But you can't pretend that I'm not an adult either." He looked at her. "And you *are* trying to baby me. But it's cool."

"You're not an adult," she said.

"Now who's being jokey."

"You know I mean that with all the love in the world. But you need to take better care of yourself. You're a mess. Even if you're all smartass and a bag of chips, you're a mess. You're hiding out and you're using your parents' money to do it."

Aaron looked at her seriously, looked away. He lit a cigarette. "My parents are loaded. It's not a big deal what I spend. If it was a big deal, I wouldn't do it. Trust me."

"It's good they support you, but that doesn't mean you should use it to escape."

He wanted to laugh at the word *support*. So many meanings; so many degrees. He thought, Well, maybe his mother supported him, but his father, that's not what that was. Maybe he *enabled* him, sure, because clearly that's what money did for him. But *supporting* was so very different than what his father did, had ever done.

"What's really escaping, Jean? Really?" He propped his chin on the palm of his hand, nearly burning a hole in the couch with the cigarette dangling from his other hand. He flicked an ash into the ashtray, balanced the cigarette in one of the little notches molded in the middle. He said, "Everyone escapes in their own way. Me. You. *Everyone*. You escape Phil and your life and who knows what else by coming down here. Savior Jean to the rescue. I escape by jumping on a greyhound. My mother escapes to her world of make believe, writing all her bullshit, and apparently now to one national park or another to chase ToTonka and run around with Pocahontas. And my dear father? Maybe he ran off to work a thousand hours a week to get away from my mother. What do I know? Same thing, just a different way to get where they want to go."

Jean nodded. "I'm not arguing, because you're right. That is exactly what I'm doing down here, if I'm honest about it. But we're not talking about me. We're talking about you. We can talk about me if you want. I have no problem with that. But we're talking about you, honey."

Aaron let his head fall back onto the couch, closed his eyes, opened them. "Jean. I love you, you know that. But that's exactly why I'm here. To get away from talking about me. I don't like it. I've never liked it." Aaron put out his cigarette, lit another one. He got up, walked to the cabinet, started downing Skittles, popping candy corn from a glass jar that had been there since who knows when. "I don't want to say that you don't understand, Jean. I don't. But you don't understand. And I know you don't."

"Try me out, honey. I know I—"

"No, Jean. You don't. You don't know. With every ounce of shit in me I know you don't."

Jean was nodding now, and for a second Aaron wanted not to care, not to have to think about Jean's emotions. But now, with Phil in the hospital, there was just no way. He could not not feel for her. He could not not feel bad for talking to Jean like that; all she had ever done was love him like he was her own son. "I'm sorry," he said. "Truly."

She smiled at him, but she was still nodding. "Don't go, baby," she said. "What would I do without you?"

But he did not answer her. Instead, the doorbell rang, buzzed low like a dying bee. Jean looked over her shoulder, saw it was one of their neighbors, the new girl with the little boy, moved in a couple doors down right around the time Aaron had moved in. The boy was holding one of those shiny order forms, and she knew they were probably there to sell stuff to a guy that wasn't buying. She said, I got it, and went to the door, ordered a tub of frozen cookie dough and a tin of Buffalo Blue popcorn. Told them to bill her over at her place, she'd take some of the chocolate caramel cookies as well, what the heck.

When she walked back inside, Aaron had changed his clothes. He had thrown on a pair of jeans (too big, of course), and a T-shirt that said "Hi, How Are You?" on it with some frog or something with big eyes. She told him his belt looked like it was trying to strangle him.

"I'm heading out," he said. He looked at her and smiled. He walked over to her. He put his thin arms around her waist, kissed her on the lips. "Thank you," he said. He walked out the front door, closed it, then stuck his head back in. "Do me a favor, sweetie. Lock up on your way out. The landlord's a real pain in the tuchus."

"Be safe," she said.

"Never," he said.

They had conversations like this, like clockwork, about once a month. If he was predictable to her, she was more predictable to him. Thirty-some years apart yet kindred spirits. Like she was the smoothed-out version of him, edges refined, slowed down, and, obviously, if he were decades older and female and losing a husband to some ghastly disease. There wasn't anything either of them wouldn't do for the other, and Aaron, caustic when he wanted to be, cherished the relationship they had. He was careful not to kick her when she was too far down.

He walked a few blocks to the bus station, caught the 12 to Fourteenth Street. He walked two avenues up to Mary's, ordered a Heineken. He went upstairs, sat on a Merlot-colored, crushed velvet sofa. It was still early, maybe eight, nine. Somewhere around there. The bar was empty, a few guys sitting in a corner, a couple of queens nursing half-empty glasses of Pinot Grigio, staring at whoever walked in the door. Rolling their fairy eyes every few minutes when someone walked by and they weren't interested.

He went through the zillion numbers on his phone, remembering faces, apartments in warehouse districts, parties in artist's lofts around the country. Smoke wafted along the ceiling, blurred the lights overhead, behind the bar. He remembered feeling lonely, feeling like he was feeling now. Like everyone was somewhere else, occupied with life, doing something with people who cared for them, made them laugh. People important to them. Family and friends, coworkers. People like that. Around you all the time for different reasons. Coming. Going.

It is times like these that remind him that he has felt lonely more times than not. In Chicago; in Iowa. Driving across the planet that was Texas. At parties. Places where everyone was happy, where everyone was drunk. Where everyone remembered all of the grand old times they'd had at other parties, when they were happy and drunk and remembering the other times before that. He has spent more than one New Year's Eve alone, naked in bed, watching Dick Clark and Lance Bass (not totally un-cute, really) and others counting down the minutes and then the seconds, fireworks exploding in the night's sky and confetti raining down over Times Square, him watching it all down below his protruding ribs, his jacked-up feet and toes, all the while his skeletal behind sinking further and further into the cum-stained sheets of one Motel 6 or another. Until, as always, he drank himself and smoked himself into oblivion, *three, two, one*, buh-bye.

And then he met Jeannie. Found her number on the last page of the *Backwood's Gazette*, first listing under "For Rent," right smack below the M4M classifieds he had been browsing just because. Within ten minutes he knew he was moving in, just by how she was looking at him. Had that lady-stopping-for-the-injured-animal-on-the-side-of-the-road look. Only asked for first month's, nothing else, even when he offered to pay six months in advance. Keep your money, she'd said. I'd just spend it anyway. And that the apartment was furnished already, he couldn't have asked for more. Even without that beautiful window right up front, looking out at the street, the black gum, the bluewood, he would have moved in. With Jeannie as his landlord, he was going to be okay. More than okay. And he was. For a long time.

Not that there hadn't been any rough patches in the past, because there were. Especially during certain times of the year. New Year's, sure. Christmas. Spring break. Especially spring break, when all the kids were free to roam, and his parents went away on their own spring breaks? When he was left alone? Or not alone, but with the Oggys, which was worse? So many years ago. But damn if that hammer didn't return. Damn if those memories didn't make him scale that ladder, dive down head first into that bottomless swimming pool of vodka, of X. Where he could numb. Where he could die and feel nothing. Where he wasn't scared of becoming everything he hated.

Because sometimes he felt like his skin was turning inside out. Getting ravenous inside, but not for food. And those sometimes were becoming almost all the time now, so bad that he could hyperventilate. So bad it felt like sixty Red Bulls and a pot of coffee.

At first, the yearnings were like flittering birds, zipping by. Like he saw them out of the corner of his eye, a flash of darkness, vanishing off into the horizon somewhere, a whisper floating in the air left behind. But more and more it felt like his skull was being crushed, filled up with lead and rocks and needles, like a cactus was growing in there and was ready to take over his body, pop out of his skin like needles in a balloon. It worried him. It worried him, because the grip he felt he'd been able to hold onto for so long grew slippery and wet. It threatened to seep over into the here, the now, and overwhelm everything that's struggled to remain balanced.

For a long time, he watched the television. He loved Springer and Judge Judy and sometimes, when the bug hit him, he watched the Cold Case shows, where kids that looked like him vanished back in the seventies in their tight Jordache jeans and retro T's, combs in their back pockets and feathered hair like too many tacky eighties rockers wore. But then, when he wanted the pain, when he needed it, needed to open the wounds, to let them breathe, he watched more sincere shows like Maury, where someone's baby daddy was always sticking it to twelve other baby mamas, and which, of course, they always proved through DNA, surprise, surprise! Or he watched Oprah, where you could put money on it someone's story would make him weep like the sap he was. But then the window, which he'd fallen in love with on that first day, six-feet wide and clear as the breeze beyond it, overtook him, and he knew it meant trouble. Because out there, walking around in that fishbowl world, laughing and crying and riding bicycles and yelling and dirty-kneed and smudge-faced and skinny and vulnerable, were the united colors of *him*. Only smaller. More vulnerable. And though he wishes he can't, he knows, tragically, that he *can* predict the future. He already *is* predicting the future. And it's a future that is dreadful.

And the next morning and all day, still buzzing with Cosmos and Appletinis, it is happening.

He is watching him. He has watched him all day. And for the past few as well, though he had not been sure until then, until that very moment, exactly why. Playing with friends; sprawled out on the lawn; lost in his make believe adventures, his claustrophobic world, enjoying, in complete innocence, the weekend. Now it is Monday, and his mother walks him to the bus stop, brushes her lips across his cheek, waves as she walks away, back home, to her car. The window is like a giant television, its characters nestled gently behind glass, living dioramic lives that he may have, at one point in time, understood. Lives that could have been *their* lives, those of his mother, his father. His. If they had gone slumming. If they were not them. If they had lived others' lives.

Her car, parked in the driveway, a newer red station wagon, sporty, tires on thin rubber, not a block away. He knows how the week will go, because all of last week Aaron has done the same thing—watch the mother and the boy, the bus come, go, the boy taking his time until the bus rumbled away, his mother waiting by the bushes, because the boy is too old for a mommy in front of other children but too young for the rest of the bad world without one.

Aaron lights a cigarette, listens to the paper burn into his lungs. His lease on Jean's window-front apartment will end soon, or he will make it end, and he will pack his bags and move on, to another city, another state. Where he will disappear all over again, vanish into obscurity behind cheap rents, line cooks, and mechanics with greasy hands and torn denim. Maybe he'll even find a new Jean with new sad eyes and a new husband who's dying of something, or maybe not dying but killing the new Jean in his own, unoriginal, unprovoked, unhurried way. But right then, right now, he is only peeking over the edge, taking notes. Observing.

Once a month, he speaks to his mother, unless she calls him when she is lonely. And this, her calling, is something, recently, that she has taken to doing more and more. And his father calls too, leaves messages, over and over, as if that makes a difference. The inconvenience of cell phones is that they follow you, even if you can't—or don't want—to be found. He does not hate his father, not before and not now, but he can't not think that without him, without the choices he has made for them, for their family, normalcy may—had it been given a chance—been possible. Without him, the devil would never have had a key. *Call me.* This is his father's message, over and over. *Call me.* Except every third call, if weeks have passed in silence, if Aaron has not texted or e-mailed. Then he says, Aaron, *please*. Just *call*.

But he had to know, his father. How could he not? How naïve could one man be about what was happening to his own child? Gifts were one thing, but lavish presents rained down on him, on Aaron, as if Aaron were Mr. Oggy's own son. As if he were his own flesh and blood. But perhaps, he thinks, has thought, perhaps Mr. Oggy's own children were not enough. Maybe they were just too close to home to smother, to suffocate, to risk being exposed for what he is, what he was then. Perhaps always has been. Maybe his father, even his mother, had read the shoeboxes full of wrinkled and stained letters Mr. Oggy sent him over the years, which he has left, intentionally, out in the open for everyone to see. Not right there on his bed, but certainly not hidden away in a closet, under mud-stained cleats, behind golf clubs he has never used. Golf clubs, ironically, his father bought for him so they, he and his father and the oh-so-beneficent Oggys, could hit the links.

It had started, artlessly, with a picture. A boy, a man. Nude in a room much like Mr. Oggy's library, which is, from what he recalls, where it, where this—*all of this*—began. This was that first year, when his father had become President of the company and Mr. Oggy had invited them over for dinner after church. Lewis, Mr. Oggy's son and named after Lewis Carroll the writer (so clever he thinks now, considering Lewis's sister's name was Alice), had been showing him the house, the two of them running around the three-level mansion, playing hide and seek and I-Spy this, I-Spy that, when they'd stumbled into Mr. Oggy's library, seemingly by chance. What a world he had built around himself, Mr. Oggy, with the kids, the house, the power to do whatever he so chose in his little fiefdom.

Once they had stumbled into the library, Lewis had disappeared. Vanished like a magician's rabbit. It was just he and Mr. Oggy behind closed doors, surrounded by walls of hard cover books—books, he thinks, that closed the room in on him, created the perfect place for Mr. Oggy's loud, warped fantasies. Books that were not for opening your mind to new things but, rather, muffling the nearby ears to forbidden ones.

Mr. Oggy had smiled. Aaron remembers Mr. Oggy had called him his "luscious, luscious" Aaron, which made him think of Dustin Hoffman in *Mr. Magorium's Wonder Emporium*, standing curiously amongst a mountain of toys and trinkets in his tight suit. He cannot recall why his father was not there with them, but he is sure that Mr. Oggy had arranged for circumstances to be so. He remembers Mr. Oggy saying, "You know, Aaron, your father is my new best friend," which Aaron understood, even if it took years to accurately comprehend. Forever Aaron pretended those years were just make believe.

Recently, his heart skips a beat. He drinks espresso until his tongue is dead with its bitterness. In between the occasional meal, he nibbles on chips, on stale bread, on the packets of dehydrated cheese and garlic sitting around on the coffee table, the kitchen counters. He has thinned out, taken to boring holes into his belt to keep his jeans from slipping down his legs; tucks his shirts in. He drinks cranberry vodkas, stays inebriated for long stretches of the day. He has even bought a gun, legally, from a shop downtown, even though he has never fired a weapon in all his life, and really only because he wanted to see if it could change how he viewed himself, which had always been less than manly. He does not keep the gun loaded, though he does play with the box of ammunition that came with it, a pleasant and unexpected lagniappe from the gun shop owner who he thought, at first, may have been a queer hater. And he has formed a strange habit even for him—biting each round, literally, with every tooth in his mouth, over and over, as if to separate each casing from each bullet, to mark each round indelibly his own.

It has taken him a long time to admit what Mr. Oggy has done. Mr Oggy took away everything from him before he'd ever had a chance to know what he had. Mr. Oggy brutalized him and victimized him, changed everything he could have ever been. All of the opportunities he'd always had, they stopped mattering. But he knows, also, that he never had a chance. Mr. Oggy was no amateur. The old man was experienced at manipulation, at all of the skills germane to the pedophile. Gifts were given, chosen thoughtfully, delivered privately. Gifts above suspicion, yet clever in their ways. And then of course there were all of the charming photographs they had taken together, random moments (or so he thought), always before the eyes of his doting parents. During dinner, the holiday parties. And how could one forget the fawning missives, their bold messages—too bold, really, now that he considers them. The man was fantastic at his game; hid in plain sight, clever boy. So much easier than it sounds, Aaron thinks, now that he has sampled the life, or at least the beginnings of it. Who, really, is at fault? How far back goes the chain?

Their *secrets*, too many to recollect. Mr. Oggy making Aaron's whole thing disappear into his mouth. Maybe Lewis knew, maybe he didn't. But like him, Lewis split as soon as he could. Threw himself into finance. Convinced himself he was completely straight, a man's man, not damaged. Who could blame him? But Aaron knew what he was. Once you crossed into that new world, your eyes opened. You saw things fresh. You saw things for the first time that had always been there, things—you were shocked to realize—that had already always been staring at you.

Lewis married, pretended everything was fine. People like him did. And half of them, you could tell what they were in two seconds if you weren't blind or pretending to be.

Later on, when he was a teenager and too big (he assumed) for Mr. Oggy's tastes, he considered putting a little red dot on the map over Mr. Oggy's opulent estate. Expose him like the rest of the pervs were exposed. Let the world know what type of man this *gentleman*, this titan of industry, really was. Show his face, front and profile, hair mussed, that dumb look all predators had in front of the camera, like the world was about to end and they'd caused it. But of course life was not as uncomplicated as that. There were other people involved. Others whose lives would have been destroyed. You couldn't let the sun in on the head vampire and not expect his victims to go without a little sizzle. And so he thought, one life damaged is better than many destroyed. He could bear the burden for everyone; in the same way his mother bore her burdens, in the same way so many in his family bore theirs. Who didn't find martyrdom at least a little appealing? He had not thought of it before, but yes, his was a cursed family. Maybe they bore more burdens than any family ever should have to bear. Except it was *his* family. You couldn't change that. Some people lived in Mayberry, others lived in Hell. You got what you got. Someone had sold their soul to the Devil somewhere down the line, and Mr. Horns and Pointy-Tail decided it was time to collect.

It was morning. He had been eating smoked salmon from a stuffed Ziploc Jean had left for him on the kitchen table. The smell coming from the pinkish plastic bag stunk up the room, but he was glad to be eating something other than pizza. Jean had friends in Alaska, and every year she sent them things they wanted, and they sent her things from there. Salmon, mostly, but her house was filled with bear carvings and fake moose poo, mini dogsleds carved from wood and beige, faux leather photo albums with the outline of maps of Alaska on the cover.

His fingers slick with the oils of the salmon, he lit his cigarette and the boy, as he did every morning at that hour, walked into his line of sight. The boy's mother trailed less each day. The boy's name, graciously bestowed on Aaron through a lovely, muted scolding: *Shane, don't eat before lunch, sweetie!*, had a new outfit on, a Junk Food rock T from the Gap, Rolling Stone tongues all over it, lips licking the flags of Canada and Mexico, Brazil. Cute little carpenter jeans, faded, a tool pocket and little boy hammer loop on the right leg sticking out like a loose thread. Maybe it was his birthday, Aaron thought. Maybe Daddy put some overtime in, hit that scratch-off, got his boy a new little outfit.

He heard the neighbors upstairs arguing as they did these days, stomping the hardwood above him, yelling obscenities at each other, her double his size, him thin and wiry, black-haired, quiet as a mute. He looked like the Arabs they paraded on the news all the time, or maybe one of the Sardinian servers that waited on him over at the Greek place downtown. He watched the bus roll up, watched Shane walk self-consciously over the rubbery steps into the faded, tangerine tube, his big doe eyes flat, which was a bit out of the ordinary. Aaron guessed it was the clothing, which he understood. New clothing, new anything, always felt like you were making a statement, showing off. Calling attention to yourself, like, Hey, everyone, look at *me*! Which was not something kids like them did.

The bus rolled away, and for a second Shane's mom seemed to look in his direction, as if she could see past the glare of the big picture window, see him sitting there on his couch, shirtless, smoking his cigarettes, one hand pressed under his jeans. As if she could smell the salmon from all the way on the sidewalk, which he knew, just by looking at her, by having gotten to know her for all these days, that the smell would repulse her, that his whole existence would make her want to retch. He froze, sinking deeper into the couch. Feeling like now things were reversed, the fish were looking beyond their reflections, their big dead eyes stabbing at him. But when the idiots upstairs shut up, she'd turned away, walked out of view, and was gone. When she did not return that day to pick Shane up from the bus stop, Aaron knew that that was it. Shane was independent. Shane was like him. Shane *was* him.

He never gained much weight, either during his school years or the brief few afterwards. He had a high metabolism, always had, and he never ate much, not for a boy with his energy, at his age. *Slight*, is what his friends called him, and he was okay with that. *Sweet*, too. Another ducky adjective. But they never called him queen. Never flamer. Because he wasn't. You couldn't tell by looking, anyway. Not at him. At least that is what he told himself. So there was never any trouble in that way. No boys showing off at his expense, calling him names, pushing him around. A rash of boy-boy sex early on, then a straight-pause (accompanied by some religion of varying denominations), then back to the realization that no, you couldn't change who you were, even if psychologists (all online, all anonymous) told you you couldn't get over your childhood traumas. The biggest *duh!* in all the world. What twits! And then, the last couple of years, the running. Hotfooting from one town to the next. Flamer paradise to flamer paradise. All over the U.S. and even good old Montreal, *Mont-Re-Al!*, him parading around the clueless and closeted Jean-Jacques, Ooh la la!, while Jean-Jacques pretended, god knows why, to be a Canadian butch, which he hadn't the slightest clue of how to pull off. All the while he, Aaron the wanderer, watched his trust fund increase rather than decrease, as if he were living his life in reverse, from its dénouement until its beginning, which he knew did not start well, and which he knew even more he never wanted to revisit. Would he have loved boys even without Mr. Oggster? Indeed. No question. So while he wished it weren't so, there were reasons to keep quiet about it. You could cheapen who you were by what had happened to you, even if you were a victim. Or especially so.

And yet the truth was that everything was not all bad. There were good times, when the eye passed right over him, when he felt safe, loved. Happy. When his mother was there and she took him everywhere and seemed to understand him, like she didn't care what he was or how damaged he could be. When all she seemed to want to do was make him happy. When she read her little make-believe stories to him at night, before his father came home from work, them sitting around the kitchen table drinking cabernet and eating stinky cheese, which for some reason was a big faux pas around his father's friends—not the cabernet nor the cheese, of course, but their pairing. She minded the smoking, but not enough to force the issue, not enough not to share one from time to time. He loved those nights, when they were friends, and not mother and son. And once they were gone, once his mother began drawing inward, drifting away to the refuge of her enormous room, creating her own space among her catchpenny gewgaws and bedroom accoutrement, pretending like the worlds in her books were more important than the world she—they—lived in, he knew it was time to go. Even if everything within him told him he was abandoning her, leaving her behind to face the demons and dragons and blackness of their home—which was enough to lose oneself in and, increasingly, void of life and absent of the living—it was time.

The day the bus was late, Aaron felt Shane's fear. At first Shane stood still as a statue, as if transforming himself into some inanimate object so he could hide in plain sight. As if that would help. But when a slight breeze rattled a scattering of dried maple leaves, the poor boy nearly jumped out of his skin. Aaron could not help but smile. He walked outside, let the screen door behind him slap against its frame so Shane could hear him coming. Aaron had once been that little boy, and he knew right then he probably looked like the scariest thing to ever walk the planet to Shane. "Hey there," Aaron said, smiling his come-hither smile.

Shane said Hi back, watched Aaron walk past him to a mailbox. The smoke swirled from Aaron's cigarette like the smoke behind a race car, twirled round and round, thinned out to nothing. Aaron opened the lid of the mailbox, swung it shut.

"Nada," he said, as if apologizing.

Shane backed away from the sidewalk, stepped onto the lawn to give Aaron room to pass. But Aaron stood there, looking at him, this beautiful boy, who looked younger than he was, probably more scared than he was. Aaron squatted butt to heel, put his hand out. "I'm Aaron," he said. "I live in that house right there."

Shane's eyebrows rose, fell. He did not extend his hand.

"You're Shane, right?"

Shane did not move, but they could hear the bus approaching, and when Shane jerked forward, Aaron stood. When the bus pulled to a stop and the door opened, Shane was quick up the black rubber steps. Aaron waved to the bus driver, then watched Shane staring at him from a seat rows and rows toward the back of the bus. He imagined Shane's legs dangling off the bench seat, Shane kicking the air nervously. When the bus ambled on, Aaron watched the line of cars that had been delayed roll away behind it, the faces of early-morning commuters drooping over coffee mugs, smoking cigarettes. An obese woman smearing lipstick on herself, staring at the rearview, wiping sweat from her neck with a cardboard-beige McDonald's napkin, looking like every other disheveled commoner he despised.

Over the years his time alone with Mr. Oggy varied. Some months it seemed he lived there, especially during the summer, when his parents took trips abroad by themselves. At Mr. Oggy's insistence, and more than once on the company's dime, his parents were sent to Saint-Tropez and Lake Como, Anguilla and on safaris in South Africa and Kenya. He even had a room in the Oggys's designated his room. At night, when everyone was in bed,

Mr. Oggy would sneak in, sashaying over the thick carpet, bare as a baby underneath his silky robes. This was many months removed from when he had first begun showing Aaron attention. By then Aaron had given up resisting, because by then there was no point. He thought about telling, or thought about considering thinking about telling, but there was no point in that either. He had tried in his way early on, protesting whenever they went to the Oggy's home for dinner. More than once he pretended to be sick, sticking his fingers down his throat, vomiting. Pretended he had homework, or that he had a friend coming over, or that he hated Lewis, which maybe he did. But in the end? In the end, what could you do?

Afterwards it became easier, accepting what Mr. Oggy wanted. Letting him do as he pleased—because he was never angry, and he never hit him. He just did what he wanted to do, touching him, rubbing on him, taking him in his mouth. Whenever he was done, once he cleaned everything up and talked to him for a little while—not about what they had done but about school, about games, other things—he would kiss Aaron on the cheek, ruffle his hair. Like his dad did sometimes. And on it went. For years. Until it stopped. Until he made it stop. Until he prevented it from ever happening again. When he took back the control, which, really, was not that hard to do. Although, perhaps even that was a delusion.

For an entire week Aaron watched the window. But Shane did not come, nor did his mother. Nor did any other children walk by. When he'd gone to the *Conoco* down the block to buy a carton of cigarettes, he'd noticed the Cadbury Crème Eggs and the Easter stuff all over the store—stuffed bunnies and purple and gold candies, blue and yellow transparent chicks stuffed with gumballs. It was spring break for the kids. Although Shane was not waiting at the bus stop in the mornings and wouldn't until the next week, Aaron bought a few packs of Mini Eggs, an Easter Egg Hunting Kit, a box of yellow marshmallow Peeps. When he got home he wrapped the presents in wrapping paper he cut out of paper grocery bags. He wrote "To Shane" on the outside of the paper bag, but didn't include a card. You couldn't do that, sign your name. Not living so close.

Things happened in Helen, like they happened at the long summers at the Oggys's. They happened, and like a lot of things, the memories faded, were grayed-out as if behind clouds. But he knows what he knows. He knows things happened. Things, back then, he wasn't sure about, but that now, after so much time, he is sure about. His life, what was it? A bumper car of pain, of destruction. Cruelty. Selfishness. So many other things. His life. Which, in the end, hadn't ever been his. But what use was there in dwelling? What use was there, if you couldn't change anything about it?

He laid everything out on the table and waited. He slipped his thin hand under the paper, ran his fingers slowly over the cellophane, slid them over its smoothness; tapped the shimmering scotch tape down where he had pasted the edges as tight as he could, which wasn't much (he was never good at things like that). He lit a cigarette, put it out. He did not want to get the smell of smoke onto the gifts. He saw someone walk by the window. His heart fluttered. But it was only Jeannie. Just Jeannie. *Shit*, he thought. Jeannie!

He grabbed the blanket that was on the couch, threw it over the gifts on the table. Jeannie knocked. He told her to come on in.

"Afternoon, Sugar."

"Jean."

"Jean, huh?" She pinched his cheek, sat down beside him on the couch. Tucked one leg under her bottom. She put a hand on his knee. They sat there, in silence, for a good thirty seconds, looking at each other, nodding. "Well," she said. "What's got you all silent movie, Love?"

"Nothing," he said. He let his eyes walk around the room, searching for anything she wasn't supposed to see, because she would ask. The Scotch Tape, a tube of wrapping paper, the little package of gift cards with the bright cartoons all over them. The ribbon. But there was nothing for her to see. Just Jean, staring at him, wondering about him as she always wondered about him. He smiled. He thought, I'm being paranoid. *Stop* being paranoid. You haven't done anything, silly Willy.

"Nothing," she said. Naturally, her eyes went to the table. Nothing was ever on the table unless it was a pizza box or a bottle of Stoli or Ketel One. Whatever was covered with the blanket wasn't either of those, she knew, just by looking, and Aaron knew it too. When she faked like she was going to lean forward and he flinched, she just laughed.

"Relax, darlin. Just because I'd give you my spleen doesn't mean I won't respect your privacy."

"It's not that," he said. "Sorry."

"No reason to be sorry, baby. Everyone's got a right. It's America."

Jean was staring at the pack of Kools he had on the table beside the blanket-covered packages. He told her go ahead. She tapped one out and he lit it with his Zippo.

"They'll kill you," he said.

She took a deep puff, made rings over her head. Karate chopped them.

She brushed his face with the back of her hand, softly, and he could tell she wanted to counsel him, to continue with one conversation or another they'd been having, but instead he said, "How's Phil? Anything new? Need me to go down there, straighten anything out?"

"Good, no, and no," she said. "Same old, same old. Doc's don't know shit. Test after test after test to hear the same nonsense. Inconclusive. That's what they make the big bucks for. To tell us they don't know shit."

"Hmm," he said.

"Hmm is right," she said.

A car rolled up across the street, a Camaro or a Firebird, something shiny and tough looking and low to the ground. They watched a woman, late twenties early thirties, walk a boy from the car to the front door. Aaron felt Jeannie watching him but rode it out. The woman kissed the boy in a half-ass swoop of her neck, knocked on the screen door, got back in the car and took off, a guy about her age with sideburns and wraparound sunglasses hitting the gas with a too-heavy foot. Lynyrd Skynyrd blasting out the window. The boy stood at the door for a minute then sat down on the steps, looked around. Aaron thought, The world is full of kids left alone.

Jeannie's face tensed up. "Fucking loser mom dropping him off, doesn't wait for the poor kid to get inside."

Aaron had never seen the boy before. Nor had he ever seen the mom, the car, or the boyfriend. He looked at Jeannie, expectantly.

"Dad's a computer guy or something." She looked at her watch. "He'll open the door eventually. Probably wearing his earphones or something. Always takes his time whenever anyone knocks."

"I've been here a long time, J. I've never seen any of them."

"The mom's had him probably since you moved in. But they go back and forth. She'll take him for a bit, tweak out, drop him back off here, get all cleaned up and miss the little man, come back and get him and do it all over again."

"Great life," Aaron said. He started to say more but now he was watching the boy, his little fingers unzipping the duffel bag his mother dropped by the steps. For some reason he was changing his shirt, pulling one off, shimmying into another. All Aaron saw was his belly and little wee-man chest, peach-yellow blended with a bit of rouge, where he was chafed or getting over some sort of irritation. He wasn't like that other boy in the neighborhood at all; this boy had a little something else in him, like if you looked at him he'd cuss you out, maybe throw rocks at you, didn't care you were an adult, a kid. Even from across the street he could see the child's eyes, his cheeks, his *je ne sais quoi*. The kid looked like he'd been sucked dry a long time ago. No happiness. No *emotion*. No nothing.

Jean was talking, saying something about Phil and then something about child services or something. How some people shouldn't have kids, shouldn't be so selfish, how this or that. But Aaron was already lost in the boy, tunnel-visioned in. Consumed by *him:* stripping petals off a gardenia bush; skipping lava rock off the lawn onto the street; spitting on a hornet's nest dangling off the side of the steps. He, Aaron, floating in that silent miasma he could fall into, had been falling into more and more, where the world disappeared and fell silent, and he was alone, or almost alone. Where maybe he didn't see talking rabbits or any of that, but where he was definitely, absolutely, in a universe far far away.

But then, the knock inside his brain, pleading, pleading, come *back!*, and he knew he needed to return from whence he'd gone, to flip the channel, to wake up, to zoom back in on Jean, get that close up, make himself *normal* again, tell her everything was all right. For a second or two he stared at her. It really was as if he'd just woken, found her there in his room, staring at him. For a moment, maybe she glimpsed, or worse, maybe that universe had, truly, regrettably, shown itself.

Jean was smoking another one of his cigarettes. She was staring out the window, watching cars go by. The boy from across the street was gone; his father had unlocked the door and the boy, picking up his bag, had walked in. Jean tapped her ashes into the ashtray. She hadn't moved, but he felt like maybe she was a hundred miles away now. She looked at him, and for a second he wasn't sure that he knew her.

She said, "An idle mind is the Devil's workshop, baby." It was her deep Jean voice, not her happy-go-lucky, it's-a-great-day-to-be-alive voice.

He said, "Why did you say that?" He was accusing her. Telling her don't go there, if you're going there. Are you going there? Do you know where you're going? Do you, Jeannie? No, seriously. Do you?

"Because it is," she said. They were playing a game now. It was normal for them, these games, except this time the topic of the game was one that made him uncomfortable.

Jean did not come back that week. Nor did she call. The neighbor upstairs, the husband with the scratches on his face, told him Phil had taken a turn for the worse. Jean was staying at the hospital twenty-four seven. And then as if instructed, he said, "Oh yea, they don't want any visitors." Thanks for the heads-up, Aaron said.

No visitors was not like Jeannie. He figured she was just giving the cold shoulder until he snapped out of his funk, said, Jeannie, I'm back! or whatever. Joined her in the real world. Jeannie's world, skewed as it was. An idle mind, she'd said. If only it were that. An idle mind he could take care of. An idle mind, he'd go build something, tear something down. If only that's what it was. An *idle mind*. What a joke. His mind was anything but idle. That was the problem. It was too *not* idle.

That whole week he stayed away as much as he could. Walked for miles through different neighborhoods, up blocks he had never known existed, much less thought of walking. Blocks with names like Jinglepot Road and Dusty Lane, Mews Avenue, Quaking Circle. Who thought of those names?

He stopped at empty libraries and read newspapers off racks; spent entire afternoons listening to ducks flapping their wings along man-made lakes in subdivisions with icterine-yellow homes, trees half his size. He walked by high schools, picking out the queer boys who maybe didn't even know they were queer yet (because they were still just Goth or "shy"), and he walked by middle schools and elementary schools, where most of the kids were locked up behind metal fencing, running around kicking soccer balls and punching tethered volleyballs round and round, the bigger kids picking on the smaller ones as they probably had since the invention of schools. When a teacher looked his way he smiled, lifted a hand, kept on walking. He walked to cafes where he could drink bottomless cups of coffee and surf the Internet, checked out all the boy-boy hookup sites and his e-mail, where the same little unopened envelopes always beckoned to be clicked open. Dad. Mom. Grandma. His cousin Hadley.

But he did not open any of the little envelopes except for Hadley's. All he could do was stare at the subject lines for a second or two, keep scrolling on down, past the spam, the e-mails from some of his small-town boy toys who would never get none of him again no matter how many e-mails they sent.

He looked at the date from Hadley's e-mail, his only cousin, his vajayjay counterpart with the dickhead dad and drunk mom living in Key West. Such a cool town. It was too bad; he would have already trekked down there if his aunt, Hadley's mom, hadn't staked her claim on Duval Street like the bitch she was. He'd only been there once, and with his family, but he knew even back then that Key West could have been his home, or at least a great substitute Shangri-La, with the ocean air and all.

Sometimes he felt bad for her, for Hadley, because he knew his parents had done something to her parents, betrayed them somehow eons ago, and that they blamed his folks for their pitiful lives. Maybe there was truth to it. Maybe there wasn't. You never knew with any family why anyone did anything, why anyone stopped talking to anyone else or resented anyone else. Everyone had their logic, unfounded, illogical, maybe just plain stupid. It happened sometimes. Maybe it happened all the time sooner or later, and all you did was get over it. Or you didn't. Either way, he couldn't ever remember anyone speaking about it, like it was taboo to even hint at what had happened. The big family mystery. Le grand kaboom that fucked them all up.

When he clicked on her e-mail the image of Hadley being Hadley somewhere in Europe opened slowly on the screen. Her face was right up on the camera, and you could practically see up her nostrils. The edge of some castle was in the picture, just off her right shoulder, and to her left some girl, probably one of her friends, staring at her, pretending to be caught doing something she wasn't supposed to be doing. The girl had a cell phone stuck to her ear.

Hadley always sent pictures like that, silly, random pictures—her being a clown by the Eiffel Tower; London Bridge zoomed in between her pale legs; hugging the tall, skinny cross in the Old Market Square at Rouen, where Joan of Arc was burned at the stake. Being her irrepressible, artsy fartsy Hadley.

She had written a few lines about where she'd been, where she was, telling him to come on out, get shitfaced and just jump on a plane, stop worrying about the end of the world. At first he'd written her a long e-mail, asking how she was doing, when she was coming back to the states, what castle was that in the picture, who the girl was. But then he'd deleted everything he had written. He wasn't ready for an onslaught of e-mails from her. He knew the more he gave the more she'd take. Probably his parents doing the pulling, bribing her with gifts, with money, which could be their way when they wanted it to be their way. Keeping her lifestyle going like they kept his going, making sure the credit lines never ran out, the bank accounts never got depleted. Instead, he wrote, "j'y suis, j'y reste, au revoir." He clicked send, sent the missive out into cyberspace. It was all he could give.

After a week of walking the city, he was exhausted. Until he'd actually walked everywhere, block by block, the city had seemed vast and promising and open. Now that he knew most of it, it was as small and depressing as everywhere else he had ever been. Nothing strange. Nothing different or surprising. Nada. Just sadness in the faces he saw sitting in the fuzzy corners of bars, the crystal clear look of too many lives full of hope, yearning for anything, *anything*, to be different than what it had turned out to be.

He walked to Shane's house and knocked on the door. He knew it probably wasn't the brightest idea he'd ever had. But what was? He would be gone soon enough, and no one really knew his name other than Jean and maybe the tenants upstairs. Besides, they had their own disastrous lives to navigate, and he doubted they knew his first name anyway, much less his last or anything else for that matter. Everyone else around there knew him as Charles Dodgson. It was a name he'd been hesitant to use at first (too clever?), but later realized it wasn't a name that well-known outside of geek or perv-ville. It was too clever, really. And besides, "everyone" was two, three people at best. A guy who lived in the house kitty-corner from his place who he'd helped jumpstart his car once; old Mr. Vann, three doors down, whose house smelled like cat piss and mothballs, even though he didn't have any cats. Maybe Mr. Vann's daughter, the schizophrenic who visited him every now and then and always came looking for Jean to help clean Mr. Vann's backyard. The daughter that scared him, because she came to the back door rather than the front one, which Jean let her do.

Shane did not open the door or come to the window, but Aaron could see him in the house, peeking from behind a wall, the dark droplets of his eyes pronounced against the golden yellow of his hair. He lifted the presents he'd packed, held them up to the window, so that Shane could see he was leaving something rather than taking, that he wasn't the boogeyman or anything, just dropping some gifts off, here you go.

But Shane did not move. He just stood there as if he were invisible, as if the wall were twenty feet high and made of Velcro.

Aaron waved bye, smiling the whole time at Shane. He backed away from the door, tripping over one of Shane's toys, a bright blue dump truck with black zebra stripes on the sides, big black rough-looking tires caked in dark mud. He fell to the ground, not heavily, more avoiding crushing the toy than anything else. He pretended to walk away, but at the end of the sidewalk, where a wall of conifer hedges separated Shane's house from the neighbor's (who was also Aaron's neighbor), Aaron turned and waited for Shane to open the door. And waited. And . . .

There was a time after it ended with Mr. Oggy that Aaron fell madly in love with drugs. He hadn't dabbled with marijuana and alcohol like most of his friends had, but instead dove headlong into harder substances like cocaine and Rohypnol, Ketamine and Georgia Home Boy, or GHB, Gamma Hydroxy Butyrate. Rave and club drugs, though raves were definitely not his thing. None of that skinny-boy, hippity hop, underground T-shirt, glowing light-stick-in-your-mouth bullshit for him. He didn't want to necessarily keep the damage going, because that was about as prescribed as you could get, and he was not a cliché Carrie. It was more easing the journey than anything else. Keeping a certain state of mind going. Avoiding another, far worse one. Only later, when it was harder to keep his drug connections from state to state, did he consider alcohol and marijuana, which were always easier to get. No one wanted to send anything through the mail. And that meth stuff? No way, Jose. Not for him.

The first time he'd been picked up by the police, they'd called his father, whom they knew from the papers and his donations to the PAL. His father sponsored spaghetti dinner fundraisers throughout the year, which brought in enough for two new cars and a mini sub-station in one of their neighborhoods. The police claimed he had drugs all over him, in every pocket, which was, according to them, a first. Called Aaron a walking Nescott Drugstore. Found him sleeping in the basement of someone's home, still zonked out after a binge. No charges were pressed, but everyone knew them in town, knew who they were. Didn't look good, obviously. The police let him go with a loitering charge, left out any mention of drugs. Nothing on there that would stick after he turned eighteen. He's just lucky no one shot him, Sergeant Huenke told his father. *Very* lucky. The insinuation of course being that he'd almost been shot, which couldn't be verified. But it was said Mr. Russell, the home's owner, was an avid big game hunter, and not too pleased with waking up to an intruder with a girl's body lying on one of his prized kudu hides, in sissy clothes to boot. But that was it. His father would fix it. Aaron knew it. Even if Mr. Russell said thanks but no thanks to roundtrip tickets to anywhere, enough was enough, reprimand or no reprimand. No yelling and hollering, which would have been too dramatic anyway. Just a disappointed look, which didn't have any affect either anymore. It was like they were in a desert now and they were all lizards walking the sand, handling their own business. *Surviving.* The second time he got picked up, Huenke said next time around, that would be strike three, no bullshit. So Aaron left.

"Nope. Not doing it. Sorry." He found himself on the telephone with his mother, who was out in Jellystone, apparently. He told her he wasn't going home, wasn't calling his father back just because his father *demanded* it. Not yet. Not until *he* wanted to, he said.

"He misses you, baby."

"*Mom.*"

"Okay. Okay."

He lit a cigarette, blew it out of the side of his mouth. "Yellowstone, mother? Really?"

"Yes, baby. Want to fly out? Love if you did. Greyhound it if you want. Whatever you want, you know that."

He says, "I don't think so." He can hear ice clinking around an empty tumbler. A lighter, scratching. The light burning of a fresh cigarette on the other end of the phone.

"Baby?"

"Yes, *mother.*" Impatience. Annoyance. Sorrow.

"I'm *here,*" she says. "If you need me."

"I have to go," he says. And then the line is dead. Soundless.

It is raining. It has rained all night. But now there is no lightning, no earth-rumbling thunder. Only the pitter patter of an outside gutter; only a whoosh of gray air; only the tinny slaps of hail against the windshields of the cars passing by too quickly along the street; the random thwacking of the mud puddles below the loblolly bays; only the frigid rain, falling from the sky in a cloudy torrent of shimmering silver, of ermine white. He has slept late; the hum of the rain, the dark sky, all of it has disrupted his schedule, but thankfully, or tragically, he is not too late. The bus pulls up, he hears the heavy squealing brakes, and out walks Shane, raindrops pouring down on his little body, his raincoat shimmering like whale skin.

Aaron walks outside, not slamming doors, ghost-like in his movements; lingering briefly, hesitantly, taking advantage of the blanketing, deafening downpour, until the bus has moved on, and then, as if he'd planned it, he is quickly after his little man, chomping at the space between them with each purposeful step. Shane's diminutive feet, socked and booted, rise in the air as if in slow motion. Up goes the backpack, up go the little jeans, the little hands, the little feet, only to land, innocently, angelically, pleasantly, in a soft-water puddle, rainwater splashing up and out, blossoming like an orchid in some black and white, indie movie. He is playing in the rain! Performing this, his pure, angelic, foolish little bop and tap of summer rain. And he is, hallelujah!, oblivious.

Aaron creeps up—but still one stride for every four of Shane's steps; left, right, left, right, and waits, again by the shrubs. But this time he is checking for signs of mom, signs of anyone, listening to the rain melt the earth, drown the anthills in smears of red and brown, run crushed beer cans along the gutter in violent clangs and knocks, down through the grates and into the cavernous sewers. When Shane sticks the key in the door, when Shane pulls his hood back (because he is now under the small canopy covering the front door), when Aaron sees his matted curls and yes, can practically smell his baby skin, feel the warmth of his neck, the tender breath of salty, sweaty skin, a voice shatters the dream and says, simply, unceremoniously, "*What the hell are you doing?*"

Which is a dagger in his heart.

That makes him suddenly, jarringly, ask himself the very same question. Yes. What *are* you doing, Aaron?

And he cannot really say. Because he does not really know. Because this—going this far down the rabbit hole—is new for him, too. Because though he has imagined it happening more times than he can recall, he had never thought, not once, that he would ever have the courage to attempt such a thing. And so he has, of course, entered the situation unprepared.

When he tries to speak, he chokes. Words fail him. His mouth opens, but it is plagued with Silence. Silent, roaring, heavy, *stale* air. A lack of purpose quivering before his lips. But he tries again. And again. Until finally, in desperation, and almost as a whisper, what comes out is, well, inadequate. "Making sure Shane gets home," he says.

But the police officer, with his big gun, his pressed uniform, his big man muscles and deep man voice—this man who is also his neighbor, and who is also Shane's neighbor—does not believe him, not completely, not absolutely, not in any remote sense of the word really, which Aaron hears in his voice, sees in his stance, is hard to miss at all in the bitterness in his eyes. A bitterness, of course, which he has seen before, which he has fought and been beaten with, that he has become inured to after oh so many years. That they, the commoners, always have.

"He's home," the officer says. Which they both know. Which they both knew.

"Good," Aaron says, not knowing what else to say. And so he says, "Good," again, neither of them moving, neither of them really knowing what more to say, to do. And for both of them this, all of it, is in slow motion. It is as if time has stopped and they, the two of them, are all that's left. It's them, one on one. Survival of the fittest. The outcome, the victor, of course, already determined.

While Aaron sees defeat, what the officer sees is this: the fucked-up neighbor kid, the druggie asshole who has been following Ms. Walker's kid across the yard every day, peeking at him from behind a bush—his bush, the one he has manicured and watered and clipped and stemmed during his free time, when he wasn't pulling overtime at Big T's Bar & Grill, or sleeping on a plastic chair in a sweltering booth at the Vanderlay Estates housing projects—unreal as it all is, crazy as it seems. Ms. Walker, poor single mom busting her ass who, one day, he will ask out on a date, to•dinner at the new French place, La Bergerie, where the owner does the right thing when it comes to law enforcement.

"You have ID?" he says.

"I'm your neighbor," Aaron says, shaking his head, lifting his limp hands. As if their domestic proximity can save him.

But there is a pause; Aaron nodding; walking backward, one finger in the air, wiping raindrops from his eyes. "I'll go get it," he says, now turning, the police officer behind him, following but maybe not following as well, allowing him to remove himself from the awkwardness, the whatever-this-is.

But he says, "I'll come with you," which he says from close behind, increasing his steps with Aaron's, who has increased his, without meaning to, without knowing he was going to. Creating this *situation*. This absurd, ridiculously volatile conundrum. This fucking crazy, *crazy thing*.

That first week, he knew Jean was going to be like a grandmother to him. Like his grandmother, Julianne. She had that way about her, Jean did, coming right in, taking over, like where have you been, mister? I was worried sick about you! Brought him a football field of lasagna, an iceberg salad with flecks of purple cabbage, half a loaf of garlic bread in silver foil, pieces of half-cooked garlic staring at him like pieces of chipped tooth. Told him no tenant was going to starve on her watch, no sir. Just because your mother isn't here doesn't mean you shouldn't be spoiled, she'd said. And then she proceeded to do just that. Treated him like he was her own son. Whenever she and Phil went out to the Steak and Shake or the Eat Here Now Chinese restaurant, Bubba's BBQ or the Hankook Taqueria, where they had Korean food *and* tacos, she always returned with doggie bags for him. Sometimes just dropped them off in a drive-by before she and Phil ran up to their place, drunk on margaritas and whiskey, to do what they did, which he tried not to think about. And other times she just sat there until she knew he ate every last bit. Which was what his grandmother did. Sat there until you finished, cleaned up after you like you were handicapped. Sometimes, he even called Jean Julianne.

So he guessed he missed her, his grandmother. The older he got the more obvious it was: he was Julianne's favorite, Hadley was Harvey's. Not that Harvey had treated him any different; he hadn't. They just naturally formed pairs like you did in school. Got into your cliques, hated the world together. Hadley and Harvey were interested in going far away, buckling in, setting sail for the horizon; he and Julianne, they just wanted to stay close, know home was nearby. Be able to turn right back around, follow the breadcrumbs. Peek in on neighbors around the corner and call it a day. Maybe his home was all the U.S., but still. Their insides did not boil if they weren't discovering new lands, spying on other galaxies that maybe they thought they could wiggle their way into. They were good with what was.

He felt bad about that, about not staying in touch with Julianne. But if he kept in touch with her she'd keep him on the phone forever. And if she did that he'd melt, answer all of her questions. And that would be that. She'd blab it all to his mother, his father. And then the rescue squad would arrive. He could see it. Saw it as clear as clear could be. The street cordoned off into a perimeter, black SUVs everywhere like in the movies; helicopters touching down on rooftops; straightedge counselors rappelling down the sides of walls in their corduroy jackets, megaphones strapped to their backs, yelling for him to come out of the house, drugs on the ground, let's hug it out, big guy. *Hug. It. Out.* No need for all the drama, gayboy; *everything's* gonna work out fine. Peachy, son. Just peach-y!

So he didn't call. And he didn't e-mail, which he knew she'd learned to do, because Hadley had forwarded one of Julianne's e-mails inquiring about him. Which, of course, he never acknowledged. And which, of course, Hadley never mentioned again.

The last real memory he has of Julianne is at Harvey's funeral. She was sniffling, sure, but he'd found it odd that she was not crying, not bawling like you saw people bawl on TV, where everyone was dressed in black and someone threw themselves onto the coffin. Everyone standing around the freshly-dug earth, the tufted grass, hands clasped, staring at their muddied shoes.

People no one knew standing around, wearing sunglasses that didn't hide their eyes as much as they maybe wanted them to be hidden. Harvey had a lot of friends from all over, more than a few colleagues from his years teaching and lecturing and writing books. There were dozens of college types dressed in the stereotypical jackets and jeans and loafers, some young and some old, and here and there even some from abroad, whispering to each other in French, in Spanish, some with their kids. He'd felt like they were staring at him, staring through him. But Julianne did not really know any of them, and because Harvey's other family had not driven up from North Carolina or South Carolina, or wherever it was they lived (and which, he remembers, Julianne could not believe, was appalled); she just stayed in her seat accepting condolences.

He remembers it had been nothing special, the funeral. A shiny black casket, flowers everywhere, a drizzle of lukewarm rain, if he recalls correctly. A carpet of Astro Turf underfoot. His mother and father latching him to them, away from Hadley and her mom and dad, but close to his aunt Sammy, who stood alone in a corner, consoling her mother, delivering mini plates of this or that to her as she sat in her rocking chair on the porch, staring out at the trees. He remembers his aunt Sammy especially, because he was afraid of her silence. He can't recall anything she said that weekend, not specifically, even though they'd all stayed together at the cabin. In fact, he could not remember anyone speaking, except when they had all said their goodbyes. Maybe there were refusals to speak, even.

He remembers the three of them, his mother and father and him, hugging Sammy and hugging Julianne early in the morning before the sun was up. Before Hadley or Hadley's mother or father had gotten out of bed. He remembers food still on the table from the night before, mini ham croissants and toothpicked cubes of cheddar, slices of salami. A Crock-pot with Lit'l Smokies in congealed barbecue sauce; half empty plates and Styrofoam bowls with smears of yellow potato salad; his mother trying to clean up as his father rushed to pack their bags. Sammy pushing his mother away, telling her without words to go, that she would clean everything up, that she would stay with their mother, his grandmother, for a while, until the storm settled, until the winds stopped, until life got back to a certain kind of normal.

It hadn't occurred to him until later, a few years later when he was feeling sorry for himself after a bad breakup, that they, his aunt Sammy and his grandmother, were widows. That they were a mother and a daughter who'd both lost the men they'd loved, the men they had chosen to marry. For a good week he thought of them. For a month he'd sent them flowers, anonymously. Only to stop sending them as soon as he'd realized how cruel flowers could actually be, when they became a symbol of a hope that never came.

That was what he felt for Jean. Jean hit the same place in his heart that Julianne hit. When Jean had disappeared that first time to visit Phil at the hospital, when she'd stayed there for a week straight without calling or stopping in as she normally did, he walked the twenty-three blocks to the hospital. He'd asked a nurse at a desk for Phil's room, and she told him, but she said he would have to come back in the morning, visitor hours were over. Thanks, he'd said. He walked to the room anyway. The halls of the hospital were dim but not dark, and it was about as quiet a place as any he'd ever been to. He could hear the buzz of the lights, and every so often he could hear the beep of machines and what sounded like the suction of pumps. He pilfered a bouquet of blue and white Irises from just inside an adjoining room, square glass vase and all, careful not to bump into the IV pole that stood by the door.

When he peeked in he could see Phil flat on the bed, his head shimmied up on a pillow, a spaghetti highway of tubes and wires all around him. Jean was asleep on a wide chair, her legs propped up on the windowsill, one Reebok hidden behind the salmon-colored curtains. She had a gray hospital blanket rolled under her head. When he'd pushed the door open her breathing picked up some. The windows were fogged up from the air conditioning being so low.

He watched Jean squirm around, push her legs farther up, her butt farther down, scrunching herself deeper into the chair.

She did not look very comfortable. But soon she was still and breathing lightly again, a slight shimmering of light reflecting off her lips where she drooled. Curling her legs in, tucking her hands between her knees like little kids did.

Phil had been a large man when he was younger, hands the size of Aaron's whole face. Now he looked like a withered catfish someone had thrown into a plastic bag. The afternoon before Phil entered the hospital, they had stopped by his place, told him they had just eaten at the new Indian dive, Swapna or Shiva something-or-other, but couldn't stomach any of it, all of it spicy as hell spit. They asked did he want the doggie bag. And then, before he'd even finished his shrimp biriyani, Jean was calling him that Phil was already in the ER, the doctors were rushing him in like his head was severed. Phil never checked out. Said he was ready like a woman was ready when she was prego and about to pop, that's how ready he was to be in the hospital. He lost half his weight in a year, and his skin pulled away from his body as if it were cellophane. The pills or the chemo or something had yanked the hair out of his skin. Left two patches of moustache where he'd once sported his bushy Fu Manchu. His face was so gone you couldn't nearly tell it was him unless you'd watched it happen. Now he looked at Phil and he looked at Jean and he just walked over to where Jean was and lay on the floor, right there at her feet. When Jean woke up in the morning she just rested the blanket right there next to him and they both slept until the nurses came in to check on Phil. And that was that. Or at least until when she disappeared again and told the crazies upstairs that she didn't want any visitors, which felt like she meant him, like she was speaking directly to him and him alone.

And when he heard that, that Jean didn't want any visitors, it was like his family all over again, the closest people to you in all the world became strangers, shut you out for who knew why, pulled a Jekyll and Hyde. Turned everything on its head. Made you feel like Quasimodo. And that's what he felt like—like he was going through it all again, dealing with the destruction and implosion of what he thought, or what he felt, could never be destroyed, could never implode. Because clearly it could. Undoubtedly it had.

"No clue," he remembers saying to Jean that first week when they became inseparable. When Phil was out of town hunting pheasant in South Dakota, and he and Jean were playing gin rummy eight hours a day over Grape Lifesavers and Retributions with just the right amount of Firewater, eating Taco Bell and microwave-defrosted Chicka-Chicka Boom-Boom from Chuy's over in Austin. "Just stopped talking to us. Like we killed their cat or something."

He was talking about his uncle James and his aunt Rachel. Not Hadley, because she still e-mailed him. Still sent pictures even back then, mostly of her yard, out her window, of leaves falling, of snow on the ground, her camera pointed towards the rooftops where, on the other side of town, she knew he and his parents lived. And Hadley, she didn't understand it either. First the yelling, her father at her mother, and then, for a bit, her mother at her. But that didn't happen until after her father had taken off, disappeared one day, like he forgot where he lived, forgot he had a family that thought he was family too. And then they were just mother and daughter in this big house that soon they could not afford. Hadley wrote to him of everything that was going on, what they sold when, which of her friends stopped hanging out with her, who her mother started calling names, screaming at over the phone. Like everyone was leaving them like her father had left them. Like he'd not only run away but ran away with all of her friends, all of her mother's friends. He knew, to this day, neither of them knew why.

"You could ask, you know. My experience, straight line's the fastest way point to point."

And Jean was right. It was the fastest way to get there. But it wasn't that easy, of course. "It's like the DMZ," he told her. "They're staring at each other ready to kill each other, but the why isn't there anymore. The why only means something to their parental units."

"Parental units or not," Jean said, "sometimes you gotta put your tail between your legs and head on home."

"She was telling me of everything they were losing. The furniture; the paintings; the cars. It was like they were selling and my father was buying." He'd shaken his head. "Had to buy Grand Central just to store the shit he bought, Jean. It was nuts."

He'd told Jean about how his father wasn't even home half the time, what was the point of filling the house with stuff he'd never even see but for a few minutes every month. His mother, she was like a character in a book, the wealthy widow with ghosts roaming the halls as she wrote in her leather notebooks about the days when she was happy, changing names, fucking up what really happened to fit into her books. Like you could make wrong right by changing who it happened to.

"How do you know that's what she wrote about?"

"I read them," he'd said. "Not all of them, because I didn't have a century, but I read a few."

"Nosey Nelly," Jean said.

"You try living in crazyville, then come back and we can talk."

He stared at the wall. He said, "She changed everything anyway, so it wasn't like I was reading her diaries. I mean, I knew who she was talking about, but she changed who said what, who did what. I knew who was who, but I guess that's how she fooled herself into writing what she wrote. Confused it all so people like me didn't know who she was talking about. But I knew. I knew."

"Still," she said. "You should do what you can. It's your family you're talking about, not strangers. And Sherlock, you shouldn't snoop on anyone, much less your folks. You know that."

He had his hands laced over his head. He nodded. He said, "It isn't my fight. It's between my parents and my cousin's parents."

"Still," she said. "It doesn't matter who broke it. It's who can fix it matters."

"I can't fix it," he said. He looked over at Jean, who was fumbling with a button on her blouse, trying to button it back up. She saw him and smiled and shook her head. She said, "Family's all you got, kid. You lose that, you've lost your own damn self."

He didn't know why he ran. He just started a slow sprint towards his place, towards the big fishbowl window, the whole time thinking, Why are you running, dumbass? You didn't do anything wrong! Everything got crazy in his head. Like it was a game but it wasn't really, because he knew this was not what he—what anyone—was supposed to be doing. You didn't run from the police unless you were a criminal. He of all people knew that.

The officer slipped on the wet grass, went down. Aaron ran inside, nearly crashing through the door. He could see the officer through the window, his faced pressed to a radio, his arm reaching to one side, something all over his face (a face which Aaron notices, awkwardly, crazily, that in its distress, is about as handsome as faces got).

He imagines the officer's voice, frantic across the airwaves, *breaker breaker one nine*, breaker *breaker one nine*, we have a six-five-four-three-two-one going down, need backup now! A voice, coming back from the station, yelling you have a *what?* And cute 21 Jumpstreet boy here yelling back, A faggy perv trying to maul a helpless, innocent tyke!, and then the whole lynch squad jumping into their Batmobiles to come get him, tear him limb from limb, spread his arms and legs and everything across the four corners of the earth. But no. What happens is much different. Less dramatic— or more, if you see it for what it is, which is not make believe, but *real*. Which isn't TV. Which is much too much for him to deal with or compute, because you don't get do-overs on shit like this.

He hadn't meant to grab the weapon, or gun, or whatever you were supposed to call it, but there it was. Worse, the cute officer man had seen it too. He was going to just run in the house, throw the gun into the other room, maybe into the garbage can or under the bed, get rid of it before Johnny Depp came barreling in asking his clever boy questions. But when he'd grabbed it off the table, the officer's eyes blew up wide and he'd hurled himself into the bushes like he was Butch Cassidy *and* the Sundance Kid, Aaron thinking what the fuck is Johnny doing, that's gotta hurt?

So now that the officer had seen the gun, Aaron put his hands up, walked towards the door to tell cutie pie that it wasn't loaded; he was just going to put it away; he didn't mean to freak him out with it just lying on the table like that. What a goof he'd been, leaving it out like that. But none of how he saw it happening was happening. The officer was yelling something, pointing at him with his gun, hiding behind a car he'd run to now, not wanting to listen at all to what he was saying because, truth be told, neither of them could hear a thing over the torrential downpour. Aaron thinking, *What* is this that has materialized here? It's the fucking *Twilight Zone* for real! Him backing away from the window now, the gun back on the table, the world outside like he was watching a movie. He reached for the phone, told the voice he needed the hotel in Yellowstone now. Please hurry, he said. *Please.*

Maybe Jean was right. Maybe family was everything, even if you ran away from them as fast as you could, didn't look back but every now and then, when you were feeling lonely or pitying yourself mid-happy hour, when everyone around you seemed to be happy and all you could think of was why them and not me? Why had joy touched their lives and pissed all over mine? Maybe he could do that, turn everyone's frowns upside down. Maybe he could be the bigger man (ironic as the thought was), get everyone back together, pull his own Julianne kumbaya somewhere out west, on neutral territory, or on some island somewhere, where you were trapped, where flights didn't leave but once every week or two. The phone rang and rang. So he dialed other numbers. Which rang and rang. And rang.

Later that evening, Mr. Man's colleagues' patrol cars in his driveway, blocking his street, pushing the neighbors aside, comforting Ms. Walker (who is visibly distraught), all he says, in the flashing blue and white and red, is this: "He stared at me, behind that window and yea, I could see he was all tore up. Crying. I think he said sorry, but I don't know. I just don't *know*, Sarge. The pain in my hip was killing me, you know? Must've hit something. I wasn't going for my gun, no. But that was it. It didn't matter. I didn't know. Until it was too late, I didn't know. And then? It was just so . . . quiet. Like all the sound in the world stopped. I didn't mean to, Sarge. But he moved. I swear I thought, It's him or me, Sarge. It's him. Or me.

Lettie and Michael

Lettie had read the book in high school, though in what grade she can no longer recall. Its opening line probably the best opening line in history, in all the books that had ever been written: *"It was the best of times, it was the worst of times . . ."* and it so perfectly described everything she had felt that day (those days), so many Christmases ago. In retrospect, how it all played out, she wished they—all of them—could go back, return to those December days, white out the ink on all the pages that had been written, and write a new story. Start a new draft of their lives from scratch, keeping the same characters but plotting their lives out differently, maintaining that sense of place that still lingered to this day but changing the dialogue, altering what mattered. And not only from that day or that month but from the backstory that had never been told, that as of yet had not been written. The history that included lines stolen from *The Godfather*, spoken by James and taken to heart by Michael (even their names were similar): *It's not personal. It's strictly business,* which was James' way of tutoring his new report, of giving his advice on how to deal with everyone from then on out. *Cutthroat*, he had said. Like Sun Tzu, he had said. He had even given Michael a signed copy of *The Art of War*, signed not by Sun Tzu, obviously, but by him. Be merciless, he wrote. *James.*

Because Michael, her Michael, was too soft then. Too *nice*, said James. Too needing an edge. And then, at the climax of the story, he had not said: "It's not personal, James. It's strictly business," because he did not have to. James knew what he'd created.

This is what Lettie remembered pre-Helen and over what was supposed to have been a happy family holiday:

- Michael receiving a phone call from MicroZoot, Inc.'s CEO, Mr. Oggy, the day before everyone— her family and Rachel's—were heading down to Georgia for Christmas. To celebrate their in-law's anniversary. And to celebrate theirs as well
- Michael changing their reservations to the very next day, smiling, looking at her while on the phone, holding something back
- Walking on pins and needles in Helen, Michael anxious to get back home; the vacation, generally, an awkward hullabaloo

And this is what Lettie remembers afterwards:
- The pain
  - of a crumbled family
  - of a devastated sister
  - devastating her, because she has become what she has always loathed

She sits now, staring at the lake, her eyes passing over the glassy water, wondering if this was inevitable, if life really is this cruel, if telling Michael to decline would have changed a thing. To just say no, to have less, to not be her sister's equal.

This lake, it is a lake she has known all of her adult life, but this is the first time she has seen it in person. A giant lake stretching to the horizon, cotton-puff clouds reflected off gray-blue ripples, steam rising like milk in the distance, hovering all along the rocky banks, blurring the horizon. Inside, she has read text behind glass; this lake, the largest freshwater lake above seven thousand feet in North America. It is a fact she had not known as a college student returning home one summer, when she had seen the lake for the first time, sitting on the coffee table in her mother's Florida room. Two pictures: one looking out to the lake, another looking in, presumably from some tourist vessel bobbing along the water. Tomorrow she will take her own pictures, and she will ask strangers to take some of her: before half-shed, muscle-laden bison; before limestone pools of ice blue and amber;

beside a bursting geyser; casually listing against wooden railing, the shadow of the hotel at her back, columns and a veranda of bright white against pale yellow, windows shaped like Cheerios. And a last picture: her silhouette against a plume of sulfur, strangers walking through fire, her nose crunched up at the waft of rotten egg.

She has come here because she has heard fabulous things, but also to see what her mother has seen, to live like her mother has lived. To be something much unlike what she is. To see things in ways she has never considered them. To see things as her mother has seen them, and not as Lettie the housewife has seen them. To finally, and without regret, let her hair down. To feel like she felt for a few moments that summer, when her mother's biker boyfriend, Knox, in his deep man voice, said, "Honey, you haven't seen a damn thing unless you been to Montana or Wyoming." And she had actually more than considered it.

He was pointing to the pictures of the lake. "Took that backstroking in the frigid waters of Lake Yellowstone," he said, which was of course a lie, and a badly worded one. If he had said, "Took that backstroking in Lake Yellowstone," she may have believed him, because he was that type of man, rugged, impulsive. If he had not clarified with "frigid waters," which was a bit much, sure, no problem, she could have allowed herself to believe it. But he had not. And then, staring at each other with nothing left to say, he had laughed. "Anyways, get your tail out here. It's worth it," he'd said.

And here she was, years later, getting her tail out there, out here, to Wyoming. Sitting perhaps in the same cushioned seats Knox and her mother had sat on, staring out at the lake, resting her feet on the vacuumed carpet, the polished hardwood. Older than her mother had been when she had been out here, taking in such wondrous beauty. And she thought, *Older than my mother.* How strange to think.

A young girl, sweet face, cute little hotel outfit, says, "Here you go, ma'am," sets coffee, an English muffin, on the table beside Lettie. "Can I get you anything else, ma'am?" she asks.

She says "ma'am" like Lettie says "ma'am" when she is addressing someone of a certain age—an age much more advanced than her own. "No," she says. "Thank you."

"Shall I charge it to your room, ma'am?"

"Please," Lettie says, all the while thinking, Stop, please stop. *Please. Stop. Calling. Me. That!*

When she told Michael she would be going to Yellowstone, flying out to Jackson Hole, he said, "Well, that'll be a great trip." He had not said, "Will you be going with anyone?," and he had not said, "Want some company?," because he knew she was going alone. That she needed to go alone. That she had planned and planned for it and that, finally, she had simply decided she was just going, and that was that. That she was going to go away. That she needed time to think, however briefly. That she needed to do it alone.

It had been hard, their lives, but mostly hers. Not hard financially, because money was never an issue. Money had never been an issue. And even if she had invited him, no way could he have been able to take the time off. Not for that long. The CEO and member of the board of an eight hundred million dollar company was not going to disappear for a month, was not going to be out somewhere where you had the chance of hiking behind a mountain and losing reception. No way. But that was not a decision he would have to make. She had made it for him. Aaron, maybe he would drive out or fly out from wherever he was, come join her for a few days either alone or with whatever new girlfriend he had. But she did not find that likely, considering she had researched and decided on Yellowstone in a matter of a few hours. What would *Lettie* not do? The old Lettie? That is how she convinced herself this was the best way. Do what she would not do. And luck was clearly on her side: a room available at the last minute, or so the woman on the other end told her.

Over tea she meets a couple, Roz and Melinda Berthold, and Mimi, their "single" friend, whom they've accosted from her life in Tacoma, Washington. Roz sells carpets wholesale, and Melinda is a stay at home mom like Lettie once was, whose children have bequeathed her the dreaded empty nest. Mimi, "recently divorced five years ago," as Melinda teases, is a free spirit, and Yellowstone is her heaven. Anywhere else on earth, Mimi would probably have not come. "But Jellystone, hah! She jumped on a plane lickity split!" says Melinda. "So I wouldn't say 'accosted.'"

"I've always dreamed of coming here myself," says Lettie.

Roz says, "We've been coming here for a number of years."

Lettie watches Roz's eyes float down to her wedding ring, which all of a sudden feels like a ten pound weight. He says, "Is there a Mr. Lettie here as well?"

"No," she says. "This is a lone wolf trip."

Mimi says, "I've found my Thelma."

Melinda says, "Roz was hoping for another boy to get into trouble with."

Lettie says, "Sorry. My troublemaker stayed home."

"I say we make tonight ladies night, then," Mimi says, and looks at Roz, who throws his hands up.

Roz says, "By all means. Take my wife, please," and smiles. "I have reading I've been meaning to do anyway. I can sit by the piano and read and drink port and look dashing."

Mimi glances at Melinda, scrunches her forehead. "And *you* didn't want to bring him."

When the hotel dining room opens, Lettie and her new friends sit down to dinner, order the salmon. Roz orders the seared duck salad. They share a bottle of Mondavi Reserve, a plate of cheese and walnuts. Roz picks up the tab and the women head to the bar, Melinda kissing Roz on the forehead as they leave him behind. Mimi orders them three Cosmotinis, and when the waitress brings their drinks, the women clink their glasses.

Mimi says, "New friends."

Lettie says, "Cheers," empties half of her martini.

After two more, the women move to a table in a corner. Melinda is clearly tipsy, but Mimi is going full throttle. After she and Mimi split the Crème Brule cheesecake, Roz walks by and collects his wife who, it is clear, is ready for bed.

Soon Lettie and Mimi are running around outside, dipping their feet into the lake, smoking Mimi's clove cigarettes in the breeze off the water. Lettie says, "I only smoked one year in all my life. Twelve months straight and then gave it up."

Mimi says, "Good for you, goody two shoes."

Lettie says, "*Seriously.*" She does not mention the occasional slips in between, when Michael was gone for weeks at a time, or when Aaron had his issues, and she felt useless and helpless to him, her tortured little baby.

Mimi says, "Tonight, sweet thing, you're my partner in crime."

Lettie says, "Uh oh," and smiles.

"Uh oh is right," Mimi says.

"This is my chance," Michael had said. "This is that next step we've always dreamed of." And he was right. It was. It was greater than they could have ever imagined it could be. But it was due to James's extending a hand. They had not sought it, but it had come. James had brought it to them. Without James, Michael would not have been hired, not have been put into the position he was put into. James's actions had aligned their stars. James's actions had made it all happen. Lettie remembers that she had, for just a second, said, "I don't know." But Michael had said, "He himself was the one made me this way." Michael was kidding, of course. But it was also true. James had made Michael relentless. He *had* made him cutthroat. Given him that last bit of drive that was missing, that last cold-hearted dagger to put in his belt. James had made his monster.

Lettie was telling this to Mimi. Telling everything to a stranger. They had boarded up in front of the hotel, climbed the steps like schoolchildren, and now the yellow bus bumped and rolled from one spot to the next, Lettie opening up like a blossoming sunflower. At Mammoth she told Mimi about Aaron, how shy he was, the spitting image of an earlier Michael, the Michael she'd met and fallen in love with. How lovely he was. But also how lost. At the little restaurant across the border in Gardiner, at the *Antler Pub & Grill*, Lettie had opened the floodgates, going as far as crying into her pink paper napkin, silly as it was. Eating a burger (which she had not done in years), Lettie told Mimi about the return home from Helen, how James and Rachel and Hadley had not known their world would come crumbling down, at least the world James and Rachel believed was to be rightfully theirs. She told Mimi how they sat there for weeks, hiking side by side with James and Rachel, she already knowing James's fate, her sister Rachel rambling on, giddily, about finally making it, reaching their goals or whatever, and her thinking, if only it were that simple.

And Mimi, disbelieving, said, "You didn't tell them right then? When you knew Michael had gotten the job?"

Lettie shook her head for a good few seconds. "No," she said. "We couldn't. We had three weeks left. Looking back, sure, we should have done it right then and there. Michael should have sat him down, put it on the table. Let the pieces fall where they fell. But it was a hurricane. We were thrown in the air. We didn't know what to do."

"Oh honey," says Mimi. "Your husband should have said 'Thanks but no thanks.'"

Of course, Mimi was right. If it were today, that's what would have happened. Lettie would have made it happen. But then, well, no. That was more out of her control than in her control. Michael had become a sort of mini James. James had created a monster. James had made him him. But Michael, it would not have been fair, telling him what he had to do. He had earned it in his way. She would never have forgiven herself, telling him what he could or could not do in that respect. That world was his world. He had earned it. He had put in the hours, not her. He had done what it took to succeed in that world, and while maybe she supported him along the way, it wasn't her sacrificing her days, giving up the daylight hours so she, so Aaron, could live their lives as they saw fit.

Lettie said, "Flying home from Helen, on that plane, all together, all that tension. Jesus. If that plane would have crashed right then and there, there probably would have been more survivors than there were after our little family reunion." She was quiet for a second, pensive. Finally she said, "Everyone's here, but everyone died back then too, you know?"

Mimi, softly: "Don't say that, honey. You don't mean that."

"It's true. I know that sounds horrible, but it's true." Lettie wanted to get up, move to another chair, one without a rip in the red backing. But she stayed still, took the pain digging into her back. *Suffer*, she thought. You've earned it.

She said, "You know those games, where you drop a metal ball into the top and watch it bounce around, left, right, left, fall into a slot?"

Mimi said, "A tilting maze?"

"No," says Lettie. "Like that, but vertical. Behind plastic. And you don't have any control. You just drop the ball in and watch it bounce around until it ends up in a slot?"

"Yes," says Mimi. She has seen such a thing.

Lettie says, "That's what my life has been. That's what it feels like."

Mimi takes Lettie's hands in hers, says, "Let's stay at Mammoth, sweetie. You and me. We'll share a room. We'll talk."

It is late, and the bus, they know, will be heading back to their hotel soon. Lettie does not hesitate, because Lettie, the old Lettie, would. But she says, "What if we can't get a room?"

And Mimi the confident says, "We'll get a room." She raises a finger, tells Lettie she'll be right back.

And it's set. Everything falls into place as everything should always fall into place. Mimi makes a phone call, twin beds, ready when they get there.

"Done," she says. "Now we can talk in peace and not worry about catching a damn bus." She looks at her watch. "Just remind me to call mom and dad or else they'll be worried about me."

Lettie says, "You need to enjoy your time here, Mimi. You don't need to do this."

Mimi says, "I love Roz and Mel. But give me them and Yellowstone or a whimpering woman and her problems and Yellowstone, and I'm going with whimpering woman seven days a week."

They share a smile, warm, like they've always been meant to be here, the two of them, sitting under the stuffed heads of snow-white mountain goat, the antlers of dead elk. Lettie says, "Thank you, Mimi," which sounds sweet on her lips, gentle, like all her life she has been waiting to say her name at just that moment.

They leave enough food on their plates to feed a whole other person. Lettie leaves half her burger and all of her fries, except the three she has nibbled on over the past hour, dipping them in ketchup, biting pieces off each fry until Mimi tells her, *For the potato's sake, just get it over with*, which tickles her.

They smoked Mimi's cigarettes under the overhang where the cars drove up and drove away, unloading elderly guests who walked into the Mammoth Hot Springs Hotel rolling their suitcases behind them, wearing their safari outfits. One guest, an elderly Asian woman, pretended to cough, as if she were allergic to cloves or smoke, as if she were catching second hand cancer from ten yards away. They had laughed. Mimi called the Asian woman a drama queen, blew smoke at her as she walked off with her much older Caucasian husband, shaking her head like what's wrong with those two. The woman's contempt made Lettie feel good, made her feel like she was twenty again.

In the evening they drank two bottles of red wine. Mimi took a shower and then ran a bath for Lettie, pouring too much huckleberry bubble bath into the water, the two of them watching the bubbles overflow as Lettie sunk her drunk behind into the tub. Mimi hit shuffle on her pocket stereo and danced a little dance to Cat Stevens' "Lady D'Arbanville," the towel on her head unraveling with each step. When Mimi bent over and pecked Lettie, slowly, on the cheek, Lettie balked, but did not move away.

He has spent years as CEO and ex-officio on the company's board of directors, and he has served on the boards of other companies, where his contributions have been many and his impact profoundly felt. His name graces the financial sections of the Wall Street Journal and the Financial Times often, and myriad dot-com editorials have his signature and mark. When he resigns from boards, the press releases are always the same: "We thank

Michael Warren for investing his valuable time, talent, passion and wisdom to help make our company successful. Unfortunately (and each year, like Google and its defections, there is always an "unfortunately"), as MicroZoot enters more of our core offerings, Michael's effectiveness as a Board member will be significantly diminished, as he will need to recuse himself due to potential conflicts of interest." Because there will be, inevitably, not only *potential* conflicts of interest but real conflicts of interest, and assuredly sooner than not. Companies that grow at MicroZoot, Inc.'s pace cannot do so by organic growth alone. Companies like MicroZoot, Inc. acquire and divest and merge and expand yearly, and they do so at an astonishing rate, yet not surprisingly, because it is a pace that has been planned months and years in advance. It is what Michael Warren was meant to do. It is his calling; there is no doubt about this. Not an iota of uncertainty in any of the milestones he has met. But things are different now, much different for him and for Mrs. Warren, as his minions call her. Now he is Mr. Michael at home (what the Hispanic servants call him), and he is Mr. Warren in the halls of MicroZoot, Inc. And to Aaron, their son, he is *Father*, not *Dad or Pop*, as his father was to him. And to Lettie, his withering light, his one true partner on this great adventure he has had the privilege to maneuver, the one person who knows the good man he once was, he remains, simply, *Michael.*

The flight to Zurich leaves near midnight, and he will be driven to Davos for his first trip to the World Economic Forum. He does not have a corporate jet to zip him across the Atlantic, and likely he never will. This lack of the jet is not due to a lack of capital but rather a proactive and deliberate inaction, a non-move, really. Too many CEOs pummeled in recent times by the votes of shareholders, the outrage of politicians accused of similar extravagance. The rage of a public at the disposal of every whim and fancy, every breaking news story any half-wit reporter is lucky to stumble upon screaming bloody murder about corporate malfeasance, every underground blog post. The whistleblowers, if they can be called that, battered and bruised but heroic in their *60 Minutes* and *20/20* profiles. This year, he will be a junior member at the *WEF*, but he will meet with titans of various industries, and he will be photographed with presidents and one particularly attractive queen. In the halls and in small rooms he will chat with colleagues, and while he will seek to network, others will seek him out as well. At the end of it all, he will drive the slippery Audi course for fun, wheels spinning out of control, and he will feel exhilaration, not only because of the freedom he feels on the ice but because he has made it, finally, to this playground of the rich, the famous, but most especially the powerful, whose company, somehow, have become his blood, the air he cannot help but breathe.

Luz, his assistant, knocks lightly on his door, says his wife, Lettie, is on the phone. Luz is from La Rinconada, a city in Spain he has never heard of, but which Luz has spoken of often, more than once over cocktails on flights around the world, and once in a hotel lobby in Pune, India. They have never become lovers, but the thought has crossed her mind, and often, his. They have never consummated, and they never will. Proximity, Michael knows, is hubris. Their intimacy are the liberties Luz takes—referring to his wife by her first name, too-long vacations, sitting on the corners of his desk when they chat on a personal level, her about her aging parents moving to Las Alpujarras, him answering relatively personal questions about his wife, her family, even Harvey, which Luz seems to have taken an interest in, and his disappointments with Aaron, his son, who wanders aimlessly, talks of art, of music, lost in his own irresponsible fantasy.

"Gracias," says Michael, who waits until Luz closes the door on her way out. Michael of course knowing his fondness for Luz comes from this lightness, this keen affection, which has always pervaded his wife's family, courtesy of stumbling bumbling Harvey, and his love for everything Castilian.

He says, "Hello?" and Lettie's voice says, "Hello."

This was five months ago. This was when she first started talking about trips away, alone, to think. Not about them, because no, they would never separate, but about her, about letting go, finding herself so she could zero back in on them, their family. Now it is déjà vu all over again. Luz walking in, telling him Lettie is on the phone again, walking out, closing the door behind her. It is as if nothing has happened, nothing has changed.

She says, "I'm having a good time. It's breathtaking out here."

"That's fantastic," he says, and he means it, because he loves her. He knows the importance of decompressing, of taking a leave of absence, which he encourages at his own company, which he has done himself earlier in his career. He says, "Pictures?"

"Lots. I'll e-mail some when I can."

"Great," he says. "Any word from Aaron?"

"A quick Hi yesterday, but that's it." Lettie, silent. *Thinking.* "I think he's found himself a little friend."

"Tell him to call me next time you speak to him. He doesn't return my calls."

"Will do," she says. There is a pause on the line. Finally she says, "I love you, Michael."

And without hesitation, because with Michael there never is any hesitation, Michael says, "I Love you too, babe," and hangs up the phone, his hand remaining on the receiver for some time.

In the beginning, he worked late and she called often. Now he works late and she calls rarely, if he has not found time during his day to say hi, or if she needs him to pick up dinner on the way home. He knows he should feel guilt, but there are too many things he must think of, too much chaos in his daily life with work. Too many other lives to consider. Later, when Luz comes in with his lunch, he will ask her to send flowers to the hotel where Lettie is hiding out, catching her breath. And when he catches her staring at him, when it's clear something's on her mind once more, when she ventures to ask yet another question about his wife's family, about the past, he will think about replacing her, finding a temp, someone who maybe he won't relate to but who will not, for whatever reason, make him feel uncomfortable.

At the end of the day, when everyone has gone but him, an e-mail arrives from Lettie, Subject Line: *Pics*, a paperclip of attachments. He has been staring out of his corner office window, at planes flying across the night sky, blinking their lights like fireflies, taking people away from this place, the red sea of brake lights down on the streets below blurring with the yellow of turn signals, the blurred glow of endless, winding traffic. He clicks the paperclip, but nothing happens. No pictures, only a gray screen, a message telling him there is no preview. He tries again. Nothing. He e-mails Lettie back quickly, tells her he can't open her pictures. Now he wants to see her. A few minutes after he clicks "send," he is surprised to see he has another e-mail, and this time he clicks the files and he is able to see.

Her face is older, but she is as beautiful as she has ever been, her tiny body toned, her arms and legs thin as noodles but firm, like a runner's. The long black hair he fell in love with, which he can still smell now, is streaked with gray; the sun shines on the child's braid dangling at her cheek—an adornment she has never worn in all the years they've been together. The landscapes around her, taupe fields stretching away, wide bodies of water, alabaster mountains, show her alone, but not meek, as they could, taken at another angle. And the last picture, *gardiner.jpg*, his Lettie smiling lightheartedly, happy as he has ever seen her, sporting a parka he has forgotten about, a parka, he knows, is heavy with memories.

He had been a coward that year, and felt like one for long afterwards. Lettie had worn the parka like skin, shedding it only to sleep, to bathe. They bought the parka the weekend before Georgia, after church on Sunday, when they'd gone shopping at the mall to gear up for a month down south. That she was wearing the parka now, years later, with no one to see, was a peek into . . . what? He couldn't be sure. But he had his hypotheses, which came to him as bullets (a trick Lettie taught him) on a blackening tenth-story window, all lit up like holiday lights in outer space:

- She missed them, everyone
- She missed him, though not very likely, given the circumstances
- She missed it—and it, of course, was being part of a family that had, at one point in time, indeed been a family

He thought, *The parka?* Is that all that remains? Is that all that is left? Is that what Lettie has to remember the family that they, in some way, destroyed? That they, in their avarice, ravaged?

The phone call from Mr. Oggy, from Graham, the CEO, as they were packing, was unexpected. Sure, they socialized at church, and sure, there was contact in meetings they had in those days, when senior staff were actually all located in the same building, on the same floor. But calling him at home? Something could not be right. And Lettie, standing right there, having answered the phone, nearly tripping over the ottoman to whisper who was calling (as if Mr. Oggy could hear even a single whispered word). Probably looking for James, he had said. But no, he was not. He was looking for him, for Michael. Had been for months, he had said. And he had—but neither of them had known it. Neither of them had thought, Yes, Michael Warren, SVP, he can make the leap. He can run the show. And even when Michael said, "But what about James?," Mr. Oggy had said, "James is a good sales guy. He is the clear choice. But he's not my President. He's not my COO. You are."

And that was that. The catalyst for everything that ever was. He's not my President. He's not my COO. *You are*. That was the beginning of the end. That was the spear through all their hearts. But you didn't know it then. He didn't know it then. Now, years later, he did know it. And she knew it. But it was done. And neither of them could undo any of it. Even talking about it had become, what? Impossible?

Who could have known?

- That James would resign "*effective immediately*"?
- That Rachel could not forgive them, try as she might?
- That Hadley would revolt a few years later, run off like her father after the divorce, but not to some feel-sorry-for-yourself town in Mexico, like he had, but instead to Europe, first to Paris and Cascais, then on to god knows where further east, riding their splendid little trains, chasing the next morning? Vanishing—not metaphorically, because that would be acceptable, but literally?

Away they went, James and Rachel and Hadley, as far as they could get from one another. And after Harvey's passing, after they'd buried Cliff (who had passed not a week later from a clot), poor Julianne was left abandoned to a house that had not so long ago brimmed with life. Left alone in a house that was no longer a home. Poor, poor Jules, he thought. What had she ever done to deserve such an end?

Not your fault, Lettie had said. And he knew, in his heart, that she was right. But that didn't make it go away. He could not not relive it every so often, because climb as he might, he was not a robot. He was not unfeeling. His feelings were many. His thoughts, they could be plagued at any time of any day. There was guilt, sure. Remorse, absolutely. These feelings could strike during board meetings, while listening to quarterly reports, out on the putting green. They could be merciless, these thoughts. Simply merciless.

The impact on them, on him and Lettie and Aaron, was no less weighty than the impact on anyone else. It was like a pendulum, swinging back and forth, a wrecking ball of actions and consequences. One *Yes* had turned into a hundred *No*s. And now, maybe it was age, maybe it was that he was lonely. Maybe it was a lot of things hidden in places in his head he had never dared venture. He wasn't sure. Whatever it was, weighed on him like, well, *weight*. Heavy, heavy *weight*. In the silence, in the emptiness of the office once his employees had gone home and the lights were turned off and all he could hear was the buzz of the lamp on his desk, all he could think of was Go! Before you drown in self-pity, just Go! *GO*! And so he went.

The flight left at nine. He was in Atlanta before midnight. He called Lettie, left a message on her voice-mail. Jumping on a flight, he'd said. Call you tomorrow. There had been a pause, but he'd hung up. He could explain later.

He picked up his rental (a Prius), and started driving north. He had not planned this—this impulsive move, this quick jaunt south, nor did the reasons why come in any concrete way. To see Julianne, was all. To make sure she was okay. To see how things had turned out for her, this wonderful woman, whose family had melted away, whose life was full of pain, overwrought with loss. All of it, of course, potentially his fault.

He slept in the car in a parking lot. He woke up at three, and then again at four and five. At six, he rolled back onto the highway, yawning, searching for coffee. He took off his tie, which he had forgotten to do in his mad rush to get on the road. He ate country fried steak and eggs at a Huddle House, asked for a large coffee to go. When he arrived at the gate at the bottom of the hill, another old man had taken the white-haired old man's place. It was early, not yet eight, but he knew Julianne would already be awake, drinking her coffee, cleaning up. Maybe she would be happy to see him. Maybe she would look much older, worn out, tired, ready to fly on up, move in with them.

"Not here," the old man said. "The cabin you're talking about, that's Frank and Imogene Cutter."

"No," he says. "I mean the house around the bend. The one that overlooks the tops of the houses down here." He points towards the hill.

The old man rubs his neck, scratches his head under his cap. He takes no pleasure in disappointing anyone. He says, "I know which house you mean, sir. Mr. and Mrs. Lipscomb's old place. It's now the Cutters'."

He sits in the car. He had not planned on this. He thanks the old man. When the old man says he can drive in, make a U-turn, head on back out, Michael says no, thanks him, backs his car out the way he came, heads back into town.

It is when he is drinking beer and eating his Jack Daniel's wings that he sees her, walking across the street, hand in hand with an older gentleman in a John Deere cap, waving at the pickup that has stopped for them, its engine revving behind red and yellow flames, this little old lady stopping this big behemoth of metal and parts, natural as can be, leading the way.

When Lettie says, "I think I'll go solo today," Mimi understands. She tells her to ring her later if she wants, that she and "the parents" are going to go check out the Canyon Talk and then do the Lupine Loop Walk. She says there's a Canyon Evening Program starting at nine-thirty, if she wants to join them just leave word at the front desk—she'll call around seven to check. Lettie tells her, we'll see.

It is early morning, and Lettie is planning her day, perusing maps, sipping tea, reading histories. She studies slides of wolves—at play, in Alpha packs, as pups, gnawing sun-bleached bones pressed down under their paws. These wolves, perhaps their fathers and grandfathers, have been reintroduced to Yellowstone after having been systematically hunted here and elsewhere for many years, threatened to near-extinction. These wolves, according to the literature, are rebalancing a damaged ecosystem. Wolves whose scraps, they've come to realize, feed others.

She flips through pictures of dying trout—Arctic grayling, westlope, yellowstone, brook, brown, lake, rainbow, all held in the pink-skin hands of bodiless men, mouths open, eyes glazed, unmoving, staying still for the camera even though, she knows, they are, at the very moment the picture is being taken, suffocating to death.

In the end, the pictures are enough. She stays close to the hotel. She has a young boy around Aaron's age, with the same patchy facial hair Aaron tends to wear, pack her a lunch: turkey sandwich, fruit, snack, bottled water. She puts her lunch into her backpack, careful not to ruffle the pages of the notebook inside. It is long overdue; she needs to return to writing, to completing that novel, to finishing what she has started so many times, to just know she can do it, have the fortitude, end what began so very long ago. Persistence is all that matters at this point.

She walks out into the summer air, heads through the parking lot and into another, which she learns is the lot where employees park their cars, because it is also where they live. The dormitories just across the way, it turns out, are employee housing. She apologizes to a young girl in a chef's hat, black and white-checkered pants, a white coat, for having invaded, for having intruded into their separate space, the area where, she knows, they are free from labor. "Totally cool," the girl says. Lettie, feeling as if she has found a friend, asks the girl for a light. She lights the broken clove cigarette she has kept from her night with Mimi, blows it out into the mountain air. Thinks about what transpired that evening.

"I love the smell of cloves," the girl chef says. "I used to smoke Djarum Blacks." She scratches her cigarette along the ground, puts the filter into her pocket, lights another. She says, "Most people don't walk back there. It's just staff. But if you go that way, you'll hit the shop. Keep along the road and it'll take you to Fishing Bridge." She is pointing to her left, down a road Lettie has driven only yesterday.

The girl finishes her cigarette, pinches the end between her fingers, which looks painful to Lettie. "I've gotta get going," the girl chef says. Lettie looks at her nametag: Amanda. From Oregon. Lettie says, "Thanks for the light, Amanda." And Amanda says, "I'm working till close. Tell your waiter you're a friend of mine. I'll hook you up with some food."

Lettie says, "Cool," and smiles, but more at having said the word *cool* than at Amanda's promised generosity. "Cool," says Amanda. Amanda walks off, waves bye, says see you later or something that sounds like see you later.

Lettie too walks off, turning every so often, trying to watch Amanda in her little uniform as she walks past the cute little post office, up some stairs off to the side of the hotel. The back entrance to the restaurant, probably.

She listens to the pines sway in the breeze, takes in the fresh air, feeling good, feeling like this place, these mountains, this landscape, is exactly what the doctor ordered. The crunch of dry twigs underfoot, the slow pace of bison along the tree line, the blue sky overhead, they are invigorating to her, and she is cognizant now of her breathing, the pinch in her right knee, that perhaps she has not slept as soundly as she would have hoped. But tonight? Tonight, she feels, may yet hold promise.

By the water, Lettie opens a blanket. She lays her notebook to one side, open to a blank page, takes a sip of the water the young man has packed for her. Some of it dribbles down her chin, and she wipes at it with the back of her hand. At first, she does not know what to write, and so she writes what she sees. She writes colors first, blue and bottle green, and russet and beige, letting the words form swaths of color palettes in her mind, letting the pen run smoothly along the paper. She writes in a sort of stream of consciousness, about mountains and water and then about Amanda, whose life she imagines is filled with adventures the likes of which she will never know. And she writes about the bald eagle with its odd white head, landing in a pine tree, panning the land from its waxy perch. When she is done writing what she sees, she writes what she remembers. At first she remembers the characters in her story, changing their names in her head to protect the innocent, whom she knows will never read her final product, this work of fiction that is ever so real.

Michael is Alejandro, and Sammy is Pilar. Harvey is Don Osvaldo el escritor, and Julianne, her mother, is Frida, like the artist, or maybe Isabel; she will decide later, on a second pass, a first revision. Her story will be set in a Castilian town but not Granada, because that is Harvey's life. She cannot steal the memories of a man who had already lost them. Yes, she thinks. I will make my world in Spain, away from here. Keep it at a distance, in another place, another time. Maybe she will even use Luz's background, if she can remember Luz's background. Maybe she can ask Luz, Michael's Luz, for assistance.

And as she thinks of her novel's setting and the characters, as the images and words come to her from Spanish lessons taken years ago, from week-long excursions through Córdoba and Toledo, Segovia and San Sebastián, she picks her settings and lays out her plot, and still there is the point of view to consider, which will be the most difficult decision she will have to make other than deciphering the novel's voice. It's always the voice that gives her trouble.

It is not yet dinnertime when she walks back into the hotel. Some of the hotel staff greet her, ask if she hasn't enjoyed her day today, such a pleasant day and all. She does not check with the front desk for Mimi's message, because it is too early, but mostly because she does not know how to think of what has happened yet, this thing at Mammoth between them. It is not guilt she feels, because it was not wrong. It was not sex. That is not what it was about, though she did enjoy it, though there was the physical touching, the feeling, as if it could be sex. And while it would be easy to simply avoid Mimi until their departure, hers and Roz's and Melinda's, she does not feel that such a discourtesy would be necessary, given everything. Given that Mimi has shown her affection, even as she exposed her. Given that Mimi did not push, even as, in some intangible way, she had pulled. But there will be no more of that, of Mimi's breath on the lobes of her ears, of *her* lips in places she would have never dreamed they would be. A one-time thing, she would tell Mimi. A slip from reality. And she would tell her, warmly, I'm glad I shared it with you, pretty girl. I am.

In the evening, she eats dinner alone, in her room, sipping tea and eating all of her gemelli, pulling out the pieces of chicken that seem inedible, though she can't put her finger on just why. She rests the empty plates outside of her door, sits at her desk, turns on the lamp. She unplugs the telephone, lays it on the floor, on top of the leather folder that lists everything there is to know about the park, the services available, what to do in an emergency, who to ring for what. In all the hotels in all the countries she has been, she has never seen the colors she sees here, in the bedspreads and the seat cushions, desecrating the fabric that has become curtains. A pinkish-tamarind of flowers and gold from floor to ceiling, down to the carpet, which is a few years too worn at best. She brings her pen to life, a quick scribble on a corner of the page, and the ink begins to flow. At first it is quiet. And then she hears a whisper, and it is Pilar chastising Carlos for leaving the courtyard door ajar, a lispy bite in her tone. And then Carlos now, clear in her mind's eye, dressed in a bright dinner suit much too profligate for the occasion, glass of vino tinto in hand, proselytizing: "The air, my dear Pilar, is for us to breathe in; it is not, amor mio, the devil's breath you make it to be."

But that, of course, is a false start. It is the writing that first comes, that will stay there, on that first page, forever in limbo, never to be written. Dialogue that will pass no knowledge, that will provide no insight into any character, that will do nothing for the plot—which itself, of course, will also never be written. A beginning too artificial, too reaching; an introduction to a world that has never existed, that never will, not by her pen anyway. And so she begins anew, listening, waiting for her characters to speak, to act, for an event to happen that will set her story off down its wonderful path, and hopefully without an arc too visible, an ending too contrived, writing too subjective, too unoriginal, too verbose. And soon it comes, the conversation she has been waiting for.

The losses are too great, Edvard is saying. "They are too great." An obvious theme, she knows. But write what comes, she tells herself. The time for editing is not now. The time for editing is later.

Lettie, realizing that sometimes characters really do have their own minds, really do lead their authors to places they maybe would not have gone if they had plotted and outlined and brought too much construction and planning, understands that her characters will not be Spanish characters with Spanish names but Nordic characters with Nordic names, and their playground will be Helen, again, which she had not expected. The story she needs to tell needs to be one closer to home, one more set in fact than whimsy. That she knows nothing of the Norse is inconsequential; her characters will be Americans with Nordic heritage; this is how she will have the authorial autonomy she will need to write what needs writing.

In her room, over the lightly stained wainscoting, she stares at the wall, then up at a black and white photograph of a ship. She imagines all of the rooms in the hotel have this picture, or ones similar to it, black and white images of the past, historical decor employed by Yellowstone's interior designers, instantly setting a scene and mood, and doing so with the utmost economy. She lets her eyes wander to a spot on the wall, a blank spot that allows her to un-focus to refocus. Edvard is Harvey, and Edvard is talking to Odin, his deceased son, who is David, Harvey's dead child. Lettie pulls names from a book someone has left in the lobby, a book about Vikings which she will, perhaps by accident (perhaps not), slip into her luggage.

But Lettie does not eavesdrop on their conversation. It is too personal, too fraught with grief. What she does pull from their talk is that David has not died in a car accident but from a drug overdose, drugs called Soma and Diazepam, overloaded in his system until he slept and never woke. It is Odin's name Edvard mistakenly calls Skjöldr. Lettie thinks, maybe Skjöldr is too much, too distracting a name. But the writing is going well, she is getting everything down that needs to be got down, and so Skjöldr it is. To get it all out of the way so she can just write and not worry, she writes down the names of everyone in her story, all at once, glancing from the book of Vikings to her list:

> Edvard is Harvey
> Odin is David, a minor character, referred to in passing
> Sigfinn is Michael
> Sigurdis is Me
> Lifdis is Mom
> Skjöldr is James
> Vigdis is Sammy
> Kari is Rachel

Soon everyone is accounted for except the children, who she will not include this go around, it's too dramatic a work, too close to reality, too near the *tragedy* of real lives lived. It is a story of adults that children need not be a part of, not living ones, anyway. Aaron does not need to be here, and Hadley does not need to be here. She will save them for a future story, one with moments of happiness, one where they live happily ever after. One where, though she is not superstitious, nothing she writes can ever influence the good or bad in their actual, real-life lives.

When Sigfinn meets Skjöldr on a bluff overlooking the mountains near Helen, when he is about to tell Skjöldr that life works in mysterious ways, and that as he, as Skjöldr has helped him rise in the corporate world, so will he help Skjöldr rise, there is a knock at the door and Lettie leaves her newfound world to answer it, knowing it will be Mimi come back. And yet, instead of shunning her in the middle of progress, as she would normally shun anyone when going full throttle on work never fulfilled, she says, "Come on in, Mims. I need an audience." And so in Mimi walks.

"We missed you today," Mimi is saying. "I hope—"

"Shh," says Lettie, smiling. "I'm making progress. And I need you."

Mimi, having lost no steps, still in lust with a soul meant to be hers in another time, another life, sits on the edge of the ruffled bedspread, leans back on her arms, says, "Go."

Sigfinn and Skjöldr, cut from the same cloth but opposite ends, drew their families away from within once the balance of power at work was destroyed.

Too much.

Sigfinn and Skjöldr worked at the same company, but their history was a history that doomed their futures from the start.

Better.

"Hmm," says Lettie. "Maybe start with someone else's story then. How about: *Edvard has woken here now, on this bed, and on this particular day, many times.*

Mimi says, "Keep going."

Julianne has aged more than Michael had pictured. Her shoulders have rounded in on themselves, her legs have bent, and the crooks in her neck, her back, have turned her face downward. But Michael knows it's Julianne, can tell by the wave of the hand, the braided ponytail she has never worn but that is, somehow, more Julianne than any of her previous hairstyles. Removed from their significant others, he thinks, the women in his life are freed through the style of their hair. And the clothing, head to toe in flowing dresses, flip flops shuffling along the road with haste, Julianne displaying the Julianne shuffle that has never gone away.

He asks for the check, drops his Amex. As usual, he has forgotten to pull out cash, which he rarely carries these days. When the waitress informs him they do not accept Amex, he rifles through his sports coat, finds his billfold, gives her a Visa. He pays, leaves a generous tip, which she cannot thank him enough for. Come back and see us, she is saying, but he is gone, walking across the street as if running from an invisible tidal wave.

From the window he can see her.

"I'm sorry," Julianne is saying, shaking her head, pulling her arms one at a time from her sweater. "I had to wait for Mr. Carter, and you know how he is. Takes his sweet old time, that one." Her voice a low hum, whispers through an open window.

The young woman is smiling, nodding her head. She says, "Mrs. Lipscomb, it's okay. Really."

But Julianne is protesting, shaking her head no, no. "I am not above the rules," she is saying. "I am not above the rules."

And the young woman, obliging: "Well, okay then, Mrs. Lipscomb. Next time I'll dock you for every minute you're late."

"Yes, ma'am," Julianne is saying. "Won't happen again. I promise."

A game they play, Michael can see. No real trouble at all.

The young woman leaves Julianne to her table, where she is writing prices on colored labels of pink and blue, ornate numbers and dollar signs, tying little strings around gimcracks, the handles of teapots and coffee mugs. He watches her from the window, wondering what has happened to her life, what the steps are when everyone goes away, when your brood disappears, when you're left to yourself and perhaps not at your prime.

When she feels a breeze and looks back, there is no one there; he is hiding, but even he is baffled why. She swears she had felt a breath. She closes the window, returns to her work, saying hello to customers as they ogle and touch what they shouldn't, as children run freely from their parents' hands, heightening their parents' nerves as they zigzag the maze of china and crystal, of things almost always on the verge of shattering, of memories yet to be made with the doodads all around them that as of yet have no meaning.

For hours he sits across the street, waiting, drinking wine, sitting now in his *Bavaria* crest T-shirt, his tie and dress shirt tossed in the bathroom trash bin. When he sees her coming out of the store, he drops a couple of twenties, having pulled out all he can from an ATM, walks out once she has passed him on the street, him with his back turned to her, watching her in the reflection of a Blimpie sandwich shop, strolling along, half the height he remembers her. Friendly as always, Julianne waves hello to half the people she meets, says "Hey, Dear," to the other half, as if she's known them all their lives. She walks along Main Street past the shops, past Alpenrosen Strasse, past the Sautee Resorts and past the Best Western and Unicoi Outfitters, right out of town.

He gives Julianne more distance, not wanting her to see him, but when she turns a corner and he runs to catch up, to not lose her, there she is, sitting on a chiseled boulder on the side of the road at the end of a long driveway, staring at him.

"If you're going to follow an old woman in Helen," she says, "you may not want to wear a suit. No one wears suits in Helen. You stuck out the moment you stepped out of your car this morning."

As he knew he would. But it had slipped his mind. Or it had never actually entered it, because he had never thought through exactly what he was doing until it was too late.

Julianne said so and so told Mrs. Coggeshall, and she told Miss Dahlia, and Miss Dahlia told Rosemary, etc. etc., on down the line, watching him move about town until he was standing at her window at work, peeking in like he was some sort of peeping tom or something. She said, "A few more glasses of wine and they'd of thought you were Cliff, bless his soul."

Julianne raises her arms, says, "I live up there now," leaning her head back towards the one-lane dirt road over her shoulder. "Come on. Help me up or we'll be here till tomorrow."

Her home is no longer a home but a guest house at the back of someone else's cabin. That he was not aware of this, that no one has ever told him, bothers him. When she sees his eyes touching everything, invading what has been private for so long, she says, "It's fine, Michael. It's where I sleep. That's all."

But even so, he thinks. Even so.

"How long have you been here? What happened to the cabin?"

"I'll tell you, but you can't tell Lettie."

"She doesn't know either?" There is a pause. There is sadness in his eyes. There is a wrinkle in his forehead. "*Jules*," he says.

"You tell Lettie and I'm done. *Poof*, Michael."

"Okay," he says. "No poof, Jules. Please."

"I Lost it," she says. "Few months after Harvey passed, bank took it back. Said the money dried up."

"Why didn't you say anything?"

"Because you would have *fixed* it." She says "fixed" as if it is a four-letter word.

"Maybe not."

"Maybe so."

"Jules. That was your dream cabin. Letting it go was not necessary."

"Sometimes letting go is the only thing that *is* necessary, Michael."

Michael could not take his eyes off her. "I thought Harvey had enough stored away?"

"That makes two of us. Apparently not. Or he did but then he didn't. Seems he left all of it to his son. Left me with a readjusting something or other." A smile appears on Julianne's face, as if something is cute, as if she is remembering something long forgotten. She says, "Now how can anyone live with themselves like that? Charging double from one month to the next? That's not readjusting anything. In my book, that's called stealing." She looked away, off out the window, off into her thoughts. "Bankers," she says.

Julianne sticks her head into what looks to be an antique refrigerator. She pulls out a pitcher of Arnold Palmer, two glasses from beside the sink. "The worst of it is he left it all to one child. Left it to his son. His daughter? She got bupkis."

"What about the books? Royalties? All that?"

"Ha," she says. "He was Harvey Lipscomb, Michael. Not John Grisham."

Julianne takes a sip of her drink, puts her glass down too quickly onto the table. She says, "So spill it. Why the gypsum you down here? Where's Lettie? Where's my grandson?"

"Lettie is in Wyoming," he says. "In Yellowstone. I don't know where Aaron is." He takes a sip of his own drink, not wanting to discuss them but wanting, instead, to return to the cabin issue. "We can get that cabin back," he says. "I'd like to get that cabin back for you, Jules."

But Jules says, "Michael. Listen to me. I don't want it back, understand? I don't."

Michael says, "*Jules*," but Julianne says, "What do you mean, you don't know where Aaron is?"

And when she says that, it sounds like an accusation of some sort, which it is. And he realizes, for the first time in a long time, that yes, there *is* something wrong with that, with not knowing where his son is, but more importantly, not caring enough to find out. Or caring but not knowing how to fix it, the one thing he's never been able to fix.

"I don't know, Jules," he says. "He doesn't talk to me like he talks to Lettie. I don't think he likes me very much." He finishes his Arnold Palmer, looks at the postcards taped to the refrigerator. Tahitian blues, Bulgarian concrete. Statues. The emerald green of a Thai jungle over which he is sure he has flown.

Julianne says, "They're from Hadley. My little traveling girl."

Michael remembers her, Hadley, but as a child, not as the continent-hopping twenty-something she has become, this child, like his but worse, who is the ghost offspring of his previous boss, his wife's estranged sister. His ex brother-in-law. The ultimate end user of the misery of which he is responsible for creating. He says, "Do you have any pictures of her? Of Hadley?"

No, she says. "I don't ever talk to her. They're addressed to the cabin, but Zippy, that's Eugene's nephew's name, he took over when they put Eugene in that home, *Century Village* or whatever down in Boca Raton. Zippy knows me. I've known him since he was yay high. He brings them over to me at my job. Been coming now for, gosh, maybe three years. She's wandering the earth, that little girl."

"Hadley," he says, remembering the little girl she was, running around, chasing after Aaron. He says, "You know, I haven't seen her since . . ." but he does not finish his thought, because this trip is about the future, and not about the past.

Julianne says, "I know, dear." She puts her icy hand onto the back of his, leaves it there. She says, "We'll have dinner,

Michael. You and I. Maybe let's call Lettie and Aaron. What do you say?"

"Sure," he says. "I'd like that."

They spent all night running scenarios in their heads, or Lettie running them in her head and then writing them down, reading them to Mimi, her first-rate critic, their feet kicked up in the air behind them, lying on their stomachs on the bed and on the floor, moving to the desk, sitting on windowsills, staring at the lights stretching along the black waters of the lake, listening to the squishy sound of the room service kids walking along the giving hallway carpets, picking up trays and dropping them off. And then they listened to the silence afterwards, for hours and hours, until early morning, when the sun rose and the new day began.

Mimi says, "Okay, sugar pie, Miss Mimi needs sleepy." She gets up, walks in her socks, carries her shoes out of the room. It is as if they are decades-long friends, as if their little Mammoth affair was only a dream they'd shared, a movie they'd watched, curled under the sheets like teenagers. She says, "Fancy a hike later?"

"Definitely," says Lettie. "And Mimi?"

"Yes?"

"Thank you."

Lying in bed, Lettie stares at the beginning of her manuscript, sitting on the wooden desk by the window, the first rays of sunlight cutting an edge of white along the spine of her notebook. Her eyes are red, tired from breaking the night as she might have broken the night during her college days, cramming for midterms. But like a new child born to the earth, the manuscript is already filled with love, and a family, her family, is living everywhere inside it. They are new to her, and they are happy, and they are troubled, and they are, in a way, strangers, but they are real, and they are hers, warts and all. They are filled with blemishes and arguments, and they are troubled by maladies and illness, and they are fragile and more than anything, they are mortal. They are human. They are imperfect, and yet, in so many ways, they are as perfect as a family can ever be.

Harvey is there, losing his mind because he is losing his memory. And mother is there, losing her husband (and not for the first time), dealing with certain horrendous accusations from the trash (or not trash, because neither she nor her mother would ever vocalize such a thing about anyone) about Harvey, losing hope that the love she shares with her children, whom she treasures more than anything, is not something they feel towards each other and probably never will. And now Vigdis is not Sammy but Sammy is Sammy, and Kari is not Rachel because Rachel is Rachel. And everyone is themselves, because this is the only way she can tell this story. And so, tired but unable to sleep, she sits back up, calls for coffee, and once again she is back at it, telling the story of her family, but this time using their names, this time being honest, letting it all out, and then, once the coffee arrives and there are no witnesses, letting the tears stain the ink but never stopping until, at last, the pain has been shed and been written, forever, down. And maybe this time for the world to see.

Finally, this novel she has wanted to write for so long, these interweaving stories that also contain her story, that have a beginning, a middle, and an end, though maybe not in that order, are coming to life. She sees it clearly now. The stories she has written in the past, that have failed, that have been rejected countless times for reasons only the rejecters know, that have never rung true even to her, they have all been practice. Years and years of practice. This she now knows. This she understands. Like a child encountering some new truth for the first time, she says, aloud, Now write, Lettie! Write! Write! *Write*!

And so she writes. She writes until she can no longer keep her eyes open, until even touching the pen to paper becomes too much. She writes about Harvey first. Why *Harvey*? she asks herself. But no, she mumbles. Don't worry about the why. Just write. Don't ask questions, just put it down. Don't lose a word. It's all important, even if it isn't.

Harvey, dead man now, complicated man, selfish, sure, but who isn't? Harvey Lipscomb, Mr. Professor, two kids who didn't necessarily care for him, one child, David, OD'd years and years ago, buried in a small grave, never visited by Harvey, couldn't if he wanted to, until he himself passed, and lo and behold, look whose plot is next door to Harv's plot. Bitter ex-wife, angry at him for the kids, not her, because she can't stand Harvey, or couldn't, once he'd left, and probably for years before that. Two sides of a very different man—Harvey with us, nice guy Harv, thoughtful Harv, considerate Harv, a man going the way of the dinosaur. And ex-hubby Harv, deadbeat dad Harv, self-absorbed, megalomaniac, I-am-the-most-underappreciated-scholar-of-my-time, Professor Harvey Lipscomb, PhD, Harv. All the same Harv. Dichotomous Harv. And at the end of it all, just Harvey Lipscomb, Harv. Imperfect human being, Harv.

And Mom. Julianne. Strong-woman-Mom. Mom I-will-fight-dragons-for-my-daughters Mom. Mom I-will-sacrifice-my-life-and-not-eat Mom, so-that-my-daughters-have-food-on-the-table-and-normal-childhoods Mom. Mom-who-will-take-the-pain-and-give-the-love. Mom-who-will-jump-in-front-of-a-truck-to-save-her-children-from-a-millisecond-of-pain Mom. Mom-the-matriarch Mom. Mom-the-glue-holding-everything-together Mom. Her Mom.

But her sisters, that is another thing. They are characters that will give her trouble. They are characters that she will have to maneuver, because like sparks near gas, how she writes about them, everything can up and combust. The potential for an explosion is there. Sammy, the obvious stick of dynamite, but Rachel, how does she begin with her? Of course, this is all in the future, all speculation for now. But what if there is forgiveness? What if Rachel rings her up one day, says, Hey, sis, I was stupid. James was stupid, and if we could find the son of a bitch he'd tell you so. We should have been happy for you guys. We should have congratulated you guys. That whole not speaking to you for years, water under the bridge! But that wasn't going to happen. Couldn't happen. Not with James off in Mexico somewhere. Not with Hadley off wherever she was. Rachel's family had imploded, and her family had been the catalyst, fault or not. Their blindness had taken away everything they could see for themselves. Her family had destroyed Rachel's. Hadn't it? Or was even this too selfish a thought to think? That she, that *they*, had that much power?

As Rachel begins to speak, the Rachel who could call her and could sit down with her, the Rachel that can have a civil conversation in this world Lettie has created (is creating), here where such a thing is possible, Lettie closes her eyes, still holding the magic pen that has allowed her to grieve overnight and for the first few exhausting hours of daylight. It is a sleep that will extend through the day, past telephones ringing and doors knocking, past daylight, until she can sleep no more, until her body says, Hey, baby ducks, it's time to get up. It's time, Miss Lettie, to get back to work.

Though she does not want to stop writing, does not want to let her characters down by forcing them to sit around idling like carless engines, staring at walls, sitting in chairs, staring at each other because they've lost their tongue, their dialogue has not yet been written, Lettie finally opens her door, lets Mimi drag her out to have a late lunch. And all the while, as she picks at her field greens and strawberries, Lettie cannot help but ignore Mimi, for though she is sitting right there, smiling, it's her family she sees at the next table, gathered all together, smiling and happy, looking around patiently, waiting for her to bring them to life. It's Harvey and Mom and James and Rachel and Hadley, and it's Sammy and Cliff, poor Cliff, and it's she and Michael and Aaron. And it's so many other people walking around whose names she can't remember, whose faces are blurred and expressionless. Whose lives want so many things, but in particular, and above everything else, simply want one thing: *meaning*.

In Helen, in the morning, Michael is awoken by the clattering of pans and the smell of freshly brewed coffee. They slept in chairs overnight, he in one and Julianne in another, facing each other from across the room. In the daylight, he can see now that these are the same chairs that had been up in the cabin—Harvey's and Julianne's plush recliners that are no longer plush. He glances around, as if he could have missed it previously, but he's not surprised. There are no beds anywhere.

Julianne turns to see Michael wiping the sleep from his eyes. "Good morning," she says.

"Morning, Jules." Michael is looking around the room, at the boxes stacked high all over, everything never unpacked or recently repacked.

She says, "I hope the recliner didn't kill your back. It's easier for me with my knees."

"I slept fine," he says. "Coffee smells good."

"Help yourself," she says. "You can pour while it's brewing. It stops brewing when you pull the pot out." She pulls out a half gallon of milk, says, "All I got. I know you like that fancy creamer stuff."

"It's fine, Jules."

She smiles, watches Michael pour too much milk into his coffee cup. She says, "No one's called me Jules in so long I almost forgot my own name." She touches Michael's face. "Go on and wash up," she says. "I'll make us some breakfast right quick." Michael watches Julianne toss a man's shirt into a basket, look around (he assumes) for anything else she needs to hide.

"Let me take you out," he says.

"No way, Jose," she says. "I haven't cooked for anyone in a long time, Michael. I'm a mother with no children and no husband to cook for. I'm cooking."

Michael doesn't say, Or boyfriend. Instead he just smiles. "I'll wash up then," he says. He takes his coffee with him into the small bathroom hidden behind a stack of boxes labeled "bedrooms 1 & 2 & 3." He washes his hands with soap that takes too long to rinse off.

After breakfast he does not call Lettie to tell her that he is in Georgia. It is two time zones back where she is, and it's still only ten in the morning. Even later he will not call her, because while it made complete sense to hop on down to visit his mother-in-law six states away, it will not make as much sense to Lettie that her husband has done such a thing. He knows it will show impulse, and it will show need, and it will show other things Michael has not been for many years. But mostly it will show an inability to handle a situation, whatever situation he's experiencing, on his own—an unambiguous weakness—which is something he himself is unsure of how to administer.

When Lettie calls in the afternoon, she assumes he is at home, or at work with the door closed, because it is quiet, just the phone buzzing lightly, practically inaudibly. This happens when he's at work or in certain parts of the house, namely the wine cellar, a few of the hallways. For some inexplicable reason, certain parts of their home are impenetrable by the signals of cell phones. But when she hears the familiar voice and the familiar tone asking Michael what he wants to eat for lunch, the tone changes. Lettie says, "What's the heck is going on?"

Michael says, "What do you mean?"

For as long as they have been married, she thinks, my husband still believes responding to a question with a question is somehow clever. She says, "*Michael.*" It's all she has to say.

"I flew down," he says. "I don't know. I had a craving for that cheese bread."

"Cheese bread, huh? Did she ask you to fly down there or did you just go?"

"I came down, Let. Your mom was as surprised as you are."

"For what?"

"I don't know. Just to come. I don't have an answer."

"Hmm," she says. She says, "How is she?"

"Good."

"She's right there next to you, huh?"

"Yep."

"Okay," she says. "Call me later."

"Say a quick hello," he says. Michael passes the phone to Julianne, who can't make heads or tails of the odd contraption. Michael holds the phone up to her ear so the mouthpiece and earpiece are where they should be.

When Lettie apologizes for her odd and inconsiderate husband, Julianne says, "Dear, I'm glad he came. Really."

Lettie says, "I'll try to come down there after here. Maybe I'll just go straight there."

Julianne says, "Take your time," which means, clearly, that Michael has already filled her in on why Lettie is in Yellowstone, gone to Wyoming on her own, for as long as she has.

Lettie says, "I'll call you in a few days, Mom," and hangs up, which lets Julianne know her daughter is less than pleased.

Michael says, "She wasn't thrilled I was here, huh?"

"She's fine. No one is making judgments."

"No one has to," he says.

Julianne begins cleaning up the plates off the table, which she had not done earlier, when they had finished eating breakfast. Seeing her browsing through her freezer, Michael says, "No way. This time we're going out. No if, ands."

Julianne swings the freezer door shut, claps her hands. "No if ands," she says, and starts getting ready to head on out into town to eat, which she has not done in much too long.

To her surprise, Michael drives them to the Nacoochee Grill. In his car, going the speed they are going, she feels like this is where they are headed, like it's where any car should always head, though why she thinks this she can't say. Something about Michael's driving is spot-on how Harvey used to drive them there, one hand on the wheel, taking in the landscape, like everything is merry and they're cruising on a Sunday afternoon, sky bright blue, clouds slow and easy. She takes a deep breath, lets it all in, and the cool breeze is like perfume—sugarberry and sassafras, pitch pine, shagbark hickory. A whiff of magnolia coming down from someone's backyard. She takes a long inhale, keeps her eyes closed. Feels the breeze on her too-dry skin. If she could live there in that moment forever, she'd be just fine with it.

When they pull into the parking lot, it is pain she feels, a tinge of it. At first it is a sharp pain, shoots up along her elbow, twitches her triceps. But the pain dulls out. It is her right arm anyway. Definitely not a heart attack, she thinks. Definitely something else. Something that can wait.

Michael sees her tense up. He puts his hand on her shoulder, which she brushes away. "Jules?"

"I'm fine," she says. "Little acid or something. Just need some Tums."

"You sure?"

He is giving her that look, which everyone seems to give her these days. It's a look that says, *You're old. The warranty has expired.* Everything's going to cost a little more.

She opens the door, steps out, slams it shut, with great effort, proving a sick woman would be incapable of slamming a door. "Come on," she says. "I'm old. I'm old. I get it."

She orders the fried calamari *and* the fried oyster Po Boy, tempting, she knows, those pains within her telling her, Go ahead, see if we care, try it. Just try it.

Michael doesn't say a word, just waits until she's done before he orders the Caesar salad wrap. But when the waiter starts walking away, he says, Sorry, actually. Can I have the Blackened and Blue with fries instead? Sure, the waiter says. It's my *fave*.

Julianne says, "All right, then."

Michael thinks "Fave" is something Harvey would have said. Or maybe he would have called it the *cream of the crop* or one *hot item* or *nonpareil*. Something like that. He says, "What the hell, Jules. You only live once."

Julianne says, "I'd start talking if I knew how to help you. But I don't. I don't know how to help myself anymore these days. I've turned myself into a content little old lady, and the fire's sizzled out."

Michael says, "Thanks, Jules. But what makes you think I'm here for help?"

"It's all over your face. You get to be my age, you can read it like a blinking neon sign."

The waiter drops off two waters, two sweet teas. Thank you, Michael says. He says, "I don't even know what I want, Jules. I have everything. Not everything, obviously. But the appearance of it, if you know what I mean."

"I know," she says. "Still."

Michael rubs his hands over the tablecloth, twirls the stem of a wineglass. "I should have said this a long time ago, Jules, but I didn't. And I don't know why." Julianne is staring at him now, eyes wide, like, Go ahead, honey, you have no enemies here. Michael says, "I'm sorry, Jules. I apologize. I don't know how we got here, and maybe it's my fault, maybe it's not. I don't know. But I am sorry."

"You have nothing to apologize for," she says. "Life happens, Michael. You know that."

"I know," he says. "But the choices we make. The choices I've made, they affect people. And some of the choices I've made—I don't know. I just wish things turned out differently."

Julianne feels the pain in her arm again, but it's a much softer pain now, muted, like someone pushing her forearm in with a thumb. Not painful, just there. Like someone trying to get her attention at a movie. She says, "I hate to sound like a bitch, Michael, but you're not God."

Not God is not a concept he is familiar with, not at this stage in the game, because if he is anything he is powerful. He is God-like. And yet he knows she is right. He isn't that powerful, not with his family. Not with their family. Not with the people who know him simply as Michael. And not with Aaron or Lettie. He says, "You're right. I know that. I guess I meant with everything that happened. With James. With Rachel."

"James is his own disaster. No one made James James but James. And I love my daughter, don't ever think I don't. But Rachel, no matter how I tried, she ended up following yours truly. Too reliant on one person too early. Put all her money on one horse, that one."

"I just feel bad. For them, of course, but for Hadley mostly. She was a good kid."

Julianne says, "She still is. Good is good and bad is bad. What someone goes through doesn't change a thing. Just because it snows outside and you can't see the grass, it doesn't mean the grass ain't there anymore."

"If you don't mind my asking, what's Rachel up to these days?"

"Working. Apparently one of her friends started a restaurant in Key West. Asked her to run it for her. By Sloppy

Joe's, I believe. On Duval Street, or off Duval Street. Somewhere around there."

"Wow," he says. "I never dreamed Rachel in a restaurant."

"Loves it," she says. "Has a new boyfriend down there. Hemingway type. Newspaperman. Fishes for marlin. Man's man, apparently. But no. I never thought she'd be one to lift a finger, tell the truth."

"And James?" He says this hesitantly, guilt in his question, which he is sure Julianne can hear.

"James," she says. "I guess we'll be here for a while." She winks at him, takes a sip of her tea. "Where oh where shall I begin?"

Julianne tells him that, from what she had been able to make out, he took off to Mexico. "Took out a suitcase full of money and just went. Left a one-line note: *Off to Mejico, Love Me.* And that was it. Not a single phone call from him after he was gone. An e-mail here or there to Rachel and Had, but flat out took off. Abandoned them, if you can believe it. Of course, we read into his not putting a comma between the Love and the Me, but that was probably giving the jerk too much credit."

"I can't," Michael said. "Really."

"I can't either. A big baby is what he is, the ass." She scratched the top of one foot with the bottom of the other. "I wanted to punch him in his fat face is what I wanted to do."

"What's he doing?"

"Who knows. Story is he flew to San Diego, rented a car, left it at the border. Walked into Tijuana like some college kid. And that was that."

"That was that?"

"Went vanished for a couple of months. Nothing. Not a word for two months. Then a broken clay pot or some such thing shows up in the mail. A hello written on the back of a piece of cardboard. And then another couple of months with not so much as a peep. You believe that guy?"

"No," he says. "I don't." And it's the truth: he doesn't.

"Me neither. Baffling, you ask me. Like he got kicked by a stupid mule." Julianne shakes her head. "A broken clay pot, can you imagine?"

The waiter drops off a basket of pumpernickel rolls, a plate of shrimp and grits. Michael tells him no, we didn't order it, but the waiter just smiles. "Mrs. Lipscomb," he says.

"Thanks, dear." She pushes the plate of shrimp towards Michael. "Owner has a crush on me." She looks over towards the kitchen, at a man half her age waving hello. She lifts a hand, drops it back to the table. "I'm what you call a cougar," she says, and laughs. "Oh me oh my." Michael, squinting as if he's in pain, closes his eyes and hopes by god he didn't hear what he heard.

When they return to Julianne's Michael sits down by the window and watches the cars drive along the road. Julianne begins unpacking her possessions, pulling out old pictures, looking for anything even remotely related to Lettie, to Michael. Anything that might mean something. She finds a box with what looks like a board game in it, but when she shows it to Michael he knows immediately what it is. He says, "Aaron and Hadley played that. Kept them busy while you and Harvey gardened."

The game had been Rachel and Lettie's idea, from what he can recall. They'd copied the swirls and curves of *Chutes and Ladders*, stolen pieces from a Parcheesi set. Mixed and matched rules from other games. The object: count down the days until Christmas, the days until New Year's, the days until the Day of the Innocents, the days until the Three Kings, and so on. All the holidays they could think of that the kids would know. Land on a certain holiday, you got points for all of the answers you could give related to that holiday. First they'd had to build the game piece by piece. They'd had to use their dictionaries, and surf the web, had to look up all of the various traditions, the types of food everyone ate, who celebrated what when. Then, once the game was done, they'd actually had to play it.

Michael says, "They hated it. But Hadley wouldn't let Aaron beat her."

"Always the tiger, that one."

"I always thought they were very similar. It's a shame they don't know each other."

Julianne says, "Mhmm." She pulls the tape off the corner of a box, but she's looking busy rather than actually being busy. Michael says, "Jules?" And Julianne looks back at Michael, throws the balled up tape into the trash bin she's been using to throw away some of the old things she's been going through. She says, "They know each other, Michael. They've always known each other."

Michael appears perplexed.

Julianne says, "They're generation Y, Michael. Internet. Phones. Brain waves. Face page. All those things the kids use these days. None of 'em have any sense of privacy."

Michael smiles. "How do you know so much about them?"

Julianne slides some of Hadley's postcards around on the refrigerator. Picks up a Romanian postcard, flips it around, puts it back. She looks at the back of one from Auckland, passes it to Michael. Typical postcard writing—Hi! Loving it! So cool! And the PS. PS, it says. Spoke to Aaron. Sends his love. So sad, that guy! Julianne puts the postcard back up on the fridge, shrugs. "Life is," Julianne says.

So sad, he thinks. My son. What would make Hadley write such a thing? Michael thinks, I thought *she* was the depressed one? I thought *she* was the one that had the issues? Aaron's a tormented artist, is what he is. Sad? Who's sad? What does she mean, sad?

Julianne says, "It's an old postcard, Michael. Kids write what they write, you know that."

Michael is silent as Julianne goes about opening windows, trying to catch a cross breeze. One of the windows gives her trouble. Michael gets up, bangs his palm against a pane. Slides the window halfway open.

He says, "I thought he was lost. Finding himself, you know. I thought maybe he would come around."

Julianne says, "Come around what?"

"I don't know. Come around."

"And do what you do?"

"Maybe. I don't know. Maybe not."

"He would never," she says, touching his arm, trying to transfer some of what's eating him to her, which seems to be working, because her arm is getting that jabbing electric feeling all over again, which Michael sees on her face. "He's never going to come around like that," she says. "That boy will be a free bird forever, honey." She takes a small scoop of grits, drinks some tea. Coughs. She wipes her mouth with her napkin. "You can't make him be what you want him to be. That one's run wild and you can't change that. You shouldn't even try."

Michael, fiddling with the salt and pepper, says, "I wouldn't, Jules. Not for a million dollars, I wouldn't. It's just not in me."

A memory. Lettie finds herself in their kitchen, hers and Rachel's and Sammy's, and her Mom's and Measly Beasley's, sitting down to dinner one night when they were all little and the linoleum was near peeled off under all of the corners and around the doorjambs. There's fried chicken on the table in a bucket, but it's not from Kentucky Fried Chicken, and there aren't any side dishes of mashed potatoes and gravy or coleslaw or mac n cheese. But there are green beans and there are cans of RC Cola and packets of ketchup everywhere. There are no potato wedges and nothing else you would put ketchup on. Her fingers are shiny with grease fat and everyone at the table has fried chicken crumbs on their cheeks. Her father has a can of something, beer probably, and her mother is walking around by the sink, throwing something into the trash can. She is wearing a denim blue gingham apron that looks like it was passed on down from probably the first pilgrim ancestor of theirs to have set foot in the new world. She sees everything peacefully, like it's a normal family having dinner, but then, to start everything up for her, Measly's beer falls to the ground and spills all over the place, and he goes ballistic, throwing first the foaming can against the wall and then the green beans, which splatter all across the beige wallpaper, all down the little banners above the little cornucopias that say "Plenty." And plenty comes.

Sammy doesn't move, even though the can hit her in the face and the green bean juice is dripping down her chin, and Rachel doesn't move and their mother, Julianne, who just turned a little and leaned her behind against the sink, shut the water off and dried her hands with a dishrag, she doesn't move either. They all just sit there, like they're watching the neighborhood boys get into it, huffing and puffing, ready to blow everyone's house down. While Lettie wants to make sure she isn't exaggerating, wants to make sure she isn't making everything up so that later, when she asks her mother if this actually happened, if what she remembers she indeed remembered correctly, she also wants to make sure she doesn't unintentionally (or intentionally) sugarcoat anything. So she writes it all down. She writes down everything she believes happened. She writes down everything as she sees it. She writes that Measly goes at it for a good fifteen, twenty minutes, throwing and breaking and kicking and yelling and pulling and grabbing and cursing like forty filthy sailors. And she writes, This is why we are who we are. And she writes, This is why mom left. But then she says, No. I'm not done. And she keeps writing about Measly, who, not even on paper, she can call *Father* without either snickering or wanting to destroy something. She also acknowledges, perhaps for the first time, that maybe her mother was wrong. Wrong not for having left Measly, but for having taken so long to do it.

And for her, for her stories, whether told in this novel she is writing or perhaps, more likely, for the memoir she *will* write, this is who Measly Beasley is at that precise moment:

- A drunk
- An angry, angry man
- Unaware of what he has and what he is about to give up
- Creating blood family that will forever despise him and want him very much dead and out of their lives

He is a man who has terrorized his family into complacence. He is a man whose bitterness has drowned the good in life, and swirled it, violently, into an ocean of bad. Over and over and over again. And as Lettie writes this, as the memories flood her heart and water her eyes, it occurs to her that still, hateful as she is to this sick man, there has always been a piece of her missing, has always been a piece of them all they have never, in all of the years since, been able to get back. Their new normal, sure, it was normal. But it didn't mean you couldn't long for what you never had. She writes, Measly Beasley was a son of a bitch. But he was our son of a bitch.

She remembers the last time she'd seen him, lying back in his tore-up recliner, which no one else ever dared sit on. Scratching himself with his big paws, maneuvering the torn areas in his boxers, a six pack of Busch beer on the end table next to his cigarettes, smoke all around him lit up in blue from the television. She remembers him watching NASCAR, not because she remembers looking at the television but because of the roar of the cars going round and round and round interminably. He'd said something crass, something hurtful to her, but she never said anything back. Just stood there looking at him. Like she knew, in the morning, he'd be gone. Maybe she had; she can't remember. But the next night, that was it. He was gone. Or they were gone. And she imagined Measly sitting wherever he was, wondering who in the world he could yell at now, and if it was like the trees that fell in the forest. Was he even making a sound if no one was there to listen? Or was he happy once he'd left? Or was it they that had gone? Did he say hallelujah and invite his friends over and thank God for his new life, this magical land of freedom without his wife, without his daughters? This second chance? She didn't know. Who could?

When Measly didn't try to find them after they'd moved, when he didn't come barreling in the door, yelling at them for leaving and not telling him where they were going, screaming at their mother to get in the damn kitchen and make him dinner for heaven's sake, she knew he was gone from their lives forever. And after a while, it didn't matter. They adjusted.

But sometimes, when she'd least expect it, Measly did come back. He came back in the sweat in Michael's gym bags, and he came back in the infrequent arguments she witnessed sometimes in supermarket parking lots, in the heated discussions she saw men and women have. She did not try to think these things; these things simply crept up, caught her by surprise. Brought her back to yesterday. Stung her like the snap of a wet towel. And whereas others, namely Rachel, namely Sammy, may have pushed the thoughts aside, she relished them, because they gave her more to write about, gave her more fuel for her books, even if she hadn't started them, even if they were just the seeds she'd hope to one day plant. One day Sammy had even peeped one of her notebooks while she was out on a hike, read probably half of the notes she had on Measly, from the days she liked to call his *Vino* period because he drank nothing but Carlo Rossi, chugging from a monstrous bottle of Paisano he kept beside his recliner. Sammy was angry.

"What's this?" she said. She was holding her notebook like it was a dead fish.

"A notebook," Lettie said, pretending to be surprised Sammy didn't know.

"Why are you writing about him?"

"Because I want to write about him," she'd said. She was feeling strong, empowered because Sammy had absolutely no right to go snooping. Funny enough, Sammy must have felt her strength, because, in her way, she backed down some, took a breath.

Sammy put the book on the table. "Well, people got their issues, Miss Madonna. Even drunk sons of bitches."

Lettie could not agree more. She said, "And I have mine, and I'm entitled to figure out why however I see fit."

But Sammy had already walked away. Seeing it now, though maybe she hadn't seen it then, Lettie sees her sister shaking her head, maybe going to a room and closing the door so she can be alone, so she can hide and figure out how everything falls into place, and who is entitled to what, from their miserable, miserable past. Maybe it is because she is older, or maybe it is because she had to endure more of Measly, she doesn't know. But Sammy definitely feels like she has a greater share in their father than she does. Like though her life may have sucked, Sammy's sucked more, and that gave her more rights over the tempestuous childhoods they'd had. As if she could *own* that part of their lives more than Lettie could.

Everyone sees things differently, Mimi is saying. "When it comes to growing up, you can bet that everyone may be living under the same roof, but they ain't in the same house."

Mimi, lying on her back on the floor, her feet up on the bed, doing some kind of stretch that looks like it would break her back if she tried. "My brother, Theodore," she says. "That guy? I'm sure Teddy would tell you that we grew up in a home without love. Without structure. But he would be wrong. Not lying, mind you, just flat out wrong."

"How so?"

"Ran out of the house every day since he was little. Just go out and run around with his friends, come home when he came home. Ate dinner alone because he got home so late, everyone always long in bed, him in front of the boob tube."

Lettie steps into the bathroom, changes out of her pajamas into shorts and a T-shirt. "Sounds like maybe Teddy was right."

"Nope. Teddy forgot that he was the one fought and kicked and spit like a snake whenever my mother or father tried to sit him down with us like a family. Completely forgot that part. Omitted it from his memory. Disremembered that my mother would take his tantrums, take his little fists in her face and neck (he was maybe six or seven, but don't let that fool you, a fist in the face is a fist in the face). Did it for a good year or two until she finally gave up. Said fine, do what you have to do. And he did. And then he blamed her for it afterwards. Blamed the both of them."

"No offense, Mimi. But a six-year old?"

"Six or sixteen, hell on wheels is hell on wheels." Lettie sits up, swirls her neck round and round like it's a ball bearing. "What I'm saying is, facts aren't always facts. Perception is a solitary thing. You own it."

"I know," Lettie says. "Trust me. I know. But it doesn't make it not odd. It baffles me, to tell the truth."

"You're a writer," Mimi says. "Nothing should baffle you."

They ordered room service. Lettie ordered a salad and Mimi the elk medallions. She tried dictating to Mimi, who sat by the window, writing furiously as Lettie started and stopped, unable to speak the thoughts that came to her in any intelligible way. It was no good, vocalizing what she needed to write. She told Mimi about the time her mother drove the three of them, Sammy, Rachel and her to a strip club to bring Measly home. It must have been three or four in the morning, because there were no cars on the street, and the traffic lights were blinking yellow. Her mother had wrapped the three of them in blankets, thrown them into the back of their yellow Hornet. Rachel was asleep when they pulled down the alley behind the club, but she and Sammy were sitting up, staring at the back of Julianne's head. They watched her calmly shut the car door, calmly walk in the back door of the club, and a few minutes later not so calmly drag their drunk father by the ear to the car. Like he was a kid. Like their mother was his mother and she was scolding him for staying out past his curfew. Maybe he was.

When they drove away from the club a big fat bearded man with a tattoo of a woman on one forearm and an eagle on the other was standing at the back door next to a half-naked redhead in an American flag bikini. The redhead was playing with the fat man's ponytail, pulling it back and forth, and he was lifting her skinny legs in the air, turning her upside down like she was light as air.

Lettie says, "She didn't care, Mimi. Wasn't embarrassed. Didn't care what time it was, didn't care where he was. Just took us and went. Didn't yell or anything. We all just went home and went to bed."

Mimi says, "Could you ever see yourself doing something like that?"

"Never," says Lettie. "But Sammy? She did it for years. *Years*, Mimi."

"I don't get it either. I would have just walked. But that's me."

Lettie shakes her head. She says, "So why did you walk?"

Lettie assumes that is what happened, that Mimi walked from her marriage, because she can see that type of strength in Mimi. Has seen it since the moment they met. Like she wore it on her chest, right there like a shiny broach, or sprayed it on like an everyday perfume, out in the open for everyone to take in. *Eau de confidence.*

"It was actually mutual," she says. "We just grew apart. He's still one of my best friends."

"Just like that, huh?"

"Just like that. No drama. No yelling or alcohol or extramarital anything."

"That's good," Lettie says. "I mean, if it has to be."

Mimi nods. "No regrets. Except the part where you question if it wasn't a mistake from the beginning. If it was so easy to walk away, you know? Makes you think you were just friends to begin with."

"Mmm," says Lettie, reaching over now to grab her parka, which seems as old as everything in the room, the bedspreads, the light fixtures. She put her arms into the arm holes, wearing the parka backwards. Pulls the sleeves out to see what it looks like inside out.

"Is it a memoir you're thinking, or are you going to try and make this a novel?"

"I don't know," she says. "I want to write fiction. But I get caught up in the facts too much. Or what's come to me claiming to be truth."

"Go with your heart, girly. Just get it done. Then put it aside for a bit. It'll tell you what it wants to be."

"Maybe," she says. "But what if it doesn't? What if it just sits there, staring at me, telling me that you can't do it? You can't put a stamp on what's already out there."

"That's on you," says Mimi. "No one can tell you that but you."

The next evening, when she is sketching out the countless settings, the places they have lived over their lives, it is Measly she comes back to. She thought she had finished with him—with writing about the terrible things he'd done over the years; writing about the smells that remind her of him, the vile sayings he'd said, what his favorite curse words were, the bad he still could do, all the complaints he'd made every single day for as long as she could remember, about his life and the shitty jobs he'd held, the shitty landlords, their crap lives and life in general, how he'd been shafted since the day he'd been born—but she hadn't. It was like this was the root of a lot of what boiled up in Rachel and especially Sammy, and in a certain way, her as well, though she didn't show it like Rachel did in the comments she made, and she most definitely did not display it as outwardly as Sammy had, becoming, in oh so many ways, the female version of Measly himself. Because she was not like her sisters. Which meant she was not like her father. Or less so, anyway. Like the later in the process they were born, the less of Measly was left to corrupt who they were. As if his atoms grew sparse within them, and the hold he had was less magnetic.

She thought of the biological aspect of it, him giving their mother less of him at conception, having less to give (which she thought was probably from the alcohol, the drugs). And her, clearly, the benefactor. Of course the thought of it repulsed her, made her shake her head. But perhaps it was true, at least in their case. Perhaps Measly was dying out, fading away, a little bit at a time. Maybe that was a good thing. Or not maybe, but undeniably. Categorically.

Measly Beasley. Their Measly Beasley. Their father. Her father. The man responsible for their existence. But what more than that? What more good was there after that? She didn't know. And likely, though she did not take pleasure in acknowledging it, she guessed not much.

Lettie does not call, and when he calls her she does not answer. He leaves a voice-mail, tells her they're hitting the hay, talk tomorrow. He does not tell her about the pain Julianne has had, because Lettie would call immediately, tell them go, get yourselves checked in, I'll be on the first plane in the morning. He does not tell her that he has told his reports at MicroZoot, has told his board, that a family emergency has come up, because none has, at least not in any way that makes sense. Does not say, Hey, everyone, I don't know what's going on in my brain right now, but some overwhelming sense of something has taken hold of me, knocked me silly, told me to look around, see what I've done. Told me to go on, dumbass, go, it's time to recalibrate.

He says none of this to anyone. Instead he listens to Julianne breathe and snore and whistle through her nose. Instead he watches her sitting upright, cold asleep, moving rarely throughout the night. Instead he listens to the few cars driving by, fewer and fewer as it turns to one, to two, to three in the morning, when no cars are on the road, and all he can hear is the wind, and maybe an owl somewhere, hooting in the darkness. What is this life we live, he thinks. Where's the joy in it?

In the morning, he thinks, I'll use deception if I have to. Whatever it takes, I'll get my boy on the phone, and I'll make him speak to me. I'll make him acknowledge that I exist. And if I have to, I'll jump on the next plane out of here and head to wherever he is, just like I did to come down here, to come check on Julianne, which no one, apparently, has done in a while. That's what I'll do, he says, whispering to Julianne, who doesn't flinch an inch, even when he says it loud enough for her to hear. That's what I'll do, Julianne. I will be a father again. You watch.

But in the morning, even though he waits until almost noon, no one answers Aaron's phone. Not the first time he calls, and not the fifth time. Not even from Julianne's cell, which he'd hoped Aaron would either not recognize or recognize and, well, maybe answer. Maybe pick up and say, in his sweet voice, Hey, Grandma. How are you?

But Julianne says, "I didn't think he would answer, Michael. He lives his life on his terms. Calls me when he wants, not when I want."

"Where is he now? Lettie says New Mexico or Texas or something."

"Sounds about right," she says. "But I'd be lying to you I told you I knew for a fact."

"I just want my son back. Just a little bit of him. I wouldn't smother him or anything." He knows he sounds desperate. Sounds too . . . not him. But he is desperate. But for his son, for his family, it's okay.

"I know, Michael."

"Because I wouldn't, Jules."

"I know."

"I just miss having my son around. I know Lettie does too. We both do."

"We all miss each other, Michael. That's a good thing, don't you think?"

"I do," Michael says. "I do."

Over tea, Michael tells Julianne he saw her with a man, the day he arrived. He says, I think it's good, Jules. You moving on."

Julianne says, "His name's Roscoe. He was friends with Harvey."

"Roscoe," says Michael, teasing.

But Julianne doesn't want the teasing. She says, looking down, almost ashamed, "There's just something there, Michael, something familiar, you know?"

Michael does. He says, "I guess we're all looking for that, Jules. It's okay. It's normal."

"Normal," she says. "Yes. What else could it be but?"

When Michael leaves, Julianne walks him to his rental car. He leans over her shrinking body, careful not to crush her in his big bear hug. As he backs out of the driveway, over the rocks and gravel, he waves, and Julianne waves back, but only for a second. She throws her hand in the air behind her, blows a kiss over her shoulder. He watches Julianne sprint as best as she can, which isn't much of a sprint at all, the phone ringing and ringing. And when she waves one last time goodbye, opens her front door, and is gone, Michael peels away, never considering that maybe, just maybe, it is Aaron calling.

But Julianne does not answer in time. She picks up, says, "Hello? Hello?" But there is no sound at the other end of the line. There are no words. Just silence. And soon, just a dial tone.

Hadley

S he was sleeping below the window in the fetal position, sun
shining over her body, and she reminded Armand of a cat.
Curled and compact, her foot fluttered like the tip of a cat's tail,
slow and undulating, sinister somehow, indefinable and, he had to
admit, somewhat frightening. Maybe it was how she held her
hands—in fists, bound almost, wrists turned awkwardly, pulled
close against her small breasts. For a moment he paused, staring.
For a moment he thought, Shall I stay? What if I stay? What if I
am here when she awakes, staring back at her? Would this be
upsetting? To her?

But Armand did not know her. How much could you
know someone after three days? Not only that, but in a foreign
country, and not only a foreign country, an Eastern European
one? He had known girls like her, or women like her back home,
and of course, on his journey, this journey. And when he thought
of the word *journey*, it was no longer a moral issue or even a
consideration issue. He glanced at her one last time, pulled his
backpack over one shoulder, and slipped out the door, silently. He
made for a cart just steps from her door, bought a freshly-made
smažený sýr and took a bite, burning his lips, dripping Edam
down the front of his jacket. He looked up at her window. This is
how he would remember Hadley the American girl, sun shining
all over her, the red roofs of Old Town Square behind her, a sad,
intriguing postcard of a life from some other decade.

She was glad he was not there when she woke. She
thought he was ugly and clumsy like typical jock-y American guys,
and ugly and big for three days through Bulgaria and Romania was
not a detriment: she would not have felt safe in Craiova or

Bucharesti, haggling with the portly taxi drivers (whose meters never worked), nor especially on the northbound trains late at night, when she felt the men had forgotten communism had ended. Even with burly Armand beside her, the marionette-bodied, hirsute passengers hanging out of the sidecar windows, smoking inexpensive cigarettes, staring back at her like she was chopped ground round, all of them were rough sketches of men at best, and they had made her nervous. The only redeeming value Armand could offer was protection, his only redeeming quality that he was part French Armenian, which made him exotic looking. But now that they were in Prague, it was a different story. In Prague she could ease up, let her shoulders down. Unwind. Kick back. The whole rest of the trip, the whole rest of wherever she was headed, now it was all going to be gravy. She was glad Armand was gone. Glad he didn't have that bogus plastic idea of chivalry some boy-men pretended to have. Sometimes it was better if they just split.

In the evening, when they'd arrived, the clerk hadn't taken any money, just gave them a key to a room and fell back asleep, head down on the reception desk. But it was Friday and she knew the hostel would fill up with Europe's weekend warriors. She walked barefoot downstairs, told the guy she wanted a private room for the week. He said he knew she came in late last night, but technically he isn't supposed to check her in until two. *But*, he says, because room empty it eez okay. My name Pavel, he says. Great, she says. She pays Pavel $362.00 for the week with a debit card—U.S. dollars, not korunas, which she still finds odd considering she's in Prague. You need something, Pavel help. Děkuji, she says.

In the hostel's kitchen she microwaves hot water for her green tea, rehydrates her dehydrated powdered milk and blueberry cereal. A lone female backpacker is making coffee, shuffling around in her tank top and shorts, dragging her bunny slippers over the cheap linoleum, keeping to herself. When Hadley is done, she rinses her mug, throws her recyclables into a bin. Early mornings in hostels are normally quiet, at least this time of year, when most college kids are still studying away, and Hadley is glad to be this alone.

She takes out a stack of postcards she has forgotten to mail along the way. From Papeete, from Moorea. From Rarotonga.

She will write her hellos on them, one after the next, will drop them in the bin at the post office after she thumbs them all with Česká Republika stamps. She will make sure to mail the Auckland postcards, send them from here as well, feeling distinctly unoriginal about sending postcards from other countries, with different postmarks, different postage, weeks and months removed from the places her recipients find staring back at them in their stacks of bills and grocery store coupons. She addresses the postcards to her friends, to one particularly friendly professor of European History, whom she got along with rather well during her senior year. Nothing sexual, a connection, a healthy—and mutual—flirtation, she is sure. And her family? Only Julianne *Superfly* Granny receives a postcard. It's funny, she thinks, how a family starts out strong, then slowly, over time, and like leaves in winter, starts falling away, one by one.

Auckland was a cool city, but she couldn't imagine living there. Something was too plain, too lacking. But Prague? Prague is different. Prague feels like Disney World. It feels like Great Adventure. And yet it also feels like home. Prague is castles and winding roads, cobblestoned streets and cheap everything. She feels she's walked into a city in a book a hundred years ago, which feels, somehow . . . right. Though she is alone, she has had friends who have worked here, who have taught English here, wrote novels here. She has friends who've studied in Prague but who've learned little except the price of Plzeň and České Budějovice at Bredovský Dvůr or U Pinkasů. Someone, she can't recall who, said there were forty thousand Americans living in Prague—*forty thousand*, which seemed—still seems—like too many. Soon she is walking Prague's alleyways, spotting the too-many—the intruding Americans—by their clothing, how they walk. Free, somehow. Unobstructed.

Prague is a good place to get lost. As in most cities she has been to, she knows if she stays away from the tourist spots she can lose herself in the Czech back alleys, away from English speakers, away from *everything*, which is what it—what *everything*— is about. She can be free—not that she wasn't before, not that anyone is after her, not that she has ever been not free. Or maybe they *are* after her. A certain few. Namely her mother, the tragic Rachel. And of course her mother's friends, Gina and Lucinda. Her Cuban Key West "sisters," or whatever. Strangers who thought they knew everything about her because her mom decided it was a good idea to not act like a mom, move to party central, tell them all about it, woe is her. Not her father, though. If she were younger, she knows she would hate him for leaving. But she's older. She doesn't hate him. She pities him. He's a disappointment. But mostly? Mostly, she misses the idea of him.

She walks through Josefov, through the Klausova Synagoga and the Španělská Synagoga, which is a Moorish Revival synagogue, built in 1868. It reminds her of the Leopoldstädter Tempel in Wien, which is in fact what the synagogue mimics, with its domed turrets, its tripartite façade. During World War II, the Germans stored the belongings of the Jews they stole from at the synagogue, like it was a big shameful closet for them to store the belongings of their victims.

In a café in Staré Město, she listens to a Czech couple argue, which reminds her of a Russian film she has watched somewhere, sometime. She imagines they are lovers in a row about another, a third party one of them has introduced to their union, though which of them has had the affair she cannot say (sadly, because she is too busy staring at their teeth, a stereotype, of course, but there it is). She pulls the torn map of Praha from her pocket, lays it across the edge of the bar, a corner of the map soaking in the dregs of spilled coffee. She runs her fingers over Karlův most, the *Charles Bridge*, up into Malá Strana, the "*Lesser side*," though she knows the translation in her guidebook is probably not entirely accurate. She leaves the coffee shop, map in tow sticking to her fingers.

Malá Strana is a quieter, slowed-down version of Staré Město. Given its proximity to Prague center, she thinks it overly quaint. When she walks across the statue'd bridge, it is like walking back in time, but only back about ten minutes. Women sit in windows waving hello to neighbors, indifferent to the fact that just above them is this enormous castle where their president lives, though conceivably only ceremonially.

She follows the Hladová zeď, the Hunger Wall, until she is at the top of Petřín hill, where she sits down on the grass, away from everyone in her own little corner. The Hunger Wall, built in the 1300's, was meant to fortify Prague Castle and Malá Strana against attacks from the west, the south. But now it is only one more thing for the tourists to gawk at. Tourists, ironically, that are not only from the west and south, but from every which direction, every country on earth. And she thinks, *As it should be.*

The breeze heavy with the perfume of roses, she reads a book she has picked up, written by a local author, a collection of Franz Kafka's, which includes "The Metamorphosis." But she is not in the mood to read about a monstrous bug. She closes the book, rests her head on its firm cover. Lies on the grass, and enjoys the summer sun on her cheeks. This was Prague. This was months ago.

Then there was Germany. And Belgium. France. A blur of hostels and Tabacs, museums with crowded art, sprawling parks flush with drunks. After Lisbon and Sintra and Faro, she is happy to be in Spain, this land that Grandpa *Superfly* Harvey has told her so much about so many years ago. She thinks about maybe renting a *piso* somewhere in the south, maybe Cádiz, Seville. She remembers the twinkle in Grandpa Superfly's eyes whenever he told of giving speeches at the universities in Spain, like he was Federico García Lorca performing his *Llanto por Ignacio Sánchez Mejías*, belting out *"A las cinco de la tarde. Eran las cinco en punto de la tarde . . ."* to outbursts of applause. It could have been yesterday, she saw in her mind, everything so clearly. She could still smell him, the musky dirt and raisin smell, the smell of sweat mixed with paraffin wax, with cedar.

Seville is . . . *nice.* After a few days she knows, however, that it is no good, it's a picture out of a magazine, *Spain for Dummies.* Too picture-perfect along the Guadalquivir, the *Maestranza* bullring's Baroque façade is simply too vomit-gorgeous. Of course, she knows what it is. It is that she has had a picture in her head for too long, an image of Granada and the Alhambra, the *Al-hamrá',* the red castle whose hallways Grandpa Superfly has laid out for her in 3-D, whose columns and muqarnas and arabesques, whose stalactite-like embellishments she has seen and memorized and re-memorized. Whose Moorish poets have carved this pearl set in emeralds into her dreams since her earliest childhood memories.

In the morning, taking one last breath of the Guadalquivir, Hadley hops the first bus of her entire trip. The ride is just over three hours, enough time to take a nap, to sightsee out her window at the rolling hills, the red clay, the desolate landscape, the interminable rows of olive trees. When the bus pulls onto Carretera de Jaen she knows they're almost at the station. She stuffs a Milan Kundera novel, *The Unbearable Lightness of Being* into her backpack, her hand over the title (it is cliché, the novel, reading it as an American abroad, she thinks), cinches the top, fastens a plastic clip, and waits for everyone on board to deboard, and head on off on their separate routes through the winding streets of Granada.

The Genil River running from the mouth of the Guadalquivir at the top of the Sierra Nevada Mountains, between the Alhambra and the neighborhood of El Albaicin, flows in a thin stream known as the Darro. It cools the air all along the road, where during the day the elders walk, and at night Granada's youth loiter. Below the Puente del Aljibillo and the Puente de las Chirimias, the Bridge of the Pipers, stray tabby cats and cats smoke-gray as the pencils of the artists along the Paseo de los Tristes, the Path of the Sad Ones, lay sprawled in the sun and lap from the Darro with their tongues.

Before she had ever seen the Darro with her own eyes, before Grandpa Superfly sank into oblivion and his own relatives talked to him like a four-year old, Grandpa Superfly Harvey Lipscomb had described in such precise detail and shown her so many pictures of it that she already knew what the riverweed felt like, knew how the temperature dropped so much when the shade of the Alhambra ran down the walls of the Carmens, along the road and down over the cobblestone, that you had to walk back into the sun to thaw out. When it hit her now, when the heat ran across her shoulders and the top of her head, warming her up and casting its bright shadow on the cats drinking the milk she had poured into paper bowls, she was back all over again in Helen. She was back sitting on Harvey's lap, listening to him tell his stories. She could not help but think, Yes, it's true. I am who he believed in. Yes, I am the only one he loved enough to trust to carry his torch. The trust—this is why he sent her his notes, months before the world scratched itself out on him, and why, out of everyone, she misses him the most.

Before there was nothing, before his beautiful brain was wholly consumed, bobbing in a structure-less ocean of confusion and disjointed memories, recollections misplaced in chronology, in time, it is apparent to Hadley, Harvey was already saving himself. She did not know it then, because she was still just a child, but looking back on it now, it's about as clear as anything has ever been. The more she's learned about him from Grandma Superfly Julianne, the more she thinks, *That* man, Harvey Lipscomb, was one smart cookie. *That* man knew what he was doing, and he knew how best to do it. But, she also thinks, Harvey was surrounded by a family of his own Romans. And the Romans, she knows, originally called the River Darro *"aurus,"* or "gold," because people panned for gold along its banks, looking for something else instead of seeing the beauty already there, the beauty in the running water, the beauty among the greens and browns and blues at the bottom of the river. Hoping to find *more* beauty in what was already beautiful, as if beautiful, after some consideration, was not beautiful enough.

When the Arabs took Granada, they called the river *Hadarro*. With the next wave of conquest, it was renamed yet again; the Christians named it *Dauro*, which bled, in due course, to Darro. And Hadley, pouring the last of the milk to meet the eager appetites of the Darro's throw-away cats, thinks, It does not matter what name its beauty is given, it does not matter if at first you do not see that beauty for what it is because you are too busy looking for more of it; it's *there*. And someone, somewhere, will love it for what it is, and not what it could be or what it was.

It was her last couple weeks in Granada, and Hadley was feeling many things. Granada had been her home for the past

many months, and her feelings about leaving were mixed. Closer
to facing her mother and maybe, if it were possible, finding and
then facing (and maybe confronting?) her father, though that, she
knew, was probably not going to happen. She was not naïve to
who she was—a bit of her mother, a bit of her father, a lot like
Harvey, who was not even blood. But yes, a lot like Harvey. A
gang of runaways, all of them. Wasn't this, really, what they had
become? A sort of less-than-hip version of Romany?

She let the last tabby lick the bowl until he flipped it on its
side and the milk wasted into the grass. She scooped the bowl up,
scratched the back of the tabby's ear, shuffled back up the side of
the bank, over the wall. She looked at the cats lying there, content,
bellies full, licking the sandy pads of their paws.

She knows Harvey's letters, his notes, were a topic of
discussion when they had arrived in the mail so many years back.
Grandma Superfly had told her mother that they were coming,
that Harvey had had her send them out, odd as it was, addressing
a box full of notes and pictures to such a young child. But it wasn't
that odd, when you considered how close they were, Harvey and
Hadley. Two peas in a pod. Even their names, but two letters off.
That's what Grandma Superfly had told her mother. It was her
father had the problem with not opening Harvey's package
immediately upon its arrival. Great guy, Harvey, but who knows
what a guy with Alzheimer's is capable of sending, he'd said. It
was the first time Hadley had ever heard of Alzheimer's. The first
time she understood Harvey was imperfect somehow. But her
mother had won. Convinced him she'd take the responsibility if
there was anything strange, anything inappropriate in there.

Still, for a long time the box sat there at the top of her
mother's closet, Harvey's writing on the label, all scribbled out in
denim crayon. *To Hadley, Love Grandpa H.* The box waiting years
and years until her mother thought her mature enough to go
through a grown professor of sexuality's notes until one day, her
fifteenth birthday to be exact, she'd pulled the aged box down and
put a bow on it and set it out on the kitchen table with Hadley's
cereal, a peculiar gift among her other presents; (Hadley had been
adamant that there was to be no party). She had looked right past

the brightly-colored and gift-wrapped jewelry and laptop and gift cards and envelopes stuffed with money, right to that old box. She could not wait to open it and rummage through Harvey's things after so many years. Just seeing the box she couldn't help but smile. The crayon writing was smudged, the letters beat up by time. But finally. Finally.

Back in her apartment her landlady, Clemen, is already showing the place to prospective renters. She can tell by the looks on their faces (a young French couple, from the accents) that they are not very enthusiastic, hesitant to go on because of the size of the rooms. But Clemen runs through the benefits of a carmen so close to Plaza Nueva, of such incredible proximity to the Alhambra. Look at the views of el castillo, she is saying. And from the room, *vaya*. Romance? I cannot even begin to explain.

It is the same speech Clemen had given her a year earlier, almost to the day. And sure, there had eventually been romance, as predicted. Clemen winks at Hadley when she is leading the couple out the front door, raises her eyebrows. She imagines Clemen thinking, *silly French*. What can they possibly know about carmens? About romance?

Clemen closes the door behind her, and not ten seconds later someone knocks. Hadley assumes it is Clemen, returned to mention one last thing, please don't forget this, that. But it is not Clemen. It is Antonio.

She has seen him often, but she has not spoken to him in months. She is surprised to see him standing there, smiling. Something different in his eyes, how he holds himself. A little less confident, perhaps, is what is showing. A little less sure than what she is used to, what he seemed, previously, to be so skilled at. Hola, he says. How are you?

She makes them iced café con leches, ice cubes stacked to the tops of their tubo glasses. They go out onto the roof. One of her neighbors' laundry is drying on the clotheslines, jeans and T-shirts and thin red panties blow in the wind. When Antonio's eyes wander to the panties, Hadley says, Calmate, tigre. Calmate.

They pull a small plastic table into the shade, put their cafes down. Antonio puts his hand on Hadley's knee, pulls away.

Sorry, he says. He looks out at the Church of Santa Ana down below, its rooftop sloping to one side. "I've been wanting to come see you," he says. "For a long time I have been wanting to come see you. But I don't know. I don't know why I could not."

She says, "You're here, Antonio." The obvious.

"I am. Yes." He lights a cigarette, offers her one. She puts her hand up.

He blows the smoke out, away from her. Into the wind, which takes it away. He says, "So you are leaving."

"Yes."

"Why?"

"I was always leaving," she says. "I love Granada. But it's not my home." She looks at him. He is disappointed. She says, "I know what you're thinking. No place is anyone's home. But anyway." The words are Antonio's. One of his cliché pickup lines.

He looks at her; she turns away. "I wanted to tell you I am sorry," he says. "What I did was bad. I did not mean to hurt your feelings."

"It's okay. I wasn't hurt."

"Well," he says. "Still."

One of the wooden clothespins snaps, a T-shirt dangles perilously by a quarter inch of cloth. Hadley gets up, clips the shoulder back up with another clothespin. She says, "Anyway, I'm leaving. In the morning. I'm glad I knew you, Gato."

Antonio lets his eyes drop, his shoulders ease. But Hadley is not affected. It's almost sad, Antonio's pitiable, feeble attempt at garnering her empathy. It is clear his game has lost its way, its impact. Seeking company with this American girl he has known, one last time. She says, "I think you'll be fine, Casanova."

He smiles, nods his head, caught at a game whose rules he no longer controls. "I will still be sad when you are gone, Hadley." He says Hadley as he has always said Hadley, with the jota, instead of the H. Hadley, but with the jarring *ja* in the beginning, like "aha!" *Jaadley.*

He kisses her on the cheek. He thanks her for the coffee. He hugs her. She stays on the roof for a while after he leaves. She hears the gate in the courtyard slam shut, his footsteps disappearing into the Albaicin, clopping off to another carmen, another girl he needs to say goodbye to. Another new lover to greet.

And soon, as if there are posters all through Granada, all of the friends in all of the neighborhoods around town come calling to say their goodbyes to Hadley. Daphne comes from Realejo and Felipa and Isi from Cartuja. Her teaching friends walk up from Bib-Rambla, surprising her with presents they've plucked from the Alcaiceria, which they know she loves. There and the Teterias, with all of the exotic teas and the sweet smell of the vanilla and orange mint and honey shisha, is from where gifts make their way. Soon everyone is there, on her roof, together. Drinking tea, and drinking wine, setting up tables of jamón and queso manchego; slicing tortilla Española and mixing Fanta Limón with vino tinto to make tintos de verano. Finally, her best friend in Granada, Agata, comes walking in with a gift-wrapped photo album already half-stuffed with pictures. Agata has made the photo album herself, picking and drying flowers over the past few months, knowing, somehow, that she, Hadley, would ultimately depart.

"Para mi hermana," Agata says, tears streaming down her tanned cheeks. Hadley hugs her for a long while, the noise of her spontaneous farewell party buzzing behind them. They sit down in a corner, away from everyone on the roof.

"It's beautiful," Hadley says, flipping through the pictures. Of them in the Alpujarras, drinking wine and eating jamón in Trevélez; of them at a corrida during the Feria del Corpus Christi (both of them looking away from bright red blood shimmering on the bull's back); of them, arms around each other at the beach in Málaga, Agata's face so red she looked like a tomato, Hadley pressing her finger to Agata's arm, turning it white, smiling.

"You know I will come visit you in America," she says.

"You better," Hadley says.

She cannot not imagine Harvey here, amongst friends, doing the things she's done. Experiencing Granada the way she has experienced it, the awkward man he was. No, Harvey would have been locked in a room somewhere, at a library in the university, at a meeting hall discoursing theories with other professors. But then,

Granada is not to her what Granada was to Harvey. It never was. It can't ever be.

She remembers when she'd first arrived. She parked herself at a café in Plaza Nueva, guide book in hand, reading through Harvey's notes (some photocopied), because Grandma Superfly did not want to risk Hadley's losing certain originals, which she kept in plastic Ziplocs in an actual safe. Call if you have any questions, she'd said. We can go through his notes together if you can't make something out.

But so far she could make everything out. Grandpa Superfly, ever the chronicler, chronicled in precise detail. He chronicled with plenty of asterisks and the †'s that looked like tiny crosses. It was as if he knew, one day, she would be holding his notes in her hands, retracing the best moments of his life. He made sure she understood what it was that had made him gush when he told his stories of Andalusia, of Spain. Of this other life he'd lived, so far from home, so many years ago.

Like a Cormac McCarthy novel, Grandpa Superfly's notes had hints of what was to come, long before you got there. At the beginning of each chapter, scrawled in Harvey's neat script, he had written words, and he had drawn dashes: *Alhambra—Patio de los Leones—UNESCO—El Mirador de Lindaraja—Ferdinand & Isabelle.* He dove deep into each, his notes like the chapters of books, of histories abridged. He wrote of his feelings at spying each Calliphal horseshoe arch, each Almohad sebka, for the first time. His emotions came out with each different piece of each different history, Moorish, Christian. Some good, some indifferent. All of it written with a profound sense of appreciation. At the bottom of one page of copious notes, Harvey had written, "*Need to be archaeologist* in next life," which she found simply adorable. Who did not want to be something else? Something Discovery-ish?

The day after she had moved into her carmen, Hadley had planned out her first day's walking trip with Harvey's notes as her guide. She wanted to relive or re-experience or re-something everything Harvey had. She wasn't going to be able to walk in his shoes, of course, but with Harvey's notes she thought she could come close. She wanted to know the life Harvey had lived, because clearly it had been Harvey at his happiest.

At first, somewhat understandably, Harvey's notes were those of a man overwhelmed. The earliest-dated entries spoke of exotic tapas and reprehensible sanitation, of people standing around at all times of the day drinking inexpensive wine and local beer. While he spoke of a city in need of updates, Hadley recognized in them the notes of a man just getting to know a city. At the top of "Entry One," Harvey had written *Granada— Alhambra—Castle—Pig legs hanging from ceilings—filth—drunk children.* But a few weeks in, it appeared Harvey had acclimated.

Hadley understood the change. At first, she had to admit, she had seen the same things Harvey had seen. At first glance, Spain seemed, well, lax in its cleanliness department. But over time his notes were more learned. They became increasingly more specific and less judgmental. The names of friends and acquaintances popped up more frequently, and Harvey chronicled personal moments away from the often imposing eyes of his academic colleagues. Some of his entries, she noticed, were written before Grandma Superfly had ever entered the picture. The young children he saw drinking from bottles and paper bags were no longer "drunk kids;" they were merely socializing in botellóns. Pig legs were no longer health hazards; now they were cured jamón, "Pata Negra." The Alhambra was La Alhambra or Al-amrā', depending on who ruled at the time, which professor Harvey had been careful to document.

The more he assimilated into the culture, the more he socialized with the Universidad's administration and lecturers, the more he had been invited to attend conferences at the Universidad, and occasionally, at functions around the city, the country. Harvey participated on panels to discuss topics of Género y Sexualidad, the historical maturation of such endeavors from country to country, around the globe. More invitations came; Harvey had become a guest speaker, written and co-written books on conclusions drawn up from the same conferences. *Books make me more appealing,* Harvey wrote at the bottom of a conference flyer. *Want me to speak again.* All of it fascinated Hadley. In her thoughts she saw Harvey walking Granada—trudging the Albaicin's cobbled streets; peeking his head guiltily out of panaderias; biting into slices of tortilla on his way out of Bodegas Castañeda, standing in front of the Muslim butcher shops, staring at the red and white striations of dangling meat. He seemed to be aware of his greater *importance* in Spain, both personally and professionally, though Hadley realized it only if she read between the lines.

That evening, it was only by coincidence Hadley saw the name on the poster. She and Agata had been sipping their vino blancos, nibbling on their primeras at a bar on Calle Elvira after Hadley had dragged Agata ten minutes south to the Huerta de San Vicente, the poet Federico Garcia Lorca's summer home. Harvey had enjoyed the ponds and gardens of the Huerta, walking the paths and eating ice cream, and apparently falling in love with some of Lorca's poems. In some of the margins of his notes, Harvey had jotted down one Lorca poem or another, and then given his go at translating what he had written. After so much time in Granada, Hadley could read Spanish, and it was clear Harvey had never come close to mastering even the basics.

"Que? What?" Agata says. She is looking at Hadley, whose face is pressed to a poster. The poster advertises an upcoming concert. At first she thinks Hadley has been admiring the graffiti on the wall behind the poster. But she notices Hadley reading the names and other information printed in red below the picture of four men, four guitars.

"That name," she says. "It's in Superfly's notes."

"It's on whose que?"

"My grandfather. He has that name in his books."

Agata says, "Your grandfather has Las Pirañas written in his books?"

Hadley laughs. "No. The guy opening for them. Miguel Ángel Ponce."

Agata says, "Ah, vale. I was curious why you were so interested in Las Pirañas." Agata watches Hadley dig in her purse, looking for a pen. She tears the poster off the wall, hands it to Hadley. "Para con el boli," she says.

Hadley looks up at her, smiles her what-did-you-just-do smile. "What if someone else wants to see them?"

Agata shakes her head. "*Nobody* wants to see Las Pirañas. Trust me." She watches Hadley study the poster, as if she can extract more information from it by staring at it. "We can go," she says. "It will be a waste of plata, but if you want to go bother him I will go bother him with you."

"The support," Hadley says. "What would I ever do without your support?" They clink their vinos. Hadley crumples up the poster, stuffs it into her purse.

Later that night Hadley goes back through Harvey's notes, searches for Miguel Ángel Ponce's name. She cannot remember exactly where she has seen it, but she is pretty sure it is in one of two notebooks—either the one with all of the maps and pictures of the Albaicin, or the one with the exhaustive cataloging of every plant and tree in and around Andalusia. In his notebooks Harvey chronicled the time he spent bending over plants and peeling the bark of trees, how curious he found the Granadinos who watched the crazy guiri doing things they would never do, as if his curiosity were a waste of time. She sees Harvey in his shorts and socks, his big hats and sunglasses, splotches of white sun block not completely rubbed in, parading around like the odd American he was. And of course, smiling and waving at the locals who waved back awkwardly, said their "holas" and "que tals." She thinks, He is odd for us too, Granadinos. He is odd for us too.

Sure enough, just as she is about to give up thumbing through the pages of Harvey's past, there is the name, scribbled in Harvey's chicken scratch. Miguel Ángel Ponce, written sideways, alongside the image of a fig tree, under "*5pm. Bring wine.*"

Nothing else is written, nothing else to provide clarity. Probably just dinner with a friend, she thinks. Nowhere else is his name mentioned. Not once. For Harvey, at least from the meticulous notes he'd kept everywhere else, the name all by itself is an anomaly. A mystery! thinks Hadley. But knowing Grandpa Superfly, it is probably not much of one. She is surprised to have remembered the name.

Of course, it is possible that the Miguel Ángel Ponce scrawled in Harvey's notebook is not the same Miguel Ángel Ponce opening for Las Pirañas. Could be, sure. But what are the chances? And after so many years? She pulls the poster out of her purse, hangs it up on the wall with thumbtacks. She stares at the poster for a bit, and then goes to sleep.

In the morning, before she makes her café con leche, before she walks down to the bakery to get her pistola of bread and her weekly palmera de chocolate, Hadley lies in bed thinking about not only Grandpa Superfly Harvey but also about Grandma Superfly Julianne, and about the rest of her family. She thinks about the good times they had early on, during family reunions, when everyone cooked too much food and certain family members drank too much and maybe didn't make fools of themselves but came close (although, sad story about Uncle Cliff, of course). All so long ago. If she had spoken to her mother recently, or if she had spoken even to her father, who was probably more lost than anyone else, burning south like a comet to the sea, she knows no answer would have come. The older she gets, the less she knows is true, because truth, as Aunt Lettie used to say, is the fiction you make for yourself while it's happening.

She has had these conversations with Grandma Superfly, and she has had these conversations with Agata. Conversations where she tears away the skin to see what she, what everyone she loves, is made of. She thinks of the many things that may have made her mother do the things she'd done, acted as she has acted. And her father? Everyone else? Only sweetboy Aaron, her tormented cousin, her peripatetic boytoy counterpart, can understand what she has been through, what she is still going through. Only he felt the effects of their elders. Only he understands what it is like to be in her position. But even he doesn't know. He belongs to that other tribe, the tribe that has won, if that's what they are. The tribe that still has members; the tribe that is still intact. Sometimes she wonders how he can be as selfish as he can, how he can use his homosexuality as an excuse to treat his parents the way he does. Sure, he had problems. Who didn't? Being gay was tough. Is tough. No doubt. But it isn't as tough as being gay ten, twenty years ago. No way. Where is that boy's strength?

Aaron had it good, all things considered. Mom there, Dad there, making bank since the dawn of time. The kind of money her father made before he'd thrown it all away. Agata said she wondered whether Hadley was not looking at things from a vantage point that was maybe a little overly self-centered. Maybe, she said. Agata also said, "Maybe your parents were never happy. Maybe they married young and woke up and didn't love each other." It's possible. Agata could be right. Maybe that's really what it was. Is. But she had plenty of memories of happiness. Lots of them. Not only with her grandparents but with her mother, her father. Because they had been a family at one point in time. A close one. Sure, her father worked more than any man or woman ever should. But whose father didn't? Sure, he was gone a lot. But what was normal at that level? There was no normal. And she liked that childhood. Loved it for the time she lived it. Who wouldn't have? How couldn't you?

She listened to neighborhood children running off to school, their voices rattling off the ancient walls below. Soon she got out of bed, got dressed. Walked down and got her bread and palmera, the sun high in the sky but the city just waking. It would be a tediously long day.

They were tipsy when the doors of the *Pata Palo* opened up. They had stopped at a few bars for dinner before the show. Agata wanted to celebrate her new freedom from her German boyfriend Paul, who was not only boring and lazy in bed but perpetually broke. He fucks like he's dead, she told Hadley. *Como un cadáver, ese tipo.* The funny thing, Agata says, is that he just said *Bueno. Nos vemos.* Just like that. Walked out. So cold, the Germans. Hadley wanted to say, That's because you've known him for a total of four weeks, Agata, but she didn't. Agata could be sensitive about her indiscretions.

They stopped at Hannigan and Sons for some shots of Jameson and to say hello to their teacher friends. Went on to El Yunque, back down to Casa Julio for some fried fish. They drank vino blancos until the lights along the street blurred slightly. They laughed a lot. They were coquettish. Hadley was nervous.

It took a while for the place to fill up. People leaned against the wooden bar, ordered bottled beer and tubos from the long-haired camarero, who may have had a slight crush on Hadley, perhaps on Agata as well.

Hadley says, "He should be on by one, no?"

"Yo que se," says Agata. "These musicians have no idea of time. They play music cuando les da la gana." She looks around. The bar is filling up, but the rest of the place in front of the stage where the musicians will play is still pretty empty. "Your Julio Iglesias is probably smoking a porro behind a garbage can on Elvira," she says. A woman behind her spills what looks like Coca-Cola on herself, and Hadley pulls Agata closer so she doesn't get burned by the cigarette the woman is holding while she dabs at the darkened spot on her sleeve.

Across the floor a man with short black hair, maybe early twenties, is setting up an amplifier on the stage. Hadley motions to him with her chin.

Agata says, "Go. Maybe we can save ourselves some time and stop this noise from killing me."

Hadley walks across the floor, avoids a group of young Dutch girls who have walked in drunk, smelling of hashish. She approaches the young man, taps him on the shoulder when it is obvious he cannot hear a word she is saying. He turns around, raises his eyebrows.

"Hola," she says.

"Hola."

She asks him if he is Miguel Ángel. No, he says. Miguel Ángel is my father. She asks him if his father is here, that she would like to talk to him. No, he says. He won't come until it is time for him to play his music. Why does she want to know? He looks at her, smiles a shy smile. He says, Am I not satisfactory? But his confidence is noticeably not one of his stronger traits.

"I don't know," she says, blushing at his sweetness, or rather because of her feeling sorry for his attempt at being more forward than what he is comfortable with. Okay, he says. Okay.

Hadley walks back to Agata, does not look back, though she knows Miguel Ángel's son is probably staring at her.

The truth is, she doesn't know what she is going to say to Miguel Ángel Ponce the musician. She has no clue what Miguel Ángel's relationship is or was to Harvey. It is completely possible that there is no relationship. For all she knows, Harvey had joined a group of people at the home of the Miguel Ángel on the paper, but not the Miguel Ángel whose son she has just somehow embarrassed.

"Y?" says Agata.

"That's his son," she says. "He isn't here yet."

"His son is cute. Maybe forget the father."

"Maybe," she says. But she is not serious. The more time she spends learning about the things that were important to Harvey, the more she can provide Grandma Superfly a history of the man she loved. Of his passions and the things he treasured, the things that excited him. Of this second country of his, and of what made him tick for so many splendid years. And perhaps fix the broken grandmother her mother, in her extreme selfishness, failed to fix.

She notices Agata looking at her. Agata brushes a strand of hair from Hadley's face, pushes it behind her ear. "Are you okay?" Agata says.

Hadley is not tearing up, but she can feel her face flush. She understands Agata's concern. After spending so much time together, they have grown to be like sisters. When Agata is sad, Hadley feels it, and when Hadley is sad, Agata knows.

"Fine," she says. And she is. She says, "I just want to have more than what I have. For Grandma Superfly. It's her birthday next month. I want to make an album for her of my grandfather's life. But I don't have much. Or I don't have enough."

"But you will, guapa. You do. You have more than enough."

And if she is honest, or not such a worrier anyway, she knows she does. She's known it for months now, but it never seems like enough. "I know," she says. She looks back at Miguel Ángel's son, plugging plugs, arranging big black boxes and microphones. "If Miguel Ángel is the wrong Miguel Ángel, I'm done. I've gone through everything already, Agata. For a whole year. There is no more to go through."

"You will have enough."

And the reality of the matter is, she does. Pictures and pictures of all of Granada, step by step, where Harvey must have walked, where he ate, laughed.

The camarero puts two Estrella Damm's on the bar in front of them. In case I am too busy soon, he says. When Hadley pulls out her money the camarero waves her off.

Groups of people are crowding in through the door. The bar begins to fill up to where they have to stand closer to the bar. Agata squeezes Hadley's arm, points with her head toward where Miguel Ángel's son is doing sound checks, tapping the microphone, saying *"Test, Test, uno, dos, tres."* A man is standing beside him now, and it is clear that this man is Miguel Ángel Ponce. Agata says, "You should go now. Before he begins."

"No," she says. "I want to listen first." But though this is true, there is also fear there, that Miguel Ángel Ponce is the wrong Miguel Ángel Ponce. That this Miguel Ángel Ponce has never had anything to do with anything in Grandpa Superfly's life. That he has simply walked into hers out of coincidence, because he happens to share the same name, which is probably not all that uncommon anyway. Or the converse: He knows everything there is to know. Both possibilities are almost too much to bear.

They sip two beers over the hour that Miguel Ángel sings and plays his guitar. Hadley considers leaving, just up and going and not letting herself be disappointed if, or when, it turns out Miguel Ángel has nothing to do with anything. And just when she is about to say to hell with it, Agata says, "Come, he's done," and they walk over to where Miguel Ángel is unplugging his instruments.

Miguel Ángel is typical height for a Spaniard, 5'8" or 5'9". His black hair tied up in a ponytail, the fingernails on both hands long, for playing the guitar. He has maybe a day, two-day old stubble on his face, specked with white, with gray. When they approach him, he smiles at them. "Señoras," he says.

It is hard to hear him. The DJ raised the volume on the music once Miguel Ángel was done, and now Techno is blaring over the speakers, thumping a monotonous drumbeat off the walls. In Castellano she asks him if he will join them outside. Si, si, he says. "Dejame terminar con esto." He points at the tangle of wires and speakers, at his guitar. Hadley looks around the crowd for Miguel Ángel's son, but he is either gone or lost somewhere by the bar, perhaps hidden by one of the wood-covered columns. When Agata starts to help him, Miguel Ángel waves her off. I'll be out in a minute, he says. Go.

Hadley asks one of the camareros for three Alhambra beers. She gives one to Agata and they walk outside, careful not to spill any as they bump through the throng of people. It must be twenty degrees cooler outside, and when they cross the alley to lean up against a wall, Hadley sees Antonio walking with a pretty blond girl with dreads, a long purple dress. Agata sees him too. She casually turns her back to him, blocking Hadley in the process. Either Antonio does not see them or pretends not to, because he just keeps laughing and talking, and he and the blond girl walk up the street and turn down an alley and are gone.

"I don't care," she says. "You didn't have to do that."

"Gillipollas," says Agata. "What a jerk."

"Really, Agata. I don't." Hadley bends down, rests the beer she bought for Miguel Ángel on the ground. She pulls half a porro out of a little box, and she and Agata smoke it until the burning paper is too small to hold. There are a few people smoking along the wall, lost in the heavy air. Miguel Ángel comes walking out with a guitar on his back. He already has a beer in his hand, but when he approaches them Hadley bends down, offers the one she bought for him.

"Que crees, que soy borracho?" he says.

"No," she says. "Sorry. I just figured, pues. No. Please. I don't think you're a drunk."

Agata says, "He's kidding, bruta."

"I'm kidding," he says. He is speaking English.

Hadley says, "You were great. Really."

"Thank you," he says. He finishes his beer, discards the bottle. Takes the one Hadley offered. He takes a swig, looks at some people coming out of the Pata Palo. "Is that why you asked me to come outside? To tell me that I am great?"

Agata looks at Hadley.

Hadley says, "No. I mean, yes. You are great. But no. I have a question to ask."

"Okay."

"It's a strange question."

"Dale, guapa."

Agata looks at Hadley, like, *Please*, get this over with.

"Did you know my grandfather? Harvey Lipscomb?"

Miguel Ángel runs the name through his head, thinking, thinking. "No," he says, flatly. "Why? Should I know him? Your grandfather?"

"I don't know," she says. "Maybe. Maybe not. It was a long time ago."

"What was a long time ago?"

"When he was here. When my grandfather wrote down your name. Or maybe not *your* name, but someone's name. Someone named Miguel Ángel Ponce. My grandfather had dinner with him. It was written amongst his notes."

"Her grandfather was a professor," says Agata, pulling gently on Hadley's hair. It is obvious that a hint of disappointment has hit her. Mostly it is the hashish and the alcohol that is catching up. "He was an important speaker and escritor," Agata says.

"In his field," Hadley corrects.

"I knew someone like this," he says, pulling an old memory, thinking it probably has nothing to do with this man, these women. "But his name is not what you told me. It was not Julio—"

"Harvey," says Hadley.

"Harvey," says Miguel Angel. "It is not Harvey this man I knew."

"Okay," Hadley says. She drops her beer into a garbage can, lights a cigarette. She feels lightheaded. She looks at Agata. She says, "I'm tired, Agata."

Agata says, "What was his name?"

Agata is holding Hadley's hand now, her fingers wrapped tightly around Hadley's, which maybe a year ago would have made Hadley anxious, or at least a little uncomfortable. But Agata always holds her hands now, especially when they gallivant around Granada, when they stumble, slightly, from café to café, bar to bar. Holding her as if holding Hadley to the earth, because if Agata didn't, it was possible Hadley might float away, drift off into the sky over the Alhambra, and disappear.

Miguel Ángel is talking to a kid with stretchy pants, a nose ring too big for his face. The kid is asking for money, a cigarette, perhaps both. He doesn't hear Agata. Agata asks Hadley if she has a picture of her grandfather, maybe it would be helpful to produce it for Miguel Ángel.

"Let's go," Hadley says.

Agata says, "Show him the picture, *por fa*. Y nos vamos."

Hadley pulls out the little leather case she carries with her, has carried, for as long as she can recall. Pictures of her family as a happy family. When she was four or five. The Brady Bunch vanity shot; the pictures of friends, half-naked, in Cabo. Pictures of Grandma and Grandpa Superfly, sitting on a porch somewhere, swinging on a swing, looking country. Holding her when she was six, seven months old.

She takes the photo out of its plastic sleeve, hands it to Miguel Ángel, who looks like he is more than done with this little reunion, this little whatever it is.

Miguel Ángel holds the picture in the palm of his hand. To their surprise, he nods. Hadley even notices a smirk, ever so slight, unintentionally visible.

"This is David," he says. "When he was young. *Joder*. Te lo juro, it's him." He shakes his head. "My old friend," he says. "Por donde andas, hombre?"

Agata looks at Hadley. "*David?*"

Hadley is looking back at her, but she has nothing to say, knows even less what to think.

Miguel Ángel says, "If you want, I can introduce you." He hands the picture back to Hadley, shakes his head, incredulous.

Hadley says, "To whom?"

"Your family, guapa. That is who you're looking for, no?"

Later that evening, on the roof at Hadley's, staring at the gingery glow of lights along the walls of the Alhambra, Agata asks Hadley what she is going to do. She is running her fingers through Hadley's hair, Hadley's head sitting in her lap. Hadley is watching the tower flags sway limply from their flagpoles in the breeze there is. Having had too much to drink earlier, and definitely too much to smoke, she had wanted to be sick. The revelation about Harvey had not helped her stomach any. But she had not vomited, and soon she outlasted her nausea. She tucked her feet under her skirt, tucked her hands under her chin. "I don't know," she says. "What the fuck?"

Agata says, "Harvey. Que malo eres. You *bad, bad* boy."

Hadley can't help but laugh, even though none of it is funny. But she always laughs when Agata tries to pronounce Harvey's name. After a few minutes, any humor she has mustered is gone. How could Harvey have done that to her? To Grandma Superfly? How could he have done it for so long? Kept such a secret? Who was this man, Harvey Lipscomb? Who was this creature that had lived these deceitful lives?

Dismayed, needing to hear it out loud, Hadley says, "It's not just us and them, Agata. He had another family, Harvey. Another one beside my family. Another one beside the one here."

"A third family? Are you kidding me?"

"*Yes.* Can you believe that? Another wife. Kids. A whole other family."

Agata strokes her hair. "*Joder.* Where?"

"South Carolina, I think. I don't know. North Carolina? Who knows."

"Do you know them?"

"No. Never. It was his big bad secret. He didn't like to talk about it."

"So you move to Spain to discover your new family." Agata shakes her head. "You are like Cristóbal Colón but backwards. And your discovery is no good."

Hadley is shaking her head now. "This is bad," she says. "It's definitely not good."

"He's dead, Hadley."

"But my grandmother isn't."

"You don't have to tell her."

"I can't not tell her. I can't do that."

"What are you going to do?"

Hadley is quiet. "Meet them," she says. "If they want to meet me. They may not."

"Wow," says Agata. She does not know what else to say.

"Wow is right," says Hadley, not believing she herself has said it.

They are quiet for a few minutes. Soon the lights on the Alhambra go out, which means it is around four in the morning. Hadley tells Agata to stay the night, she wants the company. Agata says she wasn't going anywhere anyway.

They head downstairs to Hadley's piso, their hands guiding them through the darkened stairway. In bed they talk for a few minutes, but soon fall asleep. When the sun rises it hits their faces, but they are sleeping too deeply for it to wake them.

After Agata goes home Hadley eats breakfast in the living room, by the window, studying the picture she had shown Miguel Ángel the night before. She can't tell if the picture was taken at her grandparents' home in Georgia, but there she is, maybe a year old, swaddled in Harvey the Liar's arms, right there next to Grandma Superfly.

Harvey. The *liar*. She doesn't like thinking that, but it comes, and she cannot pretend it isn't so. That he isn't a liar. Or wasn't one. Because there is no way, *no way*, that Grandma Superfly knew about this, Grandpa Superfly's family, this other one anyway, here in Spain. Did she? Impossible, thinks Hadley. No fucking way.

Now everything he had said to her—all of the stories of Don Quixote and Sancho Panza, of poets executed in wars, of heinous generals, of Boabdil or Abu Abdullah or whatever his name was, standing on that rocky prominence, staring back at the Alhambra and the valley before it, forced to abandon his love to its conquerors, whose mother had said, *Thou dost weep like a woman for what thou couldst not defend as a man*—Hadley could not help think, maybe he was not teaching her Spain's history but, rather, lamenting his own life's defeats. Maybe he was, in some clever (and sick) way, only telling her of the things he himself had lost because it was his way of mourning them, his losses. She could not help think—because it was possible—that maybe he was not really showing her, his granddaughter, love (as she wanted to believe), but teaching her things he wanted her to know, because it helped him relive his lying, his cheating, his Spanish conquests. She isn't sure. She can't say. For a second, it makes her sick. Physically *sick*.

She pulls out all of his notes. She pulls out all of the pictures Grandma Superfly has given her. She spreads them out on the tile floor. Everything she sees she sees now in a new, a different light. A light tinged and tainted. Sinister. And it is upsetting. It makes her weep. It makes her question everything. Makes her wonder what is real, if he, Grandpa Superfly Harvey Lipscomb, wasn't. If he wasn't real then, maybe nothing is now. He had been her rock. Whether he knew it or not, he'd been her rock. She thought he knew. No. He did know. And how could he have done this? How could he have built up this country, this place, this past of his, if it would do this to her? If it would destroy everything she believed was good, was honest? What the hell was this?

Again she goes through the notebooks one by one again, looking through his writing, his drawings. Seeking meaning in words that have never had meaning before. Now when she sees the maps he's drawn in pencil, she wonders if they are not maps of his trysts, do not lead to the homes of his lovers, his mistresses, if that's what they were. If they do not lead to other women whose hearts he has broken, because surely he has broken hearts. How could he not, leaving families behind as he had?

She thinks about her relationship with him. Remembers how Harvey had come strolling along (from what Grandma Superfly said), married her mother's mother, instantly took to her, to Hadley. Came in during what turned out to be the final decade plus of his life. Settled in quickly. Put down his roots for the final walk home. Took up with her, with Aaron, who she was jealous of when Harvey showed him attention. How obviously they, Grandma and Grandpa Superfly, had never had any children, but instead, he had swooped in with his humble smile, his warmth and aw shucks performances, put everyone at ease, let everyone know he had it all under control, that Grandma Superfly was safe with him, that no, she wouldn't have to go to a home, or move in with one of them when she grew older, or any of the other bad stuff that happened when you got old. That he had come to her rescue, and her to his, as it was always meant to be. *Naturally.*

She looked at the móvil number Miguel Ángel had written on the book of matches. She thinks of throwing it away, or letting it fall out the window, accidentally dropping it into the sink, where the dishes are overflowing and where, after a few seconds in the soapy water, the numbers will bleed away, and she will not be held responsible. Oops! All gone. *Damn.*

But she doesn't do any of these things. Because this, what this is, is too important to pretend, to try to escape from, to try and *deny.* That this is possible, she can scarcely fathom. That something so unbelievably cruel can really be real, it is beyond comprehension. But she can't avoid it. She won't avoid it. How could she? How could anyone?

She tosses the matchbook to the floor, next to a stack of pictures she imagines is the Alpujarras. Harvey and a group of men and women sitting at a table in the courtyard of a restaurant, holding glasses of wine, smiles on everyone's faces as they try to hold down piles of paper stacked along the table. The wind blowing the bougainvillea along a whitewashed wall; olive trees shading red-blanketed burros. She looks at all of the faces in the pictures, typical Spanish faces, olive skin, dark hair, some thin, some not so much. Some look like they come from Córdoba, pale, a bit of Moro in them, remnants of centuries past. And a hand on Harvey's. Or entwined with his. It's hard to see. Or is it she just doesn't want to?

Hadley hears Agata down below, yelling her name, warning that she is coming up. Bringing a tortilla, she says. Hadley, of course, knowing she would be there sooner or later. She could always smell the olive oil frying, the potatoes soaking, the heaviness of the eggs cooking down at Agata's in that magically unhurried way, crawling along the walls, pushing through the windows, filling the air beautifully, decadently. It didn't matter what Agata was making: Hadley always knew.

She gets the plates ready, cuts slices of the pan de barra, puts everything on the table. Folded napkins under one edge of each plate. While they eat, Agata points with her toes, asks where certain pictures were taken, who certain people are. But Hadley knows few of the faces, even less of the places they see in the pictures.

"The pile there," she says, pointing at a stack of photos, "that's my family. The other pile, no tengo ni puta idea. Nothing."

Agata takes a bite of tortilla, a bite of bread. "Are they there?"

"Who?"

"Your grandfather's other family. The ones from here."

"I don't know. I don't think so."

"Did you look?"

"No."

"Jolines, woman. What kind of detectiva are you?"

"There's women and men and kids in half the pictures, Aga. How am I supposed to know if some are his family?"

She found it odd, saying *it. His family. She* was his family. Grandma Superfly was his family.

"I don't know," she says. "Maybe there is a little boy with horrible clothing and big glasses."

Hadley slaps Agata's arm. "Funny," she says. "But what's the point? It would be guessing no matter what. I don't want to assume who is who."

Agata plays with a lighter she finds on the table. The lighter is red, has the black outline of a bull. "Did you call yet?"

"No."

"What are you waiting for? Call."

Hadley looks at the matches. "I can't. What if I don't like what I find?"

"What if they don't like what *they* find?"

Hadley looks at her. She hasn't considered the possibility. "They have nothing to worry about. I'm a prize. You know that."

"Anyway, *prize*, call him. Anda." She pushes the matchbook toward Hadley, opens her cell phone.

Hadley picks them up, puts them back down. Picks them up again. She looks at the number, dials it on the phone. She lets it ring three times. When she pulls it away from her face, Agata pushes it back to Hadley's ear. But no one picks up. Agata forces her to leave a message.

"Happy?" she says.

"Ni happy ni sad, Hadley. It's your life. I'm happy if you're happy. But si fuera yo, I would want to know who my relatives are."

Before Agata finishes talking the phone is ringing its obnoxious ring. Hadley looks at the screen; the number she just called. Miguel Ángel Ponce's number. She looks at Agata.

Agata makes her most exaggerated, *What-are-you-doing* face. "Contesta, already!"

Hadley clicks a button, says nothing. Agata yells, "*Ho-la!*" loud as she can.

Miguel Ángel says sure, maybe it *is* going to be a little awkward. But their American father has been absent so long from their lives, what does it matter? It is not a traditional happy American family, he says. Remember, guapita, they are Spanish. Their father is American, but they never really knew him. They only saw him as babies.

Hadley listens as Miguel Ángel speaks of Harvey in the present tense. She wants to say no, Harvey is gone, has been for a few years now, but she doesn't. She is not lying, but Miguel Ángel hasn't asked.

They plan to meet later that night. Miguel Ángel tells her that they, Harvey's family, have invited her to dinner. She thinks, a family is something present, not an event. Not events.

He gives Hadley an address. Tells her to be there at ten. You can bring your friend, he says. No pasa nada.

Agata has been listening, her ear pressed to the receiver. When she hears she's been invited, she nods vigorously, Yes, of course she will go. What are you, crazy?

Agata stays with her all day. They lay out Hadley's clothes. Agata brings up some of her more conservative blouses and skirts. But nothing fits Hadley as she hoped it would. She even tries on Agata's "real world" business suit, when Agata had considered actually working for a living. But the suit doesn't fit either. Finally Hadley decides she is due for a new something to add to her wardrobe anyway. Let's go to El Corte, she says.

Agata thinks El Corte Inglés is too pijo, too snobbish, but she can't convince Hadley to go anywhere else. I *hate* shopping, Hadley says. If I have to go I only want to go to one place. *El Corte* has everything.

They walk down Carrera del Genil, have almond ice cream at Helado La Rosa. They walk across the carrera, in through the glass doors of El Corte Ingles right as a pigeon leaves its mark on Hadley's shoulder. Agata laughs. "Buena suerte," she says.

Hadley closes her eyes. "Shit!" she says.

"What were you expecting?"

She tries on long skirts and dresses and camisetas and chaquetas and high heels and flats and pants. She tries on outfits as they are on the mannequins, matching everything down to the pantyhose, the accessories. She asks different salespeople to help her, until Agata finally says, "Ya, chica. Basta, joder. Pick something out, por dios!"

Hadley settles on a simple Adolfo Dominguez dress, canvas and straw sandals. Everything is *nude* in color, which makes her hesitate. But she hesitates only briefly.

"Wow," says Agata. "Por fin! My friend looks like a classy woman for once."

"I'll look pija, is what I'll look like."

"You'll look pretty, guapa. *Pretty*."

They walk back home. They have lunch at the Döner Kebap Nemrut, in Plaza Nueva. Agata has the shawarma; Hadley a falafel sandwich with too much hummus. The camarero brings them coffee, a slice of something made of phyllo dough and honey. Que aprovechen, he says.

Agata says, "What if your brothers are cute?"

Hadley says, "Shut up. *Please*."

"But if they are?"

"First, they wouldn't be my brothers; they would be my uncles. And they wouldn't be blood uncles."

"Even better."

"I don't even want to think about it, okay? I don't. This whole mess would be horrible for my grandmother. Horrible."

Agata nods. "Yes," she says. "I guess it would be."

"Yes. It would."

"Then what are you going to tell her?"

"I'm not going to tell her anything. How could I?"

"Don't you think she should know? This is more her business than yours."

"I don't know what I think she should know, Aga. I don't know anything anymore. This? It's jodido!"

A girl with a dog and knotted braids approaches their table, asks for a cigarette. The girl is wearing striped stockings under her torn shorts, about twenty necklaces. Agata waves her away. "I think you should tell her," she says. "If I were her, I would want to know. If I found out you knew, and didn't tell me?"

Hadley says, "Yes, but you like torture. My grandmother doesn't. She's old. She loved him. It would probably destroy her." She smiles at a little boy at the next table. The boy has been watching her, playing hide and seek behind a chair. "Right now, Grandpa Superfly is her prince. I can't be the one to ruin that without a good reason."

Agata says, "You aren't ruining anything. You are telling the truth. You are exposing lies. Pero lo entiendo. I understand."

At the Carmen, Agata returns to her piso to shower and take a nap. Hadley showers too, but she cannot fall asleep. She stares at the clothing she bought earlier that day. She lays the dress out on the bed, the shoes, the ribbon she is going to tie her hair up in, the little black eyeliner Agata left on the table. She picks the phone up, looks at her watch: Seven. One in the afternoon back in Helen. She wonders what Grandma Superfly will be doing now, all alone in Georgia, no Harvey, no family. Alone in that vacuous chalet.

She thinks the cabin probably has cobwebs all over it by now, hanging from the blond rafters. She imagines them thickly layered in dust, aged like everything else. She sees fruit in bowls losing their sheen; a television that has not been turned on in years; she sees everything she imagined as it would be in Miss Havisham's home in *Great Expectations*. Shriveling. Dying. Decayed.

She takes a deep breath, closes her eyes. A breeze comes in from the window, flutters the heavy curtains. She dials Grandma Superfly's number.

"Hello?" the voice says. Hadley had been about to hang up, but she knew it took her grandmother at least ten rings before she got anywhere near the telephone. She imagines her grandmother outside, spilling aphids and whiteflies into the hummingbird feeders, shooing the squirrels away so the birds can eat; imagines her sitting out on the back deck, her head asleep on one of her shoulders as she catnaps after lunch, where Harvey maybe had catnapped beside her when he was alive. When Hadley imagines her, she sees Grandma Superfly's hair flipping slowly in the wind, arms folded, keeping warm until, when it gets too cold, when the sun falls down behind the trees, when the air grows damp, she wakes up, says, *Oh, my my*, and goes inside to bury herself under a shawl, have a cup of tea before she catches a cold, freezes to death. But Hadley does not know if that's how it is at all. For a second, she just listens.

"Hello?" Grandma Superfly says again. The crackling of her elderly vocal chords. Decades of yelling, and laughter, and, well, everything. "I can't hear you," she repeats. "If anyone is there. Hello?"

"Grandma," she finally says. "It's me. Hadley."

"Hadley!" Grandma Superfly says, happy as always. "How is my little flamenco dancer?"

"Good, Grandma. I'm good." And when she hears her voice, the joy in it, she is.

"Glad to hear it, sweetie. And eating? Are you eating well, Had?"

"Too well," she says. "I'm going to float home one day if I keep eating so much."

A lie, and she is sure Julianne knows it is a lie, because she has never really eaten more than a little here or there, as if she were no larger than one of the hummingbirds that floats in front of her grandmother's trees, picking and nibbling, flying off, weightless, hovering, light as a cloud.

Hadley wants to say, Listen, Grandma, I have some questions I'd like to ask you about Harvey, about his trips to Spain, about the time he spent there, about anything and everything you know about it, or knew about it, both before and after you married him. But she doesn't. She can't. Listening to Grandma Superfly's voice, how excited she is, how easily she pulls at her insides with an *hmm*, an *oh*. How the overwhelming need to want to coddle her, to rescue her from what she imagines is now a terribly humdrum life, pulls at her over so many miles. Instead, Hadley listens.

She listens to Julianne tell her about the new groups she is hanging out in, the new knickknacks they are selling in the store this year, buying as much American as they can. "Doing their part for commerce," she says. "Just sometimes you meet some of these people losing their jobs, well. I don't know. Makes you think, I guess."

Hadley tells her about her life in Granada. About the tapas at night, drinking wine, how sometimes she sits on her roof for hours, after everyone is long asleep, stares at the Alhambra, at the top of the cathedral, listening to the carillon gong float over the cobblestone. When Julianne asks her about boys, she tells her the truth, but not about Antonio. She tells her how transient Granada is, people coming, going. But how the city is always there, always alive in its own way, which feels true (the walls, especially those in the Albaicin, seem to have eyes). I Know all about it, Julianne says. "Harvey, funny enough, said the same thing, sweetie." Which makes Hadley smile, if guiltily.

Julianne says, "Always felt Granada was special, my Harvey. Loved that place as much as anywhere. Sometimes I think more, tell you the truth."

Hadley feels a pang of something, but hides it, keeps it down inside her. "It's easy to," she says. She wants to tell her how easy it is, life there. How inexpensive everything is. How you can just breathe the air, walk, nap when you want to. Read books. She says, "You know, you could come out here. Stay with me." A bad idea, she knows. And a bit misleading, her already planning her exodus.

But Julianne does not blink. "Oh, no," she says. "Not me. That's not anything I would ever even be interested in, dear." Hadley wonders why. There is silence for a second, but eventually Julianne goes on. "You keep the postcards coming. Send some pictures. Okay? I love the pictures, Hadley. They show what's what." She's right, thinks Hadley. They do. Enough, anyway.

She stands in front of the mirror for twenty minutes after Agata finishes putting her makeup on. She does not feel like herself, does not look like herself. She can't remember the last time anything, much less makeup—rouge, lipstick concealer, eyeliner—touched her face. She runs her fingers over her cheeks. She brushes a strand of hair behind her ear. Who is this person, she thinks. Why am I pretending to be her?

But she knows. She knows that there is nothing to worry about. She knows that whatever happens, life is what it is and there is nothing she can do about what is out of her control. And this is certainly out of her control. This has nothing to do with her, isn't her fault. This is a Harvey thing. This is all him, no matter which way she thinks about it. In a way, putting that blame—if blame is what it is she is looking to shed—on Harvey, well. That is not her burden. That is not hers to carry. That is one hundred and ten percent Grandpa Superfly's.

They pick up an extravagant vino blanco, something they would never spring for if it was just them, and now they are walking along the Rio Genil, up and over a foot bridge, past cyclists riding under the soft light of lampposts. She sees the glow of a church at the foothills of the Sierra Nevada, the blackness of the river that is, during daylight, emerald green. Hadley stares at the mosaic stonework of vine and flower below their feet, feels the bumps and slopes of its pattern as they walk. "It will be okay," Agata says. "I will be right there with you."

Hadley says, "I know. Thank you." Agata takes her arm; they keep on.

When they arrive, there are not many apartments in the building, six from what Hadley can make out, only five with names beside their buzzers. The names are difficult to read, but Agata holds a lighter to the intercom, presses all five buttons with a smash of her palm, sending Hadley into a near panic attack.

Agata laughs. "What? It's normal," she says.

"It's my family, Agata."

"Your family?" Hadley gives Agata a look; a look meant to say, not now, boba. Please.

"Quien es?" the voice says.

"Hadley," Hadley says. But for a moment there is only silence. Then the voice of a child comes on, and Hadley says sorry to the woman. To the boy she says, "Soy yo, Hadley," and the boy, sounding young and old, frightening and warm, strange and yet familiar, welcoming and accusative, and so many things, buzzes them in.

And Hadley's heart, which she's never worried about until then, flutters.

About the Author

Cully Perlman was born in Miami and has travelled the world. He has been to every state in the U.S., including Alaska and Hawaii, and in his youth has worked in Yellowstone National Park and Glacier National Park as a cook. After cooking his way around the U.S., he went back to school and acquired a BA in English Literature from Florida International University, an MA in Literature in English from Georgia State University, a dual MBA in Market Strategy and International Business from Regis University, and an MFA in Creative Writing from the University of Tampa. Throughout his life, Cully has been a nomad, a lifestyle he picked up having lived in Spain with his mother and brother at an early age, but the writing life has been his lighthouse during this time, and has always drawn him to the blank page.

Cully Perlman's fiction and nonfiction has been published in Bull Men's Fiction, The St. Petersburg Review, Real South Magazine, Avatar Review, Creative Loafing, Connotation Press, The Good Men Project, Pioneertown, El Portal, and more. He was a 2013 semifinalist for his novel-in- progress, *Los Beautiful*, as well as on the short list of finalists for the 2012 William Faulkner – William Wisdom Competition for his novel, *The Losses*. He has been a finalist in Glimmer Train's Very Short Story Contest, won the Writer's Digest Dear Lucky Agent contest for a novel, and received an honorable mention in Glimmer Train's Fiction Open. Cully lives in Colorado with his wife, Susan, two daughters, and his attack dog, Kane, who, well, attacks. He snowboards (Cully, not Kane), hikes, camps, fishes, reads, and does other cool stuff that will be left unmentioned. He's also a project manager for large digital engagements.